Pengelly's Daughter

NICOLA PRYCE

CORVUS

First published in paperback in Great Britain in 2016 by Corvus,
an imprint of Atlantic Books Ltd.

1 3 5 7 9 8 6 4 2

A CIP catalogue record for this book is available from the British Library.

Paperback ISBN: 978 1 78239 877 6
EBook ISBN: 978 1 78239 878 3

Printed and bound by CPI Group (UK) Ltd, Croydon, CR0 4YY
Corvus
An Imprint of Atlantic Books Ltd
Ormond House
26–27 Boswell Street
London
WC1N 3JZ

www.corvus-books.co.uk

Pengelly's Daughter

NICOLA PRYCE trained as a chemotherapy nurse before completing an Open University degree in Humanities. She is a qualified adult literacy support volunteer and lives with her husband in the Blackdown Hills in Somerset. Together they sail the south coast of Cornwall in search of adventure.

For my husband Damian:
my very own Jim.

Family Tree

FOSSE

POLCARROW (Baronetcy created 1590)

Sir Francis m 1) Elizabeth   2) Alice   Robert
Polcarrow   Polcarrow   Polcarrow   Roskelly
b.1730 d.1782   (née Gorran)   (née Roskelly) b.1750
                 b.1749 d.1770   b.1763 m.1780

James Gorran Polcarrow   Francis Polcarrow
       b.1765   b.1781

Thomas Warren   *Land agent / Steward*
Henderson   *Butler*
Mr Moyle   *Head gardener*
Joseph Dunn   *Stable lad*

COOMBE HOUSE

(1782–1792)   (From 1792–)
Pascoe Pengelly m Eva Pengelly   William Tregellas
     b.1739   (née Trewarren)   (b.1750)
   Shipwright/   b.1748   Timber merchant/
 Shipyard owner   Shipyard owner

Rosehannon Eva Pengelly (b.1772)

Mrs Munroe	*Housekeeper and cook*
Samuel	*Man servant*
Jenna Marlow	*Housemaid*
Tamsin	*Housemaid*

QUAYSIDE OF FOSSE

Pengelly Boatyard (Est. 1760) Renamed *Tregellas Boatyard* 1792

Mr Scantlebury	*Shipwright*
Mr Melhuish	*Blacksmith*
Tom	*Apprentice*

Bespoke Dressmaker (Est. 1792)

Madame Merrick	*Dressmaker*
Eva Pengelly	*Seamstress*
Mrs Mellows	*Seamstress*
Josie	*Seamstress*
Elowyn	*General maid*

Ferryman

Joshua Tregan

Members of the Corporation

Mr Brockensure	*Mayor*
Mr Drew	*Master mariner*
Mr Tregellas	*Timber merchant*
Mr Mitchell	*Insurance agent*
Mr Wigan	*Merchant*
Mr Hoskins	*Head of the new bank*
Mr Warleggan	*Importer of fine teas*

PORTHRUAN

PENDENNING HALL (Acquired 1787)

Sir Charles M. Cavendish MP b.1743	Lady April Cavendish (née Lady April Montville) b.1750

Celia b.1773	Charity b.1774	Georgina b.1780	Sarah b.1789	Charles b.1791

Mr Phillip Randal	*Steward*
Mrs Jennings	*Governess*
Beth Tregony	*Housemaid*

HILLSIDE COTTAGES

(From 1792)	Eva Pengelly	*Seamstress*
	Rosehannon Pengelly	*Bookkeeper*
	Jenna Marlow	*Housemaid*

(From 1780) Mr & Mrs Tregony
10 children

'The tide rises, the tide falls,
The twilight darkens, the curlew calls.'

Henry Wadsworth Longfellow

Rising Tide

Chapter One

'No, Mother. Never! I'd rather salt pilchards all my life than marry that man. Mr Tregellas is corrupt and dangerous. I'm sure he tricked Father into bankruptcy...and you expect me to marry him?'

Flinching from my tone, Mother avoided my eyes. She had changed so much in the last year. Always so proud and hard-working, she was now fragile as a sparrow; her dress, with its invisible mending and reworked seams, drab and worn. She had aged, too, for her forty-five years. But it was her expression of resignation that frightened me – she was like a spring with no recoil.

'We can make do,' I said more gently, guilty I had shouted so fiercely. 'My bookkeeping's bringing in some money and your sewing's paying the rent. We're managing well enough – we can go on as we are. There's no need for me to marry – least of all William Tregellas!'

Despite the warmth of the June sun shining so brilliantly outside, the parlour was cold and musty, the small, leaded window seeming to block, rather than admit any light. It was sparse and cheerless with dark patches of damp showing brown against the lime-washed walls. Two high-backed chairs faced the empty grate and a dresser stood crammed against the wall. I knelt by Mother's feet, taking hold of both her hands. They were worn and rough, her fingertips reddened by excessive sewing. 'I'll take care of you, Mother – we'll be alright.'

'I wish it was that easy,' she said. 'Since your father died, Mr Tregellas's been very kind to us. We couldn't get Poor Relief and I didn't know what would become of us.' She began fumbling for her handkerchief. 'I told you Mrs Cousins let us have this cottage cheap, but it wasn't true.' She held her handkerchief against her mouth, as if to stop her words.

'Don't tell me Mr Tregellas's been paying our rent! Don't tell me you've accepted money from that man!'

Her shoulders sagged. 'I thought 'twould only be for a short while…' She hesitated, as if too scared to go on, '…but that's not all. There was no public gift for your father's burial – Mr Tregellas paid for it all.'

'Mother, no!'

'What else could I do?' The tears she was holding back now began to flow freely. 'Would you have your father rot with vagabonds? Lie alongside some stranger in a pauper's grave? What choice did I have? Mr Tregellas is a kind man and he's been good to us – he wants to help but you're too set against him to see any good in him. And…' Her voice turned strangely flat, '…over the past year, he's grown that fond of you…and he doesn't want to wait any longer.'

I felt dizzy, sick, the walls of the room crushing against me as the unpalatable truth began to dawn: I was being bought by one and sold by the other, as surely as if I was a slave on the market block. 'What arrangements have you made, Mother? I take it you *have* made arrangements?'

My fury made Mother wince. 'Rosehannon, think what he's offering – a position in society, a steady income…servants. He's a respectable timber merchant and he's that taken with you – it would secure your future.' Her face took on a look of longing. 'And we'd go back to Coombe House – to where your father always wanted us to live – instead of scratching a living in this damp cottage. Your father would want that.'

'Father? Approve of me marrying the man who cheated him?' I could not believe my ears. I missed Father desperately and needed his counsel so badly. Mr Tregellas had been manipulating Mother, I could see that now. He had been drawing her in like a fish on a line until he could land his catch – only, I was the catch. Bile rose in my throat. 'Perhaps you should marry him, Mother – after all, he's nearer your age than mine!'

'You know very well it's not an older woman he wants.'

'He disgusts me and I'll not marry him. And that's all there is to it.' I lifted my skirts, striding angrily to the door.

Mother's voice followed me across the room. 'That's not quite all there is to it,' she said slowly. 'He's given us until your twenty-first birthday – then he wants his answer…or he'll call in his loan.'

'But that's in three weeks' time!'

5

'I know,' she said, staring at the empty grate.

I thought I would faint. The room was spinning round me, pressing in on me. I needed to breathe the air that gave me courage. I am born of Cornwall, born from generations of fishermen and boat-builders. The wind is my breath – the sea is my blood. I draw my strength from the remorseless gales that lash our coast, the waves that pound our rocks, the gulls that scream, the wind that howls. I needed to escape the close confines of that hateful cottage.

The door to the scullery was open. Wiping her hands on her apron, Jenna left the dough she was making, following me out to the sunshine. She had heard everything, of course. No need to press her ear against the crack in the parlour door, for we had spoken loudly enough. Strands of blonde hair were escaping from under her mobcap and flour dusted her cheeks. With eyebrows raised and mouth pursed, she whistled in disbelief.

'What?' I said, pushing past her, scattering the hens in my anger.

'Will ye marry Mr Tregellas?'

'No! Of course not!'

She took my arm, leading me across the yard. The stone step behind the back gate was far enough away, but near enough if Mother wanted either of us. Over the last year we had found ourselves sitting on it, more often than not, and it had borne witness to our growing friendship. Instinctively we made our way there, the warmth of the sun beginning to take the chill from my heart. 'Here,' she whispered, her hand diving under her apron, 'these might help.'

Her dimples deepened. Wrapped inside a cloth were two apple dumplings. She handed me one and without another word, I took a bite. It was delicious – the suet light and fluffy, the apple juicy and tart. Licking our fingers, we leant against the gate, gazing across the grass to the cliff's edge. A soft sea breeze blew against our faces, rippling the grass in front of us. Behind us, our neighbour's gate began banging on its last hinge.

Jenna was three years my junior and had been our maid for seven years. I'm sure she only stayed with us because she held Mother in such high esteem. We hardly paid her and the fact she remained with us was a miracle as anyone else would have left long ago.

'It's a trap, Jenna. Nothing but a trap.'

'Then ye have to find someone else.'

Her words annoyed me. 'Why? Why's *marriage* the only answer? Why should my future depend on marriage?'

'Ye must marry…and quick too…' Her voice became coaxing, her eyes pleading. 'With yer looks, ye could get any man ye want. Ye just needs smile…flatter them…pretend to be stupid.'

'I don't see why I should pretend to be stupid just to please someone who is.'

Reproach crept into her voice. 'Have ye never wondered why ye've so few admirers? They're that scared of ye – that's why. Yer politics and wild thoughts do scare them off. Ye're beautiful and clever but ye must let go yer anger – honest, ye'd get anyone. Men are simple creatures, for all their wealth and position. Any woman can get a man…'

7

'Yes. As long as she isn't fussy!'

Jenna's frown deepened. Glancing up at the sky, she peered over to the next-door yard. 'That wind's freshening – I'll see to Mrs Tregony's wash. Her pains have started and she'll not get that lot in.'

The south-westerly was indeed picking up, wispy mares' tails blowing across the sky with a speed that heralded a storm. The clothes were already flapping on the line. Where was I to find enough money to repay our debt? My book-keeping was too sporadic, Mother's new job would not pay enough and we could expect no credit – that was for certain. Mr Tregellas had been Father's main creditor. In lieu of payment, he had been handed our old house, handed the lease of Father's boatyard, and had stepped straight into Father's shoes. Just like that. He had everything. Absolutely everything. *Let go my anger?* Jenna had no idea.

Everything about Mr Tregellas screamed treachery. I had no evidence, I just knew him to be scheming – his trap for Mother proof enough of that. I tried to think rationally. I knew I needed to discredit him, but what could I do? What would a man do? I needed evidence he cheated Father, anything at all that would hold up in court and free us from this debt.

Jenna began unpegging Mrs Tregony's washing, her apron blowing in the wind. 'They do say at Coombe House Mr Tregellas keeps everything ship-shape – not like yer father, bless his soul. His papers were always a terrible muddle, but Mrs Munroe says Mr Tregellas keeps everything in neat, tidy piles. She do say…' Her words were lost as she turned her back, but I was no longer listening. My mind was whirling. She had folded Mr Tregony's clothes and an idea was beginning to take shape.

If I disguised myself as a man, I could row across the river, walk unhindered through the streets of Fosse and break into our old house. I would search the study. Any proof, no matter how small, must surely be concealed among all those neat piles. I knew the house like the back of my hand and I knew Father's old study better than anywhere.

'Jenna, go to your mother and pick up a set of your brother's clothes – anything you can get hold of. Quickly, before he gets back from the fields.'

Jenna's hands went straight to her hips. Swinging round, she faced me with that look I knew so well. 'Why'd I do that?' she said.

'Because I say so…and don't tell anyone.'

'Why'd you want me brother's clothes?'

'Just get them, Jenna. Please?'

We had lived in Porthruan for over a year. Our cottage was one of a row of houses rising steeply from the harbour's edge. For nearly sixty years, their thick stone walls and slate roofs had huddled together, resolutely defying the vagaries of our weather. I hated the damp, the smell of rot, but at least the upstairs room was divided in two and I had to be grateful for that. I pressed my ear against the wooden partition separating our rooms and could just make out Mother's steady breathing. She was asleep.

9

It was past eleven o'clock. I was dressed carefully. My borrowed clothes chafed my legs and the heavy boots were several sizes too big, but glancing in the mirror, I felt reassured. With my height in my favour and my hair pinned beneath the cap, I would pass very well for a man. The house was quiet, the dark night perfect for concealment. Too many eyes would be watching the road so I would skirt the back of the cottages and take the cliff path.

I crossed the yard, quietly shutting the gate. The clouds were black and heavy with rain, the wind fiercer than I thought. It seemed so much further in the dark and even knowing the path as well as I did, it was hard not to stumble in the pitch black.

Down to my left, the sea pounded the rocks. Across the river mouth, the lights of Fosse glowed in the dark. Lanterns burnt on the ships in the harbour and I could just make out the distinctive rig of HMS *Thistle* which had put in to port for minor repairs. My stomach tightened. Our yard should have been doing those repairs – not Nickels. Father had fought the Corporation tooth and nail for that commission, but now Nickels had our contract, William Tregellas had our yard, and Father lay dead in his grave.

The wind was whipping my coat, tugging my collar. I hunched against its force, jamming my cap further down my forehead, my sense of disappointment deepening with every step. I knew I ought to turn back. It would be madness to row the river in such a gale, yet to turn back would be to give up too easily. Besides, if I could only get Father's boat from its hiding place, I would, at least, have accomplished something. The cliff fell steeply to my left with little, or no, protection but my eyes were becoming accustomed to the dark and I began to feel more confident. To stay safe, I would keep close to the hedge.

The path began to narrow, thorns catching on my jacket. A weathered oak, struck more than once by lightning and blown eastward by the prevailing wind, loomed in front of me, obscuring the path. In daylight the exposed roots were never a problem, but at night they snaked in front of me in uneven coils and I slowed my pace, choosing my steps with greater care.

From out of nowhere, my arm was grabbed from behind, my elbow wrenched forcibly against my back. I tried to twist, pull away, but a searing pain shot up my arm, stopping me in my tracks. I could not break free. Someone was jolting me forward, his fierce grip pushing me towards the tree. Almost at once I was forced against the trunk, my cheek pressing painfully against the rough bark. 'Thought you'd catch me?' whispered a voice in my ear.

'Let me go!' I yelled, my arm burning.

'You're going nowhere – not 'til you say who sent you.' The power of his hold left no doubt of my captor's strength. The more I struggled, the firmer I was held.

'Nobody sent me. Let me go, you're hurting me.'

His grip loosened. He spun me round, once more pinning my arms behind my back. The clouds thinned and a shaft of moonlight lit the darkness. The steel of his dagger glinted in the half-light and I held my breath, too petrified to move. 'Not quite what you seem,' he said, the tip of his dagger slowly sliding under my cap. 'Calm your terror. I'll not hurt you an' I'd not have frightened you had I known you're a woman.' He flicked his dagger and my cap flew to the ground. Released from its hold, my hair cascaded round my shoulders.

Once again black clouds plunged us into darkness, but not before I had seen he was a sailor. His waistcoat and breeches were dark, his boots muddied. He was wearing a loose-sleeved shirt which filled in the wind. Around his head he wore a scarf, fastened in a knot. Hanging from his belt was a leather pouch. He let go of my arm and, relieved to be free, I turned to face the wind, hoping to bring some order to my hair.

From the direction of the river mouth, I caught the sound of angry shouts and dogs barking. The barking was vicious, the shouts instinctively dangerous, full of menace. My assailant had heard them too. He stood straining his ears in the direction of the sound.

'They've caught my trail! Go – afore the dogs get here. They're ferocious beasts an' their blood's up – they'll attack on sight. Run!' His voice was low, urgent.

Turning his back, he reached into the base of the tree and I could just make out a coil of rope hidden among the gnarled roots. He secured one end to a sturdy root and I watched him pick up the coil and start edging towards the cliff, clearly intending to tie the rope around the tree. This was madness. I knew the tree well. Recent landslips had left the roots dangerously exposed, the ground was loose, the drop perilously steep. If he slipped, he would fall to certain death.

The men's voices were getting louder, more distinct. They sounded as if they were already at the blockhouse, heading up the cliff path and would soon reach the top. I knew I should run but something held me back. The sailor must be fleeing from the navy, or escaping the king's shilling. Perhaps he had been caught smuggling. Either way, I baulked at the flogging that awaited him. I had no faith in the justice of our system, but even less faith in the justice of an angry mob. And who was I to judge him guilty?

'Stop!' I shouted, peering at him through the darkness.

'I told you to go – those dogs'll tear you apart.'

'No. Wait!' I had to shout as the wind was blowing my words away. 'It's too dangerous to go round that side. The cliff's loose – the ground will give way. Stay there. Wait for me. I'll catch the rope. You can throw it to me.'

I worked my way round the tree until I was opposite him. The wind caught my hair, rain streaked my face. Down to my left, waves crashed against the rocks but I saw little in the darkness. 'Ready!' I said. He threw the rope. I heard it lash against the tree but could not reach it. 'Throw it again,' I shouted. I heard a thud and grabbed. The rope was rough and slippery but I gripped it firmly, pulling it securely against my chest.

Quick as lightning, he was at my side. With the rope round the trunk, he took hold of the end, twisting it into a bowline with strong, swift movements, pulling it firmly to test its strength. There was no doubt it would hold his weight. The voices were getting louder, the lanterns swaying to the rhythm of people running fast. The dogs would be ahead of them and soon approaching but I stood, too appalled to run. I could not believe the sailor was about to descend the cliff.

'Go! For the love of God, go!' he commanded. 'Take the path so your scent mixes with other trails. Run! It's my trail they're following – the dogs should stop. But run, don't stop!'

A wave of fear brought me to my senses and I stumbled blindly through the darkness, my cumbersome boots causing me to trip. As I picked myself up, a shaft of moonlight shone through the parted clouds and I glanced back, bracing myself to see the sailor begin his dangerous descent. He had not moved. He was crouching on the ground, watching me, his black eyes staring into mine. Our eyes locked in an unsmiling stare.

The barking was getting louder. I ran like never before, running in terror of the dogs, brushing against the thorns with no thought but to reach the safety of the cottage. In the yard, I stood with my back against the closed door, gasping for breath. The house was quiet, Mother and Jenna still undisturbed. As I climbed the stairs, my legs seemed like jelly beneath me. I was safe but, even so, when I pulled the bedclothes round me, my heart was still pounding.

I could not settle. The look in those black eyes kept filling my mind.

Chapter Two

Dawn broke at five. As usual, the same two cockerels vied to rouse the town. Joseph Williams was already stoking the fires in the bakehouse and, down by the harbour, an oxen cart was rumbling over the cobbles. The dairy herd would soon be gathering outside my window, but worse than that, Mrs Tregony's baby had been born during the night and the cries of her newborn infant filtered through the adjoining wall. Ducking under the bedclothes, I pulled the pillow firmly over my head.

The night had passed in bursts of terrifying dreams. One moment I was being chased by dogs, the next I was watching the sailor dangling over the cliff, his pursuers poised to cut the lifeline that held him hanging above the rocks. I could hardly distinguish the dreams from the truth. But whether he had survived, or was floating head down in the sea, was no longer my concern. I had enough problems of my own.

There would be no more sleep. The cries from next door sounded like the cries of a baby who would survive and I knew Mother would be lying awake, reliving the heartache of her lost hopes, remembering the awful silences as she cradled yet another lifeless baby in her arms. Jenna knew it too. I heard her close the latch to Mother's door.

As she entered my room, her usual, cheerful greeting died on her lips. 'Jigger me,' she cried, staring at her brother's clothes lying in a heap on the floor.

'Jenna! Don't speak so coarsely – and not so loudly.'

'I've a mind to speak more plain than that! How did them clothes get like that?' She held up the sodden, mud-bespattered clothes, glaring at me across the room. 'And what's happened to yer hair?'

'What you don't know, you can't fret about.'

'Not fret? It'll take all morning doing yer hair and all after-noon washing them clothes…and you tell me not to fret?'

She pursed her lips and began tugging at my tangled hair with more force than usual. Wincing, I said nothing – I was too busy thinking. I needed to find out exactly how much money we owed Mr Tregellas and while Mother was at work, I would take the opportunity to go through the bills and accounts. But as the day wore on, and the heat of the sun filled the yard, I began to feel listless, unable to concentrate. It was as if some magnet was pulling me back to the tree, compelling me to retrace my steps of the night before.

I could bear it no longer. I slipped out of the backyard, cutting quickly across the grassy cliff-top. Not a breath of wind blew. No one was about. Only four sheep watched me push through the swathes of flowers burning under the midday sun. Yet despite the beauty and the butterflies dancing around me, the bitter taste of injustice soured my enjoyment. This was common land, used for generations by the people of Porthruan, but it belonged to the Pendenning Estate and was soon to be enclosed. Fences were already appearing. Sir Charles Cavendish had bought the great hall with its vast estate, seven years ago. He had evicted tenants, Jenna's family among them, created a vast park, and had returned to London as our Member of Parliament. He had never been seen since. How could that be right? How could one man own everything when so many people had nothing?

Skylarks were singing above me, their song filling the air. Crossing the stile, I climbed the cliff path, the sun hot against my skin. I was wearing my green cotton dress, the lightest of my three dresses. It used to be my favourite, but now I was ashamed it was wearing so thin. Even with Jenna's care, the lace at my elbow was greying, the black stitching on the bodice faded and dull. Checking to make sure only the sheep were watching, I stripped off my fichu, removed my bonnet and despite Jenna's dire warnings, shook my hair free from its hold. It felt wonderful to be so unconfined.

Only the faintest breeze blew. There was no sign of the storm that had lashed the cliffs the night before. It was peaceful and still. Waves lapped the rocks and sunlight glinted on the sea, like thousands of glass shards. I shaded my eyes, scanning the horizon, skimming the water's edge for a lifeless body. Drawing closer to the tree, I began searching the ground, hoping not to find signs of a struggle. Nothing seemed untoward. There was no rope round the trunk, no blood stains, nothing – just a mass of muddy footprints, their indentations still damp in the shadows beneath the over-hanging branches.

Relieved, I edged round the tree, making my way to the place where I had caught the rope. The shade was so dark I saw nothing at first, but as I looked closer I saw something on the ground and caught my breath, my heart beginning to race. A beautiful red rose was lying where I had knelt the night before and my hands began to tremble as I picked it up. Breathing in its heady fragrance, I brushed it against my face, feeling the velvet softness of the petals against my lips. The scent was intoxicating, dangerous, yet the very danger seemed exciting, sending frissons of pleasure tingling through my body.

I began smiling at the audacity of the sailor. But as I held the rose, I noticed the thorns had been removed by a knife and a vision of his dagger flashed through my mind. The sailor was a violent and desperate man, and I, Rosehannon Pengelly, clever, articulate and well educated, should know better than to be beguiled by a rose from such a man.

Above me, a rustle in the leaves caught my attention and I glanced up to the overhanging branch. I jumped in fright. Through the dappled light, I saw the dark shape of the sailor standing in the tree. He was watching me. 'You're quite safe – I've no dagger this time,' he said, landing a few paces in front of me, his tall frame towering above me.

A shaft of sunlight shone on his white shirt. It was unbut-toned at the neck and loosely tucked into his breeches. His sleeves were rolled to the elbow. He was younger than I thought, probably late twenties. Around his neck was a red scarf. His face was coarsened by the sun, his chin unshaven, a small scar visible on his forehead. His hair was black, his brows dark, his expression grim and resolute. He stood staring at me through intensely blue eyes. 'By way of thanking you,' he said, pointing to the rose. 'I'm in your debt, ma'am. My name's Jim.' He bowed formally, his eyes never leaving my face.

'Jim who?' I found myself replying.

'I'm known only as Jim.'

'Then you must have something to hide,' I replied abruptly. His accent was local, his words softly spoken, but he had startled me and I did not like the way he was looking at me.

'Perhaps I'd have done better to have left you to the mob.'

'I'm grateful you didn't.' His face remained impassive, stony, his eyes lingering on my face before he looked out to sea. 'Thanks to you, I got back to my ship.'

He sounded so assured, so familiar. He had been waiting for me and, like a fool, I had walked straight into his trap. I did not like to be second-guessed and I certainly did not like to be spied on. With a sickening thud, I realised he would have seen me throw off my fichu.

'Don't insult me!' I snapped, covering my shoulders and replacing my bonnet.

'Insult you?' He sounded genuinely surprised, 'How'd I insult you?'

'What ship would be waiting in a lee gale? No boat would survive the rocks down there and no master would endanger his ship – or her crew – in weather like last night. You couldn't have had a ship waiting.' I saw his eyes widening at the truth of my words and faced him in triumph. 'You hid in the tree, didn't you?'

'That I did.' He was staring back at me, no hint of a smile.

'Why go to so much trouble – tying the rope round the tree?'

'If people see something, they believe it. If they see a rope going over a cliff, they'll think I've used it. The dogs can sniff an' bark all they like, but they'll call them off. Meanwhile I get to look at my pursuers.'

It was a clever move – dangerous but clever. 'And did you?'

'I did.' His fists clenched by his sides, a look of hatred flashing across his face. He turned away, picking up a stone, aiming it at another before sending both flying over the cliff to the rocks below.

'And did you know them?'

'No.'

His look had frightened me but the coldness in his voice now scared me. I had been very foolish to come and even more foolish to speak to him. I would leave him to his hatred. Gathering up my skirts, I began stepping over the gnarled roots. I was almost clear of the tree when his words ripped right through me. 'Goodbye, Miss Pengelly.'

I swung round. 'How d'you know my name?'

'I asked,' he replied, his face impassive.

'What d'you mean you asked?'

'In Porthruan, I asked the men in the tavern.'

'What? You just *happened* to ask who is the lady who runs around at night dressed in breeches?' I was furious – furious and scared.

'No, I asked who was the most beautiful woman in Porthruan an' they all agreed – must be Pengelly's daughter.' He was tall, assured, his broad shoulders silhouetted against the blue of the sea, his arms crossed, his head flung back, staring at me with those piercing, blue eyes. 'They also said you were proud, too clever by half, had a sharp tongue in your head, an' I'd stand no chance of winning your favour – I'd be wasting my time. Seems no man will ever be good enough for Miss Rosehannon Pengelly.' His eyes did not waver. But nor did mine.

'Well they were right,' I said, flinging the rose in the dirt by his feet.

My head was pounding. I did not have airs and graces. I did not have a sharp tongue. I was educated, certainly, but why should a woman not be educated? And why should I not have opinions? My stomach was tightening with every step. How dare he bandy my name about. What if someone had seen us? What if they were already talking about us in the tavern?

The air was thick with lassitude as I made my way slowly up the cobbles. Sleeping dogs lay stretched in the shade and only a handful of women sat in their doorways, their lace bobbins, for once, hanging idle. I nodded, even summoning up a smile where necessary, desperately hoping tongues were not already wagging, but at the bend in the road my heart sank – Jimmy Tregony stood holding the reins of a pony and trap.

Stepping out of our front door was the last man in the

world I wanted to see. It was too late, he had seen me and there was to be no escape. I had always disliked William Tregellas, but seeing him now, I hated him. He knew he was in good shape for a man of his years. His well-cut frock coat emphasised the broadness of his shoulders and his breeches, tucked into riding boots despite the heat, must have been chosen to emphasise the slimness of his hips. His silk cravat, mother-of-pearl buttons and silver buckles screamed his ever-increasing wealth, but it had not always been like this. Father would never have approved.

Mother was wringing her hands. She could barely conceal her panic. 'Oh, there you are, Rosehannon – Mr Tregellas's been waiting for nearly half an hour. Have you done all the errands I sent you on?'

'Yes, Mother, all complete,' I replied, grasping the excuse she had just handed me.

Mr Tregellas bowed slowly, his hat barely moving, his pale-grey eyes unblinking, like the grass snake I had been watching in the meadow the day before. 'Miss Pengelly, you seem unwell.'

'Yes,' I replied, relieved to have an excuse to cut short our conversation, 'this heat's given me a terrible headache. I need to go indoors to rest.'

'I can't think what madness persuaded you to go out in the first place.' He kept his eyes on my face though I had long since looked away. 'We can't have you falling ill so near to your birthday – not now I'm looking forward to celebrating it with you.' Mother's small frame seemed to shrink even further and my unease turned to nausea. I needed to breathe, but the air was hot and stifling. Mr Tregellas saw me sway and held out his hand.

'I'm fine, thank you, Mr Tregellas,' I replied, flinching from his touch. My sharp tone must have angered him. His thin lips creased into a false smile and I could hear Father's voice warning me never to trust a man whose smile did not reach his eyes. Yet Father had trusted him.

'Mr Tregellas has called to tell us Sir Charles Cavendish is expected from London,' said Mother quietly. 'The town's that packed. There's a bi-election meeting tomorrow night and there's likely to be trouble. There've been fights already, what with the navy in town – and Mr Tregellas is telling us to stay indoors.' She looked distraught, knowing any mention of the election would rouse anger in me. She was right.

'Then Sir Charles would be wiser not to distribute so much free ale and grog. People who have so little will naturally drink to excess. Perhaps if Sir Charles spent more time down here, with the people he's meant to represent, he could find better ways to relieve their misery – more appropriate ways of gaining their support.' I said it before I could stop myself. I bit my tongue but already I could see Mother wincing.

The lines round Mr Tregellas's mouth hardened. 'I can see you've been too long in the sun, Miss Pengelly. You need to rest.' His face furious, he snatched the reins from Jimmy Tregony. Mounting the trap, he lashed the whip. 'Good day,' he said curtly.

The trap jolted forward and I watched his receding back with an equal mix of fear and loathing. Holding out her hands to help Mother, Jenna's eyes were deep with reproach and, immediately, I regretted my words. My anger would get us nowhere. No, worse than that, it could plunge us into even greater poverty. They had every reason to look at me like that.

Yet why should I not have an opinion? I had the education and intelligence of any man, so why must I always stay silent? Besides, everything was not lost. I had been handed the one piece of knowledge I needed most. Tomorrow night, Mr Tregellas would be at the meeting and his study would be empty. Tomorrow would be my chance.

Chapter Three

I tried to make amends with Jenna, sitting patiently on the three-legged stool while her deft hands brought order to my hair.

'They do say Madame Merrick's a spy...d'you think she spies for the French?' she muttered, her mouth full of hairpins. 'They do say she's the centre of a smuggling gang.'

'I wouldn't put it past her.'

'...and there's talk she's the fancy woman of three rich men.'

'What? Madame Merrick? No, surely not...well maybe she is...!'

'They do say she ran off as a young woman and married an English sea captain.'

'Jenna, you must be finished by now!'

Pursing her lips, she tugged my hair and I knew I was to be held captive a little bit longer. 'Mrs Pengelly says I'm as good as any of them seamstresses Madame Merrick employs but that's only 'cos Mrs Pengelly taught me so well.'

'I hope that doesn't mean you're going to leave us and join Madame Merrick?'

'Might…depends…' Jenna tucked the last ringlet into the clasp and stood behind me, admiring her handiwork. Our eyes caught in the mirror. 'No, course I won't,' she said. 'Things will turn out right – honest they will.'

'Perhaps I need to be more like Madame Merrick?'

'Well, they do say she's that clever – everyone's buying her gowns…' She paused as Mother's voice echoed up the stairs.

'Rosehannon, what's keeping you? I can't be late…if you're not ready, I'll take the ferry on my own.'

I hurried downstairs. We needed Mother's job and we needed Madame Merrick, but as far as I was concerned, putting Madame Merrick's accounts in order was proving more trouble than it was worth. The sooner I was finished, the better.

Fosse and Porthruan glower at each other across the river mouth, Fosse confident in its greater prosperity. You are either from Fosse or Porthruan, but with the ferry so well established, people find work where they can. Father and I were born in Porthruan: Mother's family moved there when she was a small child. I was ten years old when Father moved us to Fosse and although Mother's heart will always remain in Porthruan, my loyalties will always be to Fosse.

We left the ferry and made our way past the malt house, the sweet smell of barley filling the air. It was a bright morning with a cloudless sky and even at this early hour the sun felt warm on my face. Fosse was always busy and today was no exception. The road was teeming. Tradesmen were straining under baskets piled high with produce and a cart was already blocking the way. A crowd was forming and as people pushed passed, tempers began to flare. A mule driver stared down at me, and as I returned his glare, he spat at my feet, his foul spittle narrowly missing my shoes. Two men were rolling a barrel towards us.

'At this rate we'll be late,' said Mother, stepping into the road.

'Be careful,' I cried, pulling her back as the barrel passed dangerously close.

Her frown softened and she smiled. Hesitantly, she squeezed my arm, tucking it gently into hers before continuing behind the cart. It was a small gesture, but it meant more to me than any words and filled me with such pleasure.

Our journey took us past the blacksmith and across the square. Whether Mother had really forgiven me for my rudeness to Mr Tregellas, or was just hoping I would give in to her wishes, was not important. What was important was I felt happier than I had done for a very long time. Walking arm in arm with Mother was how a mother and daughter should walk, and we had rarely done that before.

We crossed the road and I could feel my mouth tighten. Black Dog Lane, with its crowded houses and overshadowing eaves, was always rancid and foul. No sunlight penetrated the alley and the air remained damp and fetid. Holding our breath we hurried our pace, stepping over the stagnant sewer as best we could. This part of town was a disgrace, with fever at every turn. It could never be right. How could the Corporation let people live in such poverty when those who own the tenements lived in such richness?

We passed under the arch of the Ship Inn, walking quickly through the market which was already crowded with stalls, and only at the foot of the wooden, slightly rickety, staircase, held together by iron railings, did Mother let go of my arm. Madame Merrick's dressmaking business was on the first floor.

Madame Merrick was clearly busy, her eyes unusually bright. She was a middle-aged woman with an enviable figure and always dressed with care. Her green cotton gown was plain, though fashionable, her mobcap demure. Her fichu was edged with local lace, but while her appearance gave the impression of being dressed for service, the sheen on her dress, her expensive brooch, and the rustle of her fine silk petticoats were not lost on either her wealthy clients, or every other tradeswoman in town. Her height, her elegance, her aloof expression, prominent nose and beady eyes, gave her the look of a bird of prey. Already she looked as if she had her next victim in sight and was hovering, ready to swoop.

'We have *another* new fitting, Mrs Pengelly – Mrs Hoskins is coming at noon. Mrs *George* Hoskins, *no less*, the wife of the new banker.' Her French accent was only slightly discernible in her impeccable English. 'And once Mrs Hoskins has one of my gowns, *everyone* will want one.'

'What is it she wants?' It was good to see Mother's excitement. Not losing a moment, she replaced her bonnet with a mobcap and began tying her apron round her waist.

'A day dress – probably muslin as she is feeling the heat – but she has not yet made up her mind. Bring the samples, Mrs Pengelly. We can show her the new sprig that came only yesterday…and the dotted rose that arrived last week – I am confident *her* budget can stretch to that.'

Mother rolled up her sleeves but had barely made it to the storeroom before Madame Merrick called after her. 'Josie has to redo the seams on Mrs Mead's bodice to allow another quarter of an inch and Mrs Mellows will have to finish the embroidery on Mrs Wilkes's gown…only she must use more silver thread as we are getting short of the *gold*…You can sew the lace into Mrs Warleggan's evening gown only take *great* care as the silk is *particularly fine* and very easily caught.'

She drew breath, but not for long. 'And, Mrs Pengelly, keep an eye on Elowyn…that girl is probably more trouble than she is worth. Check she washes her hands properly and wears a clean apron. I'll not have my shop *stinking of pilchards*. She cannot press pilchards and work for me. If any oil gets *near* my fabrics they will be ruined.'

I glanced into the back room where Elowyn was already hard at work, her face and hands scrubbed to a gleaming shine. She caught my eye, raising her eyebrows, and I wondered whether working for Madame Merrick could be any better than working in a pilchard cellar.

Everyone in town was astonished when Madame Merrick took the lease of the first-floor warehouse next to Father's old yard. Gossip had been rife. The Corporation had given her days, maybe months, but nobody had reckoned with her extraordinary sense of business. It was as if she could sniff out new money waiting to be spent — as if she knew it was only a matter of time before all the women in Fosse would want her lighter fabrics. Even I had to admire her for that.

The early morning light was pouring through the large windows, dust dancing in the shafts of sunbeams as they lit up the tapestry back of my chair next to the bureau. I hung up my shawl and bonnet and resumed my work. Only months ago, a jumble of receipts and invoices had spilled out of these tiny drawers in a confusion that left me horrified. Madame Merrick was far better at needlework than she was at bookkeeping and only after weeks of work was I finally managing to clear her muddle. I had gone through all her papers, entering every farthing she had spent, every farthing she had earned, recording it all in a brand-new ledger.

I opened the top drawer, inhaling the smell of the rich leather binding. It was hard to explain my love of bookkeeping. Most people thought it strange for a woman to keep accounts and finding employment was proving far more difficult than I hoped. Many assumed me incapable, but money and bookkeeping had always held a fascination for me. Ever since I was a child, I recognised that figures did not lie. To have exact calculations was like taking control.

My work nearly finished, I had lost all track of time and was surprised to hear the church bells chiming eleven. I was even more surprised to see Madame Merrick and Mother leaning out of the window, their ankles exposed among a mass of white frills.

'Who's in the carriage, Mrs Pengelly? Can you see the crest?'

'No, the footman's in the way.'

'Why are they waiting in the square? How *dreadful* for them to be surrounded by such a large crowd. Elowyn, don't just stand there gawping like a fish – find out who is in the carriage.'

Elowyn scurried to the door. Mrs Mellows and Josie dropped their embroidery, rushing to the window to watch Elowyn push herself through the crowd. The landlord of the Ship Inn was positioning tables next to his cart full of barrels and a band of musicians, playing loudly on pipes and fiddles, began to cross the square. Groups of children had begun dancing to their lively jig, and as yet more people came crushing down the lanes, it was beginning to look like the circus players had come to town.

Within minutes, Elowyn came bursting through the door. She bobbed a curtsey. 'If ye please, Madame Merrick, it's Mr Roskelly, Lady Polcarrow, and the young Sir Francis Polcarrow.' Dreading she would get her message muddled, she slowed her speech, concentrating hard, 'They're waitin' the arrival of Sir Charles and Lady April Cavendish – from London…with the whole family, it is said.' Pleased she had remembered everything, she curtseyed again – twice for good measure.

'Of course,' said Mother, 'how silly of me! Mr Tregellas told us yesterday Sir Charles and Lady April Cavendish are coming to Fosse – but I didn't think they'd come by ship.'

The carriage door was opening. Madame Merrick held her

lorgnettes to her eyes and frowned. 'Mr Roskelly has a good tailor and he clearly spares no expense...those silver buckles are very fine but, dear me, *no*, that high collar is *not* to my taste.' She raised her finely arched eyebrow at Mother before resuming her scrutiny. 'I hope those buttons on his waistcoat are well secured as they are under *quite* some pressure... and if he is preparing to stand for parliament, then someone should advise him to wear a taller hat – it would add greatly to his stature.'

'That's his sister, Lady Polcarrow, getting down from the carriage – I've only ever seen her once before.'

Madame Merrick had already focussed her lorgnettes on the lady of slim build wearing a blue satin dress with matching jacket. She clearly did not meet with approval either. Madame Merrick looked incredulous. 'I will *never* understand the English. Lady Polcarrow is still a young woman, so why is she wearing such a large bustle? If you are well connected, wealthy and beautiful, why would you not wear the very latest gowns? No French woman of quality would ever be so dreadfully out of *mode*.'

Mother seemed just as surprised. 'She's never seen in public and they say she never goes anywhere – not even to the grand dos they have in Truro. She lives that quietly at Polcarrow with her son and brother and hardly ever comes out. Mr Roskelly runs the estate and does everything for her. They do say she's a devoted mother, though. That must be her son, the young Sir Francis. What is he? Must be about eleven or twelve by now?'

Madame Merrick nodded. 'He's a good-looking boy.'

'He's got his father's height and dark looks – not that he knew his father, poor boy. Sir Francis died in a riding accident when he was just a babe...' Mother lowered her voice. 'There was a lot of gossip when Sir Francis married Alice Roskelly. She was nearly thirty years younger – her father was a local squire and always the worse for drink, but she was that beautiful and nobody blamed him. We all wished him well – then there was all that trouble with his first son. It was very sad...and her, left alone with her young son...'

A fanfare echoed across the square. A few of the crowd started pointing upwards and necks began craning to watch the mastheads of a large ship inch slowly towards the town quay. From my vantage point, I could see she was a fine, two-masted schooner carrying a square rig, and my heart leapt in anticipation before diving with annoyance. Even from where I sat, I could see the bowsprit was over-large, too ornately carved, and the figurehead ridiculously gaudy, smothered in gold paint. Who else but Sir Charles Cavendish would choose to arrive in Fosse in a ship displaying all the hallmarks of a fancy London shipyard?

Madame Merrick and Mother could not have been more delighted by the latest London fashions worn by those who alighted from the ship. Madame Merrick insisted we were witnessing *true quality* but all I saw was a bad-tempered, middle-aged man, ornately dressed with a thick bandage round one calf, and a tall, very thin woman dressed in a green silk travelling dress, whose only concern seemed the welfare of the white pug dog she carried in her arms. Neither looked pleased to have arrived.

Wiping his brow in a flurry of lace, Sir Charles Cavendish was ignoring the cheering crowds, prodding his way instead to the waiting carriage where I saw him curse the footman and bark orders at the coachman. Madame Merrick was flushed with pleasure. 'But, Miss Pengelly, you cannot see *properly* from there!'

'I've seen all I need to see,' I replied. 'Sir Charles Cavendish has no business here, nor ever has.'

'Miss Pengelly! How *can* you speak like that?'

'He's only here because he wants his friend, Robert Roskelly, to join him in parliament – otherwise he'd have stayed in London.' I kept my voice calm but my heart was thumping. Madame Merrick's face puckered in disgust. Mother's hands began to tremble but I could not stay silent. 'It's wrong and corrupt, that's all. Buying his vast estate assures him of the voting rights but he cares nothing at all for the people here.'

'What foolish nonsense!' replied Madame Merrick, drawing herself up to her full height. 'We *all* depend on great men like Sir Charles – without them there would be nothing. No employment, no estates to maintain, no houses to run…no patronage, no positions, no trade contracts. You speak *foolishly*, Miss Pengelly – dangerously and foolishly.' Straightening her gown with her long fingers, she glared with undisguised dislike. 'You would be wise to curb your tongue, young lady. You have been *much* too influenced by your father's foolish talk.'

At the mention of Father, tears welled in my eyes. A lump caught in my throat. 'You didn't know Father – he was clever and articulate. He believed every man has rights, regardless of wealth or position. He believed all men should have the franchise.'

'*Pah*! Your father was a dangerous radical, a political agitator. No better than a revolutionary! *Liberté, qualité, fraternité ou la mort!* Where did it get him? What *good* is leaving your wife and daughter to starve?' Her chest rose and fell, the muscles round her mouth tight with anger. 'Miss Pengelly, you are a woman blessed with uncommon beauty. You would be wise to *use* it well. Your father was wrong to stuff your head full of his ridiculous notions – God knows, your position is precarious enough already.' She began fanning her very flushed cheeks.

Mother came through from the back, clearly trying to make amends. 'Mrs Hoskins will be here soon…I've brought the muslin and the new rolls of satin. I'm sure she'll love this…or maybe this?'

Madame Merrick was hardly listening. Her eyes were following the carriage as it pushed through the crowds. Taking a deep breath, she spoke through pursed lips. 'It is not the likes of *Mrs* Hoskins I need to patronise my business, Mrs Pengelly. I need *Lady* April Cavendish to be my patron.'

Even Mother looked shocked. 'But Lady April has the whole of London at her disposal! You saw her clothes – she wants for nothing. You really think she might buy from here?'

I was still smarting from Madame Merrick's vicious attack but the eager tone in Mother's voice cut me like a knife. It seemed such betrayal. She had abandoned all Father's principles and it hurt. It really hurt. In all the dark days since

Father's death, I had never felt so alone, and watching them bending over the rolls of fabric seemed to increase my sense of isolation. I could never be part of Mother's new life, I knew that now.

Putting away my quill, I placed the ledger carefully back in the top drawer. I put on my bonnet and stopping momentarily at the door, bobbed an indifferent curtsey. If they heard my sullen farewell, they did not look up.

There would be thunder soon – no gulls in sight, no hint of a breeze. I closed the door. This uncanny stillness was always a sign of thunder. The air was thick and suffocating, flies buzzed noisily among the nets left drying on the quayside and even the smell of dead crabs in the blackening seaweed seemed stronger than usual. I made my way through the crowd, now boisterous from beer. Notices advertising political meetings were pinned to the pillars of the wooden overhang and I managed to peer over the heads of everyone crowding round to read the posters. They confirmed what I already guessed – the meeting would start at nine. My heart started racing. I, at least, would never forsake Father.

Chapter Four

I pleaded a headache, telling Mother and Jenna I needed an early night. They were visiting Mrs Tregony, so I would seize my chance. I changed quickly into the newly washed clothes Jenna had replaced in the bottom of my trunk – time was running out, the blanket left in my bed the best I could think to do. There was thunder in the air, the wind freshening, but reaching the quayside, I felt confident I could row the river. Untying Father's boat, I slipped the mooring and drifted upstream on the incoming tide.

The river was unusually crowded, more ships than usual seeking shelter from the impending storm. Large numbers of sailors massed along the quayside, their drunken voices filtering across the water. The quays were packed three or four deep and I searched to find somewhere to moor the boat. There was hardly anywhere, just one small space and I knew it would be tight. Squeezing between two fishing boats, I secured the boat. It was the wrong end of town and a long way from Coombe House, but it would have to do.

I would cut through the alley and take the lane behind the dockside.

The alley was dark and smelt of tar, an upturned barrel lying halfway across the entrance. There had already been fights. Bottles lay smashed against the wall and I hesitated, knowing I was being foolish. I should turn back. I should return to the boat and moor further up but time was against me and I was already late. The alley narrowed, loud shouts began echoing behind me and I turned round to see the bulky frames of a group of sailors blocking the entrance. They were clearly the worst for drink and were coming in my direction.

The alley was longer than I thought, the walls towering above me. I searched for a doorway, frantically hoping for a place to hide. The sailors had seen me. They were calling out, goading me to fight, their taunts growing more vicious as their footsteps got nearer. Ahead of me, lights from the Anchor Tavern glowed through the darkness and I began to run. I had no option. The Anchor Tavern may be the last place in the world I would want to enter but it was that, or the sailors. The door to the tavern was closed. Without hesitating, I grabbed the handle, opening the heavy oak door, shutting it firmly behind me.

The stench of burning seal oil made me want to retch and I fought to control my nausea. It was hot, stuffy, the tobacco smoke thick and choking. Oil lamps hung from the densely beamed ceiling and lanterns cast shadows over the faces of sailors crammed into every corner of the rooms. Some of the men were playing dice, some eating pies; all were smoking clay pipes, drinking from large earthenware mugs. I stared through the haze, my eyes beginning to sting. On a table nearby, two men spat on their hands, shaking on a deal. On another, a ship's captain was imprinting the thumbs of two boys in a ledger. The boys, no more than eleven or twelve, looked like frightened rabbits caught in a trap.

This was my first time in a tavern and I could hardly believe my eyes. The serving girls looked just like living figureheads. In a corner a man wearing a doe-skin hat and a brown corduroy jacket was sitting legs akimbo, a serving girl sitting on each thigh. The girls' hands were everywhere, running over his waistcoat, undoing his buttons, their fingers even sliding beneath his shirt. I had never seen anything so wanton and I could hardly tear my eyes away.

Each serving girl was offering the man a large tankard of ale and it was increasingly apparent that whichever one he chose would leave the other completely desolate. Bets were changing hands and the two serving girls, with a playfulness that was turning serious, began offering him more and more inducements to be the woman of his choice. With one hand holding aloft their beer, their other hands began straying further over his body. The guffaws were getting louder, the betting more frantic, the girls re-doubling their efforts, their huge bosoms taking on a life of their own. Appalled, I looked away, but something made me uneasy. The man seemed strangely familiar.

I glanced back. To my horror, he was no longer laughing but staring straight at me. Our eyes locked and the airless room seemed to suck the breath out of me. I stood frozen to the spot, staring back across the haze of smoke. Though his clothes were different, his hair concealed, there was no mistaking it was Jim. Cursing myself for my stupidity, I pushed my way to the door, running into the cover of darkness. How could I have been so foolish? But even before I heard his footsteps, I knew he would be following me.

'Rose, stop.'

I tried to outrun him but the lane was long, rising steeply from the river's edge. My boots were heavy, weighing me down. He stayed on my heels, his footsteps right behind me. I was beginning to lose my breath and knew it would be only a matter of time before I felt his hand grab my coat. 'What in God's name are you doing, Rose?' He was breathless, too, his chest heaving as he swung me round. 'What madness is this — on a night like this?' As if in agreement, the first rumble of thunder sounded overhead.

'Let me go! It's none of your business,' I said between gasps. 'And don't call me Rose. Only Father ever called me Rose.' In the half-light of the distant oil lamp, I could just make out the lines of his face. There was accusation in his eyes.

'I hardly think I need be formal, Miss Pengelly,' he replied, 'when I've just seen you in one of the worst taverns in town.'

'I didn't mean to go there — I don't go to places like that — I was running from some sailors, that's all…' I had no reason to explain myself but he knew my name and that was dangerous.

We were standing where the lane joined the town square. A group of very drunk townsmen were weaving their way down the hill, singing and cursing as they staggered towards us. I was relieved when they passed and made to leave, but

Jim grabbed my arm, holding me back. Shapes began forming in the shadows behind them – three men were following in the townsmen's wake.

'It's the press gang,' Jim said, pushing me quickly into a doorway.

It was a small doorway, hardly room for one, let alone two, and before I realised what he was doing, he squeezed next to me, his body crushing against mine. I held my breath, desperately hoping we were enough out of the lamplight to be hidden. His hands were stretching above me, his palms resting against the lintel of the door. In the darkness, I could feel his chest rising and falling. I could smell tobacco from the tavern still clinging to his jacket. I had never stood so close to a man before, never felt a man's body pressing so firmly against my own and his strength unnerved me.

'They've passed,' he whispered, turning to go.

'Wait. My hair's caught in your button. Free it please – without pulling.' He was still uncomfortably close.

'Patience, Miss Pengelly. There, you're free.'

It was not his button which had caught my hair, but a chain he was wearing round his neck. I was amazed to catch the glimmer of a ring – a large ruby set with diamonds which sparkled even in the darkness. It was clearly worth a lot of money and I gazed in astonishment. He must have stolen it. Or had he been given it by some poor woman?

'You'd better get back to your wenches,' I said, staring pointedly at the ring. 'They'll be missing your knee to sit on.'

'That's very harsh, Miss Pengelly.'

'It's not harsh at all. It's the truth.'

I sounded cross, but it was me I was cross with. Cross, ashamed, frightened of the sensations his body had roused in me. Another rumble of thunder sounded across the river. I stepped back into the alley. 'Leave me be,' I said.

'Where're you going, Rose?'

I took no notice, walking swiftly under the arch of the stables. Time was running short. Immediately, he followed. Once again, he grabbed my arm, pulling me into the stable where the smell of horse dung mingled with fresh hay. A stable lad was calming two horses.

'What's going on? What makes a clever woman like you risk so much? If I'm to have any chance of helping you, I must know the truth.'

'Helping me?'

'You put yourself in great danger to help me, so now it's my turn to help you. What's it you're up to?'

I hesitated, the sincerity in his voice taking me by surprise. It was as if he was speaking like a friend. No, better than that, it was as if I was drowning and he was throwing me a rope. In effect, I had been drowning since Father died and I longed for someone I could trust. I had felt his strength, I could sense his power, I knew him to be clever. Something deep inside me longed to draw on this strength but I could not trust him or anyone else. I was being foolish even considering it.

'Let me pass,' I said.

Chapter Five

I made my way past the quays to the new end of town where the street was wider and the air fresher. These modern buildings were the best Fosse offered. They had covered drains and water pipes and, though rather crammed in between the steep hillside and the river's edge, stood tall and dignified with symmetrical windows, ornate shutters and porticos above the front door. Father always dreamt of owning such a fine house and when his business flourished, he poured money into obtaining the lease. Coombe House was the third in the row. I had not been back for over a year and as I stared at the familiar red bricks, I was unprepared for the intense longing welling up in my heart.

The house was strangely dark, only two oil lamps burning either side of the front door and a light coming from the basement. I crept slowly down the steps, peering in through the window. Everything was so familiar. Mrs Munroe, Sam and Tamsin had stayed with Mr Tregellas and seeing them now brought tears to my eyes. Mrs Munroe was sitting in her chair by the fireside, her huge ham-like arms working her knitting as vigorously as if she was rolling one of her prize-winning pastries. Tamsin was playing cards at the long pine table, her starched white apron and cap glowing in the candlelight.

The room was just as it had always been — a kettle whistling on the stove, a large stockpot hanging heavily from the spit. Copper moulds and fish kettles sat neatly on the shelves. A huge ham and bunches of herbs hung from the meat hooks. It was all so dear to me, so very precious — I had to stop myself from running down the steps and throwing myself through the door.

Sam was not in the kitchen: I had already guessed he would be at the cock fight in Fore Street. This was my chance. I would be quick. I would be silent. It had started to rain, so any noise I might make could be blamed on the weather.

Creeping round the back, I stood watching the silent house. There was very little space between the house and the steeply rising hill behind. Mother had tried to use it as a courtyard, but the back was too overshadowed, too dark to grow anything. Most of the larger trees had been coppiced or felled, but over the years several branches had grown outwards from the hill, leaning dangerously close to the houses. I hardly dared look. My whole plan rested on whether anyone had thought to trim the branch of the beech tree growing behind our house.

I was in luck. Even through the darkness, I could see the shadow looming above me. If anything, it seemed to have grown stronger. My old window was on the second floor

– all I needed to do was to climb the trunk and crawl along the branch. After all, it was not such an outrageous idea – I had done it many times before.

I began inching my way along the branch. The bark was dry, easy to grip and I was confident I could not be seen. All I needed to do was keep my nerve and stretch across to reach the window, but somehow it seemed more daunting than I remembered. The branch was swaying, the rain penetrating the leaves above me. The pounding in my chest was making it hard to breathe and I found it hard to balance. I had not thought I would feel such fear. I gripped the branch, staring at the casement, almost too scared to move. But I had not come this far to fail. With one hand holding tightly to the branch, I stretched out, clutching the casement as tightly as I could.

Nothing moved. The window remained tightly shut. Once again I leant across, stretching my arm as far as I could, my fingers gripping the latch, shaking the window. In my panic, I started to fumble. Nothing was shifting. The catch had always been loose and just a shake would be enough to slide it free, but it was clearly stuck, the window remaining tightly shut.

'Breaking and entry's a felony punishable by hanging. You know that, don't you, Rose?' Jim's voice came from the tree behind me. He was crouching on the end of the branch. Furious, I made my way slowly back.

'What're you doing here? I didn't hear you follow me.'

'Nobody ever does,' he said softly, the implication behind his words so unmistakable, my stomach lurched in fear. He was staring at me, no sign of a smile.

45

'Go away. Leave me alone.'

He took no notice. Squeezing past me, he began crawling towards the window, the branch dipping precariously under his weight. At the furthest end he steadied himself, holding on to the casement while he reached into his belt. He grabbed his knife and once again, I saw the cold steel glint in the dim light. With very little effort he leant across, slipping his knife into the sash, deftly flicking his wrist to loosen the catch. Immediately, the window gave way. I caught the gleam in his eye, the smile on his lips as he slid quickly across the gap, balancing on the stone sill with the agility of a cat. Making no sound, he slid the window open.

'We're in,' was all he said.

Chapter Six

In the darkness, my old room smelt musty and unused. My hands trembled so much, I could hardly strike the tinderbox. Jim heard me fumbling, 'No, Rose...don't risk a candle. Wait – your eyes will soon get used to the dark.'

'I'm not a thief,' I whispered.

'Then what're we doing here?' Through the darkness I could see him studying me.

'I'm looking for something.'

I began to make out shapes. Dust sheets were hanging like eerie phantoms, covering my iron bedstead, my washstand, my chest of drawers. I walked carefully round them, pulling back the covers, my heart aching at the touch of my old belongings. I had lived here, a young woman with plans and dreams to fill a lifetime, yet, silenced by dust sheets, my aspirations seemed to mock me from the shadows. I had not expected to feel so wretched.

'We used to live here,' I whispered, the lump in my throat catching my words. 'This used to be my room.'

'What're we looking for?' Jim's abrupt tone brought me sharply to my senses. Whether I liked it or not, I had to explain.

'My father owned Pengelly Boatyard. You must have heard about his bankruptcy.'

'No,' he said, looking away, 'I'm new to Fosse.'

'Father built a cutter for the revenue men – a really beautiful boat, the best of her kind. She was a hundred and twelve tons – eight guns and over a thousand yards of canvas. He'd designed her for speed…she was his pride and joy and ready for commission.'

'And?'

'There was some caulking to finish and warps to attach, but very little left to do…and, against all advice, she'd been fully rigged.'

'Don't tell me. She was stolen.'

'From right under our noses. The watchman was attacked and badly beaten. They slipped her out in the middle of the night and no trace has been seen of her since. I warned Father to get her insured but he never took my advice.' I tried to keep my voice low but I was conscious it was rising.

'Why'd you lose the house?'

'William Tregellas was Father's timber merchant. When the boat was stolen, Father owed a lot of money to all his suppliers. He was expecting to pay off his debts with the money from the sale, but when it disappeared his creditors foreclosed. By far the most debt was to Mr Tregellas – Father couldn't pay, was declared bankrupt, and imprisoned. Mr Tregellas was the major creditor so he was given the house and boatyard. Father didn't survive long in gaol – soon after he caught putrid fever and died.'

'An' you suspect Mr Tregellas of the theft?' Jim had got straight to the point. He was staring at me, his mouth tight.

'Yes,' I replied, grateful he had taken me seriously. 'It's dangerous using just one timber merchant – I warned Father to spread the risk but he wouldn't have it. Mr Tregellas was his friend and he trusted him. But I've always mistrusted Mr Tregellas. That's why I'm here. I need proof of his treachery before it's too late.'

'Why too late?'

'We owe him more money,' I said quickly. I had said too much already. I would have to be careful. 'If any evidence links him to the cutter, it'll be in his study.'

'Then best we waste no more time.' Jim moved quietly to the door, opening it a fraction before peering into the darkness. The house was silent, only the faint ticking of the clock downstairs. A candle must be burning in the hall as light filtered up the staircase. Nodding to Jim, I began making my way across the landing, descending the stairs to the first floor. The sight of the study door wrenched my heart. I remembered standing there as a child, reaching high as I could, leaving sticky fingerprints over the polished panels and gleaming brass knob.

We were in luck – the door opened to the pitch-black study. 'The shutters are closed – you can light your candle now, Rose. No light will show.'

The room seemed exactly as Father had left it. As the flame took hold, I could almost see him sitting by the fire, a book on his lap, pipe smoke curling in the air around him. It was as if I was a child again, sneaking into his study; watching him reading, waiting for him to take off his glasses and pretend to be surprised. He would put down his book, hold out his hands, and I would go running to him, climb on his lap, so proud and happy he had allowed me to stay. He would read to me, ask my opinion on his latest pamphlet, and I would try so hard to give him sensible answers. The pain of the memory was almost unbearable.

I put the candle on Father's old desk, placing it carefully so no wax would spill, easing open the drawers, one at a time. I searched their contents, replacing everything exactly as I had found it. With every false hope, I grew more desperate. Nothing was incriminating, all the papers unconnected with the boatyard. Even the bureau revealed nothing. Jim watched from the darkness, saying nothing, merging with the shadows, his presence strangely reassuring.

A whirring sound momentarily startled me. The long case clock in the hall struck midnight and immediately the carriage clock on the mantelpiece began sounding out the hour. The familiar chimes used to bring me such comfort but now they increased my panic. Time was running out. 'There's nothing here – but there has to be something, there has to be.'

Jim peered through a tiny hole in the shutters. 'We'd best risk no longer. Have you found anything at all?'

'Nothing to link him to the cutter.'

Holding up the candle, I cast my eye round the familiar room, searching the shadows to see if I had missed anything.

Nothing seemed out of place. The bookcases were tidy, the periodicals neatly stacked, but something caught my eye – something different. A low table, covered by a brocade cloth, stood in the corner of the room and the more I looked at it, the more out of place it seemed. I was amazed I had not noticed it before.

'This wasn't here in Father's time.' Pulling back the cloth I revealed, not a low table, but an ornately carved chest with a large lock.

Jim rushed to my side. 'The lock's too strong – I'll not be able to force it. We must find the key.'

Running to the desk, I began rummaging through the quills, knocking over inkpots in my haste, spilling the contents of the blotting sand. I had not seen a key in my search, but perhaps I had not been looking for one. I ran to the chair by the fire, searching the table, looking in the snuffbox, the tinderbox, tearing open the lid of the pipe box. There was nothing.

'It'll be a big key – too big to take with him – it'll be here somewhere.'

I was facing the fireplace. The elaborately carved mantle was too large for the room, certainly too ornate, but Father had commissioned it from one of our best carpenters and he loved it. Even when there was no fire he would stand looking into the grate, his hands resting against the mantle. I could see him standing there. Suddenly I knew where the key would be. The top of the mantle had a hidden ridge – it must be there. I hurried across the room, standing high on my toes, reaching my hand along the ledge, feeling among

51

the dust until my fingers touched cold iron. 'I've got it!' I cried.

With trembling hands, I put the key in the lock and turned it, lifting the heavy lid. It was just as I thought – the chest was crammed full of papers and I recognised two books at once. 'These are my ledgers,' I whispered, smoothing my hands across the leather bindings. 'I kept this one just before the cutter was stolen.'

'*Your* ledgers?'

'No need to look so surprised. I kept all Father's books. I was his bookkeeper.'

'Blimey, Rose. Is there nothing you can't do?'

I looked up at his hint of sarcasm, 'I can't sew,' I said tartly.

My reply seemed to catch him off guard. He threw back his head and laughed, but it was dangerously loud and I cut him short. Besides, I had seen something far more important. Among the contents of the chest were an unfamiliar ledger and a mass of letters and bills – none that I recognised. Nor could I read them. It was impossible to make any sense of them. 'These letters don't seem to be in English,' I said, putting them nearer the candle.

Jim glanced at them. 'That's because they're in French.'

'French? Then we won't know what they say,' I whispered, staring in surprise as he looked to be examining them in detail.

'I speak French,' he replied, 'an' read French,' he added, with a flicker of a smile.

'Then what do they say?' I snapped, annoyed he was enjoying a joke at my expense.

He held the letters closer to the candle. 'This one…' He stopped, glancing up at the closed shutters. Carriage wheels were rumbling along the cobbles, hooves clattering quickly towards us and we froze like statues, listening to them stop below the window. Someone was shouting, a command ringing through the night air.

'Quick.' Jim blew out the candle. 'We'll take these with us.' Throwing everything into the brocade cloth, he gathered the edges into a tight bundle, twisting it several times before he threw it over his shoulders. Almost immediately, the empty hall erupted into life. Footsteps emerged from the servants' quarters, light flooded the hall. The front door flung open and an angry voice shouted more orders. Only the large stairwell separated us from Mr Tregellas. I stood, too petrified to move – if he came upstairs to his study, we would surely hang, if he chose the drawing room, we still had a chance. 'Bring brandy to the drawing room for Mr Roskelly,' he shouted.

My heart was hammering so hard, I could hardly breathe. I felt sick with fear. We heard the drawing room door shut and I led the way, retracing our steps as silently as I could. Jim followed behind. The top corridor seemed so much longer, the distance so much further. In the bedroom, Jim eased open the window, the rain wetting our faces. The branch was swaying, swiping at us as it brushed against the glass. Jim grabbed it, helping me onto the sill, his hands steady over mine.

'Don't look down,' he whispered, 'an' be careful, it's slippery.'

I breathed in for courage. Fear gave me the strength I needed. It may have been dangerous, but far more dangerous was to be caught like the thieves we were. I reached the trunk and felt the branch dipping beneath Jim's weight.

Now all we needed to do was get those papers home.

Chapter Seven

Storm clouds raced overhead as we turned towards the sea.

'Walk. Don't run or you'll attract attention.' With the stolen books slung over his shoulder, Jim walked quickly ahead, turning almost immediately down an unlit passage. 'Keep close behind me.'

'Are you sure this is safe?'

'No, that's why we'll use it – the night watchmen never come down here.'

I hurried close on his heels, my heart racing. It was filthy, dark and narrow. I could feel my boots sinking ankle-deep in mud, squelching through fish heads lying stinking in our path. I was desperate not to stumble. Peering through the darkness, I stepped over broken crates, striding quickly over the heaps of sacking blocking the way. Men lay huddled in doorways, too drunk to move. Shuffles and grunts came from moving shadows and a woman's voice called out, enticing us over. Jim kept up his pace, going deeper into the maze of buildings, stopping only when the alley widened and we could see the quayside.

'Where's your boat?' he whispered.

'Behind the brewhouse.'

The squall had whipped the sea to an angry chop, tossing the moored boats like weightless corks. We found the boat wedged firmly between the two yawls and I needed all my strength to pull it towards us. Foam frothed against the steps, the sea rising and falling. Even the larger ships were pitching, their masts creaking in the darkness above us. Jim put down the makeshift bundle, holding the boat as I jumped in the bow. Handing me the stolen evidence, he began taking off his jacket. 'Use this to keep that dry. Don't let it get wet.' With one leg on the steps, he pushed against the boat and we began gliding through the swirling water, spray drenching us, waves rocking the boat from side to side. I wrapped Jim's jacket around the damp bundle, praying it was not already too late.

'It's a southerly – we've got wind against tide,' I shouted.

'An' it's a spring tide,' he shouted back. 'The waves are building – it's going to be rough.'

The wind was blowing straight through the gap that formed the river mouth. Jim grabbed the oars and began to pull, pitting his strength against the tide pulling us out to sea. Waves splashed against the boat, covering us with spray. My cap blew from my head, disappearing into the blackness around us. Hair swirled round my face, spray stinging my eyes. My lips tasted of salt. It was a wild night for a small boat and I should have been scared. I should have been gripping the sides in terror, fearing for my life, but for all the danger we were in, I was not afraid. I am a child of the sea. I have rowed these waters all my life and in the toughest of conditions. I become alive on the sea. I felt invincible. I had risked my life and escaped – and I was holding evidence that would clear Father's name.

The movement of the boat steadied, Jim's rowing was confident, we were making progress. For the first time in a very long while, I felt happy, carefree, and I threw back my head, relishing the wind blowing through my hair. I began smiling, laughing, looking back at Jim to share my pleasure. The smile died on my lips and I caught my breath. He was staring at me with a ferocity that made my stomach tighten, his eyes all but devouring me. For a moment I held his stare before he turned away, scowling into the darkness, redoubling his efforts against the tide. I, too, turned away, a furious blush burning my cheeks. It had been a look of naked desire and I had never been looked at in that way before. Licking the salt from my burning lips, I stared out to sea, startled by the thrill of pleasure passing through me.

I watched him from the corner of my eye. His chin, set hard with exertion, looked grim and determined. His hat had long since blown away, his hair now loosened by the wind. Dark strands streaked across his forehead, falling across his eyes. As he strained against the tide, his shirt clung to his chest. I could see the power of his muscles, the strength of his grip and I looked away. Porthruan harbour could not come soon enough.

'We'll leave the boat round the back of the smokehouse and take the cliff path,' I said stiffly. 'There's an old huer's hut on the top of the cliff – we can shelter there for a while.'

Jim nodded in agreement, his face every bit as sombre as mine.

Chapter Eight

The tail end of the squall was driving dark clouds across the moon. We left the harbour, slipping behind the bakehouse, climbing the cliff path as fast as we could. Ahead of us, the slate roof of the huer's hut shone silver against the dark sky.

The huer was Joshua Trewellyn, who lived in the cottage next to the smokehouse. For weeks he had been scanning the horizon, searching for shoals, watching, dawn to dusk, for the first sign of gannets diving headlong into the sea to gorge on the pilchards. It had been a good year for mackerel with the pilchards yet to run, but on a night like this there would be no sightings and it was no secret the lure of his bed would be too strong to resist. He would return at first light.

As a child I was once on the cliff top when the shoals came in. I will never forget the way the sea rippled and seemed to boil as the fish massed in their thousands. I remember the cry of the gulls, the diving of the dolphins, the excitement I felt as the huer blew his horn to announce their arrival. I was convinced they were my pilchards. I had seen them first and I had given them to the town. It was what everyone wanted – every ear tuned for the sound of the horn, every hand waiting to drop what they were doing; every man, woman and child, ready to run to the boats or prepare the cellars. I had watched the nets drop, the seine boats circle, the fish come glistening out of the sea like liquid silver and nothing could shake my belief that they were my fish. I suppose, ever since, I have wanted to recapture that feeling of giving people what they most need.

The wind was lessening, the clouds thinning, the steep, well-trodden path easy to climb. At the highest point, the hut stood bathed in moonlight and we stopped to catch our breath.

Jim motioned for me to wait. 'Let me see if it's empty,' he said, walking the last few yards alone. I understood his meaning. Over the last month, a large number of vagrants had come to Porthruan – it was just possible they had found it first. 'We're in luck,' he called, opening the door.

It was more of a shack than a hut. A shaft of moonlight shone through the door, lighting the cramped interior. In one corner, a small table littered with the remains of a meal, in the other, a wooden pail balanced on a stool. Along the back, a dirty mattress lay on the floor, straw bursting from it through several large holes. It was a dismal place but warm and dry and a welcome refuge, despite the rancid smell. Until then, I had not realised how wet we were. Jim saw me shivering.

'I'm afraid there's nothing by way of a fire,' he said, reaching down for the blanket lying strewn across the mattress. 'Take your jacket off and wrap yourself in this.' I hesitated, the look he had given me still fresh in my mind. 'You can trust me, Rose. I'll not harm you.' Helping me off with my soaking jacket, he wrapped the blanket round my shoulders. 'Though, you're very likely to get lice,' he added without a smile.

Lice or no lice, I felt instantly better and as the welcome warmth spread through me, I grew anxious to examine the ledgers. Sitting down on the low mattress, we dragged our stolen bundle across the dirt floor, the brocade now silver-grey in the moonlight. Jim undid the knot and reached into his jacket. He drew out the tinderbox, the remaining stub of candle. 'Have we enough?' I asked.

'Yes, though we may not get it lit – the wick's rather wet.' Rolling the wick in his fingers, he struck the flint. 'That's got it.' We were in luck, three strikes and the candle bathed the hut in soft yellow light.

He started placing the contents into separate piles, his scowl deepening. There was a lot to get through – letters, receipts, several account books, all jumbled in front of us in a tumbled mess. I helped smooth out the papers, placing them in front of him, watching him skim through their contents, any doubt of his ability to read quickly dispelled. 'Well? What do they say?'

He pointed to the first pile. 'These letters are from a sea captain based in Jersey – they are receipts for maintenance and repair of a ship called *L'Aigrette*.'

'*L'Aigrette?*'

'It's French for egret.'

'Go on.'

'These bills are for nails, tar, varnish, trunnels. This is a blacksmith's bill an' this one looks like it's from a sailmaker.' He held the bill nearer the candle, 'No, a ropemaker. An' this one's for the repair of a broken spar.'

'Why'd you pay expensive repair bills in Jersey when you've your own boatyard in Fosse?' I asked, already knowing the answer.

'This one contains expenses for the crew. Look, here it lists the master, first mate and three other sailors. This column's their food, this one…rum…this one must be wages an' this one's harbour dues…'

'When do the expenses start?' I could wait no longer. Leaning over Jim, I flicked back the pages of the neatly written entries. My fingers were trembling. 'Mai 14th 1792. Mai is May, isn't it? That's exactly two weeks after the cutter was stolen! It's got to be the cutter. This must be the proof I need.'

Jim was not smiling. 'The letters are addressed to Mr Tregellas an' it's his ship, right enough, but is it your father's cutter?' His unshaven face was dark against the shadows, his scar visible in the flickering candlelight. It was unnerving the way he never smiled, his jaw always firm, his mouth always grim. 'All this means nothing – not till you find *L'Aigrette*…' His eyes seemed to pierce mine. 'An' you'd need to identify her. Would you be able to do that?'

Able? He had no idea. Nobody did. Nobody thought a

woman capable of anything other than sewing or cooking. 'Of course I would! D'you think I don't know one boat from another? I'd know her a mile off – I know everything there's to know about that ship. I spent hours studying the plans. I helped choose the keel pieces. I watched every plank being sawn. I'd know her on sight.' I began gathering up the evidence, drawing it together in neat piles, ready to tie the edges back into a knot. Jim put his hand on my arm.

'Rose, stop, I meant no disrespect...'

The candle guttered, flickering brightly before it died, the last thin coil of smoke slowly dispersing. We were left sitting on the low mattress, bathed by the light of the moon shining so brightly in on us and I knew there could be no more reading. The thunderclouds had passed and with them the blackness of the night. It would be dawn soon. Already a grey haze was visible in the east. We had risked everything. We had stolen the evidence and had escaped uncaught. My anger was misplaced – I should be grateful to this man, not flare at him at the slightest provocation. After all, he had risked his life for me.

'Father used to engrave a rose on every ship he built,' I said more softly, 'even small fishing boats. It was our mark – our secret. I'd go searching the ship, looking everywhere until I found it, but I always found it. Even now, I could go straight to every rose, on every boat. I could go straight to the cutter and identify her.'

Jim leant against the back of the hut, wrapping another blanket around his shoulders. The thought of Father had saddened me and in the silence that followed, I thought I would cry. 'You'd climbed into that window before, hadn't you?'

I nodded. Whether it was the soft lilt in his voice, the intimacy of the hut, or the sheer beauty of the moon, I do not know. I yearned to answer. I had been holding back my feelings for so long and seeing Father's study had opened wounds I had tried to heal. 'Many times,' I replied.

'An' why was that?'

'Mother had several miscarriages and five stillbirths. I'm the only child that survived. One boy lived until he was three weeks old.' I hesitated, finding it hard to speak the words I had never spoken before. 'Father was overjoyed to have a son to carry on the yard. I was ten years old – his beloved child – but when I saw him holding his son in his arms, I knew I didn't count. When the baby died, something died in him. I knew he wanted a son, not me. It's the hardest thing, knowing you don't count.'

Jim said nothing but pulled his blanket more tightly around him, making space for me to rest against the wall. It was a friendly gesture and tugged at the emptiness I felt inside. I so wanted to talk. I wanted to tell him how wonderful Father had been, how he had taught me everything about the boats we had built. I sat back, wrapping my blanket firmly round me.

'Long after I was meant to be in bed, I would sit on the cold stairs looking into Father's study, watching his grief, getting angrier and angrier I wasn't born a boy. I knew I could be as good as any boy – I just needed to prove it. I'd watch the boys rowing the river and I was determined to join their races. It didn't take long to devise a plan to dress in breeches and row against them.'

'An' it meant climbing in and out of your bedroom?'

'Yes. You saw how easy it was.'

'An', don't tell me, you found you were good at rowing.' There was more than a hint of irony in his voice which annoyed me. I sat forward, preparing to leave.

'Well, yes, I was. And I still am, as a matter of fact. I'm a very good rower. I don't see why women are meant to be weak and feeble – some of us are very strong and able. We don't all like sitting about watching men doing things we're perfectly capable of doing ourselves.'

Jim put his hand on my arm. This was the second time he had stopped me leaving. 'Rose, I've no doubt you're capable of a lot more besides – tell me about the rowing, did you get found out?'

I leant back against the wall. 'One evening I returned to my room to find Father waiting for me. He was surprisingly calm and hadn't told Mother, but he demanded an explanation. I was eleven years old and suddenly very angry. I said if he treated me more like a boy, I wouldn't have to prove I was as good as any boy.'

'How'd he take that?'

The memory saddened me. What a hurt, lonely child I had been. 'He asked me what I proposed and I said I wanted to help him in the yard. I wanted to learn the business.'

'Did he agree?'

'Yes. From then on, I joined him every day. He set about teaching me to read and write. He taught me all about boat-building and, over the years, I couldn't learn enough. Boats, books, bookkeeping, I was like a sponge, absorbing everything. He was a self-educated man and he taught me how to learn.'

'Didn't your mother mind her only daughter spending so much time away from her?'

'No, well…perhaps. I don't know…she had Jenna to keep her company – Jenna became her companion.' Jim looked up at the catch in my voice. 'Mother taught her to sew and Jenna's much better at that sort of thing. Mother would've wasted her time trying to teach me, and besides…' I stopped.

'Besides what?'

'Nothing.' I had stopped in time. I would never tell anyone my dreams of managing my own yard.

Jim could see he had annoyed me. 'Don't let's quarrel. Tell me about your father, he seems an interesting man.' Our shoulders were touching, the warmth of his blanket pressing against mine. It felt comforting, strangely reassuring. Yes, Father had been an interesting man and I wanted Jim to know that. I wanted him to understand his actions would help clear the name of a good man. I pulled the blanket round me, the coarse wool rough against my chin.

'He was a master shipwright. He was honest and honourable. He cared so much for the men who worked for him and for those who needed his yard. I used to warn him about it, but he took no notice.'

'Of the accounts?'

'Yes. He insisted on paying the men weekly and he'd always extend credit to those in need – even though there'd be no chance of getting paid until a catch came in. Even then, there was sometimes no money to be had.'

'He was in arrears, I take it?'

'It's not so much the amount you're owed, it's who owes it. Seine boats are good business because they're owned by wealthy men and you eventually get the money, but Father never turned away drift fishermen. He knew they'd neither cash nor credit but what could he do? If he didn't mend their boats he'd be condemning their families to starve.'

'If he expected losses, why'd he not put enough by to cover them?' Jim's tone seemed suddenly dismissive – as if he thought Father foolish.

'Of course he'd have liked to! But it's not like that. Boat-building's political – it's about power and bribery. It's about greed and election promises. Contracts are awarded through political favour as opposed to any merit. You only mend or build if the Corporation lets you. You can only use Corporation-approved businesses and every member takes a cut – everything's controlled and if you challenge the system you're finished.'

'Surely contracts came his way?'

'Father would grovel to no-one, so he made many enemies. That's why he agreed to build the cutter – because his men needed work. He knew building a fast ship for the Revenue would make him unpopular with the Corporation. Their income from smuggling would be at risk, but Father wasn't put off. He took the contract to keep the yard going. He was determined to stamp out the ever increasing corruption of the Corporation…and the greed of the two big estates.'

'Then your father was a political man – a Radical?' Jim's voice sounded suddenly cold.

'Only those steeped in corruption would call him radical – others would call him a free thinker, a man of the future.' I pushed aside my blanket and knelt on the floor, gathering up the letters, pulling the cloth into a bundle.

'Others? There are others like him in Fosse?'

'In Fosse? Maybe not, but he belonged to a Corresponding Society. They believe all men are born free and have a right to live without oppression and enslavement.'

Jim's laugh was bitter. He knelt on the ground next to me, his strong hands tying the knot with ease. 'No man's free. Every man has his price – sounds like your father was a revolutionary – perhaps he'd have liked to see heads roll.'

I stared at him in horror. 'Father'd never sanction violence. He wanted democracy, that's all – the right to choose who represented him in parliament – not have some spoilt aristocrat foisted on him.'

A veil seemed to pass over Jim's eyes, his mouth tightened. 'It's a dangerous world out there, Miss Pengelly, an' thoughts like that lead to trouble – you'd do better distancing yourself from your father's politics.'

I was stunned. How could he? How dare he criticise me, or Father? 'Who are you to give me advice?' I retorted, my cheeks burning, 'An educated man, wasting his life like you? Drinking in the worst sort of taverns? Who relies on his knife and breaks into houses? I hardly think I need your advice.'

I was furious with him, but even more furious with myself. What had I been thinking? I had let him prise out my secrets.

I had let down my guard and he had thrown it back in my face. Who was he anyway? And why was he now dressed as a townsman?

'Why've you come to Fosse?' I said angrily.

He caught my glare. 'I'm searching for someone.'

'And what will you do when you find him?'

'That's my business.'

I stared at his stony face, the hate in his eyes, and suddenly felt fearful. I was a fool. I had said too much. He was a dangerous man and I could not afford to have him as my enemy. I tried to smile, soften my voice. 'Thank you for helping me, I'm very grateful, but we'll part and go our separate ways now – our paths need never cross again.'

In the east, the grey haze was streaked with pink. Before long, dawn would break, the huer would soon return. The cockerels would soon be stretching out their long necks and shaking out their feathers, ready to herald the new day. I had to hurry. Picking up the heavy bundle, I lifted it carefully onto my shoulder.

Jim was leaning against the door, his eyes following my every move. As I brushed past him, I caught his whisper. 'We will meet again, Rose. Can't you see it's our destiny?'

Jenna had not been fooled by the blanket in my bed – she had left the back door unlocked. I pushed it open, my relief so great I wanted to cry. I suddenly felt so scared. What I was holding in my hands was enough to hang me. No, it would hang us all, Mother and Jenna alongside me. I looked round, my fear mounting. They must not find it – they must know nothing about it, or they would be implicated. I crept back into the yard. I would hide it in the henhouse; it would be safer out of the cottage and I would search for a safer place in the morning.

The church clock was striking four as I tip-toed up the stairs, quarter past the hour, as I lay in bed. I felt sick with anxiety, more worried by Jim's unpredictable attitude than the theft itself – one moment he had seemed trustworthy, the next hostile and dangerous. I had no way of knowing if I could trust him to keep silent. I shut my eyes, courting sleep.

I was back in the boat, sea spraying my face. The wind was whipping the waves, the oars creaking as they dipped beneath the water. Jim was watching me, staring at me with that hungry look that had taken my breath away. Suddenly, I sat bolt upright.

I had been so preoccupied with the way he had looked at me, I had not thought how he was rowing the river. Newcomers found the tide treacherous in a southerly wind, local people knew how to do it – local people used the rips and eddy of the fast-flowing current to make the crossing safer. Jim had taken the exact course I would have taken. He rowed like a local. Like someone who had done it many times before. I remembered how quietly he had followed me to Coombe House. What an idiot I was.

I jumped out of bed, running barefoot across the yard, throwing open the henhouse. I began rummaging through the hay, desperately searching for the old sack. I drew my hands backwards and forward, loud squawking disturbing the silence. All along, I knew my search would be futile. The sack was still there but, no matter how hard I searched, the evidence had disappeared.

Chapter Nine

Thursday 27th June 1793 11:00 a.m.

Jenna pinned back the shutters, letting sunshine stream into the room. 'Honest to God…what was ye thinking, waking us all up at four this morning? Mrs Pengelly nearly died of fright…I banged me head and the chickens still ain't settled…! We never get foxes in the yard. Ye know that, I know that, yer mother knows that…and now everyone's wondering what ye were up to…Drink this and don't complain – I'm not having ye come down with a fever.' She handed me a steaming cup of nettle brew and stood, arms crossed, staring at my tangled hair. I made a face at the pungent brew, waiting for the next scolding. 'I was worried sick last night – worried sick and in two minds to tell Mrs Pengelly.'

'Don't tell her anything. Don't ever tell anyone anything.'

'Well how was I to know if ye was safe or not?'

'I am safe. And I won't be doing it again.'

'Then I'll take them clothes back.'

I looked hurriedly round the room. There was no trace of my sodden clothes. Jenna had whisked them away before Mother could see them. 'No, keep them – just in case.'

'Then ye've not finished.'

'Oh, for goodness sake, stop fussing! You do nothing but fuss. I'm fine; I'm safe and I'll keep out of any more trouble. Satisfied?'

I had to make do with a sniff and a cold shoulder, but I was not in the mood to be scolded. My head thumped, my mouth was dry, I ached all over and I was furious with myself for my lack of foresight. The fact that Jim had outwitted me so easily left me boiling with rage. 'What's the time?' I asked grudgingly.

'Just past eleven.'

'Has Mother gone to Madame Merrick?'

'Yes, but she's that worried, says she'll be home at twelve to see how ye are.'

I could tell Jenna was more than usually upset and it was not fair of me to vent my anger on her. 'I'm sorry,' I said softly, 'I'm very grateful you didn't tell her and I've no right to snap. Are we friends?'

'Could be,' she replied, 'if ye sit still enough so I can do yer hair.'

The river was intensely blue, completely still, the sun glinting so brightly it made my eyes water. Why had he stolen the evidence? What did he hope to gain? I was deep in thought as I stepped into the ferry. Either he was going to demand money from me, or he was planning to blackmail Mr Tregellas. He knew I had no money, so that was not the reason and if he blackmailed Mr Tregellas, he would be in too much danger of exposing himself as the thief. What would someone like Jim do?

I jumped at the sound of my name. I had not heard the ferryman ask for his fare.

'Gettin' out, Miss Pengelly, or are ye here for the ride?' It was Joshua Tregen. I remembered him as a thin, spotty youth who I used to row against in the gig races. I had not liked him then and I had no reason to like him now. 'Perhaps yer just wanted to watch me row, Miss Pengelly? Yer like muscles on a man, do yer?' he said, puffing up his chest, flexing his torso.

'Admire your rowing? You know very well I can row every bit as well as you, Joshua Tregen,' I said, throwing my money into the boat.

I was angry with Joshua Tregen for speaking to me like that, but even angrier with myself – it was another man's muscles I had been picturing in my mind. Losing the evidence was my main concern but something else was making me uneasy. I had found discrepancies in Madame Merrick's accounts. Several invoices for silk and half a dozen rolls of velvet and satin were missing and I was not looking forward to telling her she would need them before she could clear her books with the Custom and Excise officials.

I climbed the steps to find the shop in even more disarray than usual and Mother looking decidedly flustered. 'Oh, Rosehannon,' she cried, wringing her hands, 'thank goodness you're alright. I was that worried this morning. I wanted to send for Mrs Abbott, but Jenna said you'd just had a restless night. I suppose you were dreaming when you thought you heard a fox? Let me look at you. You look very pale.'

'I'm fine, honest, Mother – it was just a bad dream.'

'Good. I…I couldn't take it if anything was to happen to you.' She looked down at the floor, suddenly shy at her emotion and my heart ached. She seemed so fragile in her shabby dress, her spotless apron and her mobcap neatly pinned in place. Talking to Jim had made me realise how much I had shunned her as a child, always competing for my father's approval. I could see how very lonely she must have felt, left all day in a childless house, the hollow rooms echoing her empty heart. I felt terrible. She had a skill I had completely disregarded – no wonder she loved teaching Jenna to sew.

I took hold of her hands, determined to make amends. 'Nothing will happen to me, I'm very strong.' She smiled and I dropped my voice. 'You haven't told Madame Merrick I was tired this morning, have you?'

'Dear Lord, no – there's no telling Madame Merrick anything today. She's in a terrible state.'

'Is she still sulking about her precious patronage?'

'Well, yes, but ye mustn't mock, Rosehannon. She's taken it into her head she needs Lady April Cavendish and nothing'll stop her. She's heard Lady April has four daughters and she's that determined. Just think what it would mean for her business.'

'Four daughters, all as haughty and arrogant as their mother? The thought fills me with horror!'

'Hush or you'll make her even angrier. She's in a right old state because Mrs Hoskins asked for tea and now she thinks we should serve tea to all her customers. But we don't have anywhere to boil the water and we can't risk a fire – not with the fabrics in the storehouse. Madame Merrick's gone to Mr Melhuish to ask if she could keep a kettle on the boil in his forge.'

'Sounds like an unnecessary fuss if you ask me – anyway she's going to be in a worse state when I tell her about the discrepancies.'

We watched Madame Merrick striding up the steps, frowning and muttering to herself. 'Don't bother her, Rosehannon – least not yet,' Mother pleaded. 'Wait awhile, and let me talk to her when she's in a better frame of mind – you know how angry you make her sometimes. This tiswas between you does us no good.'

Madame Merrick burst through the door, a look of thunder on her face. 'Insolent man! I will *not* be spoken to like that…I am not a *seamstress*.'

Her new dress was more immaculate than ever. She strode angrily across the room, the beautiful silk robe with its fine lace underskirts swishing against the wooden floorboards. She was wearing a new lace cap threaded with satin ribbon and a beautifully embroidered fichu, held in position by a fine silver brooch, a blue gemstone glittering at its centre.

'I *will* serve my ladies tea,' she said with absolute determination. 'I will show them what a *genteel* establishment we

76

have here…whether that blacksmith likes it or not. We will just have to see what Mr Tregellas has to say – he will support me. After all, it is his yard and his decision will overrule that insolent, *half-dressed* brute.' At the mention of Mr Tregellas, she saw me flinch. 'Ah, good morning Miss Pengelly, you're very late this morning.'

'Good morning, Madame Merrick,' I curtseyed. I wanted to remain in Mother's favour but I really needed to discuss the accounts. 'I can see you're busy, and a bit preoccupied, but when you've a moment I'd like to discuss some invoices with you.' Mother let go of my hand, immediately seeking the safety of the storeroom.

'Busy! Preoccupied! *Pah*! I have a hundred and one things to do today…That cotton shipment has gone to St Austell instead of coming to Fosse and I need it if I am to finish the bodice lining for Mrs Hoskins' gown. Mrs Hoskins herself can only come for her next fitting on Saturday…though *why* I do not know as she surely has nothing better to do. When will *I* be able to go *all* the way to St Austell to fetch it? Preoccupied, you say? The lace alone will take another two days…' She stopped, her hawk eyes staring straight at me. 'Which invoices?'

'Several…Actually, there are quite a few – the rolls of blue silk, the red velvet…and that last batch of lemon satin. I can show you exactly which ones they are.'

'Never mind which ones they are – I know which ones they are. You will find them among the other receipts.'

'Madame Merrick, I've looked everywhere for them. They aren't there.'

'Then you are *mistaken*. If you look again, tomorrow, you will find them.'

'I can look now if you like but I know they're not there. You'll need them for next Tuesday.'

Madame Merrick looked horrified at my insistence. 'You will have them *tomorrow*, Miss Pengelly,' was clearly all she was prepared to say.

Mother came in from the storeroom, her eyes darting from one of us to the other. She was carrying a roll of soft grey cotton which shimmered in the sunshine. 'Look, isn't this the most beautiful material?' she said, smiling shyly, obviously trying to make amends. 'Madame Merrick's given it to me to make a dress. I can hardly believe it. See, I'm going to decorate it with this.' She laid a spool of Belgian lace gently against the cotton. 'It's going to be that beautiful. Look.' She held up the fabric, her face glowing with pleasure. 'Madame Merrick's been so kind…so generous, I feel that spoilt.'

Madame Merrick permitted herself a half-smile before turning brusquely away. I felt terrible. Mother had obviously wanted to keep things pleasant between us and my manner had been abrupt and insolent. Had Mother wanted to protect me from Madame Merrick or Madame Merrick from me? I hardly recognised myself any more. It was not my anxiety making me quick to anger; it was our poverty turning me so sullen.

I tried to make amends. 'You'll both look so lovely in your new gowns – Lady April Cavendish is bound to agree to be your patron. I know I would, if I were her.'

'Thank you, Miss Pengelly – that is very kind of you, but looking lovely is of no consequence if Lady April is never to see us.'

'What've you done to attract her attention? Have you sent her your particulars? She can't be your patron if she doesn't know you exist.'

'What *can* be done? *Everyone* is trying to attract her attention and no-one can approach her before she sends a calling-card. I am beginning to think having her patronage can only remain a dream.'

It was always the same. Madame Merrick was an accomplished dressmaker, yet her future depended on the whim of people who did not care one jolt whether she even existed – let alone prospered.

'People like Lady April care nothing for the likes of you or me,' I replied. 'They only care for their horses and dogs! You'd do better choosing your finest silk, embroidering it with your most delicate stitches and sending her a cushion for her hideous pug!' I had spoken in anger but, suddenly, I realised the truth behind my words. 'Why don't you do that? Edge it with your best lace, thread it through with your finest satin ribbons and send it to Lady April with your *compliments*. Enquire after her dear dog's welfare. After all, the poor thing's had a long sea voyage and may be incapacitated by the upheaval! You never know, it might just get her attention.' Madame Merrick's eyes sharpened. She did not smile, but nor did she raise her eyebrows.

If I had seen him coming, I would have dived into the storeroom but it was too late. Mr Tregellas was mounting the steps, two at a time, his brows contracting in a frown. I was powerless to escape. 'Good afternoon, Madame Merrick, Mrs Pengelly, Miss Pengelly.' His bow was curt, barely even noticeable.

'Good afternoon, Mr Tregellas. What a nice surprise. I trust we find you well?'

'Well enough, Madame Merrick – but in very bad humour.'

Madame Merrick raised her eyebrows. Mother's hands gripped the back of a chair and I took a deep breath, trying to calm my fear.

'What can have happened?' Madame Merrick said, closing the door before offering Mr Tregellas a chair.

Turning his back on her, he waved her brusquely aside. 'Thieves broke into my house last night and stole something of great importance.' He was staring straight at me, his cold grey eyes accusing me of theft.

'How *terrible*!' Madame Merrick sat down, fanning herself vigorously. 'And have you caught them yet?'

'No, but we will – they'll be caught and hung.'

'How did they break in, Mr Tregellas?' Mother looked shocked.

'Through a window in the back of the house – Miss Pengelly's old room, I believe.'

My heart was thumping, my stomach tightening. *He has no proof*, I kept repeating in my mind. I must not give myself away. He may have his suspicions, but he has no proof. I needed to keep calm, keep my breathing steady.

'I hope you get everything back. Was it worth a lot of money?' Mother must have been wondering whether it was something that had once belonged to her. She looked wistful but Mr Tregellas ignored her, addressing me instead.

'You look tired, Miss Pengelly. Are you unwell?'

'No, very well, thank you.'

'You look pale. Have you been overdoing things recently?'

'No, I've been very quiet. I think it's the heat.'

'Do you still row? I remember you used to scull with your father. I remember him telling me you were a powerful rower.'

I tried to laugh. 'Oh no, my rowing days are long over.' I looked down in what I hoped was a demure fashion. 'I don't imagine I'd have the strength to row these days.'

He stared at me, a pulse twitching in his forehead. His eyes were cruel, I could see that now – cruel and treacherous and dangerous beyond belief. He must have dressed in a hurry; his cravat was badly tied, his hair ruffled. His movements were restless, the rolled-up paper in his hand constantly slamming against his thigh. Reaching for his fob watch, he checked the time. 'Good day,' he said abruptly.

'Good day, Mr Tregellas. I hope you catch the thieves,' I managed to say.

'There's no doubt of that, Miss Pengelly. And I shall watch them hang.'

He was halfway across the courtyard before Madame Merrick remembered her need of a kettle. She ran quickly after his receding figure, calling him to stop. I reached for a chair, my legs no longer able to stand, and watched them through the window. They seemed to be arguing, Mr Tregellas shrugging his shoulders a number of times, Madame Merrick shaking her head and counting on her fingers. It did not look as if they were discussing the need to serve tea and, with a fast cutter at his disposal, my guess was that they were discussing the missing invoices.

Their conversation at an end, Madame Merrick walked sedately back up the steps. Arranging her fichu more comfortably around her shoulders, the blue jewel glinting in the light, her composure seemed completely restored. A look of triumph flashed across her face as she stared down at Mr Melhuish.

'From now on, ladies, we shall offer tea to *all* my customers.'

Chapter Ten

Fosse is a morning town. It faces east, catching the promise of every new dawn. By six, or seven, the sun dips behind the cliffs, leaving the town in cool, dark shadow. Porthruan is an evening town. It faces west, bathed in the setting sun, the warmth lingering on the houses, turning them a golden red. As we climbed the steep cobbles to the cottage, Mother and I were enjoying the last of the sun on our backs. The carefully cut pieces of her new dress were heavy and we stopped to catch our breath. She seemed preoccupied, turning to look down to the harbour, across to the cottage where I was born.

'I can't imagine living anywhere else,' she said wistfully.

'Nor me. Nor should we have to.' We watched the gulls swooping round the harbour entrance. I was desperate to tell her about the ledgers, but what could I say? I was a thief and had trusted a thief? No, I had to wait. I had to hope Jim's parting words meant our paths would cross again.

'Rosehannon, I've been that worried, all day.' Mother looked serious, her voice slightly trembling. 'I've been such a fool – getting us into debt to Mr Tregellas.' She put down her parcel, tucking a loose strand of hair under her bonnet. 'I thought he was honest and decent, wanting the best for us but, this morning, I saw something in him I didn't like. There was cruelty in his voice and a look in his eye I'd not seen before. It's left me thinking I've been wrong to encourage your marriage.'

My heart leapt. 'You did only what you thought best – it's me that's at fault. I've never been the daughter you deserve.'

She swung round to face me, her face full of anguish. 'Don't ye say that, not ever. Yes, ye may've been more of yer father's daughter – and perhaps we've not shared as much as we could've shared, but ye've got strengths I could only dream of having. I love all yer learning and clever thoughts – the way ye're so quick and have such spirit. Honest to God, I couldn't be more proud of ye.'

Mother had never spoken to me with such passion before, relapsing into the speech of her youth and I realised I hardly knew her. I felt suddenly so sad, as if I had never heard her speak her mind before. Bathed in the glow of the evening sun, her lovely face had pain deep in her eyes. 'Did you love Father very much?' I asked.

'Yes. Though, sometimes I wish…' She paused, looking away.

'Wish what?'

I watched her choose her words with care. 'I wish yer father hadn't been so taken by his anger – always fighting 'gainst those in authority. It weren't easy, living with someone so set against the Corporation, every day thinking he'd be arrested.

I know ye've got his passions but I think Madame Merrick's right – yer father was wrong to encourage ye. Women can't defy men, especially powerful men – ye know that. Everything we do, or have, the beds we sleep in, the clothes on our backs, the food in our mouths, the wood in the grate; everything depends on them.'

A shadow fell across the sun and I shivered. She did not need to tell me something I knew so well. 'Come,' I said, 'it's getting late – let's go home.'

From halfway up the hill we could see something was wrong. The door to our cottage was open, Jenna pacing backwards and forwards, wringing her hands in great distress. She saw us and ran towards us, clutching her skirts so high we could see her ankles.

'Oh, Mrs Pengelly, Miss Rosehannon, thank Jesu ye're home…There's been thieves. Two men – I caught the back of them when I came in. They've thrown everything all over the place – mattresses, beds, the trunk…They stripped the larder, broken pots, pulled up the floorboards – they've took the washing out the bucket and dripped it all over the floor. They emptied the hens from the henhouse…broke eggs… I've been that busy clearing up the mess, but I'm feared they'll be back.' She held out her hands, grabbing us both, pushing us firmly through the door before fastening the latch.

'What have they taken? Not that there's much to take. Did they steal our money?' Mother rushed to the dresser, taking down the pot that once held calf's foot jelly, relief flooding her face as it rattled reassuringly in her hands.

'That's what's odd – they had hold of the jar but they didn't take it. They took nothing. That's what's wrong – they'll be back.'

I was worried sick at the mention of the washing. Grabbing Jenna by the arm, I pulled her into the kitchen, shutting the door so Mother could not hear. 'Were your brother's clothes in the tub? Did they find the clothes?'

'Course not. Couldn't hang them on the line for fear of wagging tongues, could I? I hung them at Mam's. I had them with me but the men ran out the back.'

'Oh, Jenna – you're the most wonderful…clever…girl!'

Jenna's look of pleasure turned to suspicion. Hands on hips, she looked at me severely. 'Ye know more about this than ye're telling. Who're those men?'

'Never mind those men. It doesn't matter who they were – they won't be back. Not now – not thanks to you.' I caught hold of her hands and began spinning her round the tiny kitchen. I felt so relieved, so happy. She looked surprised and remained reluctant to dance, but I could not help it. Taking the clothes to her mother's had just saved my life. Round and round we spun until the room became a dizzy blur and we collapsed, spread-eagled on the floor like rag dolls.

Mother opened the door, her eyes wide with astonishment. 'What's going on, girls – all this laughing and dancing?' Could one of you please explain?

In time, the light from the candle showed Mother's frown fade and her smile return. She was never happier than when she was sewing with Jenna. It was as if they became one, each intuitively knowing what the other wanted. I pretended to read, but the reality of how close I had come to being caught left me reeling. If Jim had not stolen the ledgers, my life would be over.

The light was fading. To save on candles, Mother and I always retired early to bed. I could hear Jenna talking to someone at the front door but took no notice, pulling the bedclothes round me, glad to be safe. I was surprised to hear her footsteps on the stairs and even more surprised by her knock on my door. She was holding a candle in one hand and a basket of cherries in the other. 'I'm to give these straight to you and no-one else,' she said.

'Who're they from?'

'Mrs Tregony's third youngest but could be the fourth youngest. I can never tell. Could be the third oldest, him being so small – but it wasn't Jimmy…'

'Never mind which child it was – they clearly aren't from him. Who gave them to the boy?'

Jenna looked annoyed by my sharp reply. 'How'd I know? All I know is there's a note inside.'

A note? It must be Jim's demands. I slipped out of bed, running to her side. As she handed me the basket, I caught the twinkle in her eye. 'Go to bed…' I whispered. 'Take the cherries but leave the candle. And don't say a word to Mother.'

It was only a small note, folded in three and secured by red wax. There was no formal seal, just the imprint of a thumb.

Slipping my finger under the wax, I could hardly believe my eyes. There was just one word – *Midnight* – and beneath that a sketch of a rose. Nothing else – no date, no place, no name – just *Midnight* and a sketch of a long-stemmed rose with three leaves, exactly like the one I had found by the tree. I stared at the rose, the symbol of love, flinching at his deception. The candle flickered, the note in my hand trembled. It was strange. For once, it was not anger I was feeling, but loneliness. Not fury, but regret. Even the irony of knowing he had saved my life could not take away the hurt of his betrayal.

But this was nonsense. I took a deep breath, filling my lungs with much-needed courage. I was Rosehannon Pengelly, made of sterner stuff. I understood what he meant. I would meet this thief and I would do whatever I needed to get the ledgers back. I would show him I was not to be played with.

Searching the trunk, I found my borrowed clothes washed and pressed, hiding under several layers of greying petticoats. The church bell had just chimed eleven.

It was going to be another late night.

Chapter Eleven

Jenna would be lying awake. She slept in the kitchen, her straw pallet crammed in the scullery by day. She would be listening, waiting for my footsteps, and I knew I could not risk her hearing me leave. I stared out of my window. The drop was only shallow, hardly any distance at all – why not? Without giving it a second thought, I slipped the casement open, lowering myself gently out of the window.

Dropping the short distance to the outhouse was as easy as I thought and I waited, holding my breath, the only sound, the barking of a distant dog. The slates held firm and I made no noise, inching quietly across the roof, lowering myself onto the ground next to the henhouse. I crossed the yard, closed the gate, and started quickly along the cliff path, the moon as clear as daylight. The leaves in the hedgerow were silver-grey, the stones on the path glinting as I walked.

He was waiting by the tree, dressed in the sailor's clothes he had worn at our first meeting. Putting his finger to his lips, he took hold of my arm, pulling me quickly into the shadows beneath the tree. 'Expect to be followed – from now on, don't trust anyone,' he said.

'That's a bit rich – coming from a thief,' I replied. 'Where are my ledgers, Jim?' Despite my bravado, his words had sent a chill straight through me.

'They're safe. An' I haven't stolen them – you can have them back when you're out of danger,' his voice was brusque, almost curt.

'Did you suspect Mr Tregellas would search our cottage?'

'Of course.'

'Is that why you took them?

'Of course, William Tregellas is a dangerous man and we need to keep ahead of him.' The urgency in his tone scared me, making the blood rush from my head. Jim took my arm. 'I'm sorry, I didn't mean to fright you,' he said, more gently, 'an' I'm sure you've not been followed. Come, sit over there.'

He led me to a boulder with just enough room to sit side by side. Taking off his jacket, he placed it over the rock, his eyes never leaving my face. I was surprised by his obvious concern. 'I'm fine, honestly I am. It's completely unlike me – I never faint.'

The night was warm, only the slightest westerly blowing against my cheeks. I breathed in the scent of honeysuckle, watching the moonlight dancing on the black sea. It was too beautiful to quarrel, too peaceful to taint with anger. Jim took his hat off and looked up at the stars, 'The sailor's friend,' he said pointing to the pole star.

'Yes. But you're not a sailor, are you? And you're not a stranger to Fosse.'

The muscles in his jaw tensed. 'What gave me away?'

'The way you rowed the river.'

He glanced up, the corners of his mouth lifting to a fleeting smile. As if a mask lifted from his face, I saw pain in his eyes, anguish, a tenderness I had not expected. 'You're really quite remarkable, Rose,' he whispered.

I hardened my heart. 'You've lied to me and you have my ledgers. What is it you want?'

All trace of emotion vanished. 'D'you remember a man called Sulio Denville?'

'Yes – he was the night watchman the night Father's ship was stolen. He was a sailor recovering from a broken leg – he'd only been with us a few weeks. He begged for work and Father felt sorry for him – but I never liked him. When the cutter was stolen, he was beaten badly, covered in blood and close to death – everybody thought he'd die. Then one day he vanished. Nobody saw him again.'

'Didn't you think that odd? Didn't anyone think him involved in the theft?'

'I did wonder – and still have my doubts, but he was cleared by the authorities. When he disappeared, we thought he'd been scared off. Why d'you ask?'

'Sulio Denville's the man I've come to find.'

'Why d'you want him?'

He hesitated, his tone hardening. 'I'm a condemned man, Rose. If they find me, they'll hang me. The charge is robbery with violence, based on the lies of that man – lies and false witness but enough to get me hanged. I need to find him an' when I do I intend to make him take back every word.

Until then, I remain a dead man.' The hatred in his voice sent a chill through me. I had thought him to be running from the gallows but, somehow, I did not want to believe it. 'That blood you saw on Sulio Denville was pig's blood – they used the same ploy on me, the night I was accused.'

'Of course, pig's blood, but if you've come looking for Sulio Denville, what's your interest in Mr Tregellas? You can't just be helping me.'

'That night I hid in the tree, I'd been asking people for the whereabouts of Sulio Denville – I said I'd a score to settle. It didn't take long before I was followed an' you know the outcome – but I lied to you about not knowing my pursuers. One of them was William Tregellas.'

'And one Sulio Denville?'

'No, but I heard them talking. I was right above them an' heard every word. Mr Tregellas was angry as hell – his exact words, "*We might have to move him. If necessary, I'll arrange for it*". It's my guess they were talking about Sulio Denville.'

My head was spinning. I took a deep breath, trying to clear my thoughts. 'Is Mr Tregellas protecting Sulio Denville?'

'I thought that at first, but not any longer. I think they used him. Instead of giving him safe passage – which I'm sure they promised – I think they had him arrested for some trumped-up charge. It's my guess he's been rotting in gaol since the day he went missing.'

Mention of the gaol made me wince. The stench, the filth, the inhumanity of the place still seemed so vivid. Jim was watching me. He put his hand on my arm. It felt warm and strangely reassuring. 'Are you alright, Rose?' he whispered.

I nodded. 'That awful place brings back such pain. But why d'you think he's in gaol?'

Jim's voice took on a new coldness. 'This morning, I hid outside Tregellas's house. I knew the first person he'd go to would need to know about the theft, so I followed him. He went straight to Polcarrow — to Mr Roskelly.'

'Mr Roskelly? No wonder poor Father didn't stand a chance.'

'We've disturbed a vipers' nest, Rose. Mr Tregellas was at Polcarrow for nearly an hour — then he went straight to the gaol. From there, he went to Hoskins' Bank, then straight back to the gaol, carrying something under his jacket — no doubt a purse full of coins.'

'Bribery — or payment for services rendered.'

'When he left the gaol he leant against the wall, loosened his collar an' wiped his brow — hardly the actions of an innocent man. Then, I believe he graced you with his company.'

'He was furious. I know he suspects me.'

'But he's no proof an' never will — so long as I keep the ledgers safe. He'll not find them, Rose, have no fear. He's got nothing to go on but suspicion.'

'Were you watching him when he talked to Madame Merrick?'

'Yes.'

'Did you hear what they said?'

He shook his head. 'I couldn't catch their words. Why?'

'I think Madame Merrick and Mr Tregellas are part of a smuggling gang.'

He did not seem surprised, but his eyes sharpened. 'Have you said anything to your mother?' I shook my head. 'Good, then make sure you don't say a word. I believe she's very close to Madame Merrick.'

His words stung me. I resented his implication Mother would side with Madame Merrick. 'Well, if Sulio Denville's in gaol, you'll not get near him,' I snapped.

He met my anger with a half-smile, 'Maybe, maybe not, but they're planning to move him to Bodmin on Saturday morning.'

'How d'you know that?'

'I've had it on good authority.'

'Who?'

'Bess – the serving lass in the Anchor Tavern.'

'I hardly call that good authority!' Which one had she been? The one running her hands under his shirt or the one stroking his thighs?

Again, the half-smile. 'Her father's the gaoler. She took some persuading, but I got her to tell me the new orders.'

'I'm sure she took no persuading at all – I'm sure your charms were well received!' Suddenly the night seemed less beautiful, the air somewhat cooler.

'They're moving a prisoner from Fosse to Bodmin Goal on Saturday morning and it's my belief it's Sulio Denville. Once he's in Bodmin, there'll be no getting near him, so we've got to get him between Fosse and the moor. If we free him, we might be able to strike a deal – it's got to be worth the chance.'

I could not believe what I heard, but his face was deadly serious. 'No, Jim. You can't mean that. It can't be done.'

'It can be done – if we use you as a distraction.'

'It's far too dangerous.'

'For me, maybe – but not for you. You'd be nothing but an innocent bystander an' take no part.' His black eyes were full of danger.

'D'you have a plan?'

'Can you get a horse and wagon, or a hay wain? Something with four wheels not two? We need to get you up on the moor for a day out on Saturday morning.'

Despite my horror, I burst out laughing. 'Are you mad, Jim? What would I be doing going for a day out on Saturday? I never go anywhere. I can't go borrowing a cart and setting off on a jaunt – I've only been across the moor a handful of times. Everyone would suspect me. If your plan hinges on me finding a cart, then it's a stupid plan.' I was suddenly very cross. Cross and disappointed. He was asking too much of me. I turned my back, scowling into the darkness.

A cart! A trip across the moor! Suddenly my mind cleared. I remembered Madame Merrick and her dilemma about collecting her cotton from St Austell. If Madame Merrick needed to be at Mrs Hoskins' for a fitting on Saturday, then I could offer to collect the cotton for her. 'Wait…I think I can do it,' I said a little breathlessly.

'I knew you'd think of something,' he said, the hard lines down his face softening into a half-smile. I could feel myself beginning to burn under the glow of his approval and turned my face towards the sea, hoping the breeze would cool the heat from my cheeks. 'Can you be ready to leave Fosse at a quarter to eight?' I heard him ask.

'Yes.'

'Take the top road out to the moor.'

'And?'

'Make sure you leave at a quarter to eight. Can you go alone?'

'No, of course not!'

'Then only one other person – but not your mother. And can you wear a red dress.'

'Why?'

'Because the colour will stand out.'

His words scared me. Had he done this before? A knot began tightening in my stomach and instantly I regretted my decision. I knew nothing about him. He could be leading me straight to the gallows and I did not even know who he was. 'Who are you?' I asked sharply.

He turned his back, staring across the shimmering sea, his shoulders broad in the moonlight. 'I told you – my name's Jim. Until recently, I've been working at the household of the Governor General of Dominica. While I was there, circumstances arose making it necessary I return to England.' His voice was flat, lacking all emotion.

But what are words when actions speak so much louder? The knot in my stomach gave one further wrench. He said nothing, but his hands went straight to his chest, pressing against his heart. I remembered the gold chain, the beautiful ring that shone with such brilliance and the taste in my mouth turned sour. There are some things a woman need not be told. Cursing my weakness I turned quickly away, walking briskly back through the undergrowth.

Whatever emotions I had begun to feel, whatever notions I had started to harbour, I pushed aside as roughly as I pushed aside the gorse that snagged my clothes. He was not doing this for me. He was not helping me with my struggles – he was doing this for her.

We had an enemy in common, that was all.

Chapter Twelve

Mother looked anxious. She had obviously dressed in a hurry as her mobcap was slightly askew. Wisps of hair framed her face, the dark shadows under her eyes accentuating her pallor. She was wringing her hands against her chest. 'I think we should tell Madame Merrick you've changed your mind. I'm sure she can find someone else to go.'

'I'll be fine – I'll be back before dark. Stop worrying. Besides, I'm really looking forward to a little trip across the moor.' I hoped I sounded convincing. I had not slept either.

We had spent the previous day in deep discussion. Madame Merrick had shown great surprise when I offered to pick up her consignment of cotton, studying me keenly through her beady eyes, almost as if she suspected something. Mother immediately dismissed the idea, but when Madame Merrick confided she was worried someone else would *steal it* from right under her nose, Mother had given way and finally relented. I was to ask my friend Ben to borrow his father's cart and if we left early enough, we could get there and back before dark.

'Jenna's packed this basket with a loaf and some potted crab. She says you didn't eat anything at all yesterday and you'll fade to nothing the way you're going.'

'Jenna's just fussing.' Food was the last thing I felt like.

'No she isn't. It's a long way to St Austell.'

'It's only seven miles — and I've done it twice already when I went to buy timber with Father. It's not the end of the world!'

Mother had been born in St Austell. She had been six when she left and had never been back. In fact, Mother had not left Fosse or Porthruan since, so I knew the thought of my journey scared her. 'Take your cloak and this rug — and take this cushion…it'll be that uncomfortable sitting on the cart all day and, before I forget, Jenna's given you this flagon of ale for Ben, though whether he should drink ale, or not, I don't know.'

An early morning mist hung in the air and the warehouse felt cold as we waited. It was already half past seven and if we were to leave in time, we had only a quarter of an hour to get everything sorted. My anxiety was increasing by the minute as I knew Jim's plan depended on us leaving at exactly quarter to eight.

'I think I should come with you, Rosehannon. I'd be that happier, coming with you. It's not right for a young woman to go alone. In fact, the more I think on it, the more I'd love to see St Austell after all this time.'

My heart plummeted. 'But, Mother, we discussed this yesterday. The jolting would make your back worse – it would be far too uncomfortable for you.'

Madame Merrick was crossing the courtyard, mounting the steps. She looked impeccable in a green velvet gown with matching jacket. Taking off her hat, she greeted me with a half-smile. 'Remember, Miss Pengelly, *three* threads in the selvedge. Do *not* accept it if there are only two. I will not be fobbed off with imported cotton – though, of course, if it were *French*, that would be different. Check through *all* the roll, not just what you can see on the surface – they have a habit of putting good quality on the surface and poor quality underneath. They will try to *trick* you – especially when they see you are so young.'

'I won't let anyone trick me, Madame Merrick.'

'No, I do not believe you will – that's why I am prepared to trust you. And remember, I will *not* pay more than ten shillings a roll. They agreed eight, but no doubt they will try and sell it to you for more. Start with an offer of seven and six and act as if the cotton is not worth more. Do not let them cheat you, Miss Pengelly.'

'I won't.'

Madame Merrick opened her silk purse and counted out thirty-five shillings. Putting the coins back in the purse, she held it out to me, 'Hide it well, Miss Pengelly...no, not in the basket – put it down your bodice.' I stuffed the silk purse down my bosom and she nodded in approval.

We were still waiting for Ben. I was worried he had forgotten, or had gone into one of his trances. People were spiteful where Ben was concerned, saying he was mazed and with the pixies most of the time, which was nonsense of course. But it was true he was not like other boys. He lived in his own world – a simple world. Some actually called him simple, some said he was soft in the head and many of the boys were cruel to him, taunting him and goading him until he cried. Cruelty sickens me and ever since I found him crying in a pigpen, his feet tied together, I have tried my best to shield him.

A wagon came clattering across the courtyard and I looked up. Ben was dressed in his Sunday best, his face and boots polished to a shine. He was clearly pleased to see me, beaming his wonky half-smile, his teeth jutting from out of his crowded mouth, a bit of spittle glistening on his chin. I stared at the wagon. It was so beautiful, every inch of the painted red cart festooned with flowers. I rushed down the steps clapping my hands. 'Oh, Ben! It's so beautiful – I've never seen anything so lovely.'

Garlands of bindweed, honeysuckle and dog roses hung over the yellow wheels. Huge bunches of flowers cascaded over the sides of the cart. It was breath-taking. Ben steadied the old nag and jumped down, his smile filling his face. He handed me a bouquet of wild flowers smelling of sage and thyme. 'Fff...for yer, Miss Rose'annon,' he said shyly.

'Ben – they're beautiful.'

I was so delighted I almost forgot the time – it was a quarter to eight. I threw the basket of provisions onto the cart and swung myself onto the bench. Ben climbed next to me while Madame Merrick and Mother stood watching.

'It's like a bridal cart,' I heard Mother say. '...that boy adores her.'

'Then he should be warned,' came the quick retort. 'Rosehannon would eat him alive.'

'Oh no,' replied Mother, 'She's devoted to Ben. Ever since they were bairns, she's looked after him. Honest to God, I've watched her see off some of the biggest bullies just by crossing her arms and glaring at them – you know, the boys were that scared of her! They knew she was a force to be reckoned with.'

Madame Merrick was staring at me. 'She still is, Eva,' I heard her say.

With all the flowers and my red dress matching the cart, we made a colourful spectacle pushing our way through the crowd. We were certainly drawing our share of attention, but somehow I did not care what people thought. Ben's obvious delight was catching and now we were on our way, I began to relax slightly. It was such a rare chance to get away from Fosse and I was longing to see the moor again. Besides, we were only going to be a distraction – Jim had promised we would be in no danger.

We clattered slowly out of Fosse, Jupiter almost as excited as we were. The sun was breaking through the morning mist and I watched the town fall away beneath us, the ships' masts rising like a forest of winter trees. It was going to be a beautiful day. Ahead of us lay the twisting road, above us kittiwakes screeched as they dived to their nests and, for the first time in a very long while, I began to feel free. I held the bouquet of wild flowers to my nose, breathing in their scent, smiling at Ben. 'Did you grow these yourself?'

'Yes.'

'I thought so. They're lovely.'

Ben was one of life's gentlest creatures. He was thin, no taller than me. His jacket was too small, the sleeves ending well above his wrists, his breeches clearly too big for him.

Without the string tied several times round his waist, they would have slipped off long ago. He looked shyly across at me, through the long lashes of his watery eyes, 'I've me own garden now,' he said, smiling.

'Have you, Ben?'

'Yes, and I've put stones round…to protect it from the wind. Yer can grow anythin' out of the wind.'

'That's clever. Where's your garden?'

'Up here on the cliffs.'

My heart froze. 'But this is Polcarrow land, Ben – they've enclosed it. Surely you know that?'

'I'm nnn…not doing no harm.'

'I know, but you must be careful. If they find your garden, they might hurt you. They're very severe if they find trespassers.'

A cloud crossed his face. 'I'll be careful – I'll keep it secret.'

His words had frightened me but I did not want to scare him. He was looking so proud driving the beautiful cart and I did not want to spoil his day. Besides, he was concentrating on the track, which had thinned considerably the steeper we climbed. It was now very rutted with deep holes, sending the

103

cart lurching from side to side. I held on with both hands, grateful for Mother's cushion, watching the other travellers sharing our route. Several carts had pulled ahead, but we were caught behind a heavily laden mule pack, carefully picking its way over the stones in front.

We followed slowly, skirting the side of the hill, going inland towards the bend in the river, climbing steadily to above the tree line. Thick shrubs and gorse now lined the route, the air beginning to smell of heather and wild thyme. 'That's better!' I said, watching the mule pack turn to the left, branching down the ancient path traders and pilgrims had used for a thousand years. Our path lay straight ahead, steep and very narrow, leading to the last copse before the moor. Behind us, I heard a carriage rumble.

We entered the copse, the trees merging in a canopy over our heads, making it cold and dark. Jupiter seemed to hesitate, pulling back his ears, reluctant to proceed. Ben urged him on, soothing his fears, coaxing him through the tunnel of trees. We were almost through. Suddenly, a loud crack filled the air and a huge tree came crashing down in front of us, the branches ripping and splitting as it hit the ground.

'Hold tight, Ben!' I shouted as Jupiter reared high in the air, the whites of his eyes stark with terror. I gripped the seat, watching Ben haul on the reins. The cart was jolting from side to side, I was sure I would fall. Nothing seemed to calm Jupiter. The branches were shaking from the impact, swaying in front of us, and he stayed bucking and kicking, twisting in his harness with fear. He may have been old but his strength was considerable and we watched in horror as he broke free of the harness, bolting into the woodland, dragging the reins behind him.

A wheel jolted loose and the cart lurched to one side, balancing on the axle as I clung to the seat. Ben jumped to the ground and I thought he would right the wagon but he stood, transfixed, gazing ahead, too frightened to move. A highwayman stood on the trunk of the fallen tree, his long black cloak falling round him, his head covered by a large hat. His eyes were hidden behind a mask. Round his face was a black scarf and over his shoulders hung a large coil of rope. He stood tall and dark, like an avenging demon, holding a pistol in his outstretched hand. I screamed in fright. Ben fell to his knees, shaking in terror.

The highwayman jumped from the trunk, pointing his pistol in my direction. 'Get up…or she gets hurt.' Ben lay crouched on the ground, whimpering and moaning. He was shaking with fear, unable to move. 'Get up!' the highwayman repeated. Ben lurched to his feet, blind and stumbling, and I watched, petrified, as the highwayman grabbed his collar, forcing him towards the wood. I had to save him. I jumped from the cart and I tried to run but my foot got caught by the broken harness and I tumbled forward, grazing my hands. I looked up. Ben was nowhere to be seen. I felt frantic, looking everywhere, not knowing which way to follow.

But already the cloaked figure was striding back, his pistol pointing at my chest. With one kick he pushed over the wagon, the huge yellow wheels spinning in the air, Jenna's basket crashing to the ground. Ben's flowers lay crushed and spoiled. Reaching for his rope, the highwayman grabbed my arms, twisting me round. Instantly I recognised that iron grip.

'It has to be this way, Rose,' he said coldly.

'No, it doesn't!' I yelled as I tried to free my arm. 'What've you done to Ben?'

'Ben'll be fine.'

'If you've hurt him…'

'Of course I haven't hurt him and I won't hurt you.' He was breathing hard, holding my arms behind my back, forcing me down against the wagon and I screamed in fright, struggling with all my might against him. He took no notice and I felt my wrists burn as he bound my hands against the cart.

'For God's sake – why are you doing this?'

'Because those men building the enclosures over there are watching and they'll be called as witnesses. It must look real.'

'Don't do this to me,' I cried, tears filling my eyes. Again he took no notice but continued tying his rope round my outstretched arms. In the distance, I could hear coach wheels approaching, the crack of a whip, the beating of hooves. I thought he would stop, take shelter in the woods, but he came closer, kneeling on the ground, his huge cloak spilling over my crumpled dress.

'Forgive me, Rose. If I could think of any other way, I wouldn't be doing this.' He untied the bows of my bonnet, freeing my hair. With a tug, he loosened my fichu, pulling it from me. His face was close to mine, his scarf almost touching my cheek. I could smell the leather of his mask and I turned my face in disgust. 'Believe me, if there'd been any other way...' he said, loosening my top lace, his hands brushing against my breast.

'How dare you!' I screamed, writhing in fury.

'I'm sorry, Rose.' He sprung to his feet, vanishing soundlessly in the wood behind.

Almost immediately, the coach came hurtling round the bend, the horses thundering to a frightened stop. Dust and stones flew everywhere. The leading pair reared high in confusion – huge, great beasts, sleek and powerful, reaching high in the air, jolting the coach from side to side. 'God's teeth...Whoa...' the driver pulled frantically on the reins, trying to calm them.

There were three men. The youngest jumped from the seat, adding his volley of oaths to the noise and confusion. Grabbing the halters of the leading horses, he struggled against them as they tossed their heads. Their eyes were white with fright, their nostrils flared. 'There's a bloody tree down,' he called. 'That's why the bleedin' cart's over.'

Next to the driver, a guard sat with a blunderbuss across his lap. A thick-set man with heavy features, he seemed oblivious to the lurching of the carriage but remained chewing tobacco, slowly, deliberately, his eyes widening as he stared straight at me. I stared back, my heart sickening – it was the gaol coach, definitely the gaol coach. The front looked like any other coach but behind the driver's seat, a grid of iron bars formed a heavy cage. Small, cramped, bolted with chains. Someone was in there.

I tried twisting myself free, pulling frantically at my bindings. I arched my back, kicking, twisting, digging my heels in the dust beneath me, but nothing would loosen the ties binding me to the cart. Worse than that, the more I wrenched, the more my skirt rose up my legs, exposing my ankles. The two drivers stared with amazement and I watched in horror as they came gawping towards me, their eyes so incredulous they seemed to bulge.

'Well, I'll be damned.' Their eyes travelled over my body, taking in every detail. They were smiling, licking their lips, appraising me like a cow in a market stall.

'Untie me, you idiots.' My fear was mounting, my mouth dry. The men did not move, but stood as if statues, staring down at me, lust glazing their eyes. I was furious, so furious. Furious with them, furious with Jim, furious with myself. I had been so stupid to trust him. 'Untie me now, or there'll be trouble,' I shouted louder.

As if in answer to my prayer, a donkey cart stopped behind the coach and a huge man with auburn hair jumped quickly from it. He came running towards me, pushing past the drivers who still stood gawping. Falling quickly to his knees in the dirt before me, he stretched forward, undoing my wrists. 'Ye'll be alright now, miss,' he said quietly, 'here, let me get ye untied...'

His kindness brought tears to my eyes. I could not speak but smiled my thanks and he smiled shyly back, averting his eyes as he straightened my dress and replaced my fichu. His touch was gentle for such a huge man and as he leant over to undo my ropes, I saw the concern in his eyes. He must have been about twenty. He wore no hat, his hair tied loosely behind his neck, his complexion freckled by the sun. Over his working-man's breeches he wore a leather apron and large belt.

'What's your name?' I said at last, wiping my eyes with my sleeve.

'Joseph Dunn, miss,' he said courteously.

I rubbed the red marks on my wrists and found I was shivering. Joseph Dunn took off his jacket, placing it gently round my shoulders before helping me up. It was a thick jacket, smelling of horses and it swamped me completely.

The two drivers were still gawping. Joseph swung round to face them, his fists clenched by his sides. 'What are ye staring at?' he said angrily. 'Leave her be – ye should be ashamed at yerselves. And if that's yer coach – why's the door wide open?'

Chapter Thirteen

Porthruan
7:30 p.m.

Mother and Madame Merrick were both downstairs, still shocked by the terrible incident. Jenna had given them some camomile infusion and was sitting next to me, watching me drink mine. She looked incredulous. 'Go on... his name was Joseph Dunn...what happened next?'

'After he untied the ropes and set me free, he just turned to the drivers and asked them why the cage was empty.'

'How frightening. Go on...'

'They found the guard bound and gagged, lying face down in the dirt. The highwayman had taken the key and freed the prisoner. The two drivers searched everywhere but the highwayman and prisoner had vanished – there were no tracks – nothing.'

'Why'd a highwayman take a prisoner?'

'If I knew that, Jenna, I would have told the constable.' I sighed. It had been a long day of questioning and not all of it as well-meaning as Jenna's.

'I'm sorry ye're upset – we're all upset. Even Madame

Merrick's that concerned – well was concerned till she found someone else to collect her cotton!' She raised her eyebrows. 'She blames herself – I heard her telling Mrs Pengelly it was her what made ye put the purse down yer bodice. She knows ye was only protecting her money – refusing to give it to the highwayman…What did he look like?'

'Jenna, he was wearing a mask and had a scarf over his face. I didn't see him at all…but he was violent and cruel.' My voice broke, 'And I hate him for what he did to Ben.'

'How's Ben?' she said softly.

'Terrible. Completely petrified – and it's all my fault. He'll never trust me again.'

'That's nonsense. How was you to know there was a highway man?' She pushed back the hair that had fallen over my face, wiping a tear from my cheek.

'I should never have asked Ben to come.'

''T weren't your fault.'

It was my fault and I would never forgive myself. And I would never forgive Jim. I had found Ben in the wood, whimpering and shaking, tied to a tree. His best Sunday breeches soiled by his fear, his lovingly polished boots scuffed and spoilt. He had cried as I released him. *Couldn't do nothin', Miss Rose'annon*, he had sobbed. *Couldn't do nothin' – nothin' to save you*. I had led him straight into danger as if I had pointed the pistol and secured the ropes. I would never forgive myself.

We had tried to gather up as many of the flowers as we could, but most of them were ruined. Joseph Dunn took us home and I had cradled Ben in my arms, trying to soothe his fears. 'I'll never let anyone hurt you again,' I had promised.

An empty promise. I knew I had no chance of protecting him, not now we were grown.

The evening sunshine was fading, the room beginning to darken. It had been a horrible, violent day – one I would never forget. And behind all the violence was Jim. 'Jenna, you can take all your brother's clothes back,' I said, rubbing the marks still left on my wrists.

A look of relief flashed across her face. 'Thank Jesu…it's about time ye came to yer senses.'

'Yes,' I said. 'I've come to my senses. I'll never need them again.'

Chapter Fourteen

Sunday 30th June 1793 11:30 a.m.

A steady grey drizzle was falling against the window. I could hear church bells ringing across the river. Burying my head under the covers, I had no intention of getting up. Mother had come into my room before she had left for church, but with no will to face her, I had lain pretending to be asleep. Jenna's bucket was clattering above the clucking of the hens and I could hear her talking to Mrs Tregony over the yard wall. There would be a lot of chattering going on out there, that was for certain.

All night I had re-lived the violence of Jim's actions, the harshness of his grip, the pain in my wrists as he bound me with his rope. I could not get Ben's stricken face out of my mind, but what hurt me most was why Jim had not explained his plan to me. Why had he caught me so unaware and used me so violently? I had trusted him and he had not trusted me in return. Somehow that made it worse.

Jenna was making her way slowly up the stairs. She entered my room, a steaming bowl of soup balancing on a large tray. Putting it on the floor, she began fluffing up my pillows.

'I'm not hungry, Jenna.'

'Have just a bit.'

'I can't face it,' I said, lying back against the pillows.

'Ye must have something or ye'll fade away.' She crossed the room and opened the window. Immediately she clapped her hands. 'Shooo...Go away – that's hens' food not yers. Honest to God, that black and white tom's getting that bold ye'd think he lives here.'

'That's because you encourage him.'

'I don't.'

'Yes you do. I've seen the scraps you leave for him.'

'Well, he's that hungry, poor mite.' She frowned across at me. 'Try some at least. This'll pass – and soon there'll be no more tongue-wagging.' She started busying herself with my clothes, brushing the dust off my red dress. I hated that dress now: it felt so tainted.

'What are they saying? The truth, please, Jenna.'

'They do say the drovers saw it all. They do say the highwayman tried to rob ye with a pistol and threatened ye... but ye put up such a fight – screaming and thrashing, but ye wouldn't give him yer money. They do say...' Jenna stopped, biting her lips.

'What do they say?'

'They say the highwayman was that overcome with yer beauty that he...'

'What?'

'He was going to ravish ye...and 'twas only because the

114

gaol coach came he couldn't…and he was that cross with them, he let the prisoner go. There, ye asked, I told.'

'Then my reputation's in tatters and I won't be able to face the town.'

'Yer reputation ain't in tatters – I may not be as clever as ye, but I know that for sure. There's talk ye put up a real fight.'

'Yes, but it won't be long before they're saying I should never have gone in the first place and I was asking for trouble.'

'Maybe, maybe not – it don't matter. Drink yer broth, it'll give ye strength. And ye can't stay here all day…Ye're going to have to get out of that bed and face the gossip. We'll take no heed of what people say.'

She stood ready to defend me, standing so fiercely, sleeves rolled to the elbows, hands on hips. Suddenly, I realised how much I loved her, how much Mother and I depended on her. For so many years, I had taken her for granted, yet now I could not imagine life without her.

'Jenna, it won't always be like this,' I said, my voice breaking. 'One day I'll make it up to you. I'll make sure you're alright. One day you'll have your own cottage and a whole brood of children and chickens and as many cats as you can fit in the yard. You deserve so much better – I don't know why you stay with us.'

She sat on the bed, a slow smile crossing her face. 'I'll want a proper bed, mind, not one like this one,' she said, prodding the mattress. 'And a proper stove – not one that goes out all the time…one like Mrs Munroe's at Coombe House and I'll want a copper pan and kettle and a table…and a big rocking chair and I'll want me own pump…'

'Steady on, Jenna, I won't be made of money.'

'Then drink that broth and let me get on with yer hair.'

Jenna was right. There was nothing to do but to face the sniggers and judgemental looks, the raised eyebrows and nudges. I had done it before and survived and I would just have to do it again. I always left flowers on Father's grave on Sunday, so today would be no exception. Besides, the walk to Porthruan church was only a mile and the fresh air would clear my head.

The day was mizzling with overcast skies and a damp fog blanketing the cliffs. I decided on my warmer brown dress and my largest bonnet. Wrapping my shawl tightly round me, I headed for the church. Jim's plan had worked well, there was no denying that. He had freed the prisoner, both of them had escaped, and the men building the enclosures had given exactly the account he wanted. He had been clever, very clever.

But what was unforgivable was the way he had not confided in me. He should have warned me first. He should have told me what he intended to do and I would never have taken Ben. He had used me cruelly, with no regard for my safety or reputation, and he had left me to my fate. I would never forgive him. Without Joseph Dunn, anything could have happened.

The lane was no more than a grassy track. Pools of water had gathered in the ruts and droplets of rain still clung to the ox-eyed daisies as I picked them into a neat bunch. At the wicket gate, my heart sank. There must have been a lot of people at church that morning as the path was a well-churned quagmire. My shoes were already covered with mud, the hem of my dress already soiled and, reluctant to make matters worse, I thought I might just as well try the path that cut through the churchyard a little further up the lane – after all, it could not be any worse.

The short distance accomplished, I turned inwards, making my way through the dripping overgrowth, a damp, heavy scent filling the air. This part of the churchyard was always full of birds and today was no exception. It was always peaceful here. It was where my grandparents and great-grandparents lay buried and where we had laid Father. It was also where, one by one, we had buried my brothers and sisters. It always saddened me to see their names on the tombstone, the span of their short lives measured in hours and days. As a child I used to run my fingers over their names, trying to touch something of them, feeling guilty only I had survived. I will always feel regret for the brothers and sisters I might have had.

The square tower of the church was directly ahead, the path leading to the porch no more than ten feet away. I would seek shelter for a while. Crossing the path, my eyes were immediately drawn to two men, half hidden between the porch and the buttress. They were deep in conversation, their backs towards me. Instantly, I recognised them both and ducked behind a large tomb, holding my breath. Mr Tregellas was talking to a man whose bulky figure I would never forget – Mr Sulio Denville.

I hardly dared move. I crouched where I was, my cheek brushing against wet lichen as I watched the two men responsible for my father's downfall. Sulio Denville's huge frame was barely contained in his blue jacket. He was short, thick-set, in his late fifties. He wore the hat of a ship's master, his head beneath it shaven. Large, bushy eyebrows sliced angrily across his forehead, his chin covered by an untidy grey beard. I sank back, leaning against the tomb, fighting to stay calm.

Jim must be dead. He must be lying in a ditch, strangled by those huge hands. Sulio Denville's neck was like a tree trunk, his arms like hams – no-one could better him in a fight. Jim must be dead, this was worse than ever. Without Jim, I had no evidence. No proof against them. The slightest movement made me look round. I could just make out the fleeting shape of a man running across the churchyard, ducking behind the gravestones in an effort to remain undetected. He ran quickly, his sure-footed agility making him tread without sound.

'I didn't expect you'd be so glad to see me,' Jim whispered as he threw himself beside me.

'I'm not glad to see you, I'm just glad you're not dead. And if you didn't still have the ledgers, I'd never want to see you again.'

'It was the only way, Rose. I know I've lost your good opinion, but it had to look real.'

'I'll never forgive you – never. Not after what you did to Ben.'

'I didn't know you were bringing a simpleton.'

'He's not a simpleton, he's my friend. He's harmless and there was no need to be so cruel.' He looked tired, his stubble rough, his hair unkempt. I saw his jaw stiffen and his mouth tighten. I looked away. This was only the second time I had seen him in daylight and what I saw did nothing to dispel my unease. There was something forbidding about this man. For a brief, unwanted second I remembered the touch of his hands against my breast. 'So Sulio Denville gave you the slip, did he?'

'Captain Denville, if you notice – he's ship's master now.'

'I don't see how that's possible.'

'Sulio Denville wasn't our prisoner, Rose.'

'Oh, that's just what I needed to hear. You've just ruined my reputation and scared Ben witless – all for nothing. Great plan!'

'Somehow I knew you'd say that.' He smiled.

'How can you smile when you used me so badly and left me to the mercy of those men?'

'I didn't leave you to their mercy.' His face was serious again. 'I knew you'd be safe with Joseph. He's known throughout Cornwall for his wrestling skills – he's a champion.'

'You sent Joseph? I don't believe you. I think you're just trying to make me think less badly of you.'

'You can think what you like, but we've no time to argue. I've been following Mr Tregellas all morning and he's led me straight to the man we seek. Captain Sulio may not be our prisoner but we've found him at last. He looks well, don't you think?' He raised his eyebrow, the small scar disappearing into the creases of his forehead. 'But then, the proceeds of the black market make most men prosperous – with a fast cutter at his disposal, he can out sail the Revenue.'

'Of course! How stupid of me – he's master of *L'Aigrette*, after all.'

'Yes, an' I'm certain she'll be anchored up one of these creeks, concealed by the mist. If I follow him, I'll have a good chance of finding where they're hiding her.' He edged forward, peering round the side of the tomb.

They were still talking, standing under the overhang of the buttress. Sulio Denville was walking backwards and forwards like a caged bear, impatiently shrugging his shoulders, the frown deepening on his already thunderous face. It was obvious they were engrossed in a conversation that pleased neither of them.

I noticed Jim looking at me, his smile briefly returning. 'I'm surprised you've not asked about the prisoner you helped release,' he whispered.

'I'm sure he was very grateful – grateful and surprised!'

'The poor man was in a terrible state, wracked by coughing an' very weak. He's riddled with lice, covered in sores and as light as a feather when I carried him to safety.'

'Poor man.'

'It took me a long time to cut through his chains an' wash away the prison filth. He was hungry an' confused, sleeping fitfully, often crying out, but by daybreak he seemed much stronger an' even spoke his name.'

'You tended him all night?'

'Of course – I could never leave anyone in that state.' I was surprised to see Jim's face soften. His eyes looked surprisingly

120

tender. Lifting his hand, he placed a finger against my lips, ignoring my glare. 'What I'm about to say will shock you – really shock you, but you must make no sound. No sudden cry. I hoped to tell you this when we were far from anyone, but we haven't time – remember, don't make a sound.' I nodded and he edged closer. 'The man we saved was no ordinary prisoner. He's your father, Rose – Pascoe Pengelly.'

His words seemed to suck all breath from me. Father alive? I felt giddy, faint, barely able to take it in. Father was alive. The churchyard began whirling round me and I must have cried out for Jim's hand closed quickly over my mouth. He held me gently against his shoulder while I fought to regain my senses. Father was alive. I felt weak as a kitten, my heart racing.

Jim kept hold of me, whispering into my ear, my shock so great I could hardly hear him. 'Tregellas didn't want to risk an investigation, or a chance your father's debt could be cleared, so they told everyone he'd died. They swapped him with a prisoner who'd died of gaol fever, burying him in your father's place. Believe me, Rose, there's as much corruption in gaol as anything found outside. The guards knew the fever to be rife and your father would die soon enough. All they had to do was keep their mouths shut, call him by the other name and claim brain fever was addling his wits.'

My wonderful, beloved Father was still alive. I put my head in my hands to stop the dizziness. I still could not speak. My hands were trembling, tears stinging my eyes. Jim held me tenderly, slowly peering round the side of the tombstone.

'They've stopped talking – they're going, Rose, I'll have to leave you. I'll get you word about your father but don't tell anyone. Nobody must know. Keep it secret – especially from your mother. D'you promise, Rose?' His whisper was urgent.

I glanced round the tomb. Sulio Denville's blue coat tails were heading up the path in the direction of the shrubs. 'Yes…yes…I promise…but at least let me tend him. Where is he?'

'Safe. Trust me.'

'But…you must let me…' My plea fell on empty air. In an instant, Jim slipped from my side, ducking behind tomb-stones as he made his way silently across the churchyard.

From my hiding place, I watched Mr Tregellas walking down to the gate, my anger making my face burn like a furnace. Never before had I felt capable of direct violence, but as I knelt on that tomb, I had to hold myself in check. I wanted to run after him, lash out at him. I remembered the day he had come knocking on our door, his face full of grief, telling us he was heartbroken to lose such a dear friend. We had begged him to let us see Father, to say our last goodbye, but he had shaken his head, saying that the putrid fever was too foul and contagious to risk us going anywhere near him.

I could not imagine the horror Father had gone through, kept in filth with nothing but water and stale bread. They must have expected him to die at any moment, every day expecting he would weaken and collapse, but they did not know Father. They did not know he would cling to life, desperate to thwart them by staying alive. My beloved, wonderful, stubborn father – too strong for them to subdue, too determined to fight his cause.

A steady drizzle was blowing across the churchyard, the posy of flowers squashed in my hands. Not to place them on Father's grave would be as good as admitting I knew he was alive. The vipers were indeed loose and they would be watching my every move. Mother's flowers were where she always put them and I placed my posy next to hers, wondering who the man laying buried next to my brothers and sisters was. As I knelt, damp penetrated my gown but nothing could daunt my spirits. Father was alive.

Suddenly, I heard footsteps behind me – the soft tread of someone stopping. Even without looking round, I knew who it would be. Why had he come back? Had he seen me, or had he thought to check the flowers on Father's grave? I took a deep breath, filling myself with much-needed courage, knowing I must not give him even the slightest reason to doubt me. He cleared his throat and I looked round, staring straight into the treacherous eyes of the man who had stolen everything from us and who had not the slightest compunction about leaving Father to rot in gaol.

Chapter Fifteen

'Good afternoon, Miss Pengelly. I'd have thought you'd have had enough excitement to be out again so soon.' He hovered above me like an executioner, his hateful voice heavy with threat.

'Good afternoon,' I said, quickly covering my face in my hands.

'Come, Miss Pengelly, tears where there's usually such pride? I thought nothing could daunt the fiery spirit that keeps Miss Pengelly at loggerheads with everyone in authority.' His voice was angry, his laugh dismissive.

'You've caught me in a moment of weakness, Mr Tregellas, that's all. Most people think I'm fiery all the time, but I have moments when I'm not strong at all, far from it.' I tried to keep my voice calm.

He thrust his handkerchief towards me. 'Your face is covered with dirt.'

'But this is silk – I might ruin it.'

'It doesn't matter. Keep it – your need is greater than mine.'

'Thank you, you're very kind.' The words almost stuck in my throat. My heart was racing, banging furiously against my chest. I had underestimated this man's power, certainly underestimated his cruelty. I cleared my throat, 'I'd no idea of your kindness till only the other day when Mother told me of your great generosity. If I'd have known how indebted we were to you, I'd have made a point of thanking you – well before now. I'd no idea that, without you, we'd be destitute and Father would be in a pauper's grave...' Once again, I lifted the detestable silk handkerchief to my eyes.

'Your father was my friend as well as my business associate. I could never leave you homeless. Indeed, it was my intention to see you and your mother comfortably settled well before this. Get up, Miss Pengelly, you're wet and your dress is getting ruined amongst all that dirt.'

Rain was gathering on the capes of his travelling coat, drops falling from the edge of his wide-brimmed hat. Though his voice had lost something of its cruelty, his eyes remained cold and disdainful. Putting out his hand, he helped me rise. 'Let me take you home, Miss Pengelly. This drizzle's set to continue and your cloak's getting soaked. You'll catch a chill in those damp clothes and you're in no fit state to walk home. My trap's at your disposal.'

'Thank you, I'd be very grateful.' It was as much as I could do to stop the shudder I felt at the touch of his hand. 'You're right, I'm in no fit state to be seen – my dress is ruined.'

'It's not your appearance I'm questioning, but the fact you are out alone again so soon. Do you not learn from misadventure, Miss Pengelly?' His eyes were accusing me of collusion, staring at me; judge and jury. I stared back, this time not looking away.

'You mean the highwayman? I didn't know you'd heard.'

'Of course I've heard – the whole town's heard. It's all everyone's talking about.'

'I was very lucky the highwayman didn't steal anything. Madame Merrick's money was not touched. He was disturbed before he could take anything.'

'I cannot think what induced you to attempt anything so foolish! Especially with that crazed boy as an escort. What were you thinking? Madame Merrick was wrong to let you go, but what induced you take such a risk? That's what interests me. Why put yourself in such danger? If it hadn't been the highwayman, it would've been the vagrants or cutthroats, so why insist on going? That's what I'm curious to know.'

I said nothing but looked at the ground, stepping carefully round a puddle that had formed on the path. Despite my damp clothes, I felt perspiration trickling down my back. *He's no proof*, I said over and over in my mind. *He's no proof*. I would give myself away if I showed the slightest fear.

'Please don't press me, Mr Tregellas,' was all I could think to say.

We were making our way down the muddy path towards the wicket gate. So much depended on him believing I was innocent and my mind was racing. At the gate I stepped to pass in front of him but he stood squarely in front of me, barring my way. 'But I am pressing you, Miss Pengelly.'

'I'd rather you didn't ask.'

'But I am asking. I will know, and you will tell me.' He

interlocked his hands, clicking his fingers in front of me, the threat so obvious it made my stomach turn.

'Then you must promise not to think badly of me, because I'd rather you didn't know.'

'Indeed? I am intrigued, please, carry on.'

'Mother's told me of the great honour I might expect from you on my twenty-first birthday, but that's less than three weeks away and…as you may have noticed, I've no decent clothes. I've only this dress and two others which are worn and threadbare and I hate them being so shabby. Madame Merrick has beautiful fabrics – the most beautiful fabrics – but they're too expensive…so I thought that if I went to St Austell to get Madame Merrick's cotton, I could buy some material that we could afford.' I was talking too quickly, but I could see he was listening. There was just the slightest chance he might even believe me. I kept my eyes lowered, my voice soft.

'Mother can make even the cheapest fabric look wonderful and I was hoping that when you came on my birthday, you'd be pleasantly surprised…' I put my hand against my mouth as if reluctant to continue. 'Because…I was scared you might change your mind. There – I've said it now and I wish you hadn't made me say it.'

It was my only option. If he believed me, it would buy me time. For a moment I thought he would laugh or accuse me of lying, but he stood watching me, his unsmiling eyes showing no emotion. We walked on in silence, stopping at the wicket gate. 'Wait, while I fetch the trap,' was all he said. A blackbird was singing in the hedgerow, drops of rain were falling from the trees. Puddles pooled by the gate and I passed slowly round them, edging carefully through the mud, not knowing whether he believed me or not.

The pony and trap was making its way down the lane and I hardly dared look up. I watched him jump down and hold out his hand to help me mount. As he did so, his eyes travelled up and down my body – greedy, possessive, full of want and domination. In that instant, I knew he thought I was his for the taking, and looked down, hiding the flash of triumph sweeping through me. Wrapping my shawl round me, I stared ahead, sitting in silence as the cart splashed through the gathering puddles. As the cottage came in sight, he slowed the pony. I knew what he was going to say, even before he spoke.

'Does this mean I can tell Parson Bettison to call the banns, Miss Pengelly?'

'Could you wait three weeks, Mr Tregellas?' I replied, my carefully thought out excuse at the ready. 'You know Mother. She'll want to do everything properly – it'll take her that long to make some new dresses and she'll want Jenna to prepare a fine meal. She'll be determined to receive you in her best style.'

We reached the cottage door. Holding the reins tightly, Mr Tregellas dismounted. I knew I had to sit and smile, hide my loathing, curb my hatred. He was a thief, he had left my father to rot, yet I had to hide my anger and show no fear. Helping me down, he stood closer to me than was comfortable, pressing my fingers more tightly than was necessary. In response, I held his hand for a little bit longer than was customary. Hiding my distaste, I leant slightly towards him, almost touching him. His body tautened, his breathing deepened. A flush began spreading across his face. Beads of sweat started glistening on his upper lip.

'Good day, Mr Tregellas,' I said a little breathlessly.

'Good day, Miss Pengelly,' he said, his voice thick with desire.

Mother and Jenna stood open-mouthed, staring at my mud-splattered clothes. I brushed past, desperate to get to the safety of the cottage. I had never lied so blatantly and never, ever used my body like that. Part of me was disgusted, the other part strangely exhilarated.

I had news that would turn their worlds upside down. I wanted to tell them. Dear God, I wanted to tell them. Father was alive and we would soon have him home. I wanted to sing, dance, tell them their frowns were misplaced – they should be sharing my joy. But I would have to wait.

'I'm starving, Jenna,' I called over my shoulder. 'What've you got to eat? There must be something in this larder of yours – have you any apple dumplings?'

They followed me into the kitchen, Mother holding the sleeve she had been sewing in one hand, the attached needle in the other. 'Rosehannon, was that Mr Tregellas you were with?'

'It was, Mother.'

'What were you doing?'

'Simpering, fawning and pretending to be stupid,' I said, winking at Jenna who stared back, incredulous.

Mother's frown deepened. 'You're making no sense what-soever. What does she mean, Jenna? Could one of you *please* tell me what is going on?'

'Absolutely everything and absolutely nothing,' I said, cutting a large slice of bread and smothering it with lard. I felt invincible. I had Mr Tregellas eating out of my hand. All we had to do now was find a good attorney. We had three weeks and all the evidence we needed but, best of all, Father would soon be home with us.

'Rosehannon, you're talking in riddles – just like your father,' Mother replied, putting down her sewing, 'and it was one of his least likeable habits…and just look at the state of your dress! What'll the neighbours think? As if we aren't talked about enough already. And why were you alone with Mr Tregellas? Honest, from now on you need go everywhere with me or Jenna. What d'you mean, *simpering* and *fawning*…?'

I felt flushed with success. I wanted to put my arms round Mother and hold her to me, grab Jenna by her hands and whirl her round the kitchen. I wanted to shout that Father was alive. I wanted them to know I had outwitted Mr Tregellas and everything was going to be alright. But instead, I smiled.

'Don't you fret, Mother, I won't go anywhere on my own again. I'll be the perfect daughter. Everything's going to be alright. We're going to be so happy again – just you wait and see.'

Mother looked unconvinced, the worry in her eyes plain to see, but I felt almost light-hearted with joy. Father was alive. The impossible had come true.

Chapter Sixteen

Monday 1st July 1793 7:00 a.m.

I woke in a cold sweat. If Sulio Denville was working for Mr Tregellas, there was no-one to turn king's evidence. Mr Tregellas would flourish a bill of sale, claim he did not know it was the same ship, and insist the mistake in Father's identity had nothing to do with him. He would claim the contagious nature of his death meant he had not actually seen the body but he had relied on the prison guards for his information. Robert Roskelly would be the presiding magistrate, Father would go straight back to gaol and be hanged for escaping. It was worse than ever.

My untouched breakfast did not go unnoticed. Mother was watching me intently. As we sat in the ferry, her eyes barely left my face. I was so glad I had not told her – glad she was not feeling the same fear. Besides, what could I tell her? Father was alive but in more danger than ever? Jim was right; if she knew, she would not be able to hide her anxiety.

We reached the warehouse and began climbing the steps. Across the yard, the sound of hammering filled the air and a pang of longing filled my heart. It was as if the boatyard was beckoning me back. Glancing through the arch, I could see the men already hard at work.

'Mother, I'll only be a minute – I'm going to say hello to Mr Scantlebury.'

Father had owned this boatyard for ten years. He had left Porthruan to start out on his own and his decision had proved sound. His boats were the best to be had and the town soon knew it. His reputation grew, commissions came pouring in and we were set to prosper. We would be prospering still, if the Corporation had not taken against Father. Until that moment, it had been too painful even to look into the yard, let alone walk under the arch, and I had not been back for over a year. I could smell the sawdust, the varnish, the new paint and I breathed it in, delighting in the acrid smell of burning pitch. It was all so familiar, so very dear.

The sign *Tregellas Boatyard* made my blood boil. How dare they steal it from us? This boatyard was in every part of me, just as it was in every part of Father. We were born to build boats, my forefathers before me, each generation seeking new ways to harness the wind, new ways of pitting their wits against the power of the sea. I strode angrily under the arch, my feet following the path I knew so well.

Joseph Melhuish was wielding his hammer against the hot trivet he was forging. His furnace was blazing, with more faggots lying ready to be burnt. Even at this early hour, he was stripped to the waist, his body glistening, a pile of newly crafted shackles cooling on the stones around him. He had known Father for many years and looked pleasantly surprised

132

at my nod of greeting. Two sawyers stood gossiping in the sawpit, a huge oak trunk waiting to be planked. As I passed, I heard their sniggers and caught the insolence in their eyes. 'What are you staring at?' I snapped, glaring down at them with the full force of my fury.

'Come on, miss. Who could resist such a pretty sight?' the tallest replied, his eyes as bold as brass.

'D'you want a boat?' said the other, finding his words so funny he almost choked.

I did not find him funny. Anyone could see they were lazy and if I had anything to do with the yard they would have gone long ago. Anger made my cheeks burn. This was Father's yard and no-one would take it from us. No, I did not want a boat – I wanted the boatyard. I wanted every hoist and pulley, every plank of timber, every pole and spar. I wanted every coiled chain, every barrel of nails, every shackle, every trunnel, every pot of paint and varnish. I wanted every sack of hemp, every bag of oakum and every last handful of horse hair. I wanted it all back. All of it.

Across the yard, a three-masted lugger was having a final coat of varnish and the nameplate *Dolphin* nailed into position. The letters were bright blue, the gold background painted with elaborate red and green swirls. There were matching swirls adorning the bowsprit and two dolphins painted either side of the bow, but she was a beautiful boat – despite the finish. Mr Scantlebury came hurrying towards me, his face filled with pleasure. 'Oh, Miss Pengelly,' he cried, 'it gladdens my eye to see you.'

'And mine you, Mr Scantlebury. I shouldn't have left it so

133

long.' I must have been frowning because a shadow fell across his face and he looked at me sadly.

'No doubt you'd your reasons.' The muscles round his jowls slackened and I thought how much older he looked though he was still a fine man with a powerful frame for his fifty years. He and Father had been apprentices together and he had been Father's foreman and senior shipwright ever since we moved to Fosse.

'Tell me about this lugger,' I said. 'She's a lot fancier than anything we used to build – she's quite a painted lady – but no doubt under all that paint she's as good as anything we ever built.'

'Oh, aye, the craftsmanship's the same – though there's been many changes since your father left us.' He put out his arm and I took it, grateful for a sign of our old friendship. 'Aye, many a change and not all for the better, I can tell you. But it doesn't do to hanker for the past – we must look to our future.'

'Are you getting good contracts?'

'Oh, aye, plenty of work, though mostly repairs. This is the only boat we've built this year. She's for a consortium.'

'All Corporation men I take it!' I could not hide the disgust in my voice. When Father found out, he would spit with fury.

'Aye, each and every one of them! They're the ones with the money.'

A young lad came tentatively forward, unsure whether he could interrupt. He was wearing a leather apron and carrying a varnish brush. Mr Scantlebury nodded and the boy approached, stopping at a respectable distance to take off his hat. Trying to swap hands, he fumbled and dropped the varnish brush. As he bent to retrieve it, his hat fell off and landed on the brush, sticking to the varnish. In an agony of embarrassment he wrung his hands together, ruining the hat. Finally, he made a polite bow, his face glowing like the tip of Mr Melhuish's poker.

'This is Tom, my sister's youngest – I'm hoping to make an apprentice of him. Tom, this is Miss Pengelly.'

'Good mornin', Miss Pengelly,' Tom replied, smiling shyly. 'Our Elowyn says yer the cleverest lady in England.'

'Your Elowyn?'

'She works for Madame Merrick. She says ye add up in yer head and ye're never wrong.'

'That's enough, lad – go to the sailmakers and tell them we're ready. And put that brush down – no, not there.' As Tom's lanky frame crossed the yard, Mr Scantlebury shook his head. 'I don't hold out much hope. Mr Tregellas's taken against him and his word's final. Tom's a good lad but he's all fingers and thumbs and hasn't enough learning. I can't bear to tell my sister for she's pinning her hopes on me.'

'Is your sister well?'

'Aye, now she's left that vicious drunk and moved in with me. They're welcome to all I have but I can't promise an apprenticeship.' There was a heaviness about him which had never been there before. If only I could tell him about Father.

'Is she your design?' I said looking back at the *Dolphin*.

'Ha!' His frown returned, 'I only build boats now. No, if she were mine I'd have stepped up her foremast and steeved up her bowsprit –'twould allow for plenty of sail but keep her shorter. Not just for harbouring, but for the dues as well.' It was not like him to be so bitter.

I smiled. 'Corporation men don't pay harbour dues – you should remember that!'

We walked back across the yard and reached the office door. The boatyard leased the ground floor of the warehouse, Madame Merrick leased the first floor, the sailmakers the large loft above. Mr Scantlebury hesitated. 'I can't offer you tea or anything as genteel as that,' he said with a wink, shades of his former self showing through, 'but if you've a minute, will you come in? I could show you a new design I've been working on – though it's between you and me, mind – Mr Tregellas is not to know.'

He rolled out the plans and I could see it was his most ambitious design yet – a one hundred and twenty foot brig. I could hardly believe it. Made from oak and deal, she would have elm for the keel and fir for the two masts. His plans detailed everything, even the cordage which was often left to the sailmakers. 'She'll be nigh on four hundred tons. See the extra studding sails – and the spanker aloft on the gaff?' I nodded, following his finger as he pointed out the details. 'She'll turn with ease. She's broad in the beam and sits deep in the water – she's heavy, mind, and will withstand any sea. I reckon she'd do eleven knots.'

'You really think you could build her here?' Excitement made my heart race. It was always like this when I saw new plans. Turning dreams into reality, flat drawings into solid ships that would plough the waves and keep their crew safe. I felt so alive.

'Aye, we can build her right enough – we've the skill and the space.' He looked up as if he dared not raise his hopes.

Frustration welled inside me. I could not bear the thought that Mr Scantlebury's plans could go to waste or, worse still, be built by another yard. I would clear Father's name. I would get this yard back and we would apply to the Admiralty to build this brig.

'Where's that old Admiralty list?' I asked, rushing to the cabinet. 'The one we used for that navy repair commission?' It felt so good to be back in the office. Nothing had changed; everything was in exactly the same place. 'Here it is, look, Mr Robert Steppings – Navy Board's Surveyor of Sloops.' I waved the list triumphantly in the air.

'What're you up to, Miss Rosehannon? You've that look in your eye, like old times.'

Like old times – how good that sounded. I stuffed the list down my bodice and put my fingers to my lips. 'What list? I see no list. Keep these plans well hidden and promise me you'll not show them to anyone else. I'll tell you everything when I can, but for the moment it's our secret.' I could not wait to tell Father.

Mr Scantlebury's smile faded and his look turned grave. It was as if he knew I was concealing something. 'I'd trust you with my life, Miss Rosehannon, but be careful not to cross Mr Tregellas. He's not a man to meddle with. Cross him and you're in dangerous waters.'

'I know,' I said, smiling back at him despite his warning. I was almost at the door, 'Mr Scantlebury, I can't promise anything but send Tom to me on Saturday and Sunday morning – I'll see what I can do to help his learning.' I turned to go but another thought struck me. 'And tell Tom to bring Elowyn too – let's see if I can get them both adding up in their heads.'

He nodded but his smile said everything. I even think his back looked straighter and, for some unaccountable reason, mine seemed to be, too. My courage had returned. Whatever it took, I would get our yard back and see justice done for Father.

It was a beautiful, bright morning with clear blue skies. A sudden bright flash caught my eye and I glanced up at the window to see Madame Merrick studying me through her lorgnettes. The sun had caught the glass and though she turned hurriedly away, she saw I had seen her. My heart froze. How long had she been watching me? Worst still, had she seen me study the plans?

Chapter Seventeen

Madame Merrick made no mention of seeing me in the yard but seemed preoccupied, pacing round the room several times before returning my greeting. 'Miss Pengelly, I have placed those invoices you wanted on the bureau – they are all in *order* and dated correctly and, as you will notice, they have the *correct* excise stamp on them.' There was something very tense about the way she was watching me.

I walked over to the bureau and studied them. Some attempt had been made to make them look older than a few days, but they would fool nobody. We all knew, however, that the person they were meant to fool had just issued them so no questions would be asked. I just wondered how much she had had to pay. Smuggling, though rife, was still a dangerous pastime. 'I'm glad you found them, Madame Merrick,' I said, with just a touch of sarcasm.

'*Indeed.* Now everything is in order.'

'Where's Mother?'

'In the fitting room. Elowyn is making some adjustments

to her gown.' I smiled politely and would have gone through to the sewing room, but Madame Merrick put her exquisitely manicured hand on my sleeve, 'One moment, Miss Pengelly...*if* you please.'

She crossed to the table and pulled forward two rolls of material and several boxes of lace and brocade. I was astonished when she beckoned me over as I had never discussed fabrics with her, nor knew anything about them. 'This pale-cream material is cambric and you can see it is very light, easily laundered and *comfortable* to wear,' she said. 'This fabric, on the other hand, is the *last* of the sprig muslin and is particularly superior. You can tell by the very *fine* selvedge that it is delicately woven and therefore more *expensive*... and *consequently* I would usually reserve it for more *important* clients. However, both fabrics could be made up into a simple chemise gown with perhaps a little brocade at the neckline or lace – or even a chiffon frill.'

I watched her caress the material, carefully trying the various combinations, holding the different brocades and lace against the fabric, dismissing one and then another until she had the best combination. 'This would make a very pretty gown. I like this best. What do *you* think, Miss Pengelly?' She pointed to the green sprig muslin, a length of white cotton brocade and some green satin ribbon which exactly matched the sprig. I was astonished she was talking to me in such a way and felt rather unnerved.

'Yes, I like that best too. Who is it for, Madame Merrick?'

She held herself very upright. 'For *you*, Miss Pengelly, I would like you to have it as a *present*. Elowyn can make it up as she can do with the *practice*.' Her voice was pleasant enough and a smile crossed her face, but her eyes remained watchful. Was she buying my silence? Smuggling or not, she must know I could be no threat to her business.

'That's really very generous,' I replied, 'but why would you want to give me so much?'

'By way of a *thank you*. I heard how you defended my money when you were attacked and I know any lesser person would have handed the money straight over. You put yourself at *great* risk and I have to thank you for that. There was a *lot* of money in that purse, as well you know.'

So that was it. I put my hand to my bodice front. 'Yes, I was very scared. It was dreadful when he tried to force it from me.'

'It must have been, but that is now *over* and you will have a *beautiful* new dress.' She remained smiling and I wondered if I had judged her too harshly.

The thought of a new dress, however I came by it, filled me with joy. I had never been particularly interested in dresses, yet, as I looked at the material, I felt a thrill of excitement, imagining, for the first time, what it would be like to wear something so delicate and feminine. I unrolled a few yards of the beautiful soft sprig, holding it against my cheek, feeling suddenly shy and self-conscious. 'It's really very beautiful, Madame Merrick. D'you think it will suit me?'

'Very much, Miss Pengelly – *that* is why I chose it: jewel green to compliment your fiery looks and auburn hair.' She pursed her lips, fidgeting with the lace, drawing herself up to her full height. 'Miss Pengelly, there was absolutely *no* reason for you to go to St Austell. I insist only *my* fabrics are worn in *my* establishment.' I felt suddenly winded. Only one person could have told her that and the thought of her spying on me in the boatyard made my stomach tighten.

Mother came through from the back room, clearly overwhelmed by Madame Merrick's offer. Wiping away her tears, she repeatedly thanked her, her radiant smile almost breaking my heart. I left them to go through the various combinations of materials and lace, taking up my position at the bureau so I could begin my letter to Mr Steppings.

England's war with France was likely to take a heavy toll. Already a yard in Mevagissey was fitting out ships for troop transport and more ships would be needed. My letter was short and to the point. I reminded him we had already won one of his contracts and informed him that, should he be in our area again, or should he be willing to make the journey, we would be able to furnish him with very accurate and detailed plans of a fast new brig which we were planning to build. I assured him of our best attention and signed it with my name, making sure that Rosehannon was illegible, but Pengelly was clear. No-one would suspect it had been written by a woman. Sealing it quickly, I hid it down my bodice, confident that neither Madame Merrick nor Mother had seen me write it.

A young messenger was struggling up the stairs, carrying a huge parcel wrapped in brown paper and tied with string. Balancing it precariously on his knee, he almost toppled onto Madame Merrick as she opened the door. 'For Miss Pengelly, Madame.'

'Miss Pengelly? There must be some mistake.'

'No M-m-madame,' the boy managed to say. 'I w-w-was told to bring it here.' He waited expectantly, but as Madame Merrick seemed turned to stone, and I had no money, Mother searched her purse and produced a coin. The boy seemed pleased, bowing several times as he backed out of the door.

Madame Merrick remained incredulous, handing the large parcel over to me, and I knew I would have no privacy in opening it. I started to undo the knot but she leant forward, brandishing the small pair of silver scissors she kept hanging on a chain from her waist. 'Are you expecting a parcel, Miss Pengelly?' she asked as she cut the knot.

'No,' I replied, as surprised as she was.

As I unfolded the paper, we gasped. Wrapped in soft gauze was the most beautiful ivory silk I had ever seen. It was light and delicate, so finely woven it looked like it had been spun out of air. I released it from its folds and it lay shimmering in the sunshine. Underneath the silk were layers of exquisite lace, rolls of delicate satin ribbons and at least a dozen beautiful pearl buttons.

Madame Merrick looked as if she had swallowed a lemon. Her mouth puckered, her colour drained and she gripped the table in an effort of self-control. 'That is *Italian* silk,' she said, '…from *Mantua*…and that is the *finest* Belgian lace – *Point Duchesse*, to be exact – though I do not expect you to recognise either.'

Mother had paled. 'There's a letter,' she said, handing it to me. 'Who's it from?'

143

I looked at the handwriting, my heart sinking. 'It's from Mr Tregellas.'

'But how could he come by such beautiful silk?'

I caught the indignant fury in Madame Merrick's face. 'No doubt he has his sources,' I replied.

'Read the letter. What does it say?' urged Mother.

I broke the seal and began to read, but I had hardly got past the first line when my voice faltered.

Dear Miss Pengelly,

Please accept this silk as a token of my sincerest regard. Madame Merrick will no doubt be delighted to attend to you in person and will, I am certain, make this gown her priority.

With great expectations, I remain your obedient servant.

William Tregellas

Mother reached for a chair and I stared at the letter, wondering what would be more hurtful to Madame Merrick – his hint of our marriage or the fact he had kept back the best silk, not passing any through her hands. With silk as fine as this, even Lady April Cavendish would be beating a path to her door. Madame Merrick was gripping the table, trying to swallow the unpalatable truth. She cleared her throat, her voice uncharacteristically thin.

'Mr Tregellas has always been *very* good to me and it will be my *pleasure* to sew your dress – in fact, I will make a start straight away.' For all her imperious ways, I felt sorry for her. I would gladly have given her the silk there and then. I knew I would never wear it.

Mother remained seated, her eyes sad. 'My dear, does this mean what I think it means?'

I wanted to tell her. I wanted to shout to the rooftops that I did not give a fig for the silk; that I would never marry Mr Tregellas, but I could say nothing. Nor could I lie. I took her hand in mine and I held it tightly. It was trembling. 'We'll be just fine, Mother,' I said softly. 'You mustn't worry. Things will work out, I know they will.'

'Well, what a day this has turned out to be! First one dress and now another!' Madame Merrick was clearly rallying. No doubt she was already thinking how she could turn this to her advantage. Besides, it would not do to quarrel with the next Mrs Tregellas. Holding up her lovely sprig muslin, she leant towards me, her voice strangely conspiratorial. 'I can see you will not be wanting *this* now, Miss Pengelly.'

'Oh, but I do want it – very much,' I found myself pleading. 'That's…that is if you don't mind.'

Madame Merrick looked astonished. I had not meant to sound so passionate, but for some reason I wanted the new dress more than anything, and the thought of not having it was suddenly too awful. I looked away, embarrassed by my outburst, a furious blush spreading over my face.

My red cheeks were not lost on Madame Merrick. 'Then you *shall* have it, Miss Pengelly,' she said, slowly studying my face, a half-smile playing on her lips. 'I will ask Elowyn to start making it for you *straight* away.'

Madame Merrick had the uncanny knack of making me feel she knew exactly what I was thinking. I could not afford to make any more mistakes.

Chapter Eighteen

It was past nine o'clock. The evening was as hot as the day had been: even the usually damp kitchen was humid and sticky. Jenna was tight-lipped and flustered. Honestly, sometimes she was just like Mrs Munroe.

'Have there been any messages, Jenna?'

'Not since last time ye asked.'

'Are you sure?'

'Course I'm sure.'

Waiting to hear from Jim was driving me to distraction. My beloved father was in need of my attention, yet I could do nothing until Jim contacted me. He had all the evidence and he had Father, so why had he not got in touch? It was almost too much to bear. Pinching off a bit of pastry, I tasted it raw.

'Miss Pengelly, if ye don't mind, ye're getting under me feet. If I'm to finish making this pie ye must let me on with it.' She threw a scrap of brawn to the cat who was sitting by the open door. Devouring it, he looked up for more.

'I can see what you mean about the way that cat looks at you. D'you think he lost his ear in a fight? We could call him Scrappy…or Pesky…or how about Mr Pitt? He's going to need a name – I think we should call him Mr Pitt.'

'Miss Pengelly, unlike ye, I've *a thousand and one* things to do. Now, if ye don't mind…'

'Can you remember how to add up thousands, Jenna? Would you like me to go over it again? You used to love me teaching you calculations.'

'No, Miss Pengelly. I've enough of calculations.'

'Then I'll read you my latest pamphlet.'

'I've enough of Miss Mary Wolfstonecroft.'

'Wollstonecraft.'

'Enough of her, too.'

'Jenna, she's important. You should know all her views on the rights of women.'

'Ha! Like I've time for all that!'

'Just imagine what it could be like – a proper education for women and the right to contribute to society.'

'Perhaps ye'd like to contribute to society by passing that rolling pin.'

'You shouldn't mock – one day it'll happen.'

'Now I know ye're piximazed.'

It was no good, when Jenna was in a huff she could be very uncommunicative. Finally I plucked up the courage to ask what I had wanted to ask all afternoon. 'Has anyone left a basket of fruit – cherries, perhaps?'

She slammed down the rolling pin and Mr Pitt fled in alarm. Placing both hands on the table, she leant forward in triumph. 'I knew it – ye may've fooled your mother but ye can't fool me. All that nonsense – fawning and simpering – like I'd fall for that! Ye're up to something, Miss Rosehannon Pengelly. Ye're waiting for another love letter and it ain't from Mr Tregellas.'

'Of course I'm not! I'm a little hungry, that's all, and I wondered if there were any cherries.'

'Like I believe that! Ye've been restless all afternoon, sighing and gazing out the window – as jumpy as Mr Pitt…I know ye too well. Ye're waiting for another love letter.'

'I'm not. Anyway, that first letter was not a love letter.'

She was watching me closely and I knew she could see my face burning. This waiting was making me jumpy. Jumpy and cross. Where was Jim and why had he not contacted me? It had been such a hot day. The corridor was stuffy, the stone walls warm to the touch. I opened the front door, peering one way, then the other, vainly searching for Jim or any sign of a message. I knew he would not come in person, nor would he leave anything unattended, but he must surely contact me soon.

Dusk was gathering, women sitting in clusters outside their doors, their bobbins flying, their tongues wagging. Children played hopscotch in the dying light and in the west, a beautiful red haze was promising yet another hot day. My whole life had changed, yet nothing seemed different – just the same people doing the same things, continuing their lives with no thought of my plight. Suddenly, I caught a faint wisp of tobacco smoke wafting across the lane from the alley opposite. Tobacco smoke would not normally catch my attention, but this was a particularly distinct brand, full of vanilla and cinnamon. The exact brand I had smelt once, no twice that very day – once when I left my letter in the posthouse, once in the ferry crossing back to Porthruan. The man smoking the pipe had kept his back to me, his large hat concealing his face. I had thought nothing of it, but it could be no coincidence. Whoever was smoking that pipe was watching me, probably at that very moment.

I shut the door. How could I have been so stupid? Of course I had not fooled Mr Tregellas – he was having me watched, hoping I would lead him straight to Father. What if Jim came? What if they followed him and got back the evidence? What if they found Father?

I climbed the stairs to find candlelight showing under Mother's door. She was usually so frugal with candles. I knocked gently.

'Come in.' She was sitting up in bed, sewing the hem of her new dress.

'Is the light good enough?'

'Not really – it's just I'm so nearly finished.'

'It's beautiful – your loveliest dress ever. I love those little pin-tucks and the mother-of-pearl buttons.' I wanted to be with her. I needed her company.

'Thank ye, my dear. Madame Merrick's been that generous to me. And now it seems ye're to have *two* new dresses.' I loved the way her tone grew so intimate when we were alone, stretching back to earlier days before the veneer of Father's education and prosperity kept her from being herself.

'I know...I can't believe it,' I said, lifting the edge of the gown and sitting on the bed next to her, my feet tucked under me as if I were a child.

She was wearing her cotton nightdress and nightcap, her hair falling in a long plait down her back. The lines on her face were softened by the glow of the candle. It felt so comforting, watching her needle flash in and out of the material and I tried to calm my nerves. I must stay strong. We had come so far and I had to believe we could clear Father's name.

'I'm so happy, Mother – and I know you'll be too.' I so wanted to tell her.

'Something's changed in ye, Rosehannon – something for the better,' she said softly. 'Ye've got your old sparkle back – but I'm troubled. Only days ago, ye told me Mr Tregellas was the last person in the world ye'd marry, yet now the thought seems to bring ye so much joy.' She hesitated, biting her bottom lip. 'I'm that worried I've interfered too much – even forced ye into liking him…but has Mr Tregellas done something to make ye love him?'

Her eyes searched mine, eager for reassurance. I longed to tell her everything, but of course I could not. Neither could I lie. 'You know my head will always rule my heart, Mother. I'm not so foolish. I'll not pretend to love him, but I'm happy – and I know you will be too. We'll soon be back in Coombe House, like we were.' I bent to kiss her goodnight. 'And I want our yard back.'

'If ye're sure ye know what ye're doing,' she replied, reaching for my hand. She was smiling, but the eyes that looked down were brimming with sadness.

Night was always the time when my fears would surface. As a child I would listen to the howling of the wind, believing it to be the souls of drowned sailors returning across the oceans. I would stare at the moon, seeing demons chase across the sky and listen for the cries of children lost to the fairies in the woods. Such furtive imaginings filled my nights with fear, but the thought of the man watching me was more terrifying than any childhood terror.

The room was stuffy, airless, despite the open casement. No breeze blew. I wore my flimsiest nightgown, and lay stretched out on my bed, undoing the buttons round my neck in an effort to remain cool. I must have fallen asleep. I was woken by the sound of a soft thud and opened my eyes, my ears straining in the silence, my heart racing with the dreadful realisation that someone had just entered my room. I lay rigid, trying to control my breathing, frantically hoping I would have the strength to ward off my attacker.

Through the stillness, I heard a whisper. 'Rose, it's me, Jim.'

The night was bright, the moon large. I could see the outline of his body silhouetted against the window, his head ducking under the eaves. He took a step forward, shrinking my room with his tall frame. 'What on earth are you doing coming into my room?' I whispered, relieved, but shocked nonetheless. 'If anyone's seen you...'

'No-one's seen me, an' I couldn't use the front door. You're being watched.'

'I know, by a man stupid enough to smoke a very distinctive brand of tobacco.'

'Very stupid, but then he doesn't realise who he's up against.'

'How's Father?' I whispered, ignoring his attempt at flattery. I flung a shawl round my shoulders. 'Where is he? Is he alright? How are his wounds?'

'Improving and anxious to see you – his appetite's increased and he's a lot stronger than he was. I've no doubt he'll do well so you needn't fear – he's in good hands.'

'Did he ask why we never visited him? Poor Father, he must've thought we'd deserted him.' There was so much to ask, so much to find out.

'He knew you thought him dead.'

We were talking too loudly. I crossed the room, standing closer so our voices could not be heard. We were next to the casement. Jim put out his hand, drawing me away and I realised we could be seen from the yard below. I felt the heat of his hand through the cotton of my nightdress – it was flimsy and worn, no barrier at all, and I tensed under his touch. I backed away.

He, too, backed away but even in the darkness I could see his eyes travelling down my throat, lingering on my bosom, following the outline of my legs under my nightdress. I felt a tingle of excitement – a rush of pleasure as I watched his appraisal. 'Forgive me for coming to your room like this, but we need to talk and I'd no way of getting you a message.' He seemed to be having difficulty tearing his eyes from my undone buttons.

'Where's Father? Is he well hidden?' I said, drawing my shawl around me.

'Your father's in good hands, trust me, but I need to leave him – I've to go to Truro. My plan's risky, but it's the only way I can think to snare Mr Tregellas. That's all I can tell you.'

'*Can* tell me or *will* tell me?' I challenged.

'You've to trust me, Rose. Be at the gates of Polcarrow at seven on Thursday evening, an' I'll be there with your father.'

I had trusted him before and where did it get me? I needed more information. 'Not Polcarrow – don't take Father anywhere near Polcarrow. Mr Roskelly was the magistrate who imprisoned Father so, for goodness sake, just bring him to me and give me back my ledgers. We'll find a good attorney and make a legal case against Mr Tregellas.' I could hear my voice rising.

'No, Rose. Think. No attorney would take this on – the evidence is too weak. You've no case, an' even if you did, Roskelly's still the magistrate – you'll be playing straight into his hands. You've to trust me, one more time.' His voice was almost pleading.

The light from the moon filled the room, bathing him in light. I could see the outline of his dagger hanging from his belt. 'Why should I trust you?' I whispered back. 'You're a wanted man. It's dangerous, you're dangerous. Your dagger scares me…you're violent and…'

A flash of anger crossed his eyes. 'No, Rose, I'm not violent and I'm not dangerous. I live in a world of treachery, that's all…and I bear the scars of great violence….Yes, I watch my back an' fear to look men in the eye, and, yes, I sleep with one eye open an' one hand on my knife, but it hasn't always been like that.' His chest was rising and falling. 'I never start

153

violence and I never draw my dagger first. You judge too harshly.'

'I'm only harsh because I judge on what I see.'

The lines round his mouth tightened. 'You see wrongly. I was born with honour an' a sense of justice, now I live with dishonour and injustice – a disastrous turnaround for any man. You judge me wrongly – such is the cruelty of life.'

I thought of Ben, poor Ben, who would never hurt anyone. 'You were cruel to Ben.'

'Cruel?' he mocked, his voice thick with outrage. 'You accuse me of cruelty? You don't know the meaning of cruelty.'

He gripped his shirt, pulling it over his head and throwing it to the floor as he stood in the half-light, his bare chest rising and falling with the force of his anger. I stared at him, our eyes locking, but it was not anger I saw staring back at me – it was anguish. Anguish, outrage, pain and, for a moment, my heart seemed to stop. It was as if I was staring deep into his soul, his pain screaming at me with no sound, piercing my heart so completely. He turned his back to me and, in the soft light of the moon, I caught my breath.

'This is cruelty, Miss Pengelly,' he said, his words seemingly wrenched from his heart, 'this is man's inhumanity to man.'

Across his shoulders and all the way down his back, huge red wheals cut a criss-cross of livid scars. In places the scars formed raised knots, in others dips and craters. Putting my hand over my mouth, I stifled my cry. Nowhere was the skin smooth or the flesh untouched and I stared in horror, feeling the pain and suffering each scar must have brought. But the deepest, most-violent scar was the worst of all – circling his neck in an angry red clasp. No wonder he always wore a scarf.

I put out my hand, tracing the scars with my fingers, soothing them as if, somehow, I could hope to lessen their horror, wipe away the memory of the pain. I could not help myself. Jim stood silently, his head bowed, his back glistening with sweat, his skin hot and sticky. I tried to speak, but my emotions had gone beyond the power of words.

I followed the contours of the scars across his shoulders, breathing in the scent that sent my pulses racing the night the press gang forced us to hide. Tracing the scars round to his chest I stood in front of him, my fingers lingering over a branding mark that puckered and discoloured his breast. I had never witnessed such violence and my heart was crying. Jim stood motionless, his eyes downcast. With a cry of despair, he clasped my hand, pressing it against his heart. 'Your touch is the balm my heart craves,' he cried, his voice hoarse, full of longing.

I could feel his heart hammering against my open palm. I was shocked by the tautness of his skin, the firmness of his muscles, unnerved by the strength beneath my hand. He leant closer, his hair brushing against mine. 'I love you, Rose.' His voice was unrecognisable in its tenderness. 'I loved you the moment I first saw you scowling by the tree. I love your spirit, I love your mind. I love the way you toss your hair, how you arch your eyebrows, how you glare at me. I love your beauty, Rose. I love your body. I love everything about you. We are meant for each other, you and I – it's our fate, our destiny.'

He released my hand from over his heart, his fingers travelling upwards towards my face. Gently, he caressed the outline of my jaw, softly tracing the contours of my lips. I felt the pressure of his finger lifting my face towards him and shut my eyes, feeling his lips brush softly against my own. His kiss was tentative, like a butterfly, slowly touching one side of my mouth, then the other.

My body ached for him, every inch of me calling out to him. My heart was racing, knowing I had wanted this from the moment our eyes first locked. I tried to hold back, but his lips sought mine with an urgency that left me reeling. I had never been kissed before and had often wondered what it would be like, but never in my wildest imagination could I have known how hard and how deep a man could kiss. As we fused to one, the taste of him, the desire in him, sparked sensations in me I felt ashamed to acknowledge.

It seemed I would never breathe again. Slowly and reluctantly, he released me, our lips breaking away just enough for us to catch our breath. His arms closed around me. 'Could you find it in your heart to love me, Rose?' he whispered, his lips once more seeking mine.

I could so easily have succumbed. I could have lost myself to the velvet darkness, taken the course my body yearned to take, but his words triggered something in me, returning me to my senses. I pulled away. 'How can you ask someone to love you if they don't know who you are?'

'Does it matter who I am?' he replied coaxingly.

'Of course it matters. You're a stranger to me, Jim...I know nothing about you.'

'Couldn't you love me for myself alone?'

'No, of course not – to love someone there must be no secrets.'

'Oh, Rose,' he moaned, 'and you accuse *me* of cruelty!' He let go of my arms, turning abruptly away, running his hands through his hair. It was damp, clinging to his forehead. 'Rose, why must you always...?'

But he was not to finish. A sound caught our attention, a movement, a light flickering under my bedroom door. Mother was calling, 'Are you alright, Rosehannon?'

Dashing across the room, I opened the door a fraction to delay her entrance. Jim had grabbed his shirt and was balancing on the casement sill. I opened the door wider, to see Mother looking distraught. 'Dear Lord – ye're not well. Ye look feverish – yer eyes are burning...yer face's all flushed. And yer lips, Rose...yer lips are red and swollen.' She put her hand against my temple. 'Yer pulse is racing, yer breathing's too rapid – all the signs of a fever. We must call Jenna. D'ye feel unwell?'

'No, Mother, I'm very well – it's just hot. It's such a warm night and I can't sleep for the heat.'

Mother looked at the open window. 'It's just I thought I heard talking...'

My already beating heart beat even faster. I shrugged my shoulders, attempting to look mystified. At once, a loud and very angry caterwauling filled the yard – Jim must have landed on the sleeping Mr Pitt.

Mother jumped. 'What on earth is that?'

'It's Mr Pitt, Mother.'

Mother looked horrified. 'Mr Pitt…? Apart from the obvious, who's Mr Pitt?'

'Jenna's tomcat.' I was thinking fast. 'He crept into my room and woke me. Poor thing, I had to throw him out – it must have been him you heard me talking to.'

'It's because yer window's wide open,' she said. 'I'm not surprised Mr Pitt climbed in. Perhaps ye encouraged him too much?'

'I don't think so…well, perhaps I did.' My body was tingling from Jim's touch. I could still feel his lips pressing against mine. I could still taste him. 'I didn't mean to encourage him and I certainly won't again.'

Mother looked suddenly serious. 'We must hope he doesn't climb back in.'

'He won't, I'm sure. I'll shut my window. Goodnight, Mother, let's try and get some sleep.' One thing was certain, from now on I would sleep with my windows shut, even in the stifling heat.

I went straight to the window, my face burning with shame. I had encouraged him. I had touched his scars with a shocking lack of reserve. Even worse, I had responded to his kiss with almost no restraint. How could I? Where was the woman of reason? The one whose head always ruled her heart? I had no idea physical passion could be so sudden, so powerful, so able to take control, but I was warned now, and I would never let it happen again.

I lay awake in the stifling room, trying not to re-live every moment of our stolen kiss. Suddenly, a thought struck me and my heart leapt. He had not been wearing the chain round his neck. No chain meant no ruby ring.

Now what was keeping me awake was how extraordinarily pleased that made me feel.

Chapter Nineteen

Thursday 4th July 1793 6.00 p.m.

We could hear shouts, footsteps running down the street. Jenna threw down her sewing and rushed to open the door. I followed close behind, looking over her shoulder to see a large plume of smoke rising high above Fosse.

''Tis a fire,' she said.

'Is it near the boatyard?'

'No…higher, nearer Polcarrow.'

'Tell Mother I'm going to check the warehouse. If the wind picks up – or turns westerly, the warehouse might be in danger. Tell her I won't be long – I'll be very careful.'

Before Jenna could make any protest, I grabbed my bonnet, joining the steady stream of people rushing to the quayside. Strange though it may seem, I could not believe my luck. I had been worrying all day what excuse I would use and now I had a perfectly good reason to leave the house. With no word from Jim, I had no option but to follow his instructions and meet him where he said.

The agony of waiting would finally be over. Soon I would see Father, but the thought of going anywhere near Polcarrow filled me with fear. Robert Roskelly had risen to power on the back of his sister's marriage. He was as bad as them all – ruthless and harsh; enclosing land, putting up rents, evicting everyone who could not pay. I hated him long before he had Father jailed. Why risk going near him? Why meet at the gate-house of the most powerful and unscrupulous man in Fosse?

The boats were already heavily loaded and waiting to cross the river but I was in luck, and squeezed into a small gap just as the ferry began to leave. Men were holding empty buckets, their faces turned anxiously towards the thin black plume rising high in the air above Fosse. 'Quay's safe – seems it's Polcarrow land,' I heard someone say.

'Aye – well, if 'tis Polcarrow land, I'll not help. Let 'im burn.'

'Don't be daft. If the wind turns, town'll burn like tinder.'

The ferry docked and the men dipped their buckets into the sea, running quickly to the end of the chain, passing the buckets from hand to hand. The road was almost blocked. Tradesmen were frantically pushing carts, produce spill-ing onto the road around them. Horses were rearing, dogs barking, children crying. A basket of whelks was jerked from a woman's arms, squashed in seconds by scores of rushing feet. Everywhere was noise and chaos – men shouting furiously for people to make way for the carts laden with hogsheads of seawater.

I followed behind, heading up the steep road to the shops and houses crammed against the huge, crenulated wall encircling the great estate. The gates of Polcarrow were always kept shut but today they were wide open, a long snake of men stretching along the drive. The men were passing full buckets in their right hands, empty buckets with their left. The pace was furious, sweat streaking their faces. A group of bystanders was staring through the gates.

'They're gaining,' I heard a man say.

'Aye,' replied another. 'Looks worse than 'tis – they'll soon have it out. 'Tis only the old cottages – they're burnt to a cinder but there's nought else to catch. They'll need beer, mind. This'll cost Roskelly.'

My stomach turned. Mr Roskelly was standing outside the great house, shouting orders to the footmen and servants who were scurrying round in great confusion. They looked like ants in a disturbed nest, going backwards and forwards, almost in circles, most of them carrying buckets, some holding pitchers. Wagons full of empty hogsheads were turning to reload; others waited on the drive, the men rolling the heavy barrels down planks to the ground. Amidst the chaos, Mr Tregellas stood watching and my fear rose – this was such a dangerous place to bring Father.

A shout began spreading, 'Fire's easing. There'll be no spread.'

The smoke was lessening though there was still work to be done. I heard the church bell chime quarter past six. Not long to wait before I would see my beloved Father, but I would also have to face Jim. Since our last encounter, my nights had been full of dreams, too vivid to recall without blushing.

The confusion was lessening, the servants stopping to talk rather than rushing about, so the danger was obviously passing. I stared at the long drive sweeping up to Polcarrow, at the two lines of privet hedges clipped to within an inch of their lives. A wrought-iron fence separated the formal drive from the parkland; an immaculate lawn on one side, sheep grazing beneath the trees on the other.

The house looked ancient, forbidding, built hundreds of years ago and given to James Polcarrow by Queen Elizabeth in recognition of his valour during the Armada. Not just a house, but a baronetcy, as well, so his descendants could live in idle luxury off the backs of the poor. It always galled me that nobody recognised the same gallantry in the unarmed peasants forced into battles with nothing but their picks and shovels, or the ordinary sailors blown to pieces as they manned the cannons in ships the navy knew were not fit to sail. Where was their recognition, their baronetcy?

I stared at the ugly house, at its sombre, crenulated facade built of dark stone and slate. It stood, squat and square, on rising ground halfway between the sea and the wooded hills behind. More like a castle than a house – grey and forbidding, with turrets and pointed windows. As a child it had filled me with dread. I would lay awake, imagining the long, dark corridors leading to airless, gloomy rooms. The deep dungeons beneath it.

The church clock struck the quarter hour and I peered above the crowd. Perhaps they might not see me. Instantly, I ducked behind the man in front. Sulio Denville was making his way through the crowd, his face full of anger, his bulky frame jostling the people around him. He was heading straight for the gates and as he marched up the drive, my fear turned to panic. This was madness. Complete madness. What was Jim thinking? I knew not to greet Father too warmly. People might recognise me and to keep him safe, I would have to pretend we were on nodding terms only.

A slight thinning in the crowd gave me a glimpse of two men and I had to stop myself from crying out. Father was barely recognisable. He was stooped and frail, aged well beyond his years; his frame a fraction of Jim's who towered above him. I clamped my hands over my mouth, reeling with shock, hardly able to take in what I saw – my once-strong Father, now so weak and aged, leaning heavily on Jim's arm. His corduroy breeches made his legs look like spindles. He was wearing an old brown jacket, his grey hair hanging in wispy threads, his beard wild and unkempt. His hat was too big for him, no doubt to keep him disguised. I fought back my tears, holding back my horror. They were nearly with me.

I needed to compose myself. I took a deep breath, wiping away my tears. I wanted to run to him, throw my arms around him. I wanted to clutch him, tell him how much I loved him, how desperately I had missed him, but I held myself in check. I would have to wait. He looked up and saw me and, through my tears, I saw his joy, his love. I saw the anger, too, the regret, the flicker of shame as he took in my clothes and saw how poor we had become. When he smiled, the child in me sobbed. We could not embrace, Jim's manner made that quite clear. His face was stern, his voice brusque.

'Time enough to talk – we've to hurry,' he said looking round. 'We've an appointment to keep an' we're in danger of being late.' His clothes were crumpled, his appearance unkempt. He looked rougher, thicker stubble, his hair untidy. He was wearing the red scarf round his neck. To my horror he began leading Father towards the open gates of Polcarrow.

'Jim, no!'

'We must – it's the only way. I've discussed it with Mr Pengelly an' he agrees. Come, quickly. We're not to keep them waiting.'

I turned to Father. 'You're not strong enough – it's far too dangerous.'

'We've no option, Rose – we're in Jim's hands.' He shrugged his thin shoulders beneath the huge jacket. 'We've no choice but to trust him.' Despite his frail appearance, his voice was stronger than I dared to hope, more resolute.

Jim urged us forward. He was walking quickly and I had to hurry to catch up with him. Considering what had passed between us, I was furious with his high-handed manner and lack of explanation. We were halfway through the gates of Polcarrow before I caught his attention. 'Jim, stop…could we at least please discuss what you've in mind?' I was used to his grim expression, but I had never seen him look so agitated. He seemed preoccupied, unable to look at me in the eye – he seemed even furtive. Every instinct screamed danger and I stopped abruptly. 'I'm not going any further.'

He swung round, a glimmer of uncertainty in those blue eyes. 'You've to trust me, Rose.'

'They're all there, you know that don't you?'

'I've arranged it so. Please leave it at that. We've to hurry.'

I followed reluctantly up the drive, Father leaning on my arm. A thin line of smoke rose from the blackened rubble and as we passed the long line of men, I could hear them complain of their thirst, a number calling for barrels of beer. Jim marched ahead. Why here? This could not be right. 'Father, this can't be safe,' I whispered. 'What's he told you?'

Father frowned. 'Very little, my dear – but we've no choice. He has the ledgers and all the evidence. We're in his hands.'

Chapter Twenty

As if fearing our desertion, Jim held onto Father's arm, holding it tightly until we reached the end of the long drive. Large stone steps swept up to an elaborately carved portico. Mr Roskelly had gone and there was no sign of any servants. It was as if nothing had happened. The house looked silent, austere, the huge front door black, studded with iron rivets. I helped Father up the steps. Jim paused, staring at the elaborate iron knocker, forged in the shape of a galleon in full sail. His hands clenched into fists by his sides, 'Leave the talkin' to me,' he said, lifting the knocker.

The door was opened by a liveried footman in a powdered wig and a red jacket embroidered in gold thread. On his hands he wore cream kid gloves. At the sight of us, his eyes widened, his jaw dropped and a look of horror spread across his face. Almost too indignant to speak, he would have slammed the door in our faces, had not Jim forced his shoulder against the door, wedging it open with his boot.

'Round the back – scoundrels! Round the back!' shouted

the footman, his nose wrinkling in disgust. 'Go round the back where you belong.'

'Mr Roskelly is expecting us an' I'll use any door I please. What's your name, sir?' There must have been something in Jim's tone which made him answer.

'Henderson,' he replied stiffly.

'Well, Henderson, I suggest you open the door an' tell Mr Roskelly his guests are here. He's expecting us so I suggest you don't keep him waiting.'

Henderson opened the door, walking slowly backwards across the hall, indicating with his frown of disapproval for the other servants to watch us closely. They were all clutching at mops, no doubt still cleaning the floor after all those running feet, but at the sight of us, they stood gawping, their eyes incredulous.

The door shut behind us and I glanced at Father. Jim had brought us here with no explanation. Was he going to pay Father's debts? Perhaps he had found someone willing to lend us money so we could wipe the slate clean. He must be confident we would be safe, but why not tell us? It felt so wrong. I had been expecting a sign of tenderness, some recognition of his stolen kiss, anything I could grasp at to lessen my fear, but it was as if Jim was turned to stone. He stood staring ahead and, as I watched his back, I could sense hostility in the set of his shoulders. Something was wrong.

A heavily engraved wooden staircase rose majestically from the centre of the room, sweeping and curving as it divided in two, the highly polished handrails carved with birds and animals massing together in elaborate swirls. Gold-framed portraits of complacent gentry looked down from the walls, their hands resting on their well-fed bellies. In the corner, a suit of arms stood silently to attention, its reflection caught in the polished black and white marble floor, shining like a mirror beneath it.

The servants were watching us, some mopping, others blatantly staring, clearly intrigued by our poor clothes and unkempt appearance. I had to fight the urge to take Father, open the door and run down the drive. Somehow, I stayed, watching the evening sun flood through the oval window, sending coloured shafts of light through the candelabra hanging on chains from the ceiling above. Each one must have contained a hundred candles – more than most people would use in a year.

To my right was a stone fireplace, simply sculptured, but huge, the blackened fireback recognisable as the Polcarrow crest. Above the fireplace was a portrait of a boy holding the bridle of a fine black stallion. Behind him stretched the vast Polcarrow estates and, in the distance, the house itself, standing in its formal gardens. The boy looked spoilt, demanding, his fine clothes unsuitable for riding, the horse obviously too big for him. Jim was staring at the portrait, his face impassive.

The servants began sniggering behind their hands, casting ever bolder looks in our direction. As we waited, my fear returned. Was Jim going to blackmail them? Was that why we were here? My heart was racing. I wanted to grab Father and run, but it was too late. Henderson was coming towards us, his mouth firmly pursed. 'Mr Roskelly will see you in the study – if you'll follow me.'

I took Father's arm, following Jim and Henderson across the hall to a large oak door. The door was ajar. Henderson knocked loudly and coughed, 'Your guests, Mr Roskelly.'

'We're not to be disturbed,' a voice replied.

My legs trembled, my heart raced. I looked at Jim, desperate for reassurance, but he was looking straight ahead, the same grim expression on his face, the same taut mouth. What was he planning? He must be confident or he would never have put us in so much danger.

The room was dismal, stuffy, the wood panelling dark and oppressive. Tobacco smoke hung in the air, trapped by the blackened beams of the low ceiling above. Little light penetrated the three large windows – the thick brocade curtains hung in heavy swathes, the enormous drapes darkening the room with their voluminous folds. Three men were staring at us, watching us with evil in their eyes.

Mr Roskelly was much shorter than I remembered, stouter and more florid, with a large nose and red-rimmed eyes. He was standing behind a desk strewn with papers, his weight resting on his hands, his shoulders rounded like a bulldog about to fight. Mr Tregellas stood by the fireplace, tall and erect, his shoulders squared, his hands held in fists by his side. Across the room, barely visible in the dark recess of the wood panelling, Captain Denville's thick arms were folded like an executioner waiting his commands.

Robert Roskelly's voice was strangely high pitched. 'How dare you summon me in my own house? Who are you to demand terms?' He held a letter between his first finger and thumb, holding it away from him as if it would pollute his fine silk sleeve and delicate lace cuff. 'You've made a serious error,' he said, letting it fall from his fingers.

'I think not,' replied Jim. 'An' well you know it.'

'I know nothing of the kind. Mr Pengelly's been found to be alive which is no great import. Prisoners forget who they are when fever addles their wits – many prisoners adopt the identity of other prisoners for their own gain…and though you may rejoice, it makes absolutely no difference to the law. Mr Pengelly is still a bankrupt and as an escaped prisoner he now faces the gallows – as do you and this woman. You'll swing for this and Miss Pengelly will swing alongside you.'

The room was thick and airless. I could feel the noose tightening round my neck and I staggered forward clutching Father's arm. There was a high-backed chair only feet away and I helped Father to it.

'D'you take me for a fool?' replied Jim. 'Stop wasting my time, Mr Roskelly.' He took a step closer, standing face to face with the most powerful man in Fosse. 'Perhaps you've not read my letter? Perhaps you don't understand how much proof I have that you're behind all this deception an' fraud. Having a man imprisoned for a theft you've committed yourself an' using his ship for smuggling is a felony even you'd swing for – I think you'd best read my letter again, an' change your tone.'

Mr Roskelly's colour deepened. I could see beads of sweat on his upper lip and, for the first time, I felt hopeful. Perhaps Jim *was* in control. I looked around, my eyes drawn immediately to the space under the table. I caught my breath. Two large mastiffs lay sprawled asleep, pools of drool collecting on the floor by their mouths. They were massive creatures, clearly unchained, and I looked at Jim, trying to warn him they were there. He took no notice. It was as if I did not exist. He did not look at me, or Father. Not once. It was as if he had forgotten we were there. He had sensed his advantage and was pressing on.

'I've the ledgers, the invoices, all the correspondence regarding the stolen cutter...an' the false bill of sale with both your names on it. I've the testimony of the gaoler an' the two sailors who jumped ship last time *L'Aigrette* unloaded her smuggled goods. They're willin' to testify they served on the stolen cutter under the command of Captain Denville an' can testify they've seen you an' Mr Tregellas aboard ship many times.' In the darkness, Sulio Denville flexed his muscles. By the fireplace, Mr Tregellas's fists tightened as his scowl deepened.

'Damn you! I've had enough of your insolence,' snapped Mr Roskelly. 'What is it you want?'

'I'd have thought that obvious.'

'Nothing's obvious except you're a villain,' retorted Mr Roskelly, beads of sweat covering his forehead.

'Well, they say it takes one villain to recognise another,' replied Jim.

'What is it you want?'

Jim seemed to be enjoying the panic in Robert Roskelly's voice. He paused, and the eyes which had once pierced my soul and very nearly captured my heart turned vengeful and greedy. I had touched his scars. I had felt his pain. I had melted under his kiss. I had so wanted to trust this man, but even before he uttered a word, my heart went numb. A triumphant smile lit up his face. 'I'd have thought that was obvious, you idiot. I want the cutter.'

Chapter Twenty-one

Jim's treachery sliced through me like a knife. All colour drained from Father's face. He clutched his chest, his sunken cheeks hollow against the deathly pallor of his skin. Crying out, I ran to his side, but Jim was too quick.

He stared at me, his cold eyes hard, his hands already reaching into his jacket. He knotted a scarf around my mouth, forcing my head back. 'I've had just about all I can take from that clever mouth of yours,' he said as he tugged it tight. 'If you value your father's life, you'll be quiet for once.' I tried screaming, shouting, twisting myself free, but the scarf was too tight, the knot too firm. He was wrenching my hands behind my back, strapping them to the chair with the strength I knew so well. Once more, I felt the pain of being bound; my hands, my feet lashed to the chair with the rope he had hidden under his jacket. How could I have been so stupid? How could I think to trust him?

Father tried to defend me, his frail form lunging unsteadily forward. 'For pity's sake, she's a woman, let her go. She can't harm you.' Jim grabbed his arms, pinning them behind his back, forcing him down on the chair next to mine.

'Enough!' he shouted, binding Father's mouth with another scarf. 'I know Miss Pengelly's capabilities far too well.' Reaching beneath his jacket, he released another rope, shaking it free from its coils with a deft flick. Father put up no resistance, his frail frame bound quickly to the chair by the well-practised hands. Robert Roskelly stood watching from his desk.

'They're all yours,' said Jim, turning to face him. 'Do with them what you will.'

William Tregellas scowled down at Father. 'Your damned daughter's as dangerous as any man – and well you know it. If it hadn't been for her high-handed prying, none of this would have happened and you'd be rotting where we left you.'

'Hold your tongue, you fool,' snapped Robert Roskelly. He was looking at Jim, his face full of loathing. 'You demand the cutter, do you? I'll see you hanged first.'

Jim seemed unperturbed, amused even. With a flourish he drew out a folded paper, smoothing it against the desk. 'I've a deed of sale drawn in my favour. All I need is your signature.' He turned to Mr Tregellas. 'I thought six hundred guineas a good price – though obviously I've no intention of paying you anything. This deed's a mere formality.'

Jim's insolence was too much for Mr Tregellas. His twitch was unstoppable. 'You're a dead man,' he said, his lithe frame lunging across the room at Jim.

As if waiting for his signal, Sulio Denville darted from the shadows, pushing aside a table in his haste, sending a

175

lamp crashing to the ground. His massive shoulders seemed to strain against his jacket, as he stepped slowly forward, a dagger flashing in both hands, which he held rigid in front of him. 'Now then, sailor boy, let's see what you're made of.'

Both men closed on Jim, murder in their faces. Jim started backing away, his eyes darting from one to another as they slowly forced him towards the corner. He knocked against the large table and stopped, leaning forward, his hands outstretched, swaying from foot to foot. They knew he was trapped and both men drew nearer, Sulio Denville taunting him with his daggers, waiting to strike. As his huge frame lunged forward, Jim dived between them, somersaulting behind the two men, jumping quickly up to face them. Sulio Denville crashed against the table, William Tregellas falling heavily on top of him. They picked themselves up, cursing loudly, their faces purple with fury. Sulio Denville bent to retrieve his fallen daggers.

'Think you can take on Sulio Denville, do you? Do you? Well, you can think again.' Once more he held his knives in his hands, brandishing them in front of him as he crouched forward. They were huge knives and I watched in horror as the two men began forcing Jim back across the room to the other corner. Step by step, they closed on him again, Sulio Denville almost drooling. 'Steady does it,' he said. 'I don't like to rush a killing.'

Bile rose in my throat. I thought I would choke. I began pulling against the chair, struggling with all my might, trying to loosen the bindings. The servants must hear. Surely I could alert them, but there seemed nothing I could do. I tried shouting, screaming, yelling into the gag, but my head was bursting, my breath suffocating, and my cries remain stifled, muffled by the scarf which clamped me so tightly. I shut my eyes, waiting for the sounds of killing.

Suddenly there was silence. The three men stood motionless, frozen to the spot. At first I could not understand their sudden stillness but then I saw the pistol Jim was holding in his hand. It was the same pistol he had pointed at Ben.

'Stand back, you fools, killing me would be pointless. All the evidence – the ledgers, the letters, the men's testimonies, the affidavit signed by Mr Pengelly, everything is with the Vice Sheriff of Cornwall, Lord St John Stevens. It's in a locked box an' if I don't meet him tomorrow, he's to unlock the box an' act accordingly. There's no doubt of your guilt an' no doubt of the consequences. You've no choice. D'you really think me such a fool I wouldn't cover my back? You've no option but sign the deed.'

He pointed the pistol at Sulio Denville. 'Throw those down.'

Sulio Denville spat in disgust. His daggers struck the flagstones and Jim reached to retrieve them, the pistol pointing at Mr Tregellas. 'Now, sign the deed.'

'Not until you return the evidence.'

'I've already told you. When you've signed, I'll tell you where to meet me.'

'You really believe I'd trust you?'

'You've no option.'

'What about them?' Mr Tregellas nodded in our direction.

'Captain Denville knows what to do with them,' replied Jim coldly.

I could scarcely breathe. My heart was beating so fast I thought it would burst. Mr Tregellas walked stiffly over to the desk, glaring at Mr Roskelly as he picked up the quill, dipping it angrily in the inkwell before scratching his name. 'If you double-cross me, you're a dead man. I'll hunt you down.'

Jim watched him sign. 'Now you, Mr Roskelly – you're joint owner of *L'Aigrette*, I believe.'

'May you rot in hell,' muttered Robert Roskelly.

Yes, well may you rot in hell, I thought.

We were in the greatest danger – somehow we needed to alert the servants. Henderson had seen us come in so he must be waiting for us to leave. I had to warn him, but how? I looked across the room, desperately searching for the bell pull. Father was looking straight at me. Some colour had returned to his cheeks and though he still looked gravely shaken, he seemed to be trying to tell me something. He kept lifting his eyebrows, looking from me to the dogs. At first, I could not understand his meaning but then I realised they were still sleeping, oblivious to the commotion around them. That could not be right.

Jim picked up the deed of sale, examining it carefully before sliding it into his jacket. 'I'm obliged, gentlemen, an' should you ever run short of brandy, or silk, or salt, you're only to ask. I can't guarantee you special rates but I'd be happy to do business…'

'Insolent dog! Do you really think you'll get away with this?'

'I do. I've every intention of spending the rest of my life in comfort.' Jim examined the pistol, turning it over in his hands, polishing the barrel on his sleeve.

'Get out, you bastard.'

'I'm afraid, I'm not finished yet, Mr Roskelly – I've more business to discuss.' Jim ran a hand through his hair, straightening the scarf round his neck, brushing the dust from his sleeve. 'It may not be obvious but I've expensive tastes… an' though the revenue from this cutter will provide a fair income, it's not enough. I need a bit more.'

Mr Roskelly's eyes narrowed. 'Damn your impertinence! I'll not be blackmailed.'

Jim drew up a chair and leant back, the pistol on the desk in front of him. 'Won't you? I suggest you listen to what I've got to say. You see, I've particular good eyesight, Mr Roskelly, especially at night when no-one's meant to be watching an' people get hurt. There's always a nook or doorway to squeeze into, barrels to hide behind – as a young man, I often saw things I could turn to my advantage. Your friend, Mr Tregellas, may not know what I'm about, but you do, don't you? An' so does Sulio Denville. You'll have to go back a long time, mind, but I'm sure your memory's as good as mine.'

The room was darkening, the heavy curtains blocking the fading light. Beads of sweat glistened on Robert Roskelly's brow and I was surprised to see Mr Tregellas watching Jim as intently as Father. Jim's voice remained expressionless. 'I'm talking about eleven years ago – but you remember it well, don't you, Mr Roskelly? Mr Denville?' he glanced across the room at Sulio Denville, now lost in the shadows of the wood

179

panelling. 'I can remember it as if it was yesterday, but my memory could be dulled by a monthly stipend. A man with a regular income can forget dark nights an' false accusations of violence and robbery.'

'Dammit, man, I'll not succumb to blackmail. I know nothing of what you speak.'

Jim's voice turned hard. 'But you do. Perhaps I should refresh your memory? A young man is sent a letter. It's from his step-mother's brother and requests his company in a dangerous part of town – a place where he'd normally not go. He's seventeen, young, inexperienced an' not used to being alone on the streets, but he goes because the letter's requesting his help. The young man dislikes his step-uncle intensely, but he thinks it his duty to serve him, so he over-comes his fear, enters an alley known to be particularly dangerous, an' walks alone, fearing for his uncle's safety. But it was his own safety he should have feared. Lying in wait was a dangerous and ruthless man, one known to break a man's neck with one hand – killing hands and a ruthless heart, waiting for him as he walked towards his fate.

'Of course, they'd be clever about this death. They'd arrange for their hands to be clean, for no hint of blame to come their way. After all, there was a large estate at stake so the young man would have to die, but not be murdered. So much better to let the law of the land do the killing – far better he hangs.

'They sprung him from behind, callous an' cowardly, but that was the nature of the two men. Before the young man had a chance to defend himself, they set about beating him, kicking him, knocking him senseless to the ground – but they didn't kill him. They removed the note from the young man's jacket, safe in the knowledge that the uncle had his own note in his pocket – a good forgery, requesting him meet the young man in the very place they were now standing. All they had to do was put the uncles' purse in the young man's jacket and leave him lying in the gutter while they saw to their own injuries – light, superficial wounds on their arms and legs were all that was needed. Then they set about ripping each other's clothes and rolling in the filth, but to finish the job properly, they opened their pouch of pig's blood, drenching themselves from head to toe, before they lay in the gutter, groaning as if they were dying.'

The room was silent, everyone straining to hear Jim's words.

'It wasn't long before they were discovered, was it, Mr Roskelly? And not long before the news got out. The nephew had gone wild, viciously attacking his uncle after luring him to his death. The court heard the evidence – two men's word against one. They'd been injured to within an inch of their lives and they had the heavily blood-stained letter as proof. The young man must hang, of that, there was no doubt.' The bitterness in his voice was chilling. The words had come straight from his heart and everyone in the room had sensed it.

Robert Roskelly was staring at Jim, sweat now dripping from his brow. He cleared his throat. 'A touching story and no doubt well-rehearsed, but it means nothing to me. You've nothing to incriminate me. Nothing you've said perturbs me. And who'd believe the testimony of a wretch such as yourself? Look at you – you're filthy, you stink. You're no better than a common thief. If you think anyone will listen to you, then you're even more foolish than I thought.'

'You fear me, Robert Roskelly. I can see it in your eyes and smell it on your breath. You fear me. Yet there's more I'd accuse you of.' He pushed his chair away, standing up to face Father, addressing him from across the room. 'You remember the late Sir Francis Polcarrow who married the young Alice Roskelly? That would be about twelve years ago wouldn't it?'

Father nodded, his face the colour of ash. Jim must have noticed how frail he looked because he made his way towards him, carefully untying his gag. Father wiped his hand across his mouth, looking up at Jim with bewildered eyes.

Jim turned back to Robert Roskelly. 'The new Lady Polcarrow was young and healthy. Sir Francis had served his purpose in siring a son and if you were to carry out your ambition to be the boy's guardian and take control of the Polcarrow estate, you needed to make sure Sir Francis met with a fatal riding accident – a loose saddle, an unseen mole-hill, or a blow from a low branch? The choice was endless.

'You chose the blow from a low branch, didn't you, Mr Roskelly? How easy it must have seemed as you swung the branch that smashed his skull. You managed the murder so well. You arranged the body, making everything look like an accident and you became the solid rock your sister and her young infant needed.'

Robert Roskelly stood wiping the sweat on his brow,

glaring at Jim in undisguised fear. Jim glared back, his face dark with loathing. 'Two deaths would have been suspicious, but a tragic accident, followed by a vicious attack from a young man who was known to dislike you so much, left no-one suspecting. You were free to prosper, Mr Roskelly, and prosper you have.'

Father's cough racked his chest. Jim turned and started to undo Father's wrists. To my horror, I saw he had left his pistol lying on the desk and I could see Robert Roskelly staring at it. I tried to warn Jim, shouting into my gag, pointing with my eyes in the direction of the pistol, desperately willing him to understand, but though he looked at me, raising his eyebrows in response, he did not grasp my meaning. I tried screaming, shaking my head, but to no avail. It was too late. Robert Roskelly reached across the desk and stood holding the pistol in both hands, his laughter now filling the room. 'Not as clever as you think you are.'

Hearing the pistol cock, Jim turned round, horrified by his foolish mistake. 'Damn you, Robert Roskelly,' he said.

'I should have killed you when I had the chance. You can't fool me. Right from the start I knew there was something familiar about you. You thought your sailor's accent and vagrant appearance would disguise you, but your eyes give you away. I know who you really are. We should have killed you when we had the chance, not left you to the gallows.'

'Like you killed my father?'

'Yes, like I killed your dammed father.' Jim was behind my chair, his hands gripping my shoulders. The barrel of the pistol was pointing straight at him. 'You're a dead man,

James Polcarrow,' Robert Roskelly said. 'Your futile attempt to incriminate me has failed.'

James Polcarrow? Through my fear, my mind was reeling. I should have known. I should have remembered the scandal. I had been so blind, yet now it seemed so obvious – Jim's education, his knowledge of Fosse, his sense of vengeance, his championship of the aristocracy. But it was all too late. Whatever injustices he had endured, whatever hardship and cruelty he had suffered, he was now powerless. Robert Roskelly was walking slowly across the room, the pistol pointing at Jim's chest.

Jim's strong hands squeezed my shoulders and I screamed into the suffocating gag. We were going to die – all of us. My poor, poor mother. She would never survive this. Never.

Robert Roskelly seemed content to take his time, his red-rimmed eyes enjoying my fear. With a laugh of triumph he lined up his aim and, with a sneer on his face, he pulled the trigger.

Chapter Twenty-two

A piercing whistle filled the air. The door flung open and men came rushing into the room. I watched, amazed, as the heavy brocade curtains were thrust aside and two men stepped out from behind them.

Robert Roskelly's pistol failed to fire, his fingers still frantically pulling at the trigger. Jim waited only long enough for him to realise the pistol had no powder before he aimed a heavy blow, knocking him sideways to the floor. Mr Tregellas ran for his life, dodging from side to side, but he was outnumbered and stood no chance. Two men lunged to catch him, pulling him to the ground, pinning his arms behind his back to apply their heavy handcuffs. Jim began undoing the knots that bound me, ripping away my gag and I stood trembling, shaking, running over to Father who was staggering to his feet.

'Father, come. You look so pale. Sit over here where you'll be safe.'

Behind me, someone shouted. 'One's got away.'

Another replied, 'Follow him… Quickly! You two – down there… follow him. Take this lantern and hurry.' I recognised him now, it was the constable speaking. Across the room, a small dark hole, no more than three-foot square, stood gaping in the wood panelling. Jim stood staring at it, his face full of fury as the older of the two men walked to his side. He was a tall man, dressed in a dark jacket and working-man's breeches, but as soon as he spoke, he filled the room with authority. 'Denville's escaped, damn him. Did you forget about the tunnel, James?'

'No, Sir George, I didn't know it was there.'

'Your father never mentioned it?'

'No. Perhaps he thought I was too young. Perhaps he was going to tell me when I came of age.'

'Perhaps,' replied the man. I could see him more clearly now; his face was stern, his hair greying, his whole bearing at odds with the clothes he wore. He looked at the dogs. 'That drugged meat worked well. I was worried when that lamp crashed to the ground – I thought it would rouse them.'

'There's no chance of them waking for several hours yet and, when they do, they'll have a head from hell. I can't thank you enough, Sir George. You must have been stifled behind those curtains.' He pulled the signed bill of sale out of his pocket. 'Do you have all the evidence you need?'

'Yes, the evidence is irrefutable. Two attorneys heard the confession and with a sworn witness from you, Mr Pengelly and Miss Pengelly, we have all we need. I'll keep this bill of sale with the ledgers and letters. It may take time – and a bit of ingenuity – but I'm confident I can get your original sentence revoked. Robert Roskelly will hang for murder and we'll have you back where you belong.'

'I can't thank you sufficiently.'

'Don't thank me, James. I've put right a wrong, that's all. I blame myself for not getting you acquitted in the first place – I wish I had served you better. I'm just glad you're still young and have your life ahead of you.'

'You must not blame yourself. If you hadn't got my sentence commuted to transportation, I'd have hung long ago. I owe you my life and, now, I owe you my freedom.'

'I was lucky to count your father among my closest friends and I won't stop until I see his killers brought to justice. Welcome back, James, my boy. Welcome back.'

With the other men no longer there, Father and I seemed so out of place in that awful room, watching the two men smiling so warmly at each other. Henderson was glancing fearfully in their direction, two silver candlesticks alight with six wax candles held in his shaking gloved hands. A soft glow began chasing away the shadows but though the light was welcome, it did little to lift the gloom. Jim saw him hesitate.

'Henderson, bring brandy if you please – four glasses. I'm sure Miss Pengelly could do with a glass.' Despite his dirty clothes and unkempt appearance, Jim stood tall and commanding, his shoulders squared, his chin held high. The voice that demanded brandy was full of assurance and the eyes that watched Henderson were confident and aloof. I could see at once they were the voice and eyes of another man.

I stared at James Polcarrow, at those blue eyes confronting me across the room. They were full of challenge, full of

187

defiance. Yet it was I who should feel defiant. Why had he not trusted me? Why had he put me through so much terror? I had told him everything, yet he had told me nothing. I would never have given away his secret. Never. He had used me so ill. Not even a hint, not the slightest hint that my safety had been assured. We stood staring at each other, both of us unsmiling.

Sir George coughed politely.

'I'm sorry, Sir George. Let me introduce Miss Pengelly and her father, Mr Pascoe Pengelly. Miss Pengelly, allow me to introduce Sir George Reith, my attorney.'

'Delighted, Miss Pengelly, Mr Pengelly,' said Sir George Reith, bowing. Father bowed. I dipped a curtsey.

James Polcarrow was still staring at me. There was no sign of apology, no flicker of remorse. He had put Father and me through unimaginable terror, yet he showed no remorse? Sir George was looking from one of us to the other. Raising his eyebrows, he turned to Father. 'May I suggest a more comfortable chair, Mr Pengelly? I don't know about you, but I've been standing for an eternally long time and my legs aren't what they used to be. Allow me to help you, sir.' He put out his arm, helping Father to one of the larger chairs by the desk.

I did not see them sit down; I was staring at the stranger across the room, the knot in my stomach tightening. Henderson brought in a gleaming, filigree silver tray with a glass decanter and four large glasses. The finely cut crystal sparkled in the glow of the candles, sending bright shards of light dancing against the polished silver. I had never seen such beautiful glass, or such an elaborate tray. James Polcarrow crossed the room, picking up the decanter to pour the brandy. Holding two of the sparkling glasses in his hand, he swirled them deftly in his palm as he walked slowly towards me.

Something about the way he swirled the glass, something about his nonchalant manner, his arrogant assurance, made my hackles rise. He was acting as if he owned the place and, of course, he soon would. His power would be absolute. He would own the great house, the huge park, the vast estate. He would own all the servants, all the farm workers. He would own all the farms, all the barns, all the curates' livings. He would own the voting rights of most of Fosse, half the harbour and most of the warehouses. He would soon own the lease on Father's boatyard. He looked defiant because he *was*. I had to get out of that room.

Brushing past him in my haste, I grabbed Father by the hand, almost hurling him out of his seat as I hurried him across the room. People like James Polcarrow did not need to tell the likes of me and Father what they did. They did what they liked, to whom they liked. They felt no need to explain their actions. They used people for their own ends.

Stopping at the door, I turned to address Sir George's astonished face. 'Goodbye, Sir George – it's very late and Mother doesn't even know Father's alive. Forgive us if we don't stay for brandy, but we can't waste any more time...'
All I knew was that I had to get out of that hateful house.

Father hobbled by my side. I was going too fast, but I could not help it. I rushed him across the hall, glancing gratefully at Henderson as he opened the door. On the top step, I breathed in large gulps of air, filling my lungs so completely I thought they would burst. I could smell the sea. I could taste my freedom. The firefighters had dispersed and the park looked deserted. The sun had long dipped behind the cliffs and an evening chill filled the air, making me shiver. Across the river, the last of the sun turned the leaves of the trees a golden red. I needed to get back to Mother.

But even as our feet crunched the gravel, I heard his footsteps behind us.

'Rose, you can't leave like this – we have to talk.' He was gaining on us now, running down the long sweep of steps behind us. Clutching Father's arm, I hurried my pace. 'Rose, come back.'

'We're in a hurry to see Mother,' I shouted. If I felt like crying, I stifled it.

'Come back! You can't leave like this!' He was close behind me. I started running down the drive pulling Father behind me. He was facing me now, standing in my way. 'Rose, I forbid you to go.'

'You do *what*? You *forbid* me?' I must have looked furious. I could see him blanch, but my blood was up. 'You *forbid* me, d'you, Sir James Polcarrow?'

I caught the glance of pride in Father's eyes. It was the approval I had always sought, always yearned for. I was Rosehannon Pengelly, my father's daughter, and the only thing that mattered was that I had him back. I took a deep breath. 'Good bye, Sir James, and thank you. You've saved my father's life and you've cleared his name. We'll always remain in your debt…I wish you well but, if you don't mind, I'm going to take Father home.'

I would not stay a minute longer. Turning my back on Sir James and his hideous house, I started walking down the long drive. We were going home. Home to Mother and Jenna.

We did not talk the whole way back. I could not speak. My heart was too full. The man who held me so tenderly in his arms, who had kissed me so passionately and told me he loved me, did not exist. It was over, finished. There would never be any more Jim.

Nor could there ever be Sir James Polcarrow.

Chapter Twenty-three

Porthruan
Friday 19th July 1793 2:00 p.m.

I opened the door very quietly. 'Do I disturb you, Father?'

'No, I wasn't asleep, though I have to admit my eyes are heavy. Time was, I could read all night but my attention keeps wanderin' and it's hard not to nod off.'

'Are those new glasses any good?'

'As good as they get. You're clever to get them – even if my concentration's gone, least I can read clearly!' He held out his hand and squeezed mine. 'Time was, I thought I'd never read again and I've a lot to catch up on. We live in changin' times, Rose.' He waved his newspaper in the air before placing it carefully on the table next to him.

It was wonderful to see him ensconced in the tiny parlour, his papers and periodicals spilling around him. A dream come true, only it had been a dream I never dared to dream. My heart was bursting. His grey hair was neatly cut, his beard shaved, and though his complexion remained sallow, the hollows of his cheeks seemed slightly fuller. He still looked painfully thin, his new jacket hanging from his frame, his legs lost in his breeches, but there was the old fire back in his eyes. He smiled up at me.

'I've not made friends with your Mr Pitt – just now he spat at me.'

'He couldn't have. Mr Pitt's as soft as a lamb. He never spits or scratches.'

'Well, he's made it plain enough I'm not to his liking. Look, he's scowlin' at me.'

'He just doesn't know you yet. And you can't really blame him – that used to be his chair. That's why he's so cross. Come, Mr Pitt.'

'No, don't take him away, I enjoy his company and I like the way he doesn't grovel. His scars bear witness to a terrible life, yet there he sits, scowlin' and flickin' his tail. I love that – down but still defiant. It's good there's fight left in him – that's how I felt this past year. If he enjoys scowlin' at me, then let him. I dare say Mr Pitt and I shall become friends, soon enough – though it pains me to say those words!'

I plumped up his cushions, sitting down on the stool by his feet. 'Shall I read to you, Father?'

'No, I've had enough for now – I'd no notion the French had executed their king and declared war on us.' He shrugged his shoulders, his face turning grave, 'But now we've a minute, let me show you this letter from Sir George Reith – they've found the cutter. She's now named *L'Aigrette* and they've got her impounded in Truro, pendin' all enquiries.'

'That's wonderful! Is there any hope she'll be returned to us?'

'Aye, there is. Sir George Reith states just that – though

it'll take time, of course. When she's sold, I do believe we can hope to profit from the sale.'

I wiped away a tear. 'I never dared to hope. I thought having you back was enough but to profit from her sale...! Sir George's being very kind – I don't know how we can ever thank him.'

'Rose, you should know better than that. Don't think, for one moment, Sir George has our welfare at heart. He doesn't give a damn for our welfare.'

'Why d'you say that?'

'You'll see – read the letter. George Reith has persuaded Mr Tregellas to testify against Mr Roskelly. After all, he heard him admit to murder. Mr Tregellas will be accused of theft, but won't hang. That's how it works. Men like Tregellas always triumph – George Reith gets his sentence down to transportation and Tregellas grows rich in Botany Bay.'

I shuddered. Father could make light of it but I could not. I still saw their faces when I closed my eyes. 'What about Sir George's fees?'

'His payment will come from the sale. When that's deducted, the rest's ours.' He raised his thin shoulders and shrugged. 'Seems he's put his name up as surety and there's to be no stoppin' him – he's determined to represent us.'

'I don't know how we can thank him enough.' Mother and I had been struggling for so long and to have someone as reputable as Sir George fighting our cause was almost over-whelming. I looked at Father, expecting to see his frown soften, but there was not the slightest hint of gratitude in his face.

'Don't be a fool, Rose. Sir George Reith's only interested

194

in his friend, James Polcarrow. They'll claim gross miscarriage of justice for Sir James, demand a retrial, and produce this new evidence. Before you can blink, Sir James Polcarrow will get back his vast estates and the corruption can go on. He'll get richer while everyone else struggles to make ends meet.'

'James Polcarrow saved your life. He nursed you through that first night. Aren't you being a bit hard on him?'

'Not at all – I see the truth, that's all. He saved my life, but he didn't know it was me he was savin'. He thought I was Sulio Denville. He did nothin' that wasn't for himself alone. You have to understand, James Polcarrow's a dangerous man and I'll never forgive him for puttin' your life in such danger. No amount of time will rid him of his hatred and anger. You saw how violent he was…bindin' our wrists like that, forcin' gags into our mouths – he didn't need to be so harsh. There's cruelty there, Rose…and cruelty and power don't mix. And we all know how powerful James Polcarrow is set to become.'

'Perhaps, if he's been treated like a common thief, he might be different. He'll know what it's like to be without hope, or privilege – abandoned by society.'

'James Polcarrow? There's a laugh. He doesn't know what it's like to be born with no privilege…what it's like to be a common man. His education lifts him above everyone and his contact in high places does the rest. Think on it, Rose. All he had to do was get back to England and his rich and powerful friends would spring to his defence. You saw how the wheels of power rolled so quickly to his aid. A common man would stand no such chance — straight away, he'd be imprisoned, hung, or transported back.'

The force of his words made him cough, a loud, racking cough that shook his body: his face was ashen. He was still so weak and I reached for some ale, desperately wishing Jenna would hurry back. 'Let me get you some of Jenna's nettle tea, she's left it in the kitchen – I won't be a minute.'

'No, Rose, it'll pass. I'll soon be fit as a fiddle.' He smiled at me, his eyes tender. 'I needs be fit if I'm to get my boat-yard back. Leave me be, and let me return to my readin'.' He picked up his glasses, taking hold of the paper. More papers lay in disarray and I noticed he must have read my latest pamphlet which I had left by his chair.

'What d'you think of Mary Wollstonecraft and her *Vindication on the Rights of Women*?' I asked, delighted to be able to discuss it with him.

He did not look up. 'That?' he replied. 'You can take it away and burn it. I don't think anythin' of your Mary Wollstonecraft. She's a foolish woman – foolish and very misguided. It's fit only for the fire.'

'But, Father, I thought you'd approve of…' I said no more. His newspaper was held high across his face, blocking all conversation. Picking up my pamphlet, I folded it in half and half again, tucking it down my bodice as I walked quietly to the door.

Mr Pitt was still scowling, thumping his tail loudly on the floor. When I reached the door, he, too, stood up and turned his back on Father, following me silently out of the room.

Chapter Twenty-four

Mother and Jenna piled through the door, carrying so many parcels they had to walk sideways down the hall. Hurling themselves into the parlour, they woke Father from his afternoon rest. I followed quick on their heels.

'Tell her, Mrs Pengelly.'

'No, you tell her, Jenna – I need to catch my breath.'

'Madame Merrick's finished yer dress…it's that beautiful, honest to God…I've carried it so careful so it wouldn't crease – and look here, what Madame Merrick's made specially for ye.' Picking up a hat box, she undid the ribbons. 'I can't wait for ye to see it. What d'ye make of this?' She opened the lid, lifting out a beautiful bonnet trimmed with greeen ribbons.

'It's lovely,' I said, unable to take my eyes off it.

'It's to match yer dress…look…Madame Merrick's made flowers of the sprig…she's put mother-of-pearl drops in the middle.' It was the loveliest thing I had ever been given. 'Don't just stare at it! Try it on.'

'Yes, do try it on,' said Mother, placing the bonnet carefully on my head, rearranging my hair to frame my face. 'There, you look absolutely beautiful.'

'But why's Madame Merrick gone to so much trouble? Is it for my birthday?'

'No!' they said in unison, shaking their heads like excited children, both smiling the broadest of smiles. Mother looked so well; her new dress giving her a dignity I had not seen in her before. Or perhaps it was her bearing. She seemed taller, more upright, as if her burdens had been lifted from her shoulders.

'Tell me, then!'

'Here's Madame Merrick's letter – oh, no, I can't wait… This bonnet's a present…Lady April's agreed to be her patron! She was that pleased with the cushion…and Madame Merrick can't thank you enough. She's getting a new sign to hang over the door but, without you, she might never have attracted Lady April's attention.'

The joy on Mother's face was contagious and I had to admire Madame Merrick's tenacity, but the smile soon fell from my lips. Father's voice cut angrily through our laughter. 'Madame Merrick's become quite an influence, I see. Time was when we didn't fawn to the aristocracy – we had our pride and dignity and didn't grovel. Now, it seems, Madame Merrick dresses you in fancy clothes and plays you like puppets.'

The harshness in his voice stunned me, draining all pleasure from me. Fighting a rush of anger, I tried to bite my tongue, but the injustice of his words swelled inside me. 'Madame Merrick's been here for us when you couldn't, Father,' I said, trying to keep my voice soft. 'She's helped us put food on our table and clothes on our backs. She's helped pay the rent to keep us from the streets. She's clever and courageous and very astute, yet as a woman, she faces nothing but ridicule and censure. She may toady to the aristocracy, but she doesn't deserve your harsh words – in fact, you should be grateful to her that we've survived at all. Without her, we'd have been destitute.'

I had never spoken to Father like that. Perhaps, it was the injustice, perhaps it was because I had seen Mother's hands tremble and her shoulders sag. Either way, I meant every word and waited for his reply but he remained silent. No apology. No look of regret. I scooped up the parcels and sought refuge in my own room.

'He'll come round,' Jenna said, following me out. 'It's just different, that's what. He's come home and heard nothing but talk of Madame Merrick – it's like he's jealous, that's all. Give him time – you'll see. He'll come round.'

'Jenna, where d'you get your wisdom? You've such an old head on young shoulders.'

'Come, let's see ye in this dress. Here…go through to yer mother's room…look in the pier glass.' She took hold of my elbow, ushering me excitedly through the door.

'There,' she whispered, the last button fastened. 'Ye've got to be the most beautiful woman in Cornwall, if not England …just look at ye,' she said, wiping her eye.

The dress was in the latest fashion, the muslin soft and delicate, the bodice threaded at the neck with ribbons and lace. The waist was raised, the skirt falling softly to just above my shoes, the sleeves short, lightly puffed, edged with lace. My reflection looked unreal, beautiful and feminine. I never imagined I would wear such a dress.

'Madame Merrick says it's like the Ancient Greeks used to wear…she says it's all the rage.' She rearranged my hair, pinched my cheeks and stood back. 'This'll do perfect.'

'What d'you mean, *this will do perfect?*'

'Ye know exactly what I mean. Ye'll have to see him sometime – and when he sees ye looking like this, there'll be no stopping him. No stopping him *at all*.' She raised her eyebrows, smiling for all she was worth.

'Stop it, Jenna. I won't see him.'

'Ye have to. He's called three times in the last two weeks and he's not coming to see your father. He comes to see ye.'

'His attentions are unwelcome, I won't see him. I mean it. And I won't have you tattling and gossiping.'

I looked at myself in the mirror, feeling nothing but distaste. Father was right, I should never have questioned him – we had become puppets. Fresh off the fashion plate, and probably the envy of every lady in Fosse, the dress and bonnet had transformed me into an elegant beauty. I hated it. It was not me staring back but some empty-headed society climber and I had no intention of running a boatyard looking empty-headed. Nor had I any intention of climbing into higher society. I hated it. I felt trapped, snared, somebody I was not – somebody I would never be. 'Get me out of this dress' I snapped.

Jenna crossed her arms, her lips pursing. 'Ye're so stubborn, Miss Pengelly – so very stubborn. What are ye thinking?

Sir James Polcarrow is rich and powerful…owns just about the whole world…yet ye don't go after him when ye could have him for the taking?' She bent to pick up my old dress, shaking it severely. 'And he's brave and daring…I heard it was *him* who set fire to the old cottages and *him* who smuggled the attorneys into the house among all the confusion. He's clever, very clever, probably too clever for ye – ye being too stubborn to recognise a good catch when ye see one.'

'Jenna!'

Our heated words were interrupted by the sound of hooves on the cobbles below. The casement was wide open and we heard them stop outside our cottage. Bridles were jingling, spurs clinking and the sound of men dismounting. Jenna rushed to the window, carefully peeping from one side of the shutter. 'He's here,' she said breathlessly. 'Ye'll *have* to see him now. Please, go down and talk to him – just for my sake.'

I turned my back to the window. 'If you admire him so much, you go down and see him. If he asks after me, tell him I'm not well and have a headache.'

I was surprised Jenna did not immediately answer me back, but remained staring out of the window. I heard the front door open and Mother's voice rising in welcome as she ushered Sir James into the tiny parlour, but Jenna still did not move. The more I watched her cheeks flush, the more intrigued I became. Before I knew it, I found myself edging closer to the window.

'Now *those* be shoulders!' she said, craning her neck. 'And look at them hands – ye can tell a lot by a man's hands – look at the way he's holding them reins. If only we could see his face.' She leant further out of the window.

I glimpsed down, unable to resist. Two matching black stallions stood in front of the cottage – huge, sleek beasts, saddled in very fine leather. A young man dressed in riding livery stood holding their bridles, keeping their heads steady as they shook against the flies. There was something about the young man which made me look closer. He turned his face. 'He's Joseph Dunn,' I whispered, 'the man who rescued me after the highwayman overturned the cart.'

'Joseph Dunn? Ye told me he was handsome but ye didn't say *that* handsome. Jigger me – he's perfect.'

'Jenna!'

I must have spoken too loudly. The young man looked up at the window, grappling the reins into one hand as he took off his cap. I nodded in return but, as I turned back from the window, Jenna was nowhere to be seen. Below me, the front door opened and I glanced down, horrified. Jenna was standing on the street. She had removed her fichu and rearranged her bodice, lovely wisps of blonde hair now framing her face. A basket hung from her elbow, her skirts swaying as her hips swung. She stood smiling at the bewildered young man, her dimples creasing.

Lifting the lid of her basket, a little smile of intimacy fluttered at the corners of her wide mouth. Joseph Dunn's smile broadened to a grin. Bending his head to examine the contents of the basket, I could see his eyes widen in pleasure. All three of us knew it was not just Jenna's apple dumplings on offer.

I felt suddenly chilled, despite the sun beating so warmly against the window. Envy pricked my heart and I felt ashamed of my thoughts. He would be perfect for her. Why not let her have what I could not? She reached into her basket, bringing out an apple for each horse. I watched her pretend to be frightened by their great strength, quickly reassured by Joseph Dunn. She knew I would be watching, but she took no heed. From under those fluttering lashes, she threw me a glance and for the first time ever, I caught a look of defiance.

The crowded street was filthy with refuse. I looked down to the harbour, to the ships' masts bobbing on the incoming tide. Seagulls were swooping, diving, following the fishing boats back from the sea. I smelt the salt. How I longed to be away from this hateful cottage with its crowded rooms and stifling air. I wanted to go home, back to Coombe House.

The front door opened and Joseph Dunn sprang to attention. Sir James Polcarrow walked briskly into the sunshine and nodded at Jenna. He must have seen the nervous glance she threw in my direction and, before I could hide, he looked up and saw me, standing in the full glare of the sun, the bright rays shining on my new dress. I gripped the casement and stared back, my heart thumping. He was almost unrecognisable, his hair cropped, his beard shaven, his riding jacket stretching without a crease across his shoulders. His breeches clung to his legs, his tall black riding boots shining with polish. Round his neck he wore a silk cravat. In one hand he held a riding whip, in the other, a pair of gloves.

There was no trace of the rugged sailor who had smiled up through his lock of hair. No glimpse of the accomplished thief who had broken into Coombe House, or the rogue who sat balancing two wenches on his knee. He was handsome, no doubt about it, possibly the most handsome man I would ever see – his straight nose and square jaw chiselled like the marbles in his hall. But apart from those piercing blue eyes, he was a stranger – not the man who had so nearly stolen my heart.

I began to feel calmer. I owed him everything – Father's life, our boatyard, perhaps even our return to Coombe House. Without him we would be destitute. He had given me back everything, but Father was right – James Polcarrow had been serving his own interests. He had not trusted me and that still hurt. I would not let my gratitude cloud my judgement.

I lifted my chin, staring back at him with complete resolution. His face clouded, his jaw stiffened and I saw bewilderment, even sadness in his eyes. Grabbing the reins from Joseph, he nodded to Mother and stepped high into the stirrup, urging his horse forward before he was properly mounted. Joseph Dunn followed, cantering fast on his heels and I stood watching their retreating figures, emptiness welling up inside me.

It had to be done. It was a clean cut, no festering, and it was done.

I drew a deep breath, filling myself with much needed courage. I am born of Cornwall, born from generations of fishermen and boat-builders. The wind is my breath – the sea is my blood. I know where I belong.

Chapter Twenty-five

M other rose from the parlour table, taking a candle in her hand. 'I think I'll go to bed early. Goodnight, Rosehannon. Don't be late, Jenna – you must've done enough by now.'

'Only a little bit more, Mrs Pengelly, I'll not be long.'

'Goodnight, Mother.'

Jenna looked up through her lashes. I knew that look. 'So, do ye want to know who was at the door earlier, or not?' She was enjoying herself. Her eyes were sparkling.

'No, not really. Well, who was at the door?'

'Mrs Cousin's middle one.'

'Why would I want to know that?' A knot began tying itself in my stomach.

'Ye used to want to know. Ye'd ask all the time... *has anyone left a basket? Cherries or such like*...now seems ye aren't interested. Don't ye like fruit any more, Miss Pengelly?'

My mouth felt dry, the familiar thudding starting in my chest. 'Jenna, what are you saying?'

'A lovely basket of apples arrived not long ago – beautiful they was – red and juicy and really crisp…too good for baking.'

'Where are they?' I was finding it hard to breathe.

'What? The apples? Took them straight to Mr Pengelly – put them by his chair. He was very pleased. *Lovely*, he said, *are they all for me?*' She was wiping the simmering pan with a large cloth, turning the pan round in front of her, examining it in great detail. Finally she looked up, 'Are ye alright, Miss Pengelly, only ye don't look very well?'

'Was there a letter in the basket?'

'I do believe there was.'

'Where is it?'

'I'm not sure I can remember…' She stood wiping the pan, carefully polishing the rim. Finally, she reached into her bodice, raising her eyebrows. 'It's the same handwriting,' she said, thrusting it in my direction.

I took the note, my hand shaking. 'Thank you, Jenna.'

Her lips were pursed. 'I know what ye're going to say – ye don't have to tell me…I won't say a word!'

Chapter Twenty-six

Shutting the door of my room, I steadied the candle, my hands shaking. I stared at the note, wanting the strength to put it straight to the flame. It was identical to the one I had received before – just the word *Midnight* and a fine ink drawing of a rose on a slender stem.

The candle guttered, yet I remained sitting on my bed, staring into the darkness. The church clock struck half past eleven. I would not go. Quarter to twelve, perhaps I should. Hating my weakness, I descended the staircase, tip-toeing along the passage to the back door. Father was sleeping in the parlour, preferring his makeshift bed to the stuffy bedroom upstairs and I knew the rhythmical stream of his snores would cover the sound of my footsteps. I undid the bolts as smoothly as I could and slipped quietly into the warm night air. It was late, I would have to hurry.

The moon was a distant crescent giving no light. It felt familiar, yet strangely different as I picked my way along the uneven path. The scent of honeysuckle filled the air, a frisson of excitement shooting through me. The wind was warm, smelling of seaweed, the sky and ocean merging as one, black mass. It was a night for concealment – for smuggling. My progress was slow but, as I reached the oak, a voice whispered my name and two strong hands reached out to pull me into the recess of the tree.

I could hardly see him; his dark jacket and breeches barely visible through the blackness, his hat pulled low. He was wearing the familiar loose-collared shirt, the red scarf tied round his neck. 'I knew you'd come,' he whispered.

'I very nearly didn't. Why are you dressed as Jim?'

'Because as James Polcarrow you'll not speak to me. As Jim, I stand a chance.'

I turned to go, my heart crying. Everything had come flooding back – the way my heart skipped in his presence, the way I longed for his touch.

'Rose, you cannot fight the force that binds us.' I looked up, startled at the tenderness in his voice. 'Rose, please, listen to me. Not a moment passes without thinking of you, not a night I don't dream of you. I live an empty half-life, desperate for a glimpse of you – long endless days, counting down the hours before I can visit your parents and hope to see you. What good's my wealth and vast estates if you're not there to share them? What comfort any house if you're not in it?' I turned away. 'No, Rose, please listen – what use is my position and power if you don't esteem them? I can't live like this, not without you by my side. If you cannot find it in your heart to have me as James Polcarrow, then, please, have me as Jim.'

He threw his hat to the ground and reached for my hands, pressing them against his lips. Falling to one knee, he looked up at me through the lock of hair that fell forward across his forehead. 'Marry me, Rose. Come away with me. The *Hibernia* leaves on the tide. The ship's master is a good man – he'll give us passage. He'll marry us tonight and before dawn, we'll know the joy of perfect union. Please, Rose, do me the honour of becoming my wife.'

I fought the dizziness sweeping over me. He must have seen how my head reeled and my body swayed. He drew me closer, holding me tightly, enclosing me in his strong arms. I had not been expecting this. I do not know what I had been expecting, but never this.

His lips brushed my hair, 'Our destinies lie entwined, Rose. I know you feel it too – it's in your eyes.'

His breath was hot against my cheek, his lips a fraction from my own, I could almost taste them. I had to stop myself from reaching towards them. The touch of his hands, the passion in his voice, thrilled every part of me. He kissed my ear. 'We can start afresh, Rose. I needed to clear my name – that's done now. My father's killers have been brought to justice and we can start a new life. I know you hate everything I stand for – you and your father, but I've never sought power, nor do I seek the trappings of great wealth; God knows, I've lived long enough without them. I'll give up my baronetcy – my step-brother can have Polcarrow and we'll start again. I'll get by as a tutor and you can continue your bookkeeping.' His lips lingered against mine, brushing them softly.

Every inch of my body ached for his touch. I could feel the familiar fabric of his jacket, the familiar scent still clinging to it. One more kiss, just one more kiss. To taste the lips that sent fire through my body. One more dark, velvety kiss for me to remember. 'No!' I cried, pulling myself free. Yet even as I tore myself away, I saw the pain in his eyes and struggled to breathe. 'You're not Jim — and you never can be. Not now. You're Sir James Polcarrow and anything else would be a lie. I'll not live a lie.'

His arms loosened, his jaw stiffened. He lifted his chin and it was Sir James Polcarrow staring at me, his sailor's outfit no disguise against generations of aristocratic breeding. I took a deep breath.

'You're a baronet, born to rank and privilege — you can't pretend otherwise. How long would it be before hardship made you long for your wealth? Before someone treated you as inferior and you told them who you really were? You'd hold our son in your arms and long for him to take his rightful place in the Polcarrow lineage. You aren't Jim and you can't pretend to be — it wouldn't work and it would destroy me watching you pretend for my sake.'

'I love you, Rose — that's all that matters.'

'And when your passion's spent? When poverty makes us bitter? You'd yearn for the privilege you take for granted and blame yourself for being a fool.' I saw the mask close over his face, the deep lines set around his mouth. He turned his back and stared across the black sea. I, too, must turn my back and go. It had been a mistake to come. A terrible, terrible mistake.

He swung round, his face full of fury, 'For God's sake, Rose – if you'll not marry me as Jim, then marry me as James Polcarrow.'

I drew back, shocked. My heart was aching for the sailor who had stolen my heart, not this stranger who shouted so angrily. I did not know him and certainly did not love him. 'No, Sir James,' I said, every trace of uncertainty vanishing with the breeze. 'I can never marry you, nor do I wish to. We can never live each other's worlds – I'm the daughter of a dissident boat-builder and I'll not abandon what I hold true. Nor do I want to – I'm proud of who I am. I'm set to challenge the power of the aristocracy, not become one of them.'

'That's what I love about you.' His voice sounded strangely distant.

'You don't know me well enough to love me and I don't know you, at all. You're a stranger – your position in society is so completely different from mine. Every one of your sort would loathe me. They'd despise who I was and where I came from. You mistake love for want – and you can find that in someone else.'

The breeze cooled my cheeks and I was glad of it. I must not stay. I was doing the right thing, I knew I was, but why did it hurt so much? 'Goodbye, Sir James, I wish you well… and when Father applies for the lease of his boatyard back, please bear us no malice.'

He stared back at me, all trace of emotion gone, his face once more a sombre mask. A gust of wind caught the collar of his shirt and I remembered the gale that had blown so fiercely the night we first met. It seemed an eternity ago.

I breathed in the salty air, forcing it deep within my lungs. I am a child of the sea and the wind. I am born with a spirit, free to choose. No man will force me to change who I am. I began to feel calmer and turned to go. As I did, I caught a whisper on the wind.

'I could never bear you malice. You must know that, Rose.'

Chapter Twenty-seven

I made my way back to the safety of our cottage, my eyes dry of tears, but the moment I began mounting the stairs, I knew something was wrong. A line of candlelight showed under my door – muffled sounds coming from within.

Mother was sitting on my bed, her head bowed, clutching my nightdress to her face. She was weeping, her small frame wracked by the violence of her sobs. She looked up, hardly believing her eyes, 'Oh, Rose, my dearest, I thought ye'd left us.'

I crossed the room, throwing my arms round her, cradling her to me as if she were my child. 'I'd never leave you, never.'

Her tear-stained face glistened in the candlelight. 'I... thought...well...Sir James Polcarrow isn't the sort of man many women could refuse.'

My heart froze. Had Jenna told her about the note? Surely not, or they would have tried to stop me. 'What d'you mean, Mother?'

'Ye know very well what I mean,' she replied. 'Not many

women would be able to resist the passion of a man like Sir James Polcarrow. I may be getting old and I may *pretend* to be deaf but I'm not blind. A mother knows things without being told. When he visits, he fidgets and doesn't concentrate on what he says. His eyes always search for ye, always straying to the door, willing for ye to enter. There's a restlessness about him that speaks of passion and a wildness that makes me believe he'd throw everything to the wind if love was at stake.' She wiped her eyes, blowing her nose on her handkerchief. 'I saw the look he gave ye – believe me, not many women would be able to resist such a man.'

'Well, I'm one that can,' I said firmly.

She hesitated, as if wanting to ask me something but not finding the courage to do so. Instead, she grasped my hands and kissed them. 'I should've known ye're not to be played with. I don't know where ye get your strength, but I admire ye so much.'

'It doesn't take much strength to resist Sir James Polcarrow,' I lied.

Her gaze was strangely steady. 'I have to say, I like Sir James – very much – and I don't share yer father's disregard for him. He's served us that well and I'll always welcome him into my house.'

'I don't disregard him,' I replied, understanding her meaning, 'but what makes you think his intentions are honourable?'

'I just feel it. Despite his past, I feel he's honourable – like his father was.'

'Well, it's neither here nor there, because I'm not prepared to be summoned like a servant and treated as chattel.'

I felt her flinch. Her mouth tightened but her voice was gentle, loving, the voice of my childhood. 'Promise me, ye won't shun marriage for much longer? Without marriage ye'll have no means of support – we've no family, only a distant cousin in Falmouth. If ye don't marry, ye may end with nothing. Ye could be destitute.'

'I know, you're right, but why should we have to rely on marriage? Have you never thought we deserve the same rights as men?' She flinched again. 'Please don't take badly to my thoughts – I'm not alone. A lot of women believe we've the right to contribute to society and every right to be educated – we just need to make it happen, that's all.'

I could see I was causing her pain. She let go of my hands and smoothed her nightgown, running her fingers down the tiny pin-tucks she had sewn so expertly. I saw the fine tremor in her hands and heard the catch in her voice. 'Why don't ye let things be? Why always fight everyone, like yer father?'

'Because we must,' I said gently. 'Without protest, we've no voice and with no voice we can't make changes.' I took the candle and crossed the room, opening my chest. Hidden among my stockings was the beautiful carved box Father had given me as a child. I kept everything precious in it. I searched for my rescued pamphlet, hurrying straight back. 'Have a look at this. It's a pamphlet written by a lady called Mary Wollstonecraft. She believes all women should be educated. Here, let me read it to you – it's from *The Vindication of the Rights of Women.*'

The tallow candle was smoking badly, emitting only just enough light for me to see. Mother hardly ever read and

I knew she would find the language hard. I curled next to her, starting from the beginning, reading through to the end. Mother said nothing, but listened intently, the frown increasing on her brow. When the candle guttered, I folded the pamphlet. 'Father doesn't approve – he says it's only fit for the fire.'

'I'm not surprised!' replied Mother in the darkness, 'I don't suppose *any* man would approve! I'm not sure I approve meself or even understand the half of it, but ye can explain another time. We'd better get some sleep now.' She got up to go, carefully easing her back. 'Good night, dear child.'

'Good night, Mother.' My dearest mother. She was so fragile, so very precious to me.

At the door she paused. 'No need to tell yer father,' she said.

She could not see me smiling back in the darkness. Absolutely not. No need to at all.

High Water

Chapter Twenty-eight

Fosse
Monday 12th August 1793 7:00 a.m.

The early morning sunlight caught our new sign, *Pengelly Boatyard*, making the paint gleam with promise. But what was the point of a boatyard without commissions? I re-read the letter in my hand. Mr Scantlebury was crossing the yard, his eyes glancing nervously at me as he opened the door. 'There's thunder in your face, Miss Pengelly.'

'It's the letter we've been waiting for – from Robert Steppings.'

'Then not good news, I take it. Ah well, least we tried – though I have to say I'm a little surprised. Mr Steppings seemed much taken with the plans, even led me to believe he was keen on them – aye, well, 'tis not to be, then.'

'Oh no, Mr Steppings is much taken with your plans – he's very keen.'

Thomas Scantlebury looked puzzled. 'Then surely that's good?'

'He wants your brig to be built, but not by us. He says, here, let me read you his exact words, our "*capabilities are insufficient and we have neither the space nor manpower for the undertaking*". He insists the contract should go to Nickels!'

'Nickels!' The colour drained from his face, but not before I had glimpsed the joy in his eyes. To have a brig built to your own design and commissioned by the navy was a dream few shipwrights dared to dream. 'That's poppycock – we've all the capability we need.'

'This has nothing to do with capability. Nickels has Sir Charles Cavendish's patronage, and Sir Charles has the ear of Mr Pitt. You must've heard the rumours that Charles Cavendish gave over a hundred thousand pounds to the navy – that's how he got his baronetcy.'

'Then we stand no chance – no chance at all…' Throwing his pack roughly on his desk, he slumped angrily to the chair. His eyes would not meet mine and I knew what I had to say. I had been dreading this all morning.

'You'll have to transfer to Nickels, Mr Scantlebury. You can't let a chance like this go – they're your plans, it's your ship, and I'd never dream of stopping you.' I hoped I sounded convincing. I felt like pleading with him not to desert us, begging for him to stay. I'd promised Father I would look after the yard until he was fit enough to return, but already my actions could lose us our most trusted friend.

'Aye, 'twould be the most sensible thing…' he replied slowly. 'But, let's face it, you and I – we're a stubborn pair, no mistaking. I'll build my brig here or not at all.' He looked down, shifting his papers in an attempt to avoid my eyes. ''Tis my belief they'll come running. The plans are too good – and they know it.'

My heart soared. I should never have doubted him. 'But there's something else,' I said quickly. 'The navy want it coppered.'

'That makes sense – it'll stop the worms in the warmer seas and add to the ship's speed. They'll be coppering all their ships soon enough.'

'But it'll add ten per cent to our costs and make it hard to keep the price competitive.'

'Aye, Miss Pengelly.'

'But d'you think we can do that?'

He took off his jacket and rolled up his sleeves. Pulling a large apron over his head, he passed the ties around his waist, tying them firmly in front. Only the slightest glint in his eye gave him away. 'I couldn't do it, but then I'm not you, am I, Miss Pengelly? If anyone can find the money, you can.'

I had long been thinking how to cut costs and my head was jumping. I drew out a large sheet of paper and started writing down my ideas. From now on, I would balance the books meticulously. We would accumulate reserves and never, ever, would our boatyard go bankrupt again. For a start, no credit. Not to anyone until we were in profit. I glanced at the work schedule – all of them seine boats in for repair and maintenance and would soon be needed for the pilchards. All of them belonged to members of the Corporation and all of them would expect credit.

I took a wad of paper. I would write to each member of every consortium, outlining our new terms – cash on completion and a deposit of twenty per cent prior to any work. I knew they would threaten to take their custom elsewhere, but we had to risk it. The pilchards would soon be running and most of the other yards were already full. Surely no-one would risk having their boat unseaworthy for the shoals?

Second on the list – Father never turned away the poorest fishermen, but they never paid. That had to stop. We should mend their boats in return for labour. They could work in the sawpit. My head was spinning. Third on the list, how to use what we had more efficiently? Father gave away our bark chippings to the sailmakers to preserve the sails, but why allow them free access? It did not make sense. Tanners in Truro needed oak to dye their leather and their businesses were flourishing. The demand for oak chippings was rising.

Reaching for more paper, I sharpened my quill. I would write first to the tanneries of Truro, then to the sailmakers of Fosse and Porthruan, asking each of them how much they would pay, per cartload, and agree the higher price.

My temples were beginning to throb. I needed air and, besides, I needed to check the quality of the latest batch of hemp. Stepping out into the yard, I blinked in the brilliant sunshine, surprised to see three tall masts soaring above the houses. I had not seen the ship dock against the town quay. She was huge – quite the largest ship to dock for some time. I nodded to the men and smiled at Tom. 'She must be a beauty,' I said as we gazed up at the mastheads.

'Uncle says nigh on six hundred ton. They rowed her in – must've been tight.' He seemed so confident, turning from a boy to a youth, shooting upwards, outgrowing yet more clothes. 'She's from the Indies, I believe.'

'She's flying some handsome flags. Have you done those calculations yet, Tom?'

'Oh aye, Miss Pengelly...well...they'll be done for Sunday!'

I left Tom to his caulking and returned to the office. An idea had long been gnawing at my thoughts. We should buy timber when it was a good price and store it for future use. Father had been made bankrupt because we owed too much money to one man and timber merchants were notorious for charging high prices. A couple of boatyards dealt directly with timber suppliers, so why not us? Buying logs cheaper would not only save us money but ensure the supply we needed. We could even make a profit by selling surplus cuts back to the block makers.

What we needed was somewhere to store the timber. Somewhere the logs could season. I picked up the most recent copy of the *Fosse Gazette* and turned to the page I had earmarked, staring down at the small advertisement for a creek and surrounding woodland. It was to be sold at auction and was *unsuitable for dwellings, pasture or livestock because, being tidal, it was completely submerged at the height of the tide*.

I knew the creek and knew it would make a perfect log pool, but if I told people why I wanted it, anyone I asked would buy it for themselves. We had no money, so would have to lease it, but who could buy it? I stared at the advertisement. The creek had once belonged to the Polcarrow estate and was surrounded by Polcarrow land. Perhaps they wanted it back? The solution seemed obvious, but thinking about it made my heart hammer. I felt sick with nerves.

Could I write to Sir James? Dare I ask such a favour of the man I had shunned so completely?

I crossed to the window and stared across the yard. If I delayed, we might miss this chance for ever. Father would never ask, or even approve for that matter. I took a deep breath. This was nonsense – the future of the boatyard was too important to let Father's scruples, or my pride, stand in its way. This was purely business: I would write to Sir James Polcarrow and ask that if he was interested in buying back the creek, we would like to have first offer on the lease.

Every time I began my letter, I saw the anger in his eyes and my hand trembled. The floor was littered with my failed attempts. I had walked away, believing I would never see him again, yet here I was, already asking something from him. He would despise me. I picked up my quill, writing quickly and firmly, sealing it without re-reading it. Jimmy Tregony was sitting on the steps outside. 'Take this to the gatekeeper of Polcarrow. Be quick – tell him it's for Sir James Polcarrow.'

'Right away, Miss Pengelly.'

What had I done? What would Father think? The thought of Father saddened me. His slow return to health still kept him from the yard. He remained in the cramped parlour, surrounded by his correspondence and newspapers, but it was not the lack of opportunity keeping me from him. His constant chiding of Mother irritated me. Never before would I think to conceal anything from him, yet watching Jimmy run under the arch, I knew to keep silent. I would have to tell him – but not now. Not if Sir James Polcarrow was going to be involved.

The reply to my letter seemed exceptionally prompt. Catching his breath, Jimmy handed me a small, folded note. A jolt of pain shot through me and I stared at the same neat handwriting, my throat tightening. But a glance at the stamp of the Polcarrow crest brought me quickly to my senses. The note was brief and to the point. It suggested I came to the office at Polcarrow within the hour. It was all so quick, so sudden, but it was just as well – it would leave me very little time to change my mind and no time at all to return to Porthruan to change my dress.

Not that I wanted to. My old green dress would do perfectly well for a business discussion concerning a log pool.

Chapter Twenty-nine

I would take my letters to the posthouse on my way. Gathering them up carefully, I put them in my basket and crossed the yard. The day was getting hotter; Joseph Melhuish halfway through a jug of ale. He nodded, wiping the sweat from his brow. I could not imagine how he worked at his furnace on a day like this. Jimmy Tregony had fully recovered from his errand and joined his steps with mine. He removed his cap and smiled. 'D'ye want me to take them letters, Miss Pengelly?'

The letters were too important to let out of my sight. 'No, Jimmy. I need to pay for them but wait just a moment while I see Madame Merrick – then we can go past the frigate.'

'I've heard she's a thirty-two gunner.'

'As many as that? Well, let's count them.'

Madame Merrick looked up as I entered the room, her dress rustling as she moved. It was made of very fine silk. She was wearing a piece of cloth wrapped several times round her head. A small arrangement of feathers fluttered on one side with what looked like a diamond brooch, pinning everything in place. It was surprisingly elegant but I must have looked surprised.

'It's a *turban*, Miss Pengelly, though I do not expect you to have seen one before. Those in the *higher* ranks of society know what it is.'

'And how are the higher ranks of society, Madame Merrick? How's Lady April Cavendish?'

Mother and Elowyn stopped fitting fabric against a dress-maker's dummy. Mother had pins in her mouth. She shook her head slowly, her lips pursed not only by the pins it held. Elowyn smiled broadly.

'I believe she is quite well, thank you,' Madame Merrick replied coldly.

'She's not yet called?'

'No, but she has sent her housekeeper, Mrs Jennings.'

'And did Mrs Jennings take tea, Madame Merrick?' Elowyn's eyes widened. She clasped her hand across her mouth. Mother's frown deepened.

'As a matter of fact, she did. I have learnt to take very small steps at a time, Miss Pengelly and perhaps *you* would be wise to do the same.' The old venom had crept back into her tone. Perhaps I had been wrong to tease her. 'I hear you are planning an *ambitious* venture, Miss Pengelly – a naval brig, no less, rumoured to be the *biggest* ship yet built in Fosse.'

'We've only ever taken small steps, but to survive as a boatyard, I believe we need the courage to take bigger steps.'

'Then take care those big steps do not trample on people's goodwill, Miss Pengelly.'

227

I would have replied with defiance, but one look from those hooded eyes brought me sharply to my senses. It was as if she knew I was about to make several members of the Corporation very angry. 'Thank you, but you needn't worry – the Admiralty want Nickels to have the commission. I doubt it'll ever come our way.'

Mother gasped, but those hawk eyes remained staring at me. 'One moment,' she said as I turned to go. 'If you insist on running your father's boatyard, you must, at least, *look* as if you prosper. In return for the Mantua silk, I will design you a *working gown*. The gown will afford me no pleasure but I need not make it – Elowyn needs all the *practice* she can get. This *working gown* will be plain...no frills or ribbons...it will have a short, matching jacket, similar to a riding habit but I insist you tell *nobody* it came from *here*...'

I was completely taken aback. Though her words were said harshly, her offer was so generous I could hardly conceal my gratitude. 'Thank you...that's very kind of you.'

'It's not kind at all,' she replied, turning haughtily away. 'Mr Tregellas's silk is worth far more. If you insist I keep it, then I am merely discharging my debt to you while at the same time making a handsome profit.' She arched her exquisite eyebrow at Mother, who quickly hid her smile.

'What colour will my new working dress be?' I asked.

'Red, of course. Fiery red. Nothing else will do.'

'Fiery red it is, then,' I replied, smiling. I was almost through the door when I remembered why I had come. 'Oh, I nearly forgot. I came to say I think I ought to spend at least a couple of hours each week entering your accounts for you, because if I don't I have a terrible feeling everything will get back in a muddle again. I'll start tomorrow.'

Madame Merrick's second eyebrow shot up and Mother could no longer conceal her smile.

Mother's smile seemed to reflect the mood of the whole town. There was always excitement when a large ship put in to port, but a huge naval frigate was likely to cause as much bustle as a carnival.

'Come on, Jimmy, let's go.'

We pushed our way through the throng of people and crossed the main square. It was busier than I had expected and increasingly dangerous as carts rumbled past, heedless of those around them. We were swept along by the tide of people pushing down to the quayside and I grabbed Jimmy's hand in fear of being separated.

Every food-seller in Fosse seemed determined to gain by the ship's re-provisioning. The roads were blocked, wagons lining up two or three deep. Disorder reigned and scuffles broke out between drivers anxious to unload their carts and return with more. Sides of pigs, great rumps of salted meat, sacks of flour, piles of vegetables, barrels of ale, even hogsheads of salted pilchards, stood piled high on the wagons. The din was deafening. Everyone was shouting. Beside us, a cartload of chickens squawked in their wicker baskets. As frustration turned to anger and tempers flared, I hung on to Jimmy's hand, darting down a side alley, the huge masts of the frigate looming above us, blocking out the sun.

A delicious smell began wafting over the stench of the sewers, drawing us as surely as the masts of the ship. 'It's a hog they're roasting, Miss Pengelly. It smells so good.'

'It certainly does.'

'It's making me stomach ache.'

'Perhaps if you make yourself useful, they'll give away scraps.'

We turned the corner. Dwarfing the quayside was the biggest, most elaborately carved frigate I had ever seen. She was fully dressed in naval flags, their breath-taking colours glowing brightly in the sun. 'Each flag means something, Jimmy, that's how ships communicate with each other – that's how they give orders. And that big red flag with the jack means she's under naval command.'

'Just look at them cannons! Come on, Miss Pengelly, you said we'd count them.'

We counted thirty-two on the gun deck and ten smaller, carriage-mounted guns on the quarter deck and forecastle. We would have counted them all again if a juggler had not arrived to keep Jimmy open-mouthed for the next five minutes.

I had a chance to study the ship. Father always took me to every ship that docked in Fosse or Porthruan, saying that a boat-builder learns something new from every boat he sees. I knew he would quiz me intently about this frigate, so I started looking carefully at its construction, but with all the crowds it was hard to see the lines of the hull and with all that was going on, hard to concentrate.

Navy men were everywhere, like ants in a nest. Some were rolling barrels up the gangplanks, some stowing provisions.

230

Others were scrubbing the decks or polishing the brass. Many towered above us, high in the rigging, balancing on the footropes, tidying the sails. Above the noise of the crowd, I could hear them chanting as they set about their tasks; the sun reflecting on their white trousers. As they sang, they gazed across English soil, happy at last to cast aside the hardships of their long ocean voyage.

'Want some cockles, miss?' We were being hustled on every side by food-sellers crying their wares. I shook my head.

'Like a pie, miss?'

I shook my head, then saw the longing in Jimmy's eyes. I checked my purse. 'Just one for the boy,' I replied.

'Thank you, miss.' The pie-seller pocketed the coins and handed me a pie.

'She's a fine ship – d'you know where she's from?' I asked.

'Dominica.'

'How come she's docked? Is there a problem?'

'No problem. She's on escort duty – bringin' a rear admiral to Fosse.'

'Why would a *rear admiral* come to Fosse?'

'It's rumoured he's Sir Charles Cavendish's brother and home for a holiday!'

I gave the pie to Jimmy who immediately bit into it, the juices running down his chin. He was even more excited by the news, but for me the ship had lost some of her sparkle.

A cry went up from the sailors, high above us in the rigging and all eyes strained upwards, watching the sailors point up

231

river. In a flash, the crowd saw what they were pointing to and a huge cry swept along the quayside.

'Porpoises!' The cheer was deafening. 'Swimmin' up river – a whole pod of them – means the pilchards are massin'.' It was always the first sign.

'The shoals'll be here soon enough.'

Whoops of delight echoed round the quay and my heart jumped, catching the excitement. I clutched my basket to me. I had to get the letters posted. If the shoals were massing, the seine boats would soon be needed – I just had to hope my gamble would pay off.

I left Jimmy to the excitement, crossing the quay to push my way up to the posthouse. Passing the windows of the new bank, I caught my reflection and was horrified to see what a sight I looked. My bonnet had been knocked sideways by someone in the crowd and I stopped to adjust it. A movement in the glass caught my attention and I turned to see Jenna waving frantically in my direction. I waved back, watching as she pushed her way through the crowds towards me.

'That basket's very full, Jenna. What've you got in there?'

'I've been to Coombe House,' she said, pulling back the cloth. 'Mrs Munroe's calf foot jelly for Mr Pengelly…and these rabbit pies.'

'He'll love them. How was he this morning?'

'Not well…not really – that cough ain't shifting.'

'I know. How are they at Coombe House?'

'They're that busy getting the place aired…they asked when we'd be moving back.'

'It won't be for a while – if at all. These legal cases go on

232

for ever. Sir George may never get us back. We've no guarantee it's going to happen.'

'He must think it's going to happen – him keeping Mrs Munroe and everyone on, paying their wages and all that. Can't be that long – I think it's as like to be soon enough.' Though she spoke with optimism, she seemed preoccupied, her expression grave. It was most unlike her. She linked her arm through mine. 'If ye're going to the posthouse, I'll go with ye.'

We edged away from the bank, heading towards the square where the crowd was thin enough for us to walk side by side. She seemed in no hurry and I was surprised she waited patiently in the posthouse queue until my transactions were complete. Her basket was heavy and I thought she would want to rush home, but she remained standing close to me, her expression uncomfortably solemn. Something was obviously troubling her. 'Are you alright, Jenna?'

'Right as rain, it's just...' Grabbing my arm, she led me round the back of the town hall. There was an arched portico held up by several pillars and a number of roughly hewn benches set back against the wall. There was hardly anyone there.

'D'you need to sit down?'

'No...but ye may need to.' She had certainly got my attention. I had never seen her so jumpy. She put down her basket, fidgeting with her hands.

'For goodness sake – what is it?'

She seemed to be hesitating, but my sharp tone must have spurred her on. She took a deep breath, looking straight in my eyes, her own full of concern. 'That frigate brought Rear Admiral Sir George Cavendish – Governor of Dominica.'

'I know, Jenna. He's Sir Charles's brother. They're here for a holiday and though it doesn't fill me with any great pleasure, I can live with it – it's not the end of the world.'

'Sir George has come with his family…with Lady Cavendish and his daughter…Miss Arbella Cavendish.'

Into my mind came a moonlit night, the soft breeze blowing against my cheek. I was back on the rock, surrounded by gorse. What was it he had said? *While I was there, circumstances arose, making it necessary I return to England*. My heart thumped painfully against my chest. 'Well?' I replied.

'Ye'll hear soon enough, but I wanted ye to hear from me first. Sir George and Lady Cavendish ain't here for a holiday – they've come for a wedding. Their daughter, Miss Arbella Cavendish, is engaged to be married.' Her eyes could barely look at mine. '…Miss Arbella is *engaged* to Sir James Polcarrow – they've come to see her wed.'

A searing pain shot through me.

'Miss Rosehannon, are ye alright? Ye're as white as a sheet. Shall I get you some ale? Here, use my skirt to get some air flowing…'

The ground was swaying in front of me. I thought I would vomit. The shelter had been used as a latrine and stank in the midday sun. I wanted to cry. I wanted to scream. I needed to be alone. 'Was there anything else – or d'you think you'd better get those pies home?' I snapped.

'Can I leave ye?'

'Why ever not?' I could not look at her.

'Ye sure ye don't want nothing?'

'Nothing at all. Please, go home and take Father his calf's foot jelly.' I could not move, my body racked with pain. Two gulls were fighting over a fallen pie. With wings outstretched and necks extended, they squabbled and screamed, their plaintive cries drowning the cries from my heart. I had known all along, known he was lying. My head had been warning my heart and I had not listened. He had tried to seduce me, that was all.

Chapter Thirty

Miss Arbella Cavendish. I could just imagine her – the glittering jewel of Government House, pandered and spoilt, living off the backs of slaves, never lifting a finger other than to embroider or play the pianoforte.

Absorbed by my thoughts, I was surprised to find I had already reached the gatehouse of Polcarrow. The church clock was striking the quarter hour and I had very little time to calm myself if I was to see James Polcarrow with any sense of composure. His attempt to seduce me had been despicable. How dare he? I had been drawn perilously close to a dangerous world where powerful men saw it as sport to indulge their passions. Father was right – James Polcarrow was just like the rest of them. What if I had believed his talk of love?

The sun beat mercilessly against the cobbles. I crossed the road to seek the shade, my cheeks burning not only from the heat. Did he gaze at her like he had gazed at me? Did he hold her as tightly and kiss her as deeply? Having sought the shade, an icy chill now made me shiver. Miss Arbella Cavendish. I hated that name. I hated her and I hated everything she stood for.

A cart trundled past. Two dogs started fighting until somebody threw a stone at them. I took a deep breath and squared my shoulders. I was Rosehannon Pengelly, intelligent and strong. I was not a woman to be played with and, besides, it now seemed so simple. If Sir James Polcarrow had thought he could use me for his own gains, then I had no qualms about using him for mine. I would get my log pool.

'Miss Pengelly? Sir James is expecting you, so if ye'd follow me, I'll show ye the way.' The gatekeeper led me to a small door concealed within the outer gates. He was a middle-aged man, dressed in a red livery jacket with the gold Polcarrow crest embroidered on both lapels. He unlocked the inner door and nodded, 'Go through this door, miss, and straight up the drive.'

I was conscious my empty basket made me look like an errand girl. 'Could I leave my basket with you?' I asked. He nodded, holding his hand out to take it.

Stepping onto the drive, I was struck by how different it seemed compared to the last time I had walked up to the house. It was surprisingly tranquil. Sheep grazed the parkland and ahead of me three gardeners were clipping the privet bushes that lined the drive.

I still had nightmares about Mr Roskelly. If rumours were correct, Mr Roskelly was suffering little hardship. According to gossip, he was in a single cell in Bodmin Gaol being attended to by at least two servants. Apparently he dined like a lord, drank claret and brandy by night, and wore a freshly laundered shirt each morning. If this was true, he must be paying a fortune and it worried me that a man who wielded so much influence could buy himself out of gaol. I just prayed Sir George Reith was as good as they said he was. We had so much depending on him.

I found myself enjoying the fact that the house was so grey and ugly. In fact, the more I thought about it, the more it made me smile, wondering how Miss Arbella Cavendish would take to living in such a hideous place. I hoped she hated it.

He had never trusted me, yet he must have told her everything.

Henderson glared at me from the top of the sweeping steps and I glared back, determined not to use the trades-man's entrance. But it seemed he was expecting me and he led me disdainfully across the echoing hall to the thick oak door of Sir James's study. 'Miss Pengelly,' he announced, still glaring his disapproval as he shut the door behind me.

It was the same room I had been in before with its dark panelling, dense beams and ancient furniture, but all trace of tobacco fumes had gone and the air was surprisingly fresh. The heavy drapes, that had so easily concealed the two attorneys, had been pulled back; allowing light to flood the room. For the first time, I noticed French doors leading directly onto a wide terrace and steps leading down to a formal garden, laid with box hedges and fountains. The doors were open and the delicate scent of lavender filled the room. I could even smell the sea and feel a breeze gently cooling my cheeks.

Sunlight reached across to the fireplace, lighting up a tapestry which stood in front of the fire irons. There was no sign of the mastiffs and I was surprised to see a large book-case, crammed with books, pushed against the panel through which Sulio Denville had escaped. There were so many books and I had to fight my longing to go over and touch them, to breathe in the smell of their leather covers.

Two men were sitting either side of the desk and stood up at my entrance – one was the impeccably dressed figure of Sir James Polcarrow, the other I had never seen before.

'This is a pleasure, Miss Pengelly' said Sir James, bowing. 'May I introduce my steward, Mr Thomas Warren?'

'Mr Warren,' I said, making a small curtsey.

'Miss Pengelly.' Mr Warren bowed, his eyes appraising me like a prize cow in a show ring. When his gaze rested on my bosom, my flesh crept and I felt immediate dislike for this wiry man with his fine tailored jacket, silk cravat and silver buckles. He was middle-aged, about my height, with hollow cheeks, a grey complexion and an oily brown wig. As he smiled or, more accurately, sneered he revealed darkly stained and rotting teeth.

'Miss Pengelly, can I offer you any refreshment?' James Polcarrow waved his hand towards the chair Thomas Warren had just vacated.

'No refreshment, thank you. I come for business, not pleasure.'

Thomas Warren pulled out the chair and I immediately regretted not remaining standing. Leaning closely towards me, his fetid breath stinging my nostrils, I could feel his hands pressing against my shoulder. His caress was momentary and swiftly executed, but it made me stiffen. I was furious at his appalling liberty but Sir James had clearly not seen.

Unperturbed, Thomas Warren crossed behind the desk and stood immediately behind Sir James. Both men stood staring at me from across the desk and for the first time since I entered the room, I allowed myself to look straight into the eyes of the man who, only weeks ago, had begged me to marry him.

He must have seen my anger; I thought I saw a flicker of surprise cross those piercing blue eyes. He was dressed in a well-fitting morning jacket, an embroidered, silk waistcoat and a silk shirt with a slight ruff at the sleeves. His breeches were tightly fitted and tucked into long boots. Round his neck he wore a neatly folded silk cravat. He seemed at ease, though his colour was perhaps heightened and his hair ruffled by the hand he passed over it.

'Business, Miss Pengelly?'

My mouth hardened. 'I'd just like to know whether you're considering buying the creek that's come up for auction.'

Thomas Warren stiffened. His eyes shifted away from my bosom as a distinct shadow crossed his face. He stared at me with evident hostility. James Polcarrow was also looking intently at me. 'I haven't heard of any creek for sale.'

'It's upriver from Pont Pill. It's only a small parcel of land that floods with the tide – it has no value for pasture or crops and is virtually worthless.' I knew I was speaking too quickly and tried to slow my pace. 'But if you were thinking of buying it, I'd ask to lease it from you.'

'Why do you think I'd be interested in buying this creek?'

'It's surrounded by Polcarrow land, I just assumed you'd want it back,' I replied, trying to keep the bitterness out of my voice.

James Polcarrow's face darkened. He swung round to Thomas Warren. 'Did you know about the creek, Mr Warren?'

'Yes – though Miss Pengelly's right. The land's no worth – it's useless. I thought no more of it when I saw it was for sale.' Though he spoke to Sir James, Thomas Warren kept his eyes fixed firmly on me.

'Do you not think it is your job to inform me when there's land to be purchased and my decision what land I buy?'

'You may remember, Sir James, the creek was lost as a wager by your grandfather to his groom,' Thomas Warren replied through tight lips. 'It was a long time ago and the Polcarrow estate's never been affected by the loss.'

'Bring the map, Mr Warren, I'd like to see where this creek is.' Thomas Warren sucked in his already hollow cheeks and crossed the room to search the drawers of a large bureau. I squared my shoulders, keeping my gaze steady to meet Sir James's enquiring look.

'What good can it be to you, Miss Pengelly? If it floods it can be no good to you as a boatyard.' I sensed his challenge.

'I'd like to use it as a log pool,' I replied. 'With a boom of logs chained from edge to edge, it would hold a great deal of timber. Wood needs to season – oak needs to soak at least one year for every inch of width, so I'm planning for the future. If we can season our own logs, I can buy cheaper. The naval yards are taking everything they can and small yards are struggling to find good supplies.'

'So you propose to be a timber merchant now, do you, Miss Pengelly? Not just a boat-builder – how very ambitious.'

He spoke harshly, using the tone Jim had used when he had questioned me with such contempt. I had been free to speak my mind then, but now I bit my lip, looking coldly across the desk at the man who had thought to seduce me. There was anger in both our eyes and I heard the responding harshness in my voice. 'Yes, I do propose to buy timber. There's a rumour Nickels is using bad timber, which is good for us, of course, because he's our biggest rival, but competition's fierce and a boatyard will stand or fall on the quality of the wood it uses. If I need to deal in timber, then I will, even if I have to buy from Plymouth or Penzance. Or direct from Norway. But we'll need somewhere to season the logs.'

James Polcarrow sat back in his chair, his eyes never leaving my face, 'How is business, Miss Pengelly? Do you have contracts to build?'

'We will have,' I said, momentarily thrown by the kindness in his voice, 'but repairs and maintenance pay quicker returns. The commissions we've been offered are too low and I won't let Father go bankrupt again.'

'What's your commissioning rate, if I may ask?'

His question threw me. I took a deep breath. 'That depends on the vessels' weight and the timber used but, on average, the cost per ton could be between four and seven pounds.'

'And is that the same in every boatyard?'

'Round here the price is fairly fixed, but in London or Wales, the prices can reach ten pounds a ton. Are you thinking of commissioning a boat, Sir James?'

'No, I'm afraid not,' he said with a hint of apology, 'but why don't you increase your prices in line with other towns?'

'Surely I don't need to tell you that,' I answered tartly. 'The Corporation and Sir Charles Cavendish keep the prices low so they can sell the ships on at huge profit.' At the mention of Charles Cavendish, I saw Sir James's mouth tighten. I bit my lip. I felt like shouting at the top of my voice, that yes, we were talking about his precious new uncle by marriage – his soon-to-be family.

'And this creek, Miss Pengelly, would your father bid for it had he the money?' He had been writing something, his eyes remaining fixed on the desk, but as I hesitated he looked up, a fleeting smile crossing his face. 'I take it your father knows about all this?'

'Of course,' I lied.

'Because he would need to sign the lease.'

'I know full well I wouldn't be considered sufficiently capable to sign a lease.'

'That's not what I think, Miss Pengelly, as well you know. It's the law – that's all.'

Thomas Warren had obviously sensed the friction between us and had been silently watching, his weasel eyes darting from one of us to the other, studying our faces for clues to our hostility. In the silence that followed Sir James's remark, he stepped forward, carefully placing several rolls of parchment on the desk in front of him. He began to unroll them in turn, eventually finding the one which showed the fields and estate boundaries of the land in question. The area was larger than I expected and, as Sir James stood up to flatten the map, he seemed pleased with the discovery. I noticed, however, that Thomas Warren was looking thunderous.

'When's the auction?'

'Friday evening, Sir James.'

'You must go and bid, Mr Warren. I want this land back. Whatever it costs – do you understand?' Thomas Warren raised his eyebrows in surprise and began collecting together the unwanted maps. Scowling, he walked over to the bureau to replace them in the correct drawers.

James Polcarrow leant over the desk, carefully studying the remaining map. He turned his head, looking up at me through the shock of hair that fell forward across his face. His eyes held mine, like blue arrows piercing my defences; his words barely above a whisper. 'I'm glad you thought to ask me, Rose. The land's yours – use it how you will. I'll draw up a lease with a low rent and your father can sign it when it suits him. Is he well enough to venture out yet?' His eyes were devouring me, like they had that night on the foaming sea. There was a time I might have drowned in that look, but I did not flounder. I had learnt my lesson and would swim against the strongest current. All the same, I did not want either Sir James or Mr Warren coming anywhere near our cottage.

'Father will be well enough to come here,' I replied quickly.

The door opened. Henderson crossed the room, carrying a silver tray with an embossed calling card on it. A loud disturbance was echoing across the hall and angry voices could be heard, chastising the servants. Sir James looked enquiringly at Henderson, who caught his unspoken question. 'They're having a bit of trouble getting Sir Charles out of his sedan chair, Sir James.'

Sir Charles Cavendish. The thought of coming face to face with that man filled me with horror. Two of the most powerful landowners in the county were soon to be united and their power would be absolute. This was no place for me.

'Thank you for the log pool, Sir James,' I said, making my way across the room. At the door, I turned to hold his gaze. He had absolutely no right to look at me like that. I took a deep breath. 'And may I congratulate you on your engagement to Miss Arbella Cavendish?'

He looked as if he had been struck. His head shot up, his mouth tightened, and a scowl creased his brows as those blue eyes turned to ice.

Chapter Thirty-one

I brushed past Sir Charles Cavendish, nearly tripping over his walking stick as he stabbed the marble floor in front of me. I hardly saw him, nor did I care. All I wanted to do was get out of that house. This was the second time I had been in a hurry to leave and there would not be a third.

Halfway down the drive, I was surprised to hear my name being called. One of the gardeners had stopped clipping the hedge and was waving at me. I had not recognised him before, but I instantly knew his voice. It was Ben. Intrigued, I watched him ask permission to stop work and, almost at once, he started running towards me. Removing his hat, he stood shyly in front of me, a huge grin spreading from ear to ear.

'Ben, what are you doing here? I didn't recognise you – just look at you, you've grown so strong.' He was looking so well, I had to blink hard to force back the tears welling in my eyes.

'I'm an under-gardener now, Miss Rose'annon...I can

stay long as I like. I eat three times a day – that's why I've grown so strong!' He twisted his hat in his hands, smiling at me all the time. 'I live with Mr Moyle, h-h-he's head-gardener and he tells me what to do. He says I learn quick… he says I've a feel for flowers…he says I can stay as long as I like.'

Ben seemed to have grown. He had certainly put on weight. He stood before me in his new smock, his face a picture of pride. 'How come you're here, Ben?'

'He came up the cliff…he came to my garden but I hid. I saw him comin' and I was that afraid, cause you said they'd h-h-harm me if they found me. So I hid in the wall and wanted him to go away. I was scared they'd be angry with me.'

'Did Mr Moyle come and find you?'

'No. Sir James came on his horse. He was callin' my name sayin'…"Ben, Ben, I know youse up here". He went on callin' and callin' and I was that scared and hid. It was rainin' but he got off his horse and come lookin' for me. He said it was alright…' He smiled his huge, lopsided grin, his eyes shining. 'He said you was his friend and it was alright…he said Miss Rose'annon w-w-would want me to go. Said I was good with flowers and he'd look after me…so I come out of me hidin' place and he put me on his horse and we come here. I've been with Mr Moyle ever since.'

I wanted to cry. I wanted to put my hands over my face and howl. Howl, with gratitude, regret, with what might have been, but somehow I managed to hold myself in check. 'That's wonderful, Ben. Work hard and do everything Mr Moyle tells you, won't you? Is there a Mrs Moyle?'

'She makes lovely food. We've our own vegetables and eggs…and we've rabbits from the parkland. My job's to fetch water and carry slops…but I've stopped long enough, Miss Rose'annon. Mr Moyle don't like me wastin' time. I'm so lucky. I can't think of a nicer place to be.'

I smiled across at Mr Moyle, who was doffing his hat, watching Ben's retreating figure. I had never thought of Polcarrow as a beautiful place but, looking round, I could see what he meant. To the south, the church tower stood square against the grey rooftops. To the east, the golden shades of Porthruan were shimmering through the ship's masts. Far out to sea, white sails ploughed the waves while, to the north, the river sparkled blue in the height of the tide. To the west, purple moorland fringed the skyline. High above us, skylarks were singing.

If Ben was happily settled, then it was all the consolation I needed.

I could not bring myself to tell Father about the log pool, nor could I tell him about the bark chippings – or my letters refusing credit. I knew I would have to tell him soon enough, but I did not have the stomach for a discussion which I knew would turn into an argument. I managed a rather half-hearted description of the brig, but my heart was not in it. Besides, his tobacco smoke hung heavily in the air and my head was throbbing. Neither of us was good company so I pleaded a headache and retired early to bed.

Before long, Jenna's footsteps sounded on the stairs. 'I've

brought ye some camomile tea,' she said, tentatively pushing open the door. 'Ye've not eaten a thing tonight.'

'I'm not hungry.'

'But it was Mrs Munroe's pie.'

'Maybe that's the reason, it was too rich – I like your pies better…no, don't look so surprised, you make much better pies.'

Jenna blushed and clucked her tongue. 'Better not say that again…it's like blasphemy to say such things.'

'I know someone who *does* like Mrs Munroe's pies,' I said, stroking Mr Pitt, who was sprawling on the bed beside me.

'Don't know what's to be done with Mr Pitt – Mrs Munroe won't stand for him in her kitchen – she'll kick him out to catch rats.'

'Poor Mr Pitt – you wouldn't like that, would you?' I said, rubbing his huge belly. Mr Pitt rolled over, purring louder. It was stuffy in my room and airless, despite the open window. In the yard below, Mother was talking to Mrs Tregony. A baby was crying. 'I'm very sorry I snapped at you, Jenna.'

'Can't say I noticed,' she replied with a grin.

I smiled back. 'I saw Ben today. He's an under-gardener now at Polcarrow. He's apprenticed to Mr Moyle.'

'I know,' Jenna replied.

'How d'you know?'

'Well, I heard – that's all – ye know me and gossip. I just heard.'

There was something rather furtive about Jenna's reaction. She had spoken too quickly, not looking me in the eye and, for some reason, it reminded me of Mr Warren.

There was something thoroughly unpleasant about that man. I could not help feeling he was probably as untrustworthy as he was lecherous. What if he told other boat-builders my intentions and others tried to steal the log pool from under my nose? What if someone bribed Thomas Warren to lose the bid? There was only one thing to do – I would go and watch him bid.

But what if, being there, I alerted other boat-builders? That would be like shouting out my plan and take away our advantage. Suddenly, my mind cleared – they would notice me as a woman, but not as a man. Why not? It had worked before, so why not one more time?

I sat bolt upright, scaring Mr Pitt off the bed. 'Jenna, go to your mother's tomorrow and get your brother's clothes again – I'll need everything. You know – boots and a large cap.'

Jenna swung round, her lovely face horrified. 'Them clothes are back...and that's the end of it.'

'Jenna, get them...once more, please...and don't tell Mother.' I could not explain.

Chapter Thirty-two

Madame Merrick's accounts, though still not entirely above board, were at least in order. I was just finishing the last of the invoices when carriage wheels clattered across the yard. Elowyn slammed down the bobbins she was threading and rushed to the window. 'It's Lady Cavendish's carriage – I recognise that crest.' Her face was as white as her apron.

Madame Merrick seemed caught unaware, unable to take her eyes off the carriage. 'Eva, Eva…come quickly. Elowyn, don't just stand there *gawping* like a fish – tidy away those threads…no, Elowyn, come back…go to the door and remember to curtsey *very low* – not just a bob…and whatever you do, do *not* look them in the eye. Is it Lady April, Eva?'

Mother came running. Not knowing whether to crane her neck out of the window or first remove her apron, she decided to do both at the same time. 'I can't be sure,' she said, struggling with the ensuing knot, 'there are four ladies in the carriage. I can see Mrs Jennings but, no, I don't think it's Lady April.'

Even so, Madame Merrick's long wait for patronage seemed to be over. She flew to the looking glass to adjust her turban, her deft fingers tweaking the feathers back into place. As I watched her anxiety, I too, felt strangely nervous. My heart began thumping. It was as if some visceral warning was telling me I was about to come face to face with the last woman on earth I wanted to see. I stood staring at the four women, knowing that to leave so abruptly would draw attention to myself but to stay would be almost unbearable.

Leading the party was a tall, middle-aged woman, wearing a plain, high-necked black gown and a simple bonnet, edged in purple ribbon. She was pointing towards the steps in a confident manner and I guessed she must be Mrs Jennings. Following her was a large woman whose voluminous gown, and flying ribbons, made her look like a ship in full sail. It was hard to see her face under her very elaborate hat, but the glimpse I caught of her puckered lips suggested displeasure.

Behind them, two other ladies walked arm in arm. Mr Melhuish, his glistening, bare chest hardly concealed by his smithy's apron, bowed in greeting and I saw them glance at each other in evident amusement. They were both about my age. The taller of them was wearing a lemon silk gown, trimmed with lace, and a straw bonnet, bedecked with ribbons. She was elegant and lively but even her grace, and evident wealth, paled into insignificance compared to the woman by her side. I had never seen anyone more beautiful.

Her companion was wearing a powder-blue dress, a

cream, silk fichu and a bonnet decorated with silk flowers. Holding up her lace parasol to shade her face from the sun, her hair shone like ripe corn. As she walked, soft ringlets danced against her face. She was dainty, fragile, looking for all the world like a golden angel, and I stared at her, stabs of envy pricking my heart.

Elowyn opened the door and curtseyed so deeply I thought she had fainted. Mrs Jennings looked round the room, her severe features relaxing when she saw Madame Merrick. 'Good morning, Madame Merrick...' She had barely begun her introduction before the older woman, gasping heavily from the exertion of climbing the steps, cut her short. 'Mrs Jenkins, I cannot believe you've brought us to such an appalling place with *naked men* loitering in the courtyard – girls, no need to look again. What sort of example is that for these young ladies? And that smell of burning tar. Get me my salts. There must be other dressmakers in this hellhole of a town.'

'There may be, my lady, but they are not as good,' Mrs Jennings replied, helping Lady Cavendish to her salts. 'Madame Merrick is superior to anyone, or else Lady April would not insist we came.'

'*Madame* Merrick?' cried Lady Cavendish, her eyes widening in horror. Her jaw slackened, her chins wobbled. She stared at Madame Merrick. 'Don't tell me you have bought me to a place where there are *Frenchies*! If my husband knew I was within ten feet of a *Frenchie* he would...'

'Would what, Aunt Martha?' said the taller of the two young ladies, stepping forward. 'Send in one of his frigates? I hardly think that would solve our problem.' She smiled at

Madame Merrick. 'I am Miss Celia Cavendish, this lady is my aunt, Lady Cavendish, and this is my cousin, Miss Arbella Cavendish.' She squeezed her cousin's arm before continuing with a broad smile. 'And we are here on very important business – my cousin would like to be fitted for her wedding gown.'

A cry of delight escaped Madame Merrick's lips. Clasping her hands, she beamed with pleasure. Elowyn stood transfixed, gazing in delight and I, too, could not take my eyes off Miss Arbella Cavendish, that first spark of envy now flaming like fire.

She was even more beautiful the closer you looked. Her face was a perfect oval, her eyes as blue as the dress she wore, her lips soft and delicately pouting. Her hair brought sunshine into the room. She was poised, elegant and walked with such grace, she could have been gliding. I was mesmerised, unable to take my eyes off her, furious I could not find any fault. She curtseyed to Madame Merrick and smiled at Mother without a trace of arrogance or rudeness. My mouth went dry. I never thought she would be so beautiful – nor so fragile.

'…and this is Miss Pengelly…my *bookkeeper*.' I heard Madame Merrick say.

I curtseyed, and as all four ladies turned their astonished eyes on me, I found myself blushing, averting my gaze, deeply ashamed of my shabby dress.

'How very extraordinary,' Celia Cavendish replied, her eyes wide with surprise. 'I don't know what I would do if I had to keep accounts.'

'You would employ someone to do them, I suppose,' I found myself replying a little more tartly than I intended.

'Yes, I suppose I would, Miss Pengelly,' she said, smiling despite my abrupt tone. 'But all the same, you must be very clever. I like the idea of a woman bookkeeper — it sounds different and rather thrilling.'

I looked across at the woman whose father I hated, whose family epitomised everything that was bad with our society, yet strangely, I found myself smiling back into those lively eyes. Miss Celia Cavendish had taken me completely by surprise.

Lady Cavendish was fanning herself furiously. 'I do not know what I'm doing here. I can't believe this woman has anything like the quality of fabric we require and I, for one, consider this an appalling waste of time. What my dear sister, Lady April, was thinking in sending us here, is quite beyond me. I propose we go to Truro. Or Bath. Yes, I propose we go to Bath.'

'Aunt Martha, there's no need to rush off. Rest awhile and at least see what Madame Merrick has to offer.' Celia Cavendish's well-modulated accent was clipped with impatience.

Lady Cavendish snorted but sat nevertheless in the chair Elowyn offered, heaving the vast expanse of her dress around her and folding her arms across her ample bosom. 'Mrs Merrick,' she said through tight lips, 'let me speak plainly. I'm not talking about *fishing town fabric* — my daughter requires the very best. I am the wife of Rear Admiral Sir George Cavendish, soon to be Lord Cavendish, and my daughter, Miss Arbella, is to wed Sir James Polcarrow. We are talking about a dress fit for the next *Lady* Polcarrow.'

The colour drained from Mother's face. She put out her hand to steady herself, her eyes turning in painful anticipation towards me. I kept my face composed, even managing a smile, but my eyes must have given me away. *Yes*, they said, *so much for thinking James Polcarrow was honourable.*

Madame Merrick was clasping her hands in excitement. 'Oh, Miss Cavendish, may I congratulate you? May I wish you every felicitation? Let me assure you that, if you were to choose *me* to make your wedding gown, I would make one of the *finest* quality and of the very *latest* fashion. Allow me the honour of showing you what I can offer…but, dear me, I am forgetting myself, can I offer you tea? Lady Cavendish, do you care to take a dish of *tea?*'

Lady Cavendish screwed up her nose like a pug dog. 'Tea…! Why would I want tea? Do you have punch, Mrs Merrick?'

Madame Merrick looked thunderstruck. 'Lady Cavendish …we do not do…that is…I have not yet…*started* to serve punch. We are *soon* to get a punch bowl but at present we have *no* punch…' Her mouth was quivering.

'Tea would be perfect,' cut in Miss Cavendish. 'I would love to take tea and Miss Arbella would too, wouldn't you, Arbella? And I'm sure Mrs Jennings is ready for a dish of tea.' The impatient note in Celia Cavendish's voice was plain to everyone and I looked at her with renewed interest.

The tea duly enjoyed, Madame Merrick got down to business. Elowyn kept scurrying backwards and forwards, fetching the latest fashion plates and heavy rolls of material and with the flourish of a magician, Madame Merrick unrolled her finest silks. Her new supplier had shipped some top-quality fabric and even Lady Cavendish stopped her sulks and sat up, her attention caught at last.

'Of course, I do have one *particularly* fine roll of silk which I have put aside for my most *esteemed* customer.' Madame Merrick turned to Celia Cavendish and lowered her voice. 'You will know the lady, Miss Cavendish, as she moves in the *highest* circles – and I mean the *very highest*.' She smiled conspiratorially before turning back to Lady Cavendish. 'So perhaps, if you do not mind, Lady Cavendish, I will not show you that roll.'

'But I do mind, Mrs Merrick, I mind very much. Are you saying the future Lady Polcarrow does not deserve the very best of your silks?'

Madame Merrick pretended to look mortified. 'Oh please, do not misunderstand me, Lady Cavendish, it is just that *this* particular silk is very hard to come by. Now the blockade is so effective, few silks of *real* quality are getting through...It is the *finest* Mantua silk, you see, absolutely the *finest*, and therefore *very hard to come by*.' It was masterful; Lady Cavendish demanded to see the silk, insisting they would take it with absolutely no expense spared.

Despite myself, my eyes were drawn once again to Miss Arbella Cavendish. She seemed shy and reserved, letting her mother and cousin do all the talking. She hardly spoke, just nodded and smiled, drinking her tea gracefully. I could not get the feel of her character. I could tell instantly Celia Cavendish was full of spirit, and it was plain to see she found her aunt extremely trying, but Arbella Cavendish seemed strangely distant, staring out of the window more often than looking at the silks. She was very pale and fanned herself frequently, continually seeking the open window for the breeze, if not for the freshness of the air.

The Mantua silk could not fail to impress. As Madame Merrick held up the delicate material and let the silk fall in shimmering folds, Lady Cavendish's eyes feasted with greedy delight. She positively purred. Celia Cavendish clapped her hands in delight. 'Arbella, you're going to look so beautiful. James Polcarrow is a lucky man and when he sees you wearing this beautiful silk, well…'

Mother looked shocked and caught my eye. I wish she had not looked quite so pained. A furious blush began spreading across my face, burning my cheeks. I turned to the bureau, pretending to busy myself with the accounts.

'James Polcarrow doesn't know how lucky he is,' Lady Cavendish retorted waspishly. 'With all her beauty, Arbella could have married a Lord. She could have been a duchess. I'm not saying she's throwing herself away *exactly*, but with all her beauty she should have married a viscount.'

'Mother, please!' It was the first time Arbella Cavendish had spoken and her embarrassment was obvious. Celia Cavendish saw her cousin's discomfort and came to her aid.

'As you're going to look so lovely, I'm going to have to have a new gown, too. I have my eyes on this beautiful blue organza. Aunt Martha, what about you? You and Mother agreed your gown was hopelessly out of date and you need a new gown – if not two. You can go back to Dominica and show them what we're wearing in England these days. Where are those fashion plates, Madame Merrick – the latest ones from France?'

'Huh! France! Why do you want to wear French designs, Celia? Don't you know we are at war with France? Anyway, I'm not going back to Dominica, not for a long time. I shall be needed here. I will take up residence in Polcarrow and will oversee the rebuilding work.'

'Rebuilding? I didn't know Sir James was thinking of rebuilding,' replied Celia.

'Sir James may not yet have thought of rebuilding, but it's quite obvious Arbella cannot possibly live in that hideous, draughty place, crammed so close to the stinking town with the smell of rotting fish on the doorstep. Arbella is used to better things. She'll need a bigger house away from town, on higher ground. We will need a lake and enough parkland to ensure our privacy but at least we shall be nearer to you, Celia – you'd like that, wouldn't you? Not that we expect to spend much time down here in this ridiculous hellhole – no, Sir James will have to buy a London house, too. I can't believe he does not have a London house – but that's so typical of the man. No, I'm in no hurry to return to Dominica – and certainly not until I've made some significant changes.'

Her outburst was met with complete silence. Celia Cavendish looked stunned, Madame Merrick looked distinctly uncomfortable, Mother nervously averted her eyes and Elowyn's jaw was in danger of catching flies. Only Mrs Jennings had been watching Arbella. She saw the colour drain from her face, watched her sway slightly, and rushing from her chair, offered her arm for support. 'Are you alright, Miss Cavendish?' she said, leading her to a chair.

'Yes, quite alright, thank you, Mrs Jennings – only it's rather hot in here.'

'Perhaps you would like some more tea, Miss Cavendish?'

Arbella Cavendish dabbed a handkerchief against her pale forehead and nodded. 'Yes, thank you, Mrs Jennings, if it's not too much bother.'

I had never really understood the fuss about tea but, as we sipped the amber liquid, peace was restored and spirits lifted. Even Lady Cavendish took a dish as she contemplated the Mantua silk. The conversation became lively, at times distinctly jolly. Mother and Elowyn ran backwards and forwards with material, lace and ribbons until the table groaned under the weight of so much choice.

Celia Cavendish persuaded her aunt to order two new gowns, though agreeing on the style of these new gowns was proving difficult. Madame Merrick was quietly cajoling.

'Believe me, Lady Cavendish, *nobody* of high fashion wears a bustle any more – they're quite a thing of the past. Look, waists are getting higher and sleeves are getting narrower...'

'How can you be certain, Mrs Merrick? How do I know these plates are recent?'

'I am right, am I not, Miss Cavendish? Perhaps you can reassure Lady Cavendish this is what *everyone* of fashion is wearing in London.'

Celia Cavendish smiled. 'Yes, indeed! I love the idea that waists are rising. And even if you hate the fashion, just think of the practicalities – with no restraining stays, we ladies can loosen our corsets and no one need know.' She had spoken light-heartedly, but Lady Cavendish looked furious, her eyes narrowing as she glared at her niece. 'I'm sorry, Aunt Martha – I meant only to jest. It's just it would be so liberating not having to wear corsets all the time.'

Madame Merrick intervened, asking Arbella Cavendish if she was ready to be measured. Arbella nodded her consent and Madame Merrick pointed to the fitting room. 'Through here, if you please, Miss Cavendish.'

'Measure her here,' snapped Lady Cavendish, her tone turning decidedly sour.

As if struck, Madame Merrick raised her eyebrows, but Miss Arbella only nodded and smiled. She answered softly, with little enthusiasm, 'I'm happy to be measured anywhere, Madame Merrick.' She seemed indifferent to all the excitement and I found myself getting increasingly angry with her. It seemed her cousin was more excited than she was.

'You must make your choice, Arbella. Which design is it to be?'

Arbella Cavendish pointed to the second fashion plate and Madame Merrick began frowning with concentration as she wielded her tape measure, her deft fingers darting backwards and forwards like butterflies. Standing on the stool, suspended in air, a shaft of sun striking her blonde hair, Arbella Cavendish looked even more like an angel. Everything about her was radiant and delicate and my stomach tightened. She was looking down at me and, reluctantly, I caught her eye. I have never seen such a look of happiness and when she smiled her shy smile, I felt I was being bathed in honey.

Madame Merrick put down her tape measure. Lady Cavendish struggled to her feet, heaving herself out of the chair in order to see the finished sketch. She pointed to the measurements written alongside. 'You'd better widen the waist and add width to the bosom.'

Madame Merrick looked horrified. 'Lady Cavendish...*my* measurements are *never* wrong.'

'That may be the case but Miss Arbella has been ill these past months. The long sea voyage has not been kind to her – she's had terrible sickness. But that's now ended and her appetite has increased – quite considerably, it would seem, and I'm glad to see she is regaining her fuller figure – men do not like a skinny woman, Mrs Merrick.'

Madame Merrick shrugged her shoulders, 'I suppose I could...'

Lady Cavendish cut her short. 'What I am saying is that her gown should err on the side of looseness, rather than tightness. Therefore more allowance round the bosom, Mrs Merrick, and a corresponding loosening of the waist, *if* you please, or we will go elsewhere.'

Madame Merrick looked astonished. Celia Cavendish glanced at Arbella who, lifting her quivering chin, turned her back to everyone in the room. Only Elowyn remained oblivious to the tension. She was intent on sorting the lace from the ribbon and was carefully separating the threads. She was growing very particular about how the material was to be stored. She liked everything to be just so, and it was obvious Madame Merrick's untidy rolls were beginning to annoy her.

Chapter Thirty-three

Madame Merrick watched the ladies depart, curtseying deeply and smiling happily. She nodded quite particularly to Mrs Jennings, who glanced backwards out of the carriage as it jolted across the courtyard. She even managed a small wave from the top of the steps before crossing the room in great haste, making directly for the bottom drawer of her desk. Opening it quickly, she took out what looked like a very expensive bottle of French brandy and three rather finely cut crystal glasses. Uncorking the bottle, she poured a generous portion into all three glasses.

'There are times when only brandy will do,' she said, handing Mother one of the glasses. She turned to me. 'Will you join us, Miss Pengelly? Or does all that rightful indignation of yours forbid you a small celebration?'

I smiled, 'Are we celebrating or recovering?'

'Celebrating, of course, Miss Pengelly,' said Madame Merrick, downing the contents of her glass in one gulp, 'although I will concede Lady Cavendish is a trifle *trying*.'

With steady hands, she poured more brandy and raised her glass. 'Let us drink to the health of the future Lady Polcarrow.' Mother raised her glass and, she too, finished her drink in one gulp. Mother never drank brandy.

'I could not ask for anything more...' Madame Merrick said, taking out a delicately embroidered handkerchief to dab her eyes. 'Have you ever seen such *rare* beauty? Lady Polcarrow will be my new patroness and everyone will want to emulate her...and Miss Celia Cavendish – though not quite such a beauty – is so knowledgeable about fashion. That organza she chose is my absolute *finest* and she spotted it straight away...but then it is in her blood...she has true *breeding* you see. Her grandfather – on her mother's side – is an *earl* and her uncle is a *marquis*. You are either born to quality or not, and she is, very much so. Miss Pengelly, will you not celebrate my success?'

'To the success of your business,' I said, raising my glass, 'long may you prosper, Madame Merrick.'

The brandy was smooth, burning my throat. I had tasted brandy many times as Father always celebrated a launch with a glass of brandy. I would sit by his chair, watching the flames leap in the fire and sip the fiery liquid, feeling hot on the outside and warm on the inside. But the thought of drinking a toast to the Cavendishes galled me.

'Madame Merrick, you shouldn't have to fawn like that,' I said, before I could stop myself. 'You've more finesse in your little finger then Lady Cavendish has in her whole body. She's overbearingly rude and you deserve better. I hate to see you treated like that by a woman who has no merit.'

Mother was leaning against the table, two red spots, the size of plums, glowing like beacons on her cheeks and more hair than usual escaping from under her bonnet. She looked so happy. 'But you're wrong, my dear,' she said, her eyes shining, 'Lady Cavendish has great merit, because for every gown she buys, we'll need at least three gown's worth of fabric.' She stifled a giggle. 'Madame Merrick's set to make a profit out of Lady Cavendish and that can only be seen as merit.'

Madame Merrick dabbed her eyes. It had been the day she had long dreamt of and I decided to leave the two of them together. They had already begun fussing over the designs and were busy collecting together the chosen fabrics, when Madame Merrick's voice suddenly rang across the room. 'What *are* you doing, Elowyn?'

I looked round, anxious at the sudden change of mood. Elowyn was rolling away the fabrics. She had finished tidying the lace and was standing with the sorted rolls and several slips of paper on the table in front of her. In one hand she held a pen, in the other a measuring yard. She was writing on the slips of paper before pinning them to the rolls.

'I'm gettin' a little bit bothered 'bout not knowing how much's left on the roll,' she said in a matter-of-fact tone. 'So I'm measurin' how much we've got *left* and pinnin' a note on the end. That way…if we take away the amount we use, we'll know how much we've got left – we'll not need to measure it each time.'

Madame Merrick looked speechless. Holding her lorgnettes beneath her perfectly arched brows, she stared at

Elowyn before turning to Mother. Mother shrugged her shoulders, biting her bottom lip. 'Rosehannon's been teaching Elowyn a few calculations,' she said softly.

Madame Merrick flinched. 'Now, why does that *not* surprise me, Mrs Pengelly? I knew it would be only a matter of time before that daughter of yours took it upon herself to incite *sedition* and *riot* among my women. Calculations…for goodness sake, whatever will she think of next?'

But whether it was the brandy or just the light, the eyes that turned on me seemed less like a hawk and more like a dove. And whether it was the brandy, or Mother's smiling face, I found myself responding with a glow of warmth. Suddenly, inexplicably, I was filled with a flood of affection for this extraordinary woman who had become so very important to us both.

At the cottage there was no sign of Father or Jenna. The kitchen door was ajar and though a lardy cake stood temptingly on the kitchen table, I left it untasted, crossing the back yard instead, to search the cliff path, worried that Father would tire himself if he went too far. Almost immediately I saw him standing on the cliff top, facing the sea, a letter in his hand.

'I never gave up hope of smellin' the sea again,' he said, his back to me. 'I clung to hope even at my most desperate. Stubbornness – that's what most people call it – but I call it hope. We must always have dreams.' I felt a change in him. He was standing tall, his head held high, and I noticed he had come without his stick. 'Aye, Rose, what it is to have friends in high places!'

My heart sank. *He knows about the log pool*, I thought.

'It seems the slow wheels of justice can be speeded up if you're the Vice Sheriff of Cornwall or one of the most influential attorneys in the land. These people don't like to wait, so I'm in your debt, Rose – we're to benefit from your powerful friends.'

'How so, Father?'

He waved the letter, which caught the breeze and flapped in his hand. 'Roskelly's been found guilty of murder, aye, and guilty of false accusation, false witness, violence and assault against James Polcarrow. He'll hang and James Polcarrow has a full pardon and takes back his rightful title – not that he hasn't already! Your friend has enough money and influence to do what he likes.'

'He's not my friend, not any more than he's yours,' I replied quietly. 'What news of Mr Tregellas?'

'Tregellas turned king's evidence. He swore he heard Robert Roskelly admit to murder – like I told you, they've struck a deal. He's been found guilty of theft, violence and perjury, but he's not to hang. He's got fourteen years' transportation and, like I said, he's set for Botany Bay.'

My spirits soared. 'That means you're cleared of all wrong.'

He turned towards me and I realised he had been struggling with his emotions. His eyes, too long dull and expressionless, were glistening with the warmth and vigour I had always loved. He gave me the letter. 'Aye, we can go home. We can go home to Coombe House and everythin' can get back to normal.'

The letter from Sir George was written in a close hand. With tears blurring my eyes, I found it hard to read. The first page outlined the trials and the verdicts, the second thanked us for our written evidence, telling us he was glad he had not had to call us as witnesses. The third page thanked us for our patience, wished us all good health, assured us of his best attention and begged that if there was anything further he could do, we only had to ask. I handed the letter back.

'What about his fees?' I said, knowing Father's freedom would not come cheaply. The boatyard would not make a profit for several months and if Sir George's fees were too high, Father would be in danger of being sent straight back to the debtors' gaol.

Father reached into his jacket and produced another letter. As he held it out, I almost snatched it from his hand. I unfolded the single page, not believing what I read. Sir George had overseen the sale of the cutter, bidding had been fierce, and the final sum had reached six hundred and fifty guineas. All the money, minus sale expenses, had been deposited into the bank in Father's name. There would be no fees.

'No fees? That's impossible.'

'Course it's impossible – what attorney would ever waive his fees?' Father's voice was bitter. 'No, our fees have all been paid and we both know who's paid them.'

I felt giddy, nauseous, my stomach tightening. If I had only known, I would never have asked for the creek – as if I was not grateful enough. James Polcarrow knew all along Father had enough money to buy the creek and could bid for it himself.

'And can we return home?' I managed to say.

'Aye, even after our debts are paid, we'll be in pocket. Coombe House was falsely taken from us and we're to have the lease returned. Course, I'll repay Sir James every farthin' for the fees, but for the moment we've enough to see us straight.'

We linked arms, turning towards the cottage. James Polcarrow had cleared our debts, restored Father's fortunes and promised me the log pool. He had even redressed the wrong he had done to Ben. I should have been smiling, laughing, running ahead to tell Jenna, but Arbella's smile still lodged in my mind, filling me with a sadness I could not shake off.

At the gate Father paused. 'There's an election meetin' in the town hall tomorrow night, will you come with me? It'll be like old times.'

Like old times. I took a deep breath and squeezed his arm. Let them have each other. Let Arbella Cavendish have her happiness and let James Polcarrow deserve her. But one thing was certain. I would work day and night to free us from our obligation.

Chapter Thirty-four

Thursday 15th August 1793 7:00 a.m.

I woke to the sound of Father's angry voice filtering through the floorboards. His words were indistinct but the fury evident. Throwing my shawl round my shoulders, I crept downstairs to find Jenna with her ear pressed against the door. 'He's that cross, I fear for Mrs Pengelly!' she whispered.

'What's he saying?'

'Says she can't go to Madame Merrick's no more...says she doesn't need to work now ye've yer standing back and he's forbidding her to go – says she's to have nothing more to do with that ridiculous woman.'

'Oh no! Poor Mother!'

'She's pleading with him but he'll not be moved – says her place's at home now. Says he never wants her to work again... not now. Poor Mrs Pengelly – she's that happy there...she loves her sewing. It'll break her heart.'

I squeezed next to Jenna, pressing my own ear against the door. Mother was sobbing. 'I can't bear to hear her cry, Jenna.'

'Nor me.'

I pulled my shawl tighter round my shoulders and pushed the door. Father was standing with his back to the grate, Mother on the chair by the fire, her handkerchief held against her face. Kneeling by her feet, I took hold of her trembling hands and turned to Father.

'Don't look at me like that, Rose – this has nothin' to do with you. I don't see why your mother's makin' such a fuss. She's no need to wear herself out, sewin' all hours, strainin' her eyes, hurtin' her fingers. I'll provide for my family. She needs have nothin' more to do with Madame Merrick.'

His words were spoken harshly and I felt Mother wince, the tremor in her hands increasing as I held them in mine. I looked down, worried Father would see the anger in my eyes. His dislike for Madame Merrick had turned to jealous hatred and I knew if I was not careful I could make things worse. But I was too cross to hold my tongue.

'Madame Merrick's doing her best in a difficult world and you know better than most how hard it is out there,' I said, as calmly as I could. 'Worse still, she's a woman on her own, fighting against great odds…but she was there for us when we needed her most and she needs us now. Mrs Mellows is ill, Josie has been called to look after her sister and Elowyn has only just started, so Mother is vital to her.'

I could tell Father was listening to me and I tried to keep the anger from my voice. I felt indignant he had not listened to Mother, hardly letting her speak, as if she had no voice. 'Yesterday, Madame Merrick took orders for four new dresses and without Mother she won't be able to fulfil her order. Everything could be lost – her hard-won reputation will collapse and her business will fail. It would be like Mr Scantlebury deserting us when we needed him most.'

Father snorted in contempt and I could see he was about to dismiss my comparison, but somehow his look seemed to spur me on. 'You wouldn't desert any fellow worker who needed you, Father, so you shouldn't expect Mother to desert Madame Merrick. At least let her finish these gowns – they'll take no more than two weeks.' As long as he never found out whom the gowns were for, I thought we stood a chance.

'I see you take your mother's side,' he said, looking from one of us to the other, his face stony. It was the first time I had stood up to him for Mother's sake and I knew he was thinking the same. 'You've two weeks, Eva,' he said at last, 'then you finish with that place.'

He slammed the door behind him and we breathed a sigh of relief. Mother's smile was weak, but the hand that gripped mine was as hard as iron.

I deliberated all day, deciding, in the end, to wear my new sprig gown to the election rally, even though I knew it would infuriate Father. Somehow I was prepared to face his disapproval. Jenna was spending an extraordinarily long time coaxing my hair into compliant ringlets, but even I could see the benefit of my patience.

'There ain't another woman in the whole of Cornwall with yer beauty.'

'There is,' I replied sadly. 'There's someone with far greater beauty.'

'That's nonsense and well ye know. Ye'll turn every head – they'll be drooling like dogs over a bone. Did I tell ye Mrs Pengelly's got me some material? I'm going to make meself a new gown.'

'You deserve so much more, Jenna.'

I entered the parlour expecting a furious reaction. Father's face turned ashen, his eyes hardened. I took a deep breath, my words at the ready. 'They must think we prosper, Father. The town needs to know you're back in business.'

He said nothing, just picked up his hat and headed for the door. Will Tregony was waiting to take us to the harbour and, as we climbed into the cart, the slanting rays of the evening sun caught my dress. Disloyalty to Father still tainted my enjoyment of it, but it was not vanity prompting me to wear it. I had taken Madame Merrick's advice – we had to look prosperous. We needed to show the town that Pengelly Boatyard was back in Father's hands.

The town hall was already crowded; grooms calling out, carriages jostling for position. Arms were waving, whips lashing, coachmen growing increasingly frustrated by the groups of bystanders blocking the way.

'Are you feeling well enough for this, Father?'

'Course,' he replied. 'Just like the old days – you and me against the corruption in our town.' He smiled, putting out his arm and I could see he had forgiven me. But as we pushed our way through the crowd, my earlier courage began to fail and I saw myself for what I really was — ridiculously over-dressed. My dress was too bright, my hair too formal, my bonnet too fancy. What was I thinking? I wanted to turn back, but Father was gripping my arm, ushering me towards the door.

The hall was full and unbearably stuffy. Rush lights were lit against the walls and candles were burning in the over-head chandeliers. I could hardly breathe through the tobacco smoke clogging the air. I felt terribly out of place, growing increasingly anxious for a place to sit. Chairs had been placed down a central aisle, but most were already taken. The noise was deafening and I looked about, unsure where to go.

A gradual hush spread through the room, people stop-ping mid-sentence and looking in our direction. It began to become obvious we were the centre of their attention, everyone staring in amazement. It was horrible, quite the worst thing to happen. Two men were approaching us — Mr Mitchell and Mr Hoskins, the bank manager, who must have known Father's money had just been deposited into his bank. Both were Corporation men and I held my breath, hoping Father would bide his tongue. We had no reason to be there, Father was a leaseholder not a freeholder, but to my amaze-ment both men bowed to us in turn. Mr Hoskins even offered me his arm.

'Miss Pengelly, allow me, there are seats free at the front. Let me see you settled into one of them.' I took his arm, somehow walking up the aisle as if it was an every day occurrence but my legs were shaking and my heart racing.

Everyone was nodding or bowing in our direction and I saw the calculating glint in their eyes. I was right to wear my new gown.

'Course, this is all nonsense,' Father whispered as we sat down. 'They're not pleased to see me back, they just want to distance themselves from William Tregellas and Robert Roskelly. They've as much to hide and they're scared it'll come to light.'

Father had dressed with care. He was wearing a new, brown, corduroy jacket and matching breeches. The buckles on his shoes shone, as did the buttons on his waistcoat. His necktie was plain but neatly tied and his hat sat comfortably over his new wig. He looked well, despite his cough. His eyes had lost their sunken look, his cheeks had filled and although he was still far too thin, he looked like a man who was ready to resume his role in life.

But it was not so much his physical wellbeing that worried me, more the absence of his old humour. He had lost the ability to laugh and was even now scowling across at Thomas Nickels, who was talking to Mr Drew, the new warehouse owner, and Mr Warburton who had been recently appointed as burgess to the Corporation.

'I see Nickels' amongst friends,' he muttered.

A commotion drew everyone's attention. We were too near the front to see the election party as they walked up the aisle but, as they reached the makeshift stage and began climbing the steps, they passed so close I saw them clearly. Leaning heavily on a stick, Sir Charles Cavendish ascended with difficulty, puffing and blowing in his agitation. Following him, was a middle-aged man, elaborately dressed in a blue frockcoat. He heaved his huge belly up the stairs, his ornate wig sitting heavily on his head, his face as red as Sir Charles's.

'That's George Wyndham – the new candidate,' murmured Father. 'Just like the last – a business associate and long-term friend of Sir Charles Cavendish.'

Behind him walked a younger man whose elaborate attire seemed more fitting for a court occasion than a town bi-election. He was tall and haughty; his bored and disdainful expression hardly helped by the huge mole on his chin. He stood staring down at the chair he was offered, grimacing at the thought of having to sit on it. Lips pursed, eyebrows raised, he flicked his lace handkerchief across the chair. Still unconvinced, he ventured down with great disdain, lifting his coat tails behind him, sitting straight-backed and uncomfortable as he laid his cane across his knees.

'He'd whip us like he whips his servants,' Father whispered. 'Who is he?'

'Viscount Vallenforth – father's the Earl of Mount Eddscombe.'

A gradual murmur replaced the respectful silence which greeted the arrival of the election party, everyone staring at the empty chair remaining on the platform. 'There needs be at least one other candidate – even if the whole thing's rigged,' whispered Father. 'Wyndham will get elected, but it looks better if they can *say* the seat was contested!'

The hum grew louder. Mr Wyndham smiled confidently at Sir Charles, who looked down at his fob watch and nodded to the town clerk. No other candidate was needed, it seemed, so the town clerk jumped up, clearing his voice to start proceedings. Suddenly, the door of the hall flung open and the sound of hurried footsteps rushed up the aisle. Mr Wyndham's jaw dropped, Sir Charles gripped the edge of his chair.

James Polcarrow bounded up the steps, taking them two at a time. He stood, impeccably dressed, though slightly breathless, glaring across the stage at the astonished mayor. The hall fell silent. 'Mr Dunwoody may not see fit to contest the election,' he said, looking pointedly at Sir Charles, 'but I do. I seek to represent this town, just like my father did before me and my grandfather did before him.'

Chapter Thirty-five

The hall erupted, everyone shouting at once. Sir Charles's fury was evident. Summoning over the mayor, he began shaking his head, forcibly banging his stick on the floor. Mr Wyndham's face went from red to purple and even Viscount Vallenforth showed his displeasure by twitching his cane. The shouts grew stronger. A number of men started stamping their feet, waving their papers high in the air. The more the noise level rose, the more hounded the mayor looked. Still shaking his head, Sir Charles was made to concede and Sir James Polcarrow took possession of the empty chair.

'This is better,' I heard Father say, but I could not reply. James Polcarrow sat down, looking quickly up to survey the hall, and I felt the blood rush to my cheeks. The bright ribbons on my bonnet were acting like a beacon and his eyes were drawn straight to me. I saw them widen in surprise and looked quickly away.

Viscount Vallenforth got to his feet and the room went silent. 'Gentlemen,' he said in a bored tone, 'as a representative of His Majesty's government, I am here to endorse the government's candidate, Mr George Wyndham – a man with impeccable credentials.' With that, he sat down and replaced the cane across his knees.

Sir Charles must have been expecting a longer speech. He seemed caught unprepared. The evening was obviously turning out very badly and his displeasure was evident. He hesitated, frowning at the crowd, as if waiting for something. At length, a single cry went up. 'You'll see us right, Sir Charles.' It was a half-hearted cry, with all the insincerity of a paid supporter.

'Not enough grog as yet,' muttered Father with a hint of a smile.

'Gentlemen, I have known Mr Wyndham for over twenty years,' began Sir Charles. 'He is a man of great courage and great vision – clearly a man of business.' There were murmurs of approval, Sir Charles lifting his hand as if to stop them. 'His rise to prominence lies in his ability to predict the future of our country. He believes, as do I, that we must steer this country to greater prosperity.' A roar of approval made Sir Charles nod in agreement.

Father leant towards me. 'I'm surprised he didn't say Mr Wyndham could walk on water.'

'Hush, Father, or you'll be arrested and thrown back in gaol.' Jugs of ale were being distributed round the hall. Father took one, raising it to me in mock salute.

'To our Mr Wyndham,' he said, smiling with his old sarcasm.

I felt suddenly tense, glancing up at Sir James, anxious to

see if he had seen Father's mocking salute. For some reason, I could not bear for him to think ill of Father. But Sir James was staring straight ahead, his finely chiselled profile set in a firm, unyielding frown.

Mr Wyndham got to his feet, motioning to a servant to bring a decanter and glass. The contents consumed, he wiped his mouth with the back of his hand and began speaking in an unfamiliar accent. I believe he came from the Midlands.

'Viscount Vallenforth, Sir Charles, what's a man to say after such praise has been lavished on him? But it's true. My prosperity is well known – and my prosperity will lead to your prosperity. It's no secret I own a vast number of shipyards and a vast number of ships. It's no secret I've a vast number of contacts. Contacts I'll use for this town, gentlemen. You'll grow rich. You'll prosper. You'll reap huge rewards in having me as your representative in Parliament. *Contacts for Contracts* – those are my words and that's my election promise.'

An excited uproar met these closing remarks. Everyone except Father and I jumped up, clapping their hands, stomping their feet; greed and self-interest showing on every face. Mr Wyndham smiled, holding up his hand to quieten the crowd though it was obvious he was lapping it up like a cat with cream.

Father remained unimpressed. 'Sir Charles best be careful – he'll be late for the dinner he's hostin' for the squires and freeholders. There's no more than a handful here who can claim voting rights. It's a sham and till we get the vote, it'll remain a sham. Universal suffrage must come, Rose – it has to.'

Mr Drew and Mr Warleggan raced up the steps to shake Mr Wyndham's hand. Everyone was slapping each other's backs, congratulating themselves for their very good fortune. Jugs of ale were once more passed round the room. The noise was unbearable, the smell of stale sweat beginning to be intolerable. I looked at Father, alarmed at how flushed he had become. He was sweating profusely, his eyes feverish, and I decided we should leave. I looked for the easiest way out, but my eyes once again caught those of James Polcarrow.

He was staring at me with the same look he had given me on the cliff top – that look which held such pain. I felt winded, unable to breathe, as if a knife was ripping through me, making me reel. I stared back into those reproachful eyes, my heart hammering. He seemed so hurt, so alone, his eyes accusing me of deserting him. I had to tear my eyes away.

The mayor and town clerk were trying to bring some order to the proceedings, Sir Charles and Mr Wyndham both consulting their fob watches. Father shook his head and would not hear of leaving. 'No, Rose, not as things are gettin' interesting.'

James Polcarrow stood to address the crowd, his face as dark as thunder. The effect was immediate, the fury in his face making even the paid hecklers hold their tongues. Eyebrows rose and an expectant silence filled the hall. The mayor cast a look of desperate resignation at Sir Charles and cleared his throat. 'Gentlemen, if you could resume your seats, our next candidate to speak is Sir James Polcarrow.'

James Polcarrow began slowly. 'Gentlemen, I've been away

from this town for eleven years and on my return I find the port in decline and the spirit of its people broken. I find poverty the like of which we have never seen before. I find dwellings fit only for rats and I find corruption and self-interest in those who have thrust themselves into positions of power.'

A shock of disapproval greeted his words but James Polcarrow stood resolute. 'What have you done to this town, to its people?' he said, raising his voice to be heard. 'Or should I ask what have you done *for* this town? I'll tell you what you've done – you've done nothing but serve your own interests. We are blessed with one of the largest natural harbours in Cornwall yet the port is in decline.'

He waited for the outcry to die down. 'It is woefully under-used – merchants cannot capitalise on its deep waters; the roads are nearly impassable. Why haven't you invested in a new turnpike, or a canal to Truro? Or new quays? Why haven't you grasped the opportunity that the mines offer? Importing coal or exporting copper? Why no trade in lime-stone? So many lost opportunities.'

He held out his finger, sweeping it along the lines of chairs, seemingly pointing at every man present. 'The answer lies in your own self-interest. The Corporation has grown greedy and, while you prosper, the town starves. While you dine on suckling pig, the town's children scratch limpets from the rocks.' A cry of outrage filled the hall, almost everyone jumping to their feet, clenching their fists. Amidst all the stamping and waving of papers, Father's colour drained. James Polcarrow took no notice of the angry shouts but lifted his hand, his voice calm above the protest. 'Perhaps those of you who protest so loudly are members of the lucky few who benefit from gifts of favour?' The mood had changed. A number of reddened faces glared back at James Polcarrow but there were those who had started to smile.

Father was not one. 'What's the man up to?' he said. 'Gamekeepers don't turn poacher!'

I could not reply. A deep hollowness filled me, a terrible, terrible longing.

James Polcarrow stared down at the members of the Corporation, 'Perhaps you hope to prosper from the new warehouse that will store your salt? The Mediterranean trade is threatened and our fishermen are looking to sell their pilchards to the Indies. They'll need twice as much salt to sustain the longer voyage and you'll be happy to supply it – at your own price.'

Sir Charles Cavendish could take no more. Grabbing his cane, he heaved himself out of the chair. Mr George Wyndham likewise got to his feet, followed by Viscount Vallenforth. 'This is preposterous,' he fumed. 'I'll not listen to another word.' He turned to the mayor, who looked just as furious. 'Finish this debacle at once.'

James Polcarrow stopped the mayor with a look. 'I know I keep you from an important dinner engagement, Sir Charles, but I'm not finished and if you leave now, Mr Wyndham will never know of what I am about to accuse him.'

George Wyndham's face was purple with rage. 'There's nothing you can accuse me of,' he retorted, his eyes showing the fear his voice belied.

James Polcarrow stood tall. He shrugged his shoulders, his face turning stony. 'You can either stay to defend yourself, or you can leave me to what I have to say. Either way, I've not finished.'

Chapter Thirty-six

The three men resumed their seats, knowing the mood had changed. Hushed whispers and incredulous faces stared back at James Polcarrow, but there were more smiles than frowns.

His voice soared across the hall, 'Your election promise may be *contacts for contracts*, but will you really share your boatyard contracts with the ship-builders of Fosse? And if you *did* bring our boatyards commissions, would you pay the highest rate or keep the cost deliberately low so that the excellent ships they build can be sold on at a huge profit?' I heard Father's sharp intake of breath. He was staring at Sir James in amazement.

'Would your new contracts be for warehouses to profit from the West Indies sugar trade? Why are we not putting our efforts into refining our own sugar beet that grows so well on this land? Others are trying it, so why not us? Why should sugar merchants and warehouse owners profit, while the labouring poor starve through want of employment?'

A murmur of assent filled the hall; heads were nodding. James Polcarrow's voice turned hard. 'Because Mr Wyndham will profit from the warehouses, just as he profits from the manufacturers who forge his leg irons…from his shipyards that build his slave ships…from the plantations that break the back of every slave that toils under his remorseless lash. Because that is how he makes his money and that, to me, is abhorrent. I will not sanction slavery. That is why I stand against him.'

No need for paid hecklers or false supporters. I had never been in such an angry crowd. James Polcarrow sat in his chair, glaring ahead, his jaw clenched. Father was trying his best to be heard above the now-deafening shouts and I could only just make out what he was saying. 'That's done it – he's just thrown away any chance he might've had. Those who were waverin' will be against him now. It may delay their dinner, but they'll finish him.'

Raising his hand, George Wyndham stood motioning the room to be quiet. 'So, gentlemen, it seems we've an abolitionist among our ranks,' he said, with evident enjoyment. 'Sir James forgets his duty to his country. He'd stem the prosperity of the very country he seeks to represent. Prosperity that builds schools and hospitals. He'd join the lily-livered dissenters and radicals and campaign against the very thing that drives our glorious country to greater prosperity. He'd seek to ruin the economy that spurs our industries and widens our trade and hand it all to the Portuguese or to the Spaniards – or most likely, the *French*.'

Mr Wyndham stabbed his pointed finger in the air. 'He'd hand it all to the *French* who would steal our prosperity. Stop exporting guns and manufacturing will collapse. Trade will cease. There'd be no cotton, no sugar, no rum and no more tobacco. In short, the government would lose the tax that pays our navy to defend these very shores against our enemies.'

Beads of sweat glistened on his brow, his face flushed. I thought his anger might choke him. Wiping his handkerchief across his face, he stepped forward, inviting the audience into his confidence. 'I'd not vote for a man who puts the welfare of savages above the safety of his country. Who puts my wife and children in danger. These slaves, gentlemen, are born to slavery. They labour under benevolent masters who have only their best interest at heart. They're well looked after... they have employment – a better situation than many of our own labouring poor. They thrive in the heat of a vertical sun. Slaves have been with us since Abraham walked this earth and if the Church approves of slavery, why can't Sir James Polcarrow?'

He sat down amongst an ovation of cheers. Sir Charles Cavendish gave a nod of approval and even Viscount Vallenforth stirred himself enough to turn in his direction. The town clerk stood up to end proceedings but James Polcarrow was already on his feet, holding up his hands.

'Man's inhumanity to man sickens me,' he replied, with quiet loathing. 'I've seen first-hand the brutality of your so-called benevolent masters. I've burnt in the midday sun watching men beaten to death and woman abused. The slaves you speak of are born with the right to be free, with the same right to freedom that you were born with – but you have enslaved them.' He turned to face the hall, his face full of recrimination, 'And you have enslaved them, because every one of you who does not rise against the slave trade is implicit in their slavery. So, yes, I am an abolitionist and proud to call myself one. Nor will I stop, until every slave ship ceases its heinous trade – until every shackle is broken and every slave freed. I'll not eat a spoonful of sugar, or drink a drop of rum. Nor will I chew or smoke tobacco and I entreat those of you with any decency, or humanity, left in you, to do the same.'

His tone held both accusation and despair. He sat down, staring at the stunned crowd.

A cry rang across the hall. 'God love you, Sir James.' Sir Charles and Mr Wyndham flinched, but it was a sole voice and died quickly on the speaker's lips.

Members of the Corporation rushed to help the scowling Mr Wyndham down the stairs. Men bowed and cleared the way for Sir Charles Cavendish to leave the hall. Alone on the platform, James Polcarrow remained sitting in his chair, seemingly drained of all emotion. I could not speak, the lump in the back of my throat made me want to choke. He seemed so alone. Of all the people in the hall, I was the only one who knew his suffering. I had felt his scars. I had smoothed my hands over his jagged wounds, touching man's inhumanity to man.

Father got up and stretched his back. 'That was a pretty speech from your friend. Course, it means nothing. Total hypocrisy. He lives off the back of labourers so what's different? Give him longer and he'll revert to type. They always do.'

Chapter Thirty-seven

Father sat at his desk, rustling the pages of his newspaper. Mr Scantlebury looked up and caught my eye. I thought he would be delighted Father had returned to the yard, but he seemed preoccupied, even a little distant.

'Nothin' amazes me any more,' said Father looking over the top of his newspaper, his glasses balancing on the end of his nose. 'Why's Sir Charles throwin' his clout behind Mr Wyndham and not his future nephew-in-law? Even if the damn fool's declared himself an abolitionist, blood's thicker when it comes to family – never more when you've neighbourin' estates.'

When neither Mr Scantlebury nor I said anything, Father resumed his reading. He was clearly in a buoyant mood even if he was more interested in the affairs of the town than those of the yard. After a short pause, he once again peered over the outspread pages, 'What's even stranger is why Sir George and Lady Cavendish persist with the engagement of their daughter to Sir James Polcarrow? Who'd want to marry their daughter off to a man who's just ruined his political chances? Why persist in the marriage? I've heard that daughter of theirs could snare anyone she wanted.' He folded his paper, 'Fortunately, it's not my problem – I've more pressin' matters to attend to.' He reached for his coat and hat and walked towards the door. 'Tell your mother I'll not be home tonight. I may be gone a few days.'

'Where're you going?' I called after his retreating back.

'Mevagissey,' he shouted over his shoulder. He started to whistle as he crossed the yard. I looked straight at Mr Scantlebury and was not reassured by the look on his face.

'He'll not be reasoned with. He's taken a notion we should put up our labour costs. Says it's time all yards charge the same – unity of brotherhood – he calls it. What one yard charges, all should charge – brotherhood, fraternity and equality – somethin' like that.'

I caught my breath. 'What does he intend to do?'

'He's for starting a Friendly Society…wants everyone to commit to chargin' higher costs.'

'But someone will always undercut – someone will build for less.'

'Your father says 'tis time working men stand shoulder to shoulder, to protect their rights. *Together is strength* – that's how he put it. He's after a spirit where working men work with each other, not agin' each other.'

'But those commissioning new ships will just refuse to pay higher costs – they'll go elsewhere.'

'Not if the charges are the same. He says we're to withdraw

our labour – if no-one builds boats till they get the price they demand, they'll have no choice but pay.'

My unease was turning to alarm. What was Father thinking? 'But, Mr Scantlebury, the yard can't survive even a short period of no work. Father will be arrested for inciting riot and we'll go bankrupt – all we've worked for – all our plans – your new brig – everything will be lost.'

'Since he fought off bankruptcy, people think very highly of your father – they believe he knows what he's about, and your father can be very persuasive – you know that.'

The thought that anything could jeopardise the yard and threaten our future made my stomach sicken. Father could have no idea what he was about to unleash, no idea what poverty Mother and I had lived through. And the fact he had not discussed it with me worried me even further – it was not like Father to be so secretive. There was a time when I would have been the first to know, and his abrupt departure meant I could no longer tell him about the log pool. I had been hoping to persuade him to come to the auction, but now I would have to go alone. I just hoped Jenna had remembered her brother's clothes.

Noise in the yard attracted my attention and I looked up to see wagons laden with varnish and paint pull heavily to a stop. Tom hurried to supervise the unloading, checking each consignment, carefully marking everything off against his order sheet. Mr Scantlebury stood beside me. 'His apprenticeship's been the making of him,' he said softly.

'One day he'll be every bit as good as his uncle.'

'As long as we've a yard.'

'We must have a yard, Mr Scantlebury,' I replied firmly. 'What would you say if I could get us a log pool?'

Thomas Scantlebury's eyes crinkled. 'Ye gladden my heart, Miss Rosehannon – ye always do. ''Twould mean a ready supply of logs and we'd buy when the price was low but let's be honest, lass…how will ye get us a log pool?'

Chapter Thirty-eight

Mother and Jenna were meeting Mrs Munroe to discuss our return to Coombe House and were not expected back until later. Father was in Mevagissey, so I had plenty of time to dress in my borrowed jacket and breeches. This time, I took much greater care, using several more pins to keep my hair in place, even rubbing a piece of blackened coal above my lips and around my jaw. It was far from perfect but it took the pallor from my chin and with my hat pulled down and my collar pulled up, I thought it would do quite nicely.

Thomas Warren, with his sideways looks and weasel eyes, had set my alarm bells ringing. I did not like the man, I did not trust him and I needed to know if my instincts were right. But I was late – the auction would start at eight so I had twenty minutes to get to the Ship Inn.

Boarding the ferry proved no problem but halfway across the river, the sea mist, hovering at the entrance of the harbour, began creeping silently across the water. Even Joshua Tregen stopped his banter and began to concentrate as he rowed through the fading visibility. Dark hulls loomed from nowhere and muffled shouts began echoing across the water. I began to take heart. Whereas this sea fog was the last thing most people wanted, it was exactly what I needed to slip unseen into the auction.

Most auctions took place in the Ship Inn. I had been to an auction before when Father had bid for a hoist, so I was confident I knew where to go. The lamps shone like solid spheres of light, beckoning me from across the square and I made my way quickly through the thickening mist, grateful not to be seen.

Pausing only briefly to draw courage, I opened the heavy oak door and made my way down the corridor to where at least thirty men crushed into a tiny back room. It was unbearably smoky but dark and suited my purpose. The shutters were firmly closed, lanterns casting small pools of light and, as my eyes grew accustomed to the dark, I grew confident I would remain undetected. A number of men had already taken off their jackets and my borrowed clothes felt hot and heavy. Perspiration ran down my back. The man beside me peered at his fob watch – five minutes to go and, as I dodged his sharp elbow, I peered through the half-darkness, searching for Thomas Warren.

I have always been glad of my height, but as I stood on my toes to scan the room my view was blocked by a huge man standing in front of me. He had great bulky shoulders, a shaven head and a tattooed snake creeping up his neck from beneath his collar. The snake was poised to strike and even in the half-light I could see the venom in its eyes.

Most of the men were facing away and, as I searched for Thomas Warren, my anxiety grew. A voice from the front announced the auction was starting, so I squeezed further forward, peering at the faces around me. Some I recognised as tradesmen, but most were strangers. The dimness of the light and thick smoke made it hard to make out faces, but my heart leapt as I saw Thomas Warren in the furthest corner.

He was sitting at a table, deep in conversation. His companion was smartly dressed, his head bent, his tall hat pointing at the crowd as if to keep us at bay. He looked up and my initial dislike spiralled to hatred. He was Philip Randall, steward of Pendenning Hall, Sir Charles's land agent. Very few people in Fosse or Porthruan could look at him without fear or loathing. His forced eviction had left Jenna's family homeless – he had showed no pity, just trampled his way into their homes and lit the fires. The cottages were in the way of the great park. A lake was to be created; whole families left without homes for the sake of the view.

I tried to think rationally. Thomas Warren and Philip Randall would obviously know each other – they were both powerful men and had been stewards of neighbouring estates for many years, but watching their hunched shoulders and urgent conversation, their deepening scowls and obvious displeasure, I felt increasingly uneasy and ducked behind the man with the tattooed snake, afraid they would see me watching.

'The door, if you please,' a man's voice rang out and the crowd surged forward, stragglers pushing their way into the last remaining spaces. The door slammed and I heard the key turn in the lock.

'You know the rules, gentlemen,' the voice of the auctioneer boomed. 'The door'll remain locked till the auction's completed. It'll stay locked throughout the proceedings an' only be opened after the final bid. All bids must be financially sound, all bids are binding an' must be paid by ten o'clock tomorrow or the sale will be rendered void.'

He was sitting at the table, one hand searching through the many papers strewn in front of him, the other taking hold of a chain which hung from the beam above. One of the lamps was extinguished, making the room even darker and with so many people cramming into the space, I began to feel suffocated. 'First auction is for the freehold of the land known as Tideswell Creek, just upriver from Pont Pill. It comprises the creek an' a small stretch of dense woodland. The creek submerges in the tide an' the land can only be accessed by the river. Gentlemen, I'll start the auction. Is the door locked?'

'Yes, Mr Owen,' came a voice from the dark.

'The rules are those of any candle auction – we'll burn one inch of tallow an' the last bid before the candle's extinguished is the winning bid. This bid will be binding.' A murmur of assent went round the room.

The remaining lamp was extinguished and darkness engulfed us. A flint was struck and the chain rattled, hoisting the candle over our heads. The tiny flame wavered, gradually steadying as it penetrated the darkness above us. Like everyone else, I lifted my eyes to the flickering light. A copper plate had been placed under the candle, hiding it from view, and all I could see was the surrounding glow. Bidders could only guess the rate at which it would burn and I had no idea how long that might be. Twenty minutes, maybe fifteen? Only those at the front had seen the width of the candle and I took heart that Thomas Warren had positioned himself so close to the table.

The first bid came promptly, then the second, then the third. The voices came from the back of the room. Thomas Warren cleared his throat. 'Two guineas,' he shouted.

'Two pounds, ten shillings,' came the responding bid.

'Three guineas,' replied Mr Warren.

'Four guineas,' came the immediate reply.

The room grew silent, everyone staring at the glow of the candle. Shadows danced across the ceiling, dark shapes leapt from the corners. This was a game of nerves – if a person bid too soon he would give away his interest and would raise the price. I only hoped Thomas Warren knew how long to wait.

'Four pounds, ten shillings,' came a voice from the back of the room.

Trickles of sweat ran down my back. My face was burning and I began to regret my decision to use coal dust to darken my chin. The bids seemed to stop. The room was silent.

'Five guineas,' shouted Phillip Randall.

Another bid from the back. 'Six guineas.'

'Seven guineas.' Phillip Randall's reply was instant.

'Eight guineas.' was the immediate response.

The flame floundered and the room plunged into darkness. Murmurs grew louder as everyone peered through the dark. I caught my breath. The copper plate was swallowed by blackness but, as we waited, the faintest light began to show and I stared at the tiny flicker, willing it to glow. The flame spluttered, gained in strength and once again cast eerie shadows in the darkness.

'Nine guineas,' shouted Phillip Randall.

I knew Thomas Warren's token bid would not be repeated. He had no intention of securing the land – he was in league with Phillip Randall who clearly wanted it. The log pool was slipping from my grasp. Frustration welled inside me. I was a woman and counted for nothing. I had no right to property or land. I was nobody. I could do nothing but watch my dream being snatched away.

Why did I not ask Mr Scantlebury to come with me? Anger burnt my cheeks – anger against myself as much as against the injustice of my situation. But I could not, would not, lose this creek. Suddenly, it seemed so simple. I was dressed as a man, I would bid – the slimmest chance, maybe, but I would have to take it. My mind was racing. My timing would have to be perfect. Thomas Warren and Phillip Randall would be alerted and would bid against me. Surely the whole room could hear the thumping of my heart.

I remembered the huer's hut when Jim and I huddled round the candle. We had an inch of candle and I remembered it flared just before it died. Did all candles flare at their dying? If they did, I would watch for a change of brightness. I strained my eyes, knowing if I called too soon, all would be lost. Then I saw it – the slight surge of a final flare. 'Ten guineas,' I shouted as the room plunged into darkness.

'Ten guineas,' came the voice of the auctioneer. 'Sold to the gentlemen in the middle. Your name, sir? Get a lamp lit, for God's sake. We've got more than enough to get through.'

A lamp was lit and I knew I must make my way to the auctioneer's table. Thomas Warren was looking in my direction, his face distorted by rage. For a moment, I thought he must have seen me but he was looking at the huge man in front of me. I saw him mouth the words 'get him' and I ducked to one side, my heart pounding. The tattooed man turned his great bulk away from me and I breathed with relief.

Thomas Warren was no more than five feet away and I felt my fear turn to panic. With my head down, I pushed forward, concealing myself as best I could, leaning forward to speak to the auctioneer.

'Ten guineas for a worthless piece of land?' The auctioneer was clearly flustered. He looked down at his papers. 'You've paid well over its value but who'm I to complain? I'll add my cut. What name?' He was hampered by poor light, the noise level rising, and he was getting cross. People were crushing against the table, knocking his papers, and beads of sweat were glistening on his brow. He seized the document he sought, reaching for his quill. A pair of glasses balanced on the end of his nose but he did not glance up, his eyes remaining fixed on the parchment in front of him.

I pulled my hat lower and took a deep breath. 'Sir James Polcarrow,' I said, my voice barely above a whisper.

'Speak up, boy. You his steward?'

'No, sir, but he sent me to learn the ropes.'

'He should know better than send a boy to do a man's work. I'll get the deeds sent round tomorrow.' He cleared his throat, 'If we could have quiet, please, gentlemen. The next piece of land's a lease and release on Bodmin Moor – a dwelling house with a messuage of twenty acres. Could we have the door shut? The rules of the candle auction clearly state no-one must leave or enter whilst the bidding is in progress. No draughts and no lights.'

I had only seconds to get out of the room. Diving low, I pushed my way through the astonished crowd, ignoring their angry rebukes, making frantically for the door. I grabbed the sleeve of the man holding the latch and squeezed through the narrowing gap. But even as I ran down the corridor, I could hear a volley of oaths behind me.

Chapter Thirty-nine

Youths blocked the way to the front door so I turned quickly, stumbling down the ill-lit hall, ducking under the lintels as the passage narrowed. The footsteps behind me were growing louder and I knew my only chance would be to hide. I could smell malt and a low, vaulted room opened before me, a rush light casting shadows over the barrels stacked against the wall. I would squeeze behind the barrels. I looked around. The back door lay straight ahead of me, the handle within my grasp. I reached towards it and opened the door, a blast of icy air sending shivers down my spine. All at once, I was encased by a wall of fog, so thick, it was impossible to see my hands in front of my face.

'Damn it, we'll lose him in this fog,' came a voice behind me.

'It's a blind alley – she can't escape.'

'She?'

'Pengelly's daughter – Sir James's whore!' Thomas Warren

was only feet from where I stood. He raised his voice, 'There's nowhere to run, you conniving whore. Did you really think you'd get away with it?'

I fell to my hands and knees. Every seafaring person dreaded the fog which came from nowhere, wrecking ships and leaving children fatherless, yet now it might just save my life. But a blind alley? I crept slowly forward, keeping close to the side of the inn. The cobbles were wet, soiled by slops, empty barrels and sacks lying across my path. I knew I must not make a sound. Thomas Warren was thrashing the air behind me, his stick swiping at everything within his reach. A barrel crashed to the ground and rolled beside me.

'Get the dogs – we'll flush her out like a vixen. Be quick, for God's sake – we need to get her back to the auction and expose her for the lying whore she is.' His voice turned in my direction, 'Did you hear that, my beauty? The dogs know what they're about – they'll make short work of you.' He laughed as he struck a flint, the glow barely visible through the solid fog. 'But I like a chase,' he said, sucking on his pipe, 'By God, I like a chase and when I catch you, I'll have you – see if I don't.'

I began inching across the yard, desperately trying to keep my bearings. I had no way of knowing which direction I was going – but for his voice, I could have been heading straight for him. The cobbles were rough and broken in places. I could not tell how far I crawled, perhaps twenty feet. Suddenly, my hand came up against a solid wall and I ran my hands quickly over the stones, standing up to explore how high they went. The wall stretched well beyond my reach and I knew it was the huge wall that encircled the Polcarrow estate. There would be no climbing it.

The sound of muffled barking was getting louder, the same petrifying sound I had heard when Jim had been chased. I remembered the size of the dogs as they lay drugged and began crawling faster along the damp stones. They were wet, slimy, covered with moss, and stinking of urine. The wall seemed to go on forever, but my hand knocked against something hard and my hopes soared – a huge barrel. I ran my hands round it. It seemed full, the lid securely fastened. I dug my huge boots against the iron rim, hoisting myself to the top and knelt precariously on the lid, clutching the rim.

The pipe glowed in my direction. 'Give yourself up, you stupid bitch, before I turn angry – you won't like it when I'm angry.' There was the sound of loud hawking and spittle hitting the ground. 'It's me or the dog – not that there's much difference – they say I'm a dog when my blood's up…'

Crouching on the barrel, I tried to calm my breathing. The air was freezing, the fog penetrating my jacket, but the chill I felt was fear. Steadying myself, I ran my hands against the wall, reaching high on my toes, stretching as far as I could. A part of the wall felt different – bumpy, even crumbly. Brick not stone. Part of an outhouse. My fingers made contact with the top of the wall and I knew I just needed a foothold.

I had no choice but to give away my position. The bricks were old and I dug at them, scratching with my nails. I began gouging out the mortar, hollowing out a patch until a small area began to crumble. I rocked the loosening brick, clawing with my fingers, gripping it with a strength born from desperation. It went crashing to the ground and I felt for the space. It was all I needed. I wedged my cumbersome boot into the gap and reached above me with all my strength. With one push I gripped the top of the wall and heaved myself up, my foot kicking over the hogshead, sending it clattering across the cobbles, the yard echoing with the sound of vicious barking.

'She's behind the barrel – spread out, I want this bitch caught.'

Somehow, I steadied myself on top of the wall. It was no more than a foot across, the fog smothering me, making it hard to keep my balance. On one side Thomas Warren, on the other, the long drop to the Polcarrow estate where dogs roamed freely at night. The Polcarrow gatehouse would be to my left. To my right would be the churchyard.

Inch by painful inch, I felt my way along the narrow wall, stretching like a cat over the crenulations as they heeded my progress. Only when the barking faded, did I dare to stop, and only then did I realise I was shaking uncontrollably.

Chapter Forty

Close beside me the church clock struck ten. Across the graveyard the mist was lifting, the church just visible through the thinning fog. Hazy shapes swirled round the tombstones – the very essence of my childhood terrors, but I paid no heed. I was in far greater danger from the living.

Clutching the top of the wall, I lowered my legs and dropped to the ground, crouching behind a large tomb, listening from the shadows. A mule brayed in the distance and I heard hurried footsteps run towards the quay. These fogs could go as quickly as they came, but while it lasted, I stood a chance. I had to get home. I had to hide the clothes that would incriminate me.

As the fog thinned, the streets became busier. Keeping to the edge of the street, I skirted the houses, hiding in the shadows of the overhanging gables. An oil lamp half-lit the town quay, its suffused light trapped by the swirling mist. A brazier glowed red on the quayside and groups of people stood hunching their shoulders against the cold. I could not tell whether they were warming themselves, or waiting for the ferry, so I ducked into a doorway, concealing myself behind a crate. The crate was full of fish guts, its smell so appalling I had to fight the urge to retch.

Across the river mouth the hazy lights of Porthruan could just be seen; the splash of oars indicating the return of the ferry. The wharf dropped steeply to one side and with the town quay filling up with people, there was nowhere else to hide. I would stay where I was, crouching behind the stinking crate. If there was room in the ferry, I would leave my hiding place and make a dash before it pulled away.

A scent of tobacco came sifting through the air; the foul, pungent smell, mixing with the stench of fish guts. It was sickly-sweet, the fumes laced with vanilla and cinnamon. The exact smell, the same distinctive brand. I drew back, my heart thumping against my chest. It was coming from a doorway not four feet away. I had to think. I had to calm my terror. Running would draw too much attention. I would have to control the shaking in my legs and walk calmly back the way I had come.

A group of men were crossing the quay and I saw my chance. Pulling my hat low, I slipped from the doorway, falling silently into step as they walked towards the old jetty. The passage was dark and narrow, the wharf towering above me on one side, the river falling away to the other, but I kept pace, grateful one of them was holding a lantern. The noise of their footsteps made it hard to hear if I was being followed but, somehow, I resisted the temptation to look round.

'Aye, 'tis clear enough – 'tis lifting.'

'Aye, well – 'till tomorrow then. Goodnight, Jack.'

One by one, they left the group to board their boats and I found myself alone on the creaking jetty. In places the wood was rotten, jagged gaps revealing the black sea beneath me. It was very slippery, the planks wet from the fog and I walked with care, not knowing where I was going. At the end of the jetty, I stopped, not believing my eyes. A small rowing boat was hitched to the rail, its oars still locked in place. The owner would only be gone for a short while and I stared at the small boat, knowing I had little time to decide. I could swim or I could row. I had never swum the river before, but neither had I ever stolen a boat.

With the fog thinning, I could hesitate no longer. I untied the painter and pushed the boat into the calm black water. As I grabbed the oars, salt stung my hands. I had not noticed the grazes before, or the blood that covered my fingers. With the first stroke, I steadied the boat. With the second I turned. With the third, I pulled clear of the jetty. With the fourth, I headed for home.

My feet flew along the cliff path as my mind raced. I would have to warn Sir James Thomas Warren could not be trusted. First thing in the morning, I would tell him about the auction and warn him of my suspicions. High on the cliff top, I breathed the salt-laden air. The fog had all but lifted, dispersed by the soft breeze now blowing across the sea. The sky was cloudless, the moon and stars bright above me. I stared at the huge moon, with its knowing face, the ache tightening around my heart. But I would be safe soon, the cottage lay ahead of me, only fifty yards further and I would be safe. I opened the back gate.

I saw a movement in the shadows. A huge man loomed at me, lunging through the darkness and I screamed in terror.

'It's Miss Pengelly,' said a voice as strong arms reached out to steady me. 'Are ye alright, Miss Pengelly?' His voice was familiar but I could not place it.

'No, she's not alright. She looks terrible,' said Jenna, rushing to my side. 'She looks fit to drop – quick get her in.'

I was shaking, my legs barely able to walk as they helped me through the door. I was clutching Joseph Dunn, but somehow I could not let him go. I clung to him, my whole body trembling. 'I'm sorry,' I said at last, 'it's just…I'm so glad to see you.'

'Ye're as white as a ghost,' said Jenna, taking off my hat and freeing my collar.

'I'm fine, really I am…don't wake Mother.'

'She's not here – with all that fog and Mr Pengelly being in Mevagissey, Mrs Munroe persuaded her to stay at Coombe House – we're alone.'

Joseph Dunn lit a candle and for the first time I caught a proper look at him. He was a huge lad – that was for certain. His hair was cut shorter than I remembered and stubble shadowed his chin. He had a pleasant face, covered with freckles and eyes that lit up when he smiled. He was smiling at me now, the same respectful smile that had made me warm to him before. His shirt was unbuttoned, his chest exposed, and a vast expanse of finely worked muscles clearly visible beneath his loosened garment. He must have seen my look of surprise, as the next moment he turned his back, hurrying to restore some order.

Jenna was not wearing her cap; her luscious blonde curls foaming in abandon around her. Nor was she wearing a fichu and her soft shoulders shimmered in the flickering candle-light. The top of her bodice was undone. Indeed, the top five eyelets gaped open, the soft curve of her beautiful bosom rising invitingly from beneath the lace. She saw my gaze and hastily tightened her laces.

'How very convenient Mother's not here,' I said. 'Clearly you've been beside yourself with worry over me.'

'Well, yes, we have,' replied Jenna defiantly. 'Joseph was just thinking he should go search for ye.'

'Yes,' replied Joseph rather shyly for such a big man, 'I was just...' He paused, his face full of remorse. 'I'm sorry, Miss Pengelly, it's me ye should blame...we thought ye were just delayed by fog...I'd no idea ye were...' He looked discreetly at my clothes. 'I'll leave ye now.'

'No, don't leave, wait.' An idea was forming in my mind. 'Joseph, if I give you a letter, will you take it to Sir James?'

'Course, I will, Miss Pengelly. I'm to collect him from Pendenning Hall at half past eleven. He's been dining with Sir George and Lady Cavendish and I'm going there direct. I'll give him yer letter tonight.'

'What time's it now?'

'Quarter to eleven.'

'Wait just a moment, Joseph. Jenna, come with me – help me out of these clothes.' I knew I was being brusque but we had very little time. 'Don't ask, but we'll have to burn them.'

'Burn them?'

'Or put them in a sack and Joseph can throw them to the beach – either way your brother must never wear them again...don't look like that; I'll pay for new ones. Quickly!'

Relieved to be rid of the heavy breeches, I struggled into my old dress. I could see Jenna was horrified but I had no time to explain. My mind was racing – what should I write? I dashed down the stairs, taking two at a time, nearly tripping over in my hurry.

'Bring another candle, Jenna, and get those clothes wrapped up.'

I searched the parlour for a piece of paper while Mr Pitt watched me from Father's chair. Papers lay strewn across the table, piled high on stools, spilling across the floor. I grabbed a quill, dipped it in the inkpot and balanced my letter next to Mr Pitt. He seemed pleased to see me and began to purr. What could I write that would not incriminate myself?

I liked Joseph and always felt safe in his company, but what if Thomas Warren saw him first and demanded the letter? I would not sign it, of course, but how could I tell James Polcarrow everything in so short a space? I began to write, but my hands were shaking and I smudged the ink. I reached for another piece of parchment. Sir James would have to know about Thomas Warren's treachery. He would also have to be told about the man with the pipe – somehow that seemed important. I began again.

311

'It's gone eleven and Joseph's to go. Will ye be much longer?' called Jenna through the door,

There was only one thing I could do. In the middle of the page, I wrote the word *midnight* and, underneath, I sketched a rose on a long stem. It was not a perfect drawing, and nowhere as good as the ones I had been sent, but it was the best I could do. I folded it in three, dripped a small pool of wax to seal it and, as the wax hardened, pressed my finger into the soft, warm ball. I was trembling.

Back in the kitchen, Joseph was smartly dressed, his livery jacket buttoned tightly to his neck, his hat square on his head. He was holding the sack of clothes.

'Joseph, that day you rescued me from the highwayman, did you really come across me by chance?'

He looked me straight in the eyes. 'Not at all,' he replied, his gaze not wavering, 'Sir James sent me.'

'Then, please give this to Sir James the moment you see him. Promise me you'll not give it to anybody else.'

'Course,' he replied, as if offended.

He was out of the door and the kitchen expanded. Jenna handed me a plate heaped with bread and cheese. Pushing a mug of ale towards me, I caught hold of her hand.

'Jenna, take care.'

'Nothing would've happened.'

'It might. One day it just might. You know full well all sense vanishes when passion takes over...'

'No, I don't,' she replied smiling shyly, 'but perhaps ye do.'

Her words made me burn with shame. I did know. I could still feel the hungry searching of his lips. 'Of course I don't,' I lied. 'But Jenna, promise me, you'll be careful. Joseph Dunn will batter down your defences and you'll be caught like everyone else who can't keep their bodice laced.'

'Ye know I'm not like that. I know what I'm doing. Not like some. Not like…' She stopped abruptly, turning her face away, but I had seen her expression – defiant yet concerned. I felt strangely chilled.

'Not like who, Jenna?'

'Eat yer cheese, Miss Rosehannon, don't let's quarrel.'

'Not like who, Jenna?' I repeated, pushing away my plate.

There was pity in her eyes now. Her voice softened. 'Well, I suppose ye might as well know – ye'll hear it soon enough when it becomes common gossip. Beth Tregony works up at the hall – she's under-maid at Pendenning…well, she swears, on her life – her hearing it for herself and all that…'

A knot was tying itself round my stomach. I knew what she was about to say.

'She heard Lady Cavendish scolding Miss Arbella for her foolishness…Miss Arbella is with child, Miss Rosehannon – she's with child and no doubt about it. Beth Tregony heard it all. It's why they chased back after Sir James in all that haste and why they're insisting on the marriage. There, ye asked, I told. Are ye alright?'

The walls of the room were spinning round me. 'Of course I'm alright.'

She watched me from across the room while I feigned indifference. The words *more allowance round the waist* were ringing in my ears. I must have gone through the motions of rising. I must have left the table. I think I even cleared

away my plate, but I was hardly aware what I was doing.
I was Rosehannon Pengelly; clever, articulate, known to
be rational, yet the very last flutter of hope had just died in
my heart.

Chapter Forty-one

I waited by the tree, hoping he would not come. I should have waited until morning, never sent for him in such a hurry. I had read about the Indies, the turquoise seas and mangrove swamps where flowers were the size of plates, butterflies the size of small birds. Where the nights were warm and lovers kissed to the sound of the cicada. I should have waited. He was betrothed to another woman and she was carrying his child.

A slight rustle made me look up. James Polcarrow was staring at me, his face unsmiling. How long he had been watching me, I could not guess, but when I saw him, I felt my mouth tighten and my expression harden. 'I didn't think you'd come,' I said abruptly.

'I'll always come if you need me. What's happened, Rose? Why were you scowling?'

I felt my cheeks redden. I had been thinking of what must have happened on those sultry, moonlit nights. 'I thought it important to warn you Thomas Warren is not to be trusted,'

I said quickly, 'but I don't know what I was thinking when I sent you that note — it was very foolish and I should have waited for morning. Forgive me, it was a mistake.'

I turned my back but he grabbed my elbow. 'What's wrong, Rose? You're never foolish and I've never known you make a mistake. You sent for me and I'm here — tell me what the trouble is.'

I stared at him through a wave of hostility. He was dressed as Jim — the jacket, breeches, shirt and scarf, just the same as they had been on the night we first met, even the dagger hung from his belt. Only his skin looked less weathered and his hair more groomed. He stood searching my face, his expression every bit as dark as our first encounter.

'Why are you dressed as Jim?' I asked coldly.

'I'm thinking of your reputation.'

'My reputation?' I laughed, 'since when has that bothered you?'

'Rose, don't play games. Something important must've happened. Tell me what it is.'

He put his hand on my elbow, leading me to the rock where we had sat a lifetime ago. The wind smelt of oceans, of exotic, faraway places, of frangipane and hibiscus, of mimosa and flowering bougainvillea and for once I did not want to breathe its salty air. He took off his jacket, laying it on the stone. His shirt caught the wind, ruffling his hair and I hated him for the pain I felt.

I told him everything, except what Thomas Warren had called me, and he listened without interruption, his frown deepening. I watched the familiar hardening of his jaw. 'Rose, nothing you do will ever surprise me – you're a woman without equal, but you were very foolish to put yourself in such danger.'

I chose to ignore his remark. What I did was my own concern. Below us, the waves lapped the rocks. Above us, the moon smirked. It was on a night like this I had fallen so deeply in love with him and it was on a night like this I discovered I had a rival. She had prior claim. She was beautiful, well connected and rich. And she was carrying his child.

'Why d'you think they want the creek?' My tone was abrupt.

'I don't know. Have you seen it recently, Rose?'

'No, but I know the stretch of water well. We often used to row there and we'd pull in to the creek to rest. It's just above Pont Pill and curves with the river – it's a natural stopping place...' I thought for a moment, 'a lot of boats stop there...'

'What is it, Rose?'

'That awful day when you scared Ben and me witless and you left me to the fate of the gaolers – well, I remember looking down on the river and it didn't strike me as odd then, but I remember there was a large ship anchored in Tideswell Creek.'

'I didn't leave you to the fate of the gaolers, as well you know,' he said, looking straight at me, his eyes black in the moonlight.

'I don't care whether you did or didn't,' I said, looking away, 'it's all in the past.' I pulled my cloak round me and stood up. 'I've told you everything and I'm tired – I've had a terrible night and I want to go home.'

As I turned to leave, he caught my elbow, once more drawing me to him. His touch was firm, but something in my expression must have warned him off. He let me go. 'I need to see this creek. Can you show it to me?'

'Anyone can show it to you – I'm surprised you don't know where it is.'

'No, I mean tonight…I want to see it now. The tide's on the rise and there's a full moon – it would be easy to navigate the river.'

'Tonight? Why?'

'Because Thomas Warren and Phillip Randall are up to something and I need to know what it is. They'll be there first thing tomorrow morning and they'll hide what they don't want seen – I need to get there first.'

The thought of Thomas Warren made me shudder. I was tired, my fingertips still painful, my body beginning to ache. The last thing I wanted was a long row upriver – especially in the company of James Polcarrow. 'I'll tell you where it is and you can go yourself,' I replied.

'Come with me, Rose.'

Even through the darkness I could see the pleading in those black eyes staring so intently into mine. It was the look that filled my nights. He would be lying alongside me, his head on the pillow next to mine. His hair would be ruffled, his eyes hungry for me. His hands would be playing with my hair. I would smile at him and he would smile back – that brilliant smile that would light up his face.

318

'No,' I replied firmly.

'Please, Rose. It would be like old times.'

'There were no old times – there were just lies.'

He turned, scowling into the distance. When he spoke, his voice was hard. 'If you show me the creek tonight, I'll halve the rent of the log pool.'

'Quarter it,' I replied.

'Rose – that's practically giving it to you for free.'

'I know.'

'You drive a hard bargain, Miss Pengelly,' he said, with no trace of a smile. 'First you make free with my money and now you propose to rob me of any ensuing profit. But it'll have to be. Come, or we'll miss the tide.'

Chapter Forty-two

I sat in the bow, the boat gliding upriver on the fast-flowing tide, only the splash of our oars breaking the stillness. Moonlight shimmered on the water, turning the river silver-grey. The banks were dark, shadowed by the overhanging branches of the densely wooded slopes. Owls hooted across the water and I drew my cloak around me – every child knew the dangers of getting pixilated if you went into the woods at night.

It was so different in the moonlight, so beautiful. The salt-laden air gave way to brackish dankness, the vegetation changing from drying seaweed to damp woodland. Debris floated alongside us – planks and half-submerged barrels, brush handles, pieces of old rope bobbing in the flowing current.

Distance was deceptive and our exact position difficult to locate. It seemed much further than I expected but, as we rounded the bend, I recognised the curve where the water grew shallower and knew we were nearing Tideswell Creek. 'We're here.'

'I'll aim for that overhanging branch and we'll crawl along it. Can you manage that?'

'Of course,' I replied, annoyed he could think otherwise.

With a turn of his oars, he manoeuvred the boat alongside the branch, pulling to test its strength. 'That should hold.'

I heaved myself onto the branch, cursing the folds of my gown as they got in my way. 'It's so much easier to wear breeches,' I muttered. He laughed, smiling across at me, as my frown deepened. 'Well, you should try being all trussed up – laced to within an inch of your life!' I snapped. The glimmer of amusement increased and I turned away.

It would make a perfect log pool. The mud smelt of rotting vegetation, seaweed hung from the branches of the surrounding trees and half-submerged trunks lay washed up along the river's edge. I crawled along the branch, the wet bark soiling my skirt. 'It's pretty overgrown, Jim – I mean, Sir James,' I said, furious at my mistake.

'No, call me Jim,' he said softly, smiling at me through the darkness.

'There is no Jim.'

'At least call me James,' he said with irritation, 'surely you can do that?' For a moment, we stood in angry silence, listening to an owl hooting in the distance.

'D'you think we're in danger?' I asked at last.

Those black eyes were staring at me. 'I'd never bring you knowingly to danger but I can't be sure. I've no idea why they want this land.' His voice dropped to a whisper. 'Do you want to stay here, or come? I need to take a better look.'

From out of nowhere, dark wings swooped noisily above us and I jumped in fright. 'I didn't come all this way to be left behind,' I said. 'And don't laugh at me, James – it's not my fault my mind's full of Mrs Munroe's fanciful stories.'

His voice became serious. 'Tread only where I tread – there may be traps for trespassers.' He reached for a thick branch, gripping it with both hands, stabbing the ground in front of him. 'I mean it Rose, these traps kill. Walk only in my footsteps.'

The wood was overgrown, the ground soggy as I lifted my sodden skirts, plunging my shoes into the muddy indentations left by his boots. Brambles whipped my cloak, snagging my dress and, as I struggled to climb over a fallen tree trunk, James held out his hand to steady me. I nearly reached for it. I so nearly reached for it, but I shook my head, knowing I would never let him touch me again. Our eyes met and I saw his mouth tighten in annoyance.

The trees had started to thin, the wood opening into a recently constructed clearing. Moonlight flooded the open space, making it as bright as day. At the end of the clearing, a wooden building was visible against the surrounding trees, a bonfire flickering on the ground in front of it. Wood-smoke drifted towards us; two men sitting by the fire, their backs silhouetted against the flames. We pulled quickly back, darting behind a tree. A sizeable track led from the clearing down to the river but we had seen no sign of this path from the creek and James crept forward to get a better look. Kneeling on the ground, he felt the stones with his fingers.

'*Cart ruts*,' he mouthed, making no sound.

'*Are they charcoal burners?*' I mouthed back.

'I don't think so,' he whispered, beginning to undo his jacket.

A large rope was slung across his chest and I watched in alarm as he whisked the rope over his head and began refastening his jacket. Pulling his hat low, he took off his scarf, tying it over his mouth to conceal his face. Scooping up some earth, he began rubbing it over his hands, disappearing into the darkness in front of me. 'Stay here! Conceal yourself under your cloak and promise me – on your father's life – don't follow. I'll come back, but don't move. Do you promise?'

The rope shone in the moonlight, like a snake in his hands. Twisting it quickly, he tied a knot, once again coiling it and hoisting it over his shoulder. He felt for his dagger and with no sound at all, he was swallowed by the blackness of the wood. I was alone and no amount of owls, or bats, or evil spirits, could have added to my fear. I drew my cloak around me, desperately hoping the vegetation would be enough to give me cover. My hands were shaking, my fingertips sore with gripping my cloak. I was not well hidden – I would have to find denser undergrowth, but it was too late. One of the men rose from the fire and began looking in my direction. He began walking towards me.

'I tell ye, I heard something.' His knife flashed in the moonlight.

'Probably just a fox.'

'It was voices, I tell ye.'

'Leave be. Ye're so edgy these days – ye'd jump at your own shadow.'

'Quiet…listen.'

He was halfway across the clearing, clearly visible in the moonlight. He was tall, thin, turning from side to side, his arms poised to fight. In one hand, he held a knife, in the other a pistol. I shrunk further under my cloak – petrified my petticoat would be showing beneath my skirt. I need not have worried – Jenna's carefully starched white cotton was indistinguishable in the mud.

The man swung round, raising the pistol, 'Who's there? Come out or I'll shoot.'

'It's an owl, ye idiot,' came the voice from the fire. 'Have some ale. Ye've been that jumpy all night.'

'Ye know our orders – no-one gets through. And I tell ye, I heard voices.' He cocked the pistol, once more turning in my direction.

He could not have been more than ten yards away when a sudden crack filled the air. A rope flew out of the woods, whirring across the clearing, wrapping itself round the man. His arms were pinned to his sides with such ferocity the knife and pistol fell from his hands. The rope tightened, jerked viciously, dragging him sideways until he stumbled and fell. James leapt from the darkness and secured a gag. The watchman could do nothing but stare, petrified, as his faceless assailant began winding the rope round him with lightning speed. Before the other watchman had even turned, James grabbed the fallen pistol and vanished in the darkness.

'Samuel?' The man by the fire rose, 'Samuel? For chrissake stop messin' about. Where've ye gone?'

He began edging towards the sound of grunting, pistol poised. Immediately, he was gripped from behind, cold iron pressing against his temple. He dropped his pistol, standing frozen to the spot. The pressure on his arm would leave him in no doubt who was the stronger and the watchman was clearly no fool. He put up no resistance, stumbling only with fear as he was forced against a nearby tree.

I heard, rather than saw, the ropes being bound. So that was how he did it. That was how the gaoler had been pulled from the cart, how Ben had been forced against the tree. James Polcarrow's chest was still heaving. He pulled his scarf down to breathe and I stared at him, once again, shrinking from the hand he offered.

'Rose, what did you expect? Your life was in danger – don't you realise they'd have killed you? These are ruthless men and whoever hired them will be every bit as ruthless – probably more. I didn't hurt them. They'll just have a few bruises and a lot of explaining to do.' He saw I was shaking and took a step forward, his jacket brushing against my cloak. 'I should never have put you in such danger. If anything happened to you...' his voice caught.

We stood in silence, touching but not touching. 'Where did you learn that rope trick?'

'It's what the native men of the Americas use. I was taught it by a man who saved my life. He taught me everything – how to merge with the darkness, how to follow without being seen, how to anticipate people's movements. He taught me to survive, Rose, and that's all I do. I never instigate violence – you should know that. Come, I'll get you back to safety.'

I knew we had to go back. I should never have come, but his words tore at my heart, reminding me of when he had said them to me last. His jacket hung open, the top buttons of his shirt undone. I could see a fine layer of sweat glistening on his chest. He removed his hat and wiped his brow. Dark stubble covered his chin and I felt the pain of intense longing. A terrible, desperate, yearning for Jim – for how things might have been.

This night would soon be over. This moonlit, stolen night, would soon be over. Somehow, I could not bear for it to end. 'Are those watchmen very securely tied?' I asked, forcing myself away from the warmth of his jacket.

'They aren't going anywhere until someone undoes them.'

'Then we'd be fools not to look in the building – I wouldn't be able to sleep if I didn't know what was in there. They must be smuggling.'

'The distribution's all wrong,' he replied, quickly. 'There are no roads to take the goods away – only fields. Let's take a look.'

The building was much larger than it looked and as we rounded the back, we stared in amazement. Covering everything was a fine layer of white powder. It shimmered in the moonlight, like snow in mid-summer. 'What is it?' I asked.

'Dust from kaolin. They call it china clay. They'll have dug pits up on higher ground, and be using the stream to wash the clay. They're drying it up there and bringing it down in its powder state.'

A heavily indented track led through the wood and two large wagons stood piled high with hogsheads. Spare cartwheels leant against the building and bridles and harnesses hung from iron hooks. James looked furious. 'Those hogsheads are waiting to be shipped, Rose. Do you see what's happening? They need an outlet to the sea and you've just thwarted their attempt to access the river. It's the obvious route – the river's deep here, they'll be planning on building a jetty.'

'But surely those are your fields, your stretch of moorland?'

'Is it *still* my land, Rose? Robert Roskelly and Thomas Warren are both self-made men. They've had years to sell off leases and make lucrative deals. Who knows what they've done in my absence. Like this creek.'

A terrible thought crossed my mind. 'How did the last owner of the creek die, James?'

'That's what I was thinking. Robert Roskelly may be in Bodmin, but his influence is far from stemmed.' His eyes softened, 'Come, you've had more than enough for one night, I'm getting you home.' He gripped my hand and did not let go.

Nor did I want him to.

Chapter Forty-three

I sat in the stern as he rowed me back. I should have sat in the bow where our eyes could not meet. I should not have watched the grip of his wrists, the pull of his muscles. I should never have imagined the touch of his hands or watched the toss of his head or the tightening of his mouth.

If I had sat in the bow and watched the river, my heart could have hardened. I could have parted with indifference, but as we climbed the cliff path and the cottages came into view, my heart was aching. To the east, the grey light of a new day revealed the night was nearly over. At the back gate, we stood facing each other. Behind us, clothes were flapping on Mrs Tregony's line, the hinge creaking as the gate blew gently in the breeze. I had to say goodbye but no words would come. James, too, seemed reluctant to go. It was as if an invisible web was binding us together.

'Rose, let's sit and watch dawn break.'

Without waiting for my reply, he took off his jacket and laid it on the step. He drew me down and we sat, side by side, like the friends we were, and the lovers we could never be. Just this night, I promised myself – just this one stolen night. When day breaks and the cover of darkness lifts, she can have him back. It will be over.

We sat in silence, the breeze against our cheeks. 'Who was the man who saved your life?'

James Polcarrow stared ahead. At first I thought he would say nothing but he cleared his throat, his voice flat. 'A slave called Chevego, in a place called Virginia.'

'Were you transported to Virginia?'

'It's where I ended up. I was transported to Baltimore in Maryland, only I wasn't transported – I was sold as an indentured servant. The convict trade to Baltimore and Virginia was meant to be over – or at least those who fought against the disgorging of English thieves and cut-throats believed it to be. But there were still those who saw profit in the trade of convicts. I don't suppose it mattered where I was sent, or who sold me – it would've been the same. I ended up in the hands of Captain Pamp, the master of the Swift, a particularly cruel man. He saw profit in selling us as indentured servants and claimed to be bound for Halifax, but his destination was always to be Baltimore.'

A look of loathing settled on his face.

'Rumours began circulating we were bound for Africa and the mood was fierce. Many of the convicts were hardened thieves, some even murderers. There was mutiny and though some escaped, most were recaptured. Captain Pamp quelled further unrest with his own unique brand of cruelty. We were flogged and starved, kept crammed in the hold and fettered in irons. The filth of Newgate still clung to us and the stench was unbearable. We rolled on the heaving ocean, awash in each other's filth. Disease spread quickly, the dying racked in pain, their bowels like water, their vomit thick with blood. I couldn't count all those that died.'

He ran his hands through his hair. They were trembling.

'Those of us who complained were treated worse. I shouted at them to unshackle a dying woman. A rat was gnawing her feet and I could hear her screaming. I was whipped to within an inch of my life and thrown in the cell they called the black hole. It was no bigger than an iron basket, I couldn't stand, or lay. I spent seventy days trussed and handcuffed, hardly able to move, my skin chaffed and bleeding. I nearly starved but I was determined to survive. I was determined to return one day and expose the brutality and injustice of our system. I wanted to hold Captain Pamp to account.'

'And when you got to Baltimore?'

'It was Christmas Eve, thick ice had slowed our progress, but when we docked in Baltimore those of us who survived were sold as indentured slaves – business was slow, the people of Baltimore suspicious. I was painfully thin, wracked by a cough and had no trade. The privileged life of a landowner – as you'd be the first to point out – equipped me for neither physical labour nor artisan work. They wanted printers or blacksmiths, coopers or wheelwrights. I was passed by.

'After months of being paraded in chains and clamped in leg irons, Captain Pamp cut his losses and sold us to a dealer bound for Virginia. We were taken to a tobacco plantation along the St James River, ostensibly as servants, but slaves in any other language.

'Man's inhumanity to man knows no bounds. How can we be considered civilised when people condone slavery? It's hell, Rose – a living hell. Endless days of living hell with slave owners inflicting the severest torture. Unpardonable cruelty and unrelenting pain, just grinding on, remorselessly, day after day, year after year. You can't imagine the filth, the hunger, the constant whipping and lashings, the raping of women, the abuse of men. But it's the smile on their faces as they inflict this living hell which haunts me, Rose.

'It's back-breaking work under a burning sun. The relentless heat, the flies. No shoes. No hat. No water. Just the faraway look in the men's eyes and their singing. Their heart-wrenching, agonising singing about a land where they were free and a home they'll never see again. Runaways are brought back and flogged, yet every day you plan your escape.'

I wanted to put my arms around him, to soothe away the pain, but I sat motionless, my heart breaking.

'I was chained to Chevego when we saw our chance – a fleeting oversight of a careless overseer. We dived into a ditch and waited all day, expecting any time to be found and flogged. But dusk fell and we crawled to freedom. Through thousands of acres of tobacco plants.

'Can you imagine how hard it is to break free of chains? It took us weeks, travelling by night, hiding by day. We were weak, our progress slow, and only when we chanced on a hut with an axe, did we manage to smash the iron bands that held us together. 'He looked up, pain deep in his eyes. 'I'd have starved if Chevego hadn't known what plants to eat. His people were Native Americans who live by the land. We'd no language in common but words were unnecessary. He taught me how to walk unheard, how to use the rope, how to hide from danger.

'We stayed constantly on the lookout. Everyone has to carry discharge papers, or have signed permission to travel. Bounty money's good – people are always on the watch for runaway slaves. Chevego taught me to trap animals and catch fish, how to use animal skins and sharpen flints but I knew he was getting restless. One morning I found him putting dried meat into his pouch. His homeland was calling, he needed to return to his people. He was my only friend and I can't tell you how hard it was for me to watch him walk away.'

He had lowered his voice to no more than a whisper. 'I made my way to Charlestown, Virginia. It's a new town with money being invested in buildings. I found work for a pittance, no questions asked, no papers needed. I even found lodgings and kept my head down. My plan was simple. I'd earn enough money to return to England. Somehow, I'd prove my innocence. I was determined to expose Robert Roskelly for the murderer he was. Do you really want to know all this, Rose?'

'Of course I do.' The pain was almost unbearable.

'There's a criminal network who arrange for convicts to return to England. Their fee's substantial, of course, but when I thought I had enough, I met a man on the docks and my hard-earned money was exchanged for a ticket back to the 'old homeland' – that's how he put it. The ship was to sail on the tide. Two days out at sea, we were attacked by a French privateer seeking English blood.

'I survived by speaking the French taught to me by my tutor. I spoke just enough to convince them I wasn't English and I survived – but swapped one hell for another. The life of a privateer is brutal and murderous and, once again, it was living hell. The crew were captive men and the captain knew we'd jump ship at any opportunity. He kept us out at sea and when we docked, kept us locked below decks. I didn't step foot ashore for more than two years. Two years, Rose, of endless looting and plundering, of drunken violence, lashings and disease.

'But I learnt to survive and rose through the ranks. My French was fluent by this time and I learnt to navigate. Then chance stepped in. Sickness was rife, sailors dying and we needed more men. As land took shape, I went to the captain and persuaded him we needed more men. I said I knew what I was about and laughed as I touched my knife. He needed men like me. He gave me a jug of rum and slapped my back.

'Our raiding party set out at nightfall. As we rowed ashore, I felt the first glimmer of hope. The last eight years of my life had been cruelly stolen – my youth, my education, my prospects ripped from me, but I was alive and heading for dry land.'

'Where was it?'

'Havana – a lawless hotbed of vice. Each man in that raiding party slipped silently into the darkness but to survive in a place like that, you needed the sort of skills Chevego had taught me. I hid in the shadows, stepping over the victims of stabbings and, for over a year, I lived without trace.'

He wiped his hand across the back of his mouth, his hand shaking. 'Then, one night, a chance encounter brought me face to face with an Englishman – a Cornishman, to be precise. We were fleeing from the same Spanish sailors and as we dived behind a mud shack, our knives drawn, he asked me my business and where I was from. He spoke with a Cornish accent and for the sake of our shared heritage, he invited me back to his lodgings. His name was Denzel Creed.'

I could see uncertainty in his eyes, 'Do you really want to hear all this, Rose?'

'Of course I do, James,' I whispered, trying to keep the sadness from my voice. 'Was Denzel Creed a good man?'

'No he wasn't, but we talked of Cornwall. He was on his way to be tutor to the Governor of Dominica. The son was destined to follow his father into the navy but until he started his commission, he needed a tutor. As we talked, my resentment grew. I had been expected to go to Oxford. I was a baronet's son, educated and well read, yet my education was long forgotten.

'His boat was to sail in two weeks and I asked him to let me stay and read the few books he'd brought. I wanted to reacquaint myself with Virgil and Plato, smell the leather bindings, imagine I was back in my father's library. He said I could do what I liked, so for two weeks I sat reading what I could. My brain was like a parched sponge.

'Denzel Creed was never at the lodging. He was a gambling man, a heavy drinker. The early hours would see him lying drunk in the roadside. Then, one morning, after he'd not come back for two days, I went in search of him and found him lying in a ditch, the knife wound black with flies.

'You can guess the rest, Rose, but don't judge me harshly – it's what happens. Any time you could be robbed or murdered and your identity stolen. If I hadn't pretended to be him, someone else would have taken his papers.'

'I'm not judging you,' I whispered, 'I'd have done the same.'

A silence fell between us. Above us, pink streaks lit the grey sky. Dew had settled on the step, and across the silence, the first hesitant crowing of a cockerel. I knew my time was up. I would have to go and quickly, too – before he spoke her name. I wrapped my cloak round me but, as I prepared to stand, he gripped my hand.

'Hear me out, Rose – let me finish.'

No, not her name. Please do not speak her name.

His voice was soft, hardly above a whisper. 'I settled well as a tutor, relishing every book in the library. Frederick Cavendish was slow and indifferent, but it suited my purpose. I studied for myself, tirelessly pursuing knowledge.' My mouth was dry. I really, really did not want to hear this. '... and for nearly eighteen months, I was drawn by the magnetic beauty of Arbella Cavendish – Frederick's twin sister. She could dazzle a man from across the room and I was drawn, like a moth to a lamp, unable to take my eyes off her.

'Finally, I could no longer keep my thoughts to myself and I sought her out. I chanced upon her in the garden, hiding from her maid, and I seized the opportunity to tell her how much she meant to me. She was kind but very firm. She told me her parents expected her to marry "well", not throw herself away on a penniless tutor. She *valued* my company but it was out of the question and I was never to mention my feelings again.

'Rose, you were right when you said I'd not be able to stand by if someone dismissed me as inferior. The long years of abuse and servitude, of hiding and pretending to be someone else came boiling to the surface and I spoke in anger. Before I could stop myself, I told her who I really was.'

The knot in my stomach tightened. I turned away, but he reached for my hand, forcing me to look into his eyes. 'I don't love her, Rose. I've never loved her, I can see that now. I was infatuated with her beauty, in love with the idea of love, but I've never yearned for her like I do for you. I love *you*, Rose. We are destined to love one another. She and I are like strangers – nothing else. There's nothing between us – no warmth, no love, no spark.'

He held my fingers to his dry lips. 'I ache for you,' he whispered, turning my hand over to kiss my palm. 'Every night I dream I'm holding you in my arms. I imagine you're lying beside me – your hair spilling over the pillow. You smile at me and I smile back and my heart bursts with the love I have for you. Then dawn breaks and my heart breaks, too, knowing that, somehow, I have to get through the day without you.'

I could not believe what he was saying. How could he do this to me? To her? I pulled my hands free, tears of disappointment springing to my eyes. How dare he make love to me! Sir James's whore, had he heard that too? I stood up, grabbing the latch, clutching it with desperate hands, but before I could open the gate, he blocked my way.

'Rose, stop running away. We're meant for each other.'

I stared in disbelief. 'I thought you came back to clear your name – to restore your reputation and live with honour.'

'Why should we deny ourselves happiness for the sake of *honour*? For some *foolishness* that happened long before I met you? Arbella means nothing to me and our marriage would be a sham. Would you have me trapped in a loveless marriage, wanting you every day? Longing for you every night?'

I began struggling with the latch, my hands shaking. He took a step closer, pulling me to him. I could feel the warmth of his body, the touch of his lips against my hair. His voice was tender. 'Let me love you, Rose. Let me cherish you the way you deserve. I'll end my engagement to Arbella. She and her family can return to Dominica and I'll willingly never see them again.'

How could he say that? How could James Polcarrow be prepared to abandon a woman who was carrying his child? A man who lived by such ideals, fighting for justice, standing alone against the Corporation? A man who would unshackle the slaves? I had been wrong in my judgement of James Polcarrow and Father had been right. Everyone knew the consequences for Arbella Cavendish. If he was capable of abandoning Arbella and his unborn child, then he was not the man I thought he was, and not a man I could love.

'No, Sir James,' I said, my voice taking on a tone I hardly recognised, 'I've refused you before and if you think I'll change my mind, you're mistaken. You should be grateful for what you have, rather than hanker after something you can never have. We've a business arrangement, that's all, and I'm grateful to you for that – but that's all there is between us.'

His arms loosened their hold as he swung swiftly away and I hurried through the gate, slamming it shut behind me. In my bedroom, my first instinct was to bar the window. I reached for the shutters, drawing them towards me. In the distance a cock crowed and I thought of betrayal. I ripped off my dress, throwing myself on the bed, my sobs so violent they wracked my body. I could hear a woman wailing – a deep, visceral cry, full of longing, and I realised it was me. I gripped my pillow, holding it against my chest, burying my face deep within it, curling myself into a ball as if I was a child. I had never cried like this before. Never ached so terribly.

I did not hear Jenna open the door. She held me to her, rocking me gently. I laid my head on her shoulder and clutched her to me, needing the warmth of her body to take the chill from my heart. My tears subsided though my chest still heaved and I lay exhausted, all emotion spent. Without a word, she tucked the blanket round me, pushing a matted strand from my face. When she judged me asleep, she tiptoed from the room, retrieving my torn dress from the floor.

I never saw that dress again.

Chapter Forty-four

Monday 19th August 1793 8:00 a.m.

I watched Tom load the last of the bark chippings onto the cart. He was anxious to get going and even the oxen seemed to pick up his excitement. They pulled restlessly against the harness, shaking their heavy heads, their nostrils flaring in the early morning drizzle.

'You'll take care, won't you, Tom? The ruts will be awful if this rain continues – they could be dangerous. You mustn't get stuck.'

'I'll be careful, Miss Pengelly, but we're not that loaded – we'll be fine. Besides, I wouldn't go if I was worried.'

'Make sure you speak to Mr Ferris, not his foreman. The tannery's behind Pydar Street but I think there're several there, so be sure you find the right one.'

'We won't let you down. Seth's been to Truro several times and we're grown men – I think we can handle the journey without gettin' into too much trouble!'

Along with the stubble on his chin, Tom had grown in confidence, but going to Truro was fraught with difficulties and I was not that reassured. Part of me wished I was going with them, but there was work to be done and I was secretly glad Father had not yet returned from Mevagissey. Sending our bark to Mr Ferris was just the first thing on my list.

All the accounts had been settled promptly, the yard was now empty of repairs, and within the week we would begin to build Mr Warleggan's recently commissioned lugger. Mr Scantlebury's plans were spread across Father's desk. It seemed strange that Mr Scantlebury – a man with much less education than Father – always drew careful plans while Father always worked to a model. It seemed the wrong way round, but the combination worked well. Our ships were renowned for their robust construction and I could see this lugger would be no exception.

I was alone in the office. Mr Scantlebury was with the sail-makers, trying to convince them that a dipping sail would reduce the wear on the new lugger's canvas and, for some reason, Mr Melhuish had not yet fired up the forge. It seemed strangely quiet. No banging, no hammering, no sound of sawing, no smell of pitch. All eerily quiet on a mizzling day, with the north wind bringing with it the smell of wet fields and rich manure.

I stole a quick look at my reflection.

Jenna had dressed my hair in a new style and I was still coming to terms with the way it looked. Most of my hair was looped behind me but she had left a series of tightly rolled curls surrounding my face. They bobbed up and down as I walked and were slightly disconcerting. It made me feel strangely light-headed, but it was not just my hair that drew me to the window. Jenna, Mother, and Elowyn had worked tirelessly over the last two days to finish my new *working gown*, as Madame Merrick insisted on calling it. And though my reflection was slightly distorted, I was thrilled with what I saw.

The cotton was a deep ruby red and though it did not shine, it had a richness which *spoke of quality*. The style was simple, the waist not too high to be overly fashionable. The sleeves ended just below my elbow and, as Madame Merrick was adamant I would be taken more seriously if I wore no frills, were edged in velvet, not lace. The only embellishments were the delicately embroidered patterns on either side of the jacket collar. At first I thought they were flowers but, when I looked more carefully, I saw Elowyn had meticulously worked my initials, *RP*, in black silk thread.

I gave a little twirl, to admire the way the gown fell from the back, and returned to my bureau. We had ordered surplus resin and had stocked up on tar and oakum as well as paint and varnish. The flax and hemp had been moved to another storeroom and Tom had cleared the cellars of unwanted clutter. Together, we had created quite a storehouse and word was getting out that we had good supplies.

Footsteps made me look up. Thomas Warren and his huge henchman were striding across the yard. My pen dropped from my hand as the room began to sway around me and I bent forward, putting my head between my knees to stop my sudden dizziness. Perhaps they would not see me? If they looked through the window, they might think the office empty.

The door burst open and I saw the silver buckles on Thomas Warren's shoes as he waited for me to acknowledge his presence. I felt sick with fear but pretended I was searching for something, 'Good morning, Mr Warren, this is a pleasant surprise,' I managed to say, steadying myself against the bureau.

My eyes were immediately drawn to the face of the huge man I had only seen from behind. There was something familiar about his coarse, pock-marked face and bulbous nose. Over his shaven head he wore a brown felt hat and though he wore the dress of a townsman, he looked as rough as a vagrant. 'How can I help you?' I said, summoning as much courage as I could. 'I'm afraid Father isn't here at the moment.'

'Still acting, Miss Pengelly?' Thomas Warren seemed to spit the words. 'You're good at acting, aren't you? I take my hat off to your brilliant performance, both now, and at the auction. You may've fooled the auctioneer, but you didn't fool me.' He walked slowly across the room, leaning on my bureau with both his hands, his face too close to mine. His skin was grey, dark shadows beneath his eyes.

'What auction?' My laugh sounded hollow.

'You know what I mean, you lying bitch. And you know what I've come for.' He motioned to his companion, who likewise crossed the room to stand in front of me, flexing his fingers until they cracked. They were huge, calloused hands with tattoos across the back of each finger. 'We want the creek you stole from us. We know it was you, so stop this ridiculous charade...'

342

I tried not to flinch. 'I *stole* from you? You accuse me of something I know nothing about and now you're threatening me?'

'You dare stand there with your jumped-up airs and intolerable conceit, thinking you're so clever. Yes I'm threatening you, you stupid whore. Accidents will happen. Fires will burn. Boats will get ruined. People will get hurt. Tell that to your idiot father who's no more sense than to get himself ruined again.' His twisted smile revealed broken, tobacco-stained teeth. 'You need a lesson, Miss Pengelly. Zack – go about your business.'

I saw the responding smile on Zack's face and my heart froze. In a flash, he swooped forward, swiping his huge arm across my bureau, sending everything crashing to the ground. I jumped back, watching helplessly as the papers I had been working on landed in a jumbled mess, my ledger landing with its beautiful calf skin cover creasing along the spine.

I was too terrified to do anything. Zack walked over to Father's desk to repeat his violence. Once again he reached his huge arm across the desk, sweeping everything to the floor in one long movement. Within seconds, Mr Scantlebury's drawings lay crushed beneath the weight of books and journals. 'Stop!' I yelled at the top of my voice. 'You can't do this.'

Thomas Warren seemed to be enjoying my distress. 'I can do exactly as I like,' he said.

He meant it too. Again he motioned to Zack, nodding his head towards the large bookshelf which stood at least eight feet tall against the wall. It was crammed full of documents; years of accounts and numerous boxes containing everything that was important to us. Mr Scantlebury's plans were stored on the bottom shelves while Father's irreplaceable models balanced on the top. It meant nothing to them. Thomas Warren's obedient henchman grabbed the bookcase and went to pull it from the wall.

An angry red mist started blurring my eyes. 'Get out of this office. Now!'

Thomas Warren raised his hand. Zack held the bookcase poised in the air. Only the slightest pull and everything would go crashing to the ground.

'Get out, both of you...or I'll...'

'Do what?' whispered Thomas Warren as he leant towards me. My stomach heaved. He was staring at my bosom. Beads of sweat were glistening on his brow. 'Do what, you stupid whore? Believe me, I've only just begun. There's a lot more I plan to do – a lot more.' He lowered his hands towards his groin and clenched his fists, one on top of the other – pink and solid against his breeches. He started gesturing at me, violently thrusting them up and down as he walked towards me. It was an obscene gesture and absolutely terrifying.

I began backing away, tripping over my chair, disgusted by what I saw, but Thomas Warren lunged towards me, up-turning my bureau, forcing me into the corner. He grabbed my wrists, pushing them against the wall, pinning himself against me, his disgusting tongue flicking in and out of his mouth like a snake. His foul brown tongue, in his foul mouth, darting at me, like a reptile.

I felt the thrust of his groin as he pressed against me, crushing himself against the folds of my beautiful new dress, his hands grabbing me round the back of my thighs as he forced himself against me. I turned my face in disgust, but he held me with such force I could not free myself.

'Don't struggle, my beauty – would be a shame to ruin this new hairstyle of yours.' His foul tongue wrapped itself around one of my curls and he drew it into his mouth, sucking deeply, like a baby.

From the corner of my eye, I saw movement in the yard. A man was crossing it with a large bag in one hand and a scrap of paper in the other. The heavy rain was wetting the paper, making it difficult to read. He must have been looking for somewhere because he was shaking his head, puzzled, as if he had lost his bearings. To my horror, he turned, heading in the opposite direction, hunching his shoulders against the sudden deluge which now threatened to soak him completely. He was leaving as quickly as he had come.

Thomas Warren must have seen me looking. He swung round to see the man's retreating figure. His grip loosened on my thighs but just before he put his hand over my mouth, I managed to scream with all my might – a loud, blood-curdling scream that pierced my ears and resounded round the office. Thomas Warren pushed me deeper into the corner, clamping my mouth so tightly I could hardly breathe. I struggled against him, kicking and gasping, but I was held too firmly and could make no further cry. He may have been no taller than me, and slight of build, but his strength was immense and I was completely powerless.

Zack let go of the bookcase, concealing himself in the recess behind the shutters. To anyone passing, the office would look deserted. The clock on the wall ticked loudly. It was strange hearing the clock tick. Usually the yard was so noisy, so full of activity and I had never noticed it before. Thomas Warren pressed himself harder against me, forcing me further into the corner, the bristles on his cheek scratching against my skin. He reeked of sweat and tobacco, the stench of his fetid breath making me want to retch. I strained my ears, desperately praying the man I had seen passing had heard my scream.

Footsteps stopped outside. Within seconds, the door burst open and the stranger entered with a blast of cold air and a flurry of rain. Thomas Warren immediately let go, taking a step back. The stranger walked further into the office, his face incredulous at the chaos in the room. The capes of his travelling coat and his tall hat dripped pools of rain onto the floor beneath him. Seeing me, he threw his bag to the floor and stood glaring at the two men, his hands resting on his hips, his fists, at once, clenching.

'What's happening?' he demanded, glancing at the heap of papers and overturned bureau. 'Do you require my assistance, madam?'

I said nothing but ran towards him, tears of relief filling my eyes.

'No, she doesn't,' Thomas Warren replied. He straightened his jacket and grabbed his hat. 'We're just leaving.'

Zack was clearly not ready to leave. Glowering across the room, he flexed his huge hands once again, clicking the joints of his fingers. For a moment, I thought he would run at my rescuer but he cleared his throat and spat on the floor. Such insolence was clearly too much for the stranger, who squared his shoulders and clenched his fists, undaunted that his opponent was yet a head taller than himself and considerably heavier.

'Madam, do you want these men apprehended?' he asked with authority.

I shook my head, petrified of the fight that would ensue. I just wanted them out of the office. The stranger's chivalrous act may be well meant, but to pit himself against two such violent men would be asking too much.

'No, let them pass – thank you. It was merely a misunderstanding...over some business...but now it's resolved,' I managed to say. 'But don't leave. Please stay and dry yourself, you look soaked to the skin.'

It must have been the quiver in my voice that made the stranger look so intently. He was much younger than I thought at first – not yet thirty – with a sailor's burnt complexion, if not a sailor's manner. His bearing and accent was that of an educated man and the eyes which looked deeply into mine were intelligent and kind. I could see he was reluctant to let my assailants go, but as I nodded my assent and tried to smile, he stood begrudgingly aside, holding open the door.

Thomas Warren took hold of one of Father's umbrellas, opening it so violently I thought the spokes would shatter. He paused at the door, his face furious. 'It's not yet resolved,' he said through gritted teeth. 'She knows what she has to do.' He turned to my rescuer with the same threatening air, 'And you, *sir*, whoever you are, would do better to stop your interference.'

Chapter Forty-five

My rescuer took off his hat and threw his travelling coat against the chair. He was a tall man with a commanding figure, his eyes hazel, like his hair. They were kind eyes, soft and intelligent, with crinkle lines already forming at the corners. But he was not smiling. He was looking at me with great concern.

'Madam, allow me,' he said, straightening the chair. 'Please sit down, you look very shaken.'

'I'm fine, thank you. It's just a silly disagreement.'

'This is more than a disagreement' he said, pointing to the mess. 'This is violence against a person and a person's property. Did they hurt you, miss…?

'Pengelly…my name's Rosehannon Pengelly.'

'Morcum Calstock, Miss Pengelly – at your service,' he said, making a formal bow. 'Shall I get someone to help you, or would you perhaps like me to walk you home?'

'No, Mr Calstock,' I said, trying to stop my legs shaking. 'Thank you for your kindness but it takes more than a few crumpled papers to intimidate me.' I hoped my smile looked convincing.

He smiled back. He had a beautiful smile, strong and confident yet strangely intimate and reassuring. His face was browned by the sun, his hair tied behind his neck. It was almost blonde in places as if the sun still shone on it. His jaw was square, his forehead broad, his nose straight with a slight snub at the end. His was one of the friendliest faces I had seen – and one of the most handsome.

'What if they come back, Miss Pengelly?'

'They won't come back. They want a log pool but Sir James Polcarrow owns the land and they're angry – they've taken it out on me but they'll soon realise their mistake.'

Morcum Calstock looked relieved, though I could tell he was still anxious. 'At least let me help you restore some order,' he said, returning my bureau to its upright position. 'Allow me to be your servant, Miss Pengelly.' His smile revealed strong, beautifully straight teeth.

Papers were strewn all over the office and, as we bent to pick them up, my fear subsided. Smiling at each other, we retrieved the papers, placing them once more in neat piles on the bureau or Father's desk. We were almost finished, only Mr Scantlebury's plans remained on the floor. Morcum Calstock laid them on the desk, smoothing his hands over them with a reverence I found touching. 'These are fine drawings,' he said, 'and beautifully executed. Are they your father's?'

'No, they're Mr Scantlebury's – he's our master ship-wright.'

'He's a steady hand and a real flair for detail,' he said examining them closely. 'I'd be proud, very proud if I'd done these.'

'Are you a shipwright?' I asked, my heart leaping.

'No – I'm a land agent by profession but I've secret dreams to be an architect.'

'Then you must follow your dreams,' I said, throwing all etiquette to the wind. I must have sounded harsh. Or disappointed. Or even envious. He glanced up from studying the plans, looking curiously, as if he detected there was something I was not saying.

'And you, Miss Pengelly? Do you have dreams?'

I hesitated, yet there was something about this man which made me feel comfortable. Something solid and steady – like a dependable rock. He had just put himself in grave danger on my behalf and here we were, discussing dreams. It was as if all formality was over and we were already well acquainted. 'Yes, I do have dreams, though it's highly unlikely they'll ever be realised. One day, when Father's no longer capable, I'd like to run his boatyard. Can you ever see that happening?'

A thoughtful expression crossed his handsome face. 'We live in changing times, Miss Pengelly, who knows what the future may bring? If we don't dream we dare not hope.'

Outside, the deluge of rain had dwindled to faint drizzle. A tiny patch of blue was breaking through the grey sky – it would be sunny again soon. I found I was smiling. If Jenna had been there, I would have danced round the room with her. Morcum Calstock had taken me seriously; he had not scoffed at my dreams. The office restored, Morcum

350

Calstock smiled as he picked up his bag and his still-dripping coat.

'I can't thank you enough, Mr Calstock,' I said, walking him to the door. 'I'll always be in your debt, and if there's any way I, or Father, can help, please ask.'

'Well, you could just point me in the right direction for Mrs Abigail's lodgings,' he said, his eyes creasing into their laughter lines. 'I thought it was down here – I was looking for it when I heard you scream.'

'It's a bit difficult to find…here…let me draw you a quick map – it'll be easier than if I give you complicated instructions…' The map completed, I could hear whistling and looked up. Father was back from Mevagissey and crossing the yard.

Jenna's food had done wonders for his health. He looked well – still too thin, but strong and upright. His new jacket and breeches made him look prosperous, his hat lent him gravitas, his new side whiskers a distinct look of wisdom. He was carrying a leather case and, for a moment, a pang of disappointment surged through me. Gone was the father I remembered. In his place was someone I hardly recognised – more a politician than a boat-builder.

Father must have seen me hand Morcum Calstock the scribbled map. He stood, eyeing us intently. 'This is Mr Calstock, Father.'

'D'you want to commission a boat, Mr Calstock?'

'Alas, sir, I don't have the funds.'

'Is it employment you seek?'

'It is, sir, but not in a boatyard. I'm a land agent – I seek employment but I'm only passing through your town. I need to go inland – to the moors – to where there're large estates.'

'Large estates? Why spend your life labourin' for some wealthy landowner with too much money and too much land?' Father said with a smile. 'Workin' for a pittance at someone else's beck and call all your life? Have you never thought to work for yerself, strike out on your own? Be your own man not some lackey, jumpin' at orders, touchin' your forelock and doin' another man's work.' Though his words were harsh, Father could be charming and persuasive. He smiled kindly at Morcum Calstock, patting him on the back as if he was his son.

'My father's a steward, and his before him – it's the family business, so to speak.'

'But still, you must make your *own* life, Mr Calstock – be beholden to no man. I build boats to my own design. I have freedom of choice, but in your job you'll have no freedom. We're born free – yet you'd shackle yourself to some overfed aristocrat? Times are changin'; we don't need to wear shackles of our own makin' any more. Perhaps we can persuade you Fosse is a place you could prosper – come back and see us.'

Mr Calstock smiled broadly. 'I'd like that, sir,' he said, bowing. He turned to me, his hazel eyes sparkling, 'Good day, Miss Pengelly. I hope we shall meet again.'

'Good day, Mr Calstock.' I replied, almost wishing he was not going. But for this man, things would have been very different.

Suddenly, I found myself blushing under Father's fierce scrutiny. Flinging his hat on the chair, he crossed to his desk, barely glancing at the plans as he placed his case on the top of them.

'How was Mevagissey?' I asked.

'Mevagissey's much the same.'

'Did you meet with the boat-builders?'

He chose to ignore my question, 'Where's Thomas…and the men?'

'Mr Scantlebury's with the sailmakers and he gave the men leave – work on the new lugger starts tomorrow and the repairs are complete.'

'So you had the yard to yerself. That was convenient.'

'I met Mr Calstock by *chance*, Father – he was looking for Mrs Abigail's lodging house.'

'No need to quarrel, Rose. Your Mr Calstock seems a nice man – obviously educated and with a hint of independence about him which shows promise. Aye, you needn't worry, I liked the look of him. Fact is, I hope we see more of him.'

Father sifted through his letters. 'What's this?' he said. 'Why've I got the honour of a letter with the Polcarrow seal?' My heart sank. Everything was happening too quickly. I had wanted Mr Scantlebury to suggest the log pool and Father to approach Sir James. Now that was impossible. He slammed the letter onto his desk. 'Condescendin' bastard!' he muttered, 'interferin', meddlin', condescendin' bastard. Why'd I want a log pool? And he dares suggest a rent so low it's an insult. He *requires* I contact him at my earliest convenience, does he?'

I took a deep breath. This was worse than ever. Father could be roused to terrible temper and I could never reason with him in this state. Besides, we really needed Mr Scantlebury to tell him it was his idea. I hoped he did not hear the quiver in my voice. 'He may have got wind of the new brig contract... perhaps he thinks it would be advantageous if you had your own log pool.'

Father swung round. As he guessed the truth, I saw his flash of anger, saw him bite his tongue. Part of me wanted to run to him, throw myself at his feet, but I was not a child any more. I was a grown woman, struggling in a man's world, and even I doubted I should be there. I could still smell Thomas Warren's foul spittle on my damp curl, still feel his thrusting pelvis.

Father's eyes turned to my new dress. 'Are you expectin' to go where your new gown will be appreciated? Like Polcarrow? I'd momentarily forgotten I had a daughter with friends in high places. Perhaps we should go together, to celebrate our good fortune in being offered a log pool at such an advantageous rate?'

'I've no wish to go to Polcarrow,' I said furiously, 'and I've absolutely no intention of seeing Sir James again. I'm grateful for his past help but you're wrong to call him my friend.'

Father's eyes softened. 'Rose, my dear,' he said, taking off his glasses, 'perhaps we'd best start again. My business in Mevagissey was very useful. I visited St Austell and intend to go to Polperro. We've set in motion a Friendly Society — there's a need out there for greater unity and men are interested. We'll soon gain strength.' He smiled and pinched my cheek, a gesture that used to make me blush with pride. 'And you look beautiful, Rose. I love your new gown.'

I did not blush with pride but smiled to hide my fear. Friendly Societies were beginning to be thought seditious and Father's actions could prove dangerous. He could lose everything and he would take good boat-builders with him. As if it was not hard enough already.

Thomas Warren's threats were still ringing in my ears. 'Did you take up the insurance with Mr Mitchell?'

Father looked surprised. 'I've done what you insisted.'

I could tell he was lying. Just like the last time. Just like the time we lost everything because he had thought it not necessary to insure the cutter.

'So everything's covered: boats, warehouse, storerooms – covered for theft and fire as well as storm damage? Father, please don't tell me we're still not insured. You promised me never again.'

'I'll do it this afternoon.'

'Father – we need to be insured,' I began feeling really alarmed.

'Then we'll do it together,' he said, watching me carefully. 'First, you can accompany me to Polcarrow, then we'll sort out the insurance.'

Was there irritation in his eyes? A note of impatience in his voice? I could not tell. Somehow I felt he was testing my loyalty and I knew I could not refuse. If accompanying him to Polcarrow would guarantee our getting insurance, I had no choice but to go.

Chapter Forty-six

On the way to Polcarrow, bells began peeling as shouts echoed across the town. The pilchards were running – they were to the south of Gribbon Head, heading straight for Polridmouth Bay. It was a lee shore, but hardly any wind and they were there for the taking. Rumour had it the shoal was so huge, the sea had turned silver.

I held Father's arm, pressing against the tide of people running past us, and entered the gates of Polcarrow, relieved to be leaving the mayhem. Once again, I found myself walking up the immaculately manicured drive, climbing the imposing sweep of steps to the large front door. To my surprise, Henderson was expecting us.

With the same stiff reserve, though not the same discourtesy, he opened the door, asking us to wait while he informed Sir James of our arrival. Father stood squarely, his feet apart, his hands behind his back, staring in disdain at the elaborately carved staircase. The chandeliers gleamed, the marble floor shone, the highly polished furniture reflected the fine blue and white china vases, but something was different.

A large portrait of a woman had been hung above the fireplace. She was tall, beautiful, wearing a flowing white gown, her wide hat covered in white feathers. Her hands were pressing lightly against a tree, her head and shoulders turned towards the viewer. Her smile was playful, her eyes seeming to sparkle with mischief. Under her hat, black curls foamed around her. She looked young, carefree and confident. At her feet, a spaniel with fluffy ears and huge brown eyes looked adoringly up at her. The lady had been picking flowers. Next to the spaniel was a basket, not full of formal flowers like lilies or roses, but wild flowers from the fields around her. It was a beautiful portrait, radiating warmth, and somehow changing the whole atmosphere of the hall. Henderson saw me looking at it.

'Who's the lady in the portrait?' I asked.

'Lady Elizabeth Polcarrow – Sir James's mother. She died shortly afterwards. Now, if ye'll follow me, Sir James's waiting.'

We entered the study to find the room in disarray. Mounds of papers were heaped on the desk and drawers in the bureau lay open. Piles of documents and huge, leather-bound rent books lay open on the floor. Maps, held flat at the corners, covered the carpet. Sir James Polcarrow was buttoning up his silk frock coat, tidying himself for our arrival. His hair was dishevelled, his face sombre. He bowed formally but his eyes turned quickly to Henderson.

'Is Mr Warren in his office?'

'No, Sir James. No-one's seen him.'

'I want to be informed the moment he arrives.' He turned to Father, 'Good day, Mr Pengelly, I hope I find you well. Miss Pengelly,' he said, avoiding my eyes.

'Do we intrude?' replied Father with a slight bow, 'you look busy.'

'Certain irregularities, that's all…well, a dammed sight more than irregularities, but I'll get to the bottom of them. My steward's missing and I've reason to believe he may not return. In fact, I have every reason to believe he's been dishonest.'

Dishonest, violent and lecherous, I thought, but I said nothing. Father's presence stopped me from speaking. Nor could I look at James Polcarrow and James Polcarrow was certainly not looking at me.

'Then you'll be needin' a new land agent,' said Father.

'And quickly,' replied James Polcarrow, scowling at the papers strewn around the room.

Something was wrong; Father was smiling his most charming smile, 'Well then, you're in luck. I know a land agent lookin' for a position.' He paused, his voice turning at once conspiratorial. 'Though I don't know him as well as Rose does – he's *her* particular friend but I'm sure she can vouch for his credentials. Your Mr Calstock would be just perfect for the position, wouldn't he, Rose?'

I turned away, blushing furiously. James Polcarrow stiffened, his hands suddenly clenching on the desk. 'I'm afraid I need a steward with experience. I'm about to build cottages for my workers – each cottage with a third of an acre. I intend to put in drainage and water pipes so I need a man who knows what he's about, not some callow youth looking for a chance to raise his standing!' He sounded bitter, dismissive and I swung round, facing him for the first time.

'Morcum Calstock's no *callow* youth,' I replied crossly. 'He's an authoritative and very capable man. He's kind and courageous and, besides, he wants to…' I stopped mid-sentence, both of them staring at me. I could not reveal Mr Calstock's dreams of becoming an architect – he had told me that in confidence and I had no right to betray his confidence.

A half-concealed smile played on Father's lips but James Polcarrow looked furious. 'He wants to what, Miss Pengelly?'

'It's of no consequence,' I replied, turning my back, walking towards the French window. I needed air. My face was burning and I needed to feel the breeze. The rain had passed, the sun slowly emerging from behind the clouds. The air smelt damp, earthy and renewed. On the path a lady was playing with a small spaniel puppy, just like the one in the portrait. She was throwing a ball to the puppy, laughing with delight, her hair glowing as it caught the sun.

Father cleared his throat. 'Though, I have to say, Mr Calstock shows great interest in our yard and I may've need of his services myself. I'm sure it won't take much to persuade him to join us – and a man like that would certainly be an asset.' He smiled, adding, as if in afterthought, 'I hope we don't end up fightin' over Mr Calstock, Sir James.'

Father's smile was a little too fixed and, for a moment, both men stared at each other with thinly veiled hostility. James Polcarrow ran his hand through his hair. 'Indeed,

Mr Pengelly, I've no desire to fight, as you put it. On the contrary, I have here your lease. I've drawn it up myself – the words are taken from a similar lease so it'll be binding. I just need your signature and our business will be complete.' He picked up a parchment from his desk, his scowl deepening.

Father stood with his hands behind his back, his feet apart. 'Thank you, Sir James, but I've no need for your lease. I'm sure it's kindly meant, but I've no desire for your creek and no need for a log pool.'

I stared at Father in astonishment. How dare he refuse something so freely given and so badly needed? How could he be so pig-headed? Of course we needed that log pool. Anyone with an ounce of sense could see that. Boatyards were going to the wall and only those with sufficient resources were surviving. It was as if he had no sense at all.

'Father…!' But I was too proud to plead, too ashamed of what James Polcarrow must be thinking. Furious, I bit my tongue.

James Polcarrow was staring at me, a slight rise in his eyebrow. 'And what about you, Miss Pengelly? Do you think my proposition is a good idea?' He was shielding me from my father, protecting me. I began to speak but Father interrupted me, his voice impatient.

'We can leave Rose out of this, Sir James – she's a woman and knows nothin' of business.'

I felt suddenly struck, winded. I could not believe what I had heard. I would know nothing? I had no ability, no sense of business? All those years of striving for Father's approval, trying to make up for the son he always wanted, reading his pamphlets, desperately hoping he respected my judgement and valued my opinion! Who was it who had got the business running again? The letters sent? The new contracts? How dare he?

Anger burnt my cheeks. It was all for nothing, the worst kind of betrayal, and to humiliate me in front of James Polcarrow made it even worse. *I* was responsible for getting the commissions. *I* balanced our outgoings with our income. For years, *I* had chased unpaid bills, and bargained for better deals, haggling over the price of our materials. At that moment, I hated Father. I hated him for what he had led me to believe and what he had just taken from me. But I would not be so easily silenced.

'Father, with the rent so low, we should take it. Other boatyards will jump at the offer – if Nichols gets the lease, it would work against us.'

'I'll make my own way in this world and I don't need Sir James's charity. I work an honest day and I pay men to do like-wise. The days of serfdom are passed. Men shouldn't depend on patronage and favour. My yard'll prosper an' I'll not have other men think I prosper because of James Polcarrow.'

'I offer a business proposition, Mr Pengelly, that's all.'

'And like a lap dog, you think I should be grateful for the scraps you throw? Accept with blind obedience and remain faithfully at your heels?'

'No, of course not. I ask nothing of you and expect nothing in return.'

'I know very well what you expect in return.'

James Polcarrow's already thunderous face darkened.

'Have a care, Mr Pengelly. They're already calling you an English Jacobin. These are dangerous times and you're treading a dangerous tightrope.'

'Better to tread a tightrope of me own makin' than to dance to another man's tune.'

'You risk imprisonment.'

'I risk enslavement.'

James Polcarrow could no longer contain his fury. His eyes flashed. 'You don't even know the meaning of that word, or if you did, you wouldn't use it so lightly. I'm sorry you're not taking up my offer – it seems our business is at an end. Good day, Mr Pengelly.' He turned his back, his hands clenched by his sides.

What had Father done? What pig-headed stubbornness had made him refuse? James Polcarrow had just offered Father probably the most valuable lease in Fosse. James Polcarrow knew its worth. He could have kept it for himself and yet he had been prepared to offer it to Father. And to be met with such rudeness! I was furious. Furious with Father's overblown self-importance. And to humiliate me like that about Mr Calstock – a man I had only just met?

I marched in front of Father, storming across the hall, my footsteps echoing in the vast expanse. *Knows nothing about business?* Who did he think had kept the boatyard from bankruptcy for so long? If Father had been left in charge, no bills would have been paid, no accounts settled and our boatyard would have been bankrupt long before Mr Tregellas stole the cutter – and even that would not have ruined us, if Father had been insured.

I was so furious I thought I would go straight home but, reaching the bottom step, I breathed in the earthy dampness and slowed my pace. I could not let history repeat itself. I would have to see Father secure the insurance.

Ben was running towards me, his boots caked with mud. He had a smudge of earth across his left cheek. 'Are ye alright, Miss Rose'annon? Only you look s-s-so sad. Don't be sad.'

'I'm not sad, I'm cross – but it's lovely to see you.'

'We're diggin' up where the old cottages burnt down. See all those men with w-w-wheelbarrows? We're making it flat so we can make a new garden.'

Following his pointing finger I saw the charred rubble of the old cottages had been cleared and work was in progress. A team of men were levelling the ground, their wheelbarrows carting and dumping great mounds of earth. Mr Moyle looked to be measuring while the lady gave directions. Father came slowly towards us.

'Hello, Mr Pengelly, we're buildin' a new garden.'

'So I see, Ben.'

'It's goin' to be sunken with arbours an' arches an' a sundial in the middle – but the best bit's the wall round it! A wall! Ye can grow just about anythin' with a wall round it. Oh look, here's Hercules…'

In great danger of his large paws tripping over his long ears, the little spaniel puppy was charging across the grass, his sole intention to reach Ben. Tail wagging, body shaking, he threw himself at Ben's feet, rolling over with all four legs in the air, his little round belly soft and inviting.

''Tis Lady Polcarrow's dog – look how soft he is…but he's my friend an' likes to have his tummy tickled.'

Father looked puzzled. 'Lady Polcarrow's dog? Is that Lady Polcarrow?' We looked across at the auburn-haired lady, watching her point to the ground, then up to the air as if indicating an arch. I must have spent too long in Madame Merrick's company because my first thought was how dowdy her gown was. 'I'm surprised Sir James lets her remain – I'd have thought he'd have sent her packin' a long time ago.'

'Oh no,' cried Ben, 'd-d-don't say such things…Lady Polcarrow's a lovely lady and Sir James is very kind to her – and he's kind to Master Francis. He bought them Hercules – he mustn't send them away…he mustn't…' He grabbed the puppy and clasped him.

Once again, I was furious with Father's lack of judgement. 'Of course he won't send her away – not now he's given her a garden.'

''Tis not her garden, 'tis his garden – he asked her to plan it, that's all. He wants a rose garden…he wants a red rose always on his desk…but ye can get lovely yellow and orange roses…so we're growin' them all – but we'll pick the red ones for his desk.

Father was watching me, his eyes boring into mine. He cleared his throat, 'Why'd he want a *rose* on his desk?' I said nothing but I could feel my cheeks flushing. His eyes narrowed. 'There are rumours in this town which I've chosen to ignore. Take care, Rose. Sir James is a determined man and men like that *always* get what they want.'

I could not believe my ears. 'How dare you!' I retorted.

Ben's stricken face crumpled. He flinched as if in pain. The puppy started whimpering but I could not stay to comfort them. Grabbing my skirts, I ran down the drive, frustration making my blood boil.

Damn the insurance. Damn Father. And damn James Polcarrow.

Chapter Forty-seven

Wednesday 21st August 1793 11:00 a.m.

I still could not settle. I had spent the previous day walking the cliffs, lying in the flower-filled meadow, watching the skylarks singing above me. I had sat by the sea's edge, clambering over rock pools, disturbing the crabs, all the while nursing my grievance. Yet somehow I had returned to the yard.

The keel pieces had arrived and the new sawyers were preparing the pit. Father and Mr Scantlebury were going over every inch of the elm trunks, searching for flaws, but I hardly cared. Even the good news that Mr Ferris was prepared to offer upward of thirty shillings a cartload for our bark chippings did not excite me the way it should have done. Father's words still hurt and resentment was taking its toll.

It was hot and airless: I needed to get out. Besides, the thought of Thomas Warren's threats still rang in my ears and I needed to check if Madame Merrick was properly insured. A fire in the warehouse would ruin her, and if Father did not value me – or even pay me for that matter – then I was free to go when and where I liked.

Without even glancing at the new timber, I crossed the yard. Tom and Mr Melhuish were deep in conversation, shackles of various sizes lying in piles around them. Tom saw me and smiled. Mr Melhuish nodded. I would have nodded back, but there was a playfulness in his glance of appraisal, his eyes lingering too long on my new gown. I was just about to turn my back when I saw his smile fade and a frown cross his face.

Mr Calstock was walking towards me, a small packet held carefully in his hands. He was wearing a well-cut corduroy jacket and doeskin breeches, a simple cravat and the same tall hat. He bowed in greeting, the sun catching the light in his hair. 'Good morning, Miss Pengelly, I hope I find you well.'

'Very well, thank you, Mr Calstock,' I said, smiling, suddenly very glad to see him.

He, too, stood smiling. Nodding to the other two men, he held up the parcel he was carrying. 'These are for you, Miss Pengelly – they're sugar bonbons. I hope you like them.'

The pouch was made of fine cream silk, tied with pink ribbon, and as he placed it in my hands, I felt a rush of almost child-like pleasure. 'Sugar bonbons...for me, Mr Calstock?'

'Sugar-coated almonds. They're to say thank you for directing me to my new lodgings – your map was excellent and my room's very comfortable. They're meant for your desk, but I see you're leaving. Can I have the pleasure of accompanying you somewhere, Miss Pengelly?'

'I'm only going up those steps, Mr Calstock.'

'Then I'll just have to accompany you to the steps,' he said, proffering his arm, 'though I'd prefer it was further.'

This was only the second time we had met, yet somehow I felt at ease with this handsome stranger who had rendered me such a service. I liked his eyes. I liked the way he looked at me. He was not pushy – just kind. He spoke and treated me with respect and his friendliness was refreshing. Compared to the way Mr Melhuish's eyes had become so bold, I could not take exception to the way Mr Calstock smiled at me at all.

Tom had worked wonders on Madame Merrick's rickety steps. Elowyn had insisted Madame Merrick's grand customers could easily fall and hurt themselves and Madame Merrick had taken heed, but even more impressive was the freshly painted red sign, gleaming above the door. Madame Merrick's name was clearly displayed in large gold letters: underneath were those of her patrons – Lady April Cavendish, Miss Celia Cavendish and Lady Cavendish.

I took a moment reading the colourful new sign before climbing the staircase, leaving Mr Calstock smiling up from the ground below. I was just about to say goodbye when a grand carriage came slowly across the yard, stopping right next to the steps below. Tom and Mr Melhuish immediately stopped their conversation, all of us watching the immaculately dressed footman dismount from the back and run quickly to the door to pull down the steps for the three ladies inside.

First to emerge was Miss Celia Cavendish. Shaking the creases from her beautiful cream gown, she looked around, shading her eyes from the sun. Tom bowed very low, his awe plain to see and Mr Melhuish bowed likewise – though not so low. Celia Cavendish adjusted her bonnet and turned, briefly acknowledging their greeting with a discreet nod, before looking up at the gleaming new sign, smiling as she saw her name.

Miss Arbella Cavendish leant carefully out of the carriage with immediate effect on the watching men. *Like moths to a flame.* Her pale-lemon gown glowed in the sun, her blonde ringlets dancing as she turned back for her parasol. As she descended the steps, the footman's pride at being hers to command showed clearly in his face. He danced her attendance, following her with his eyes as Mrs Jennings descended the coach unaided.

They began climbing the steps to Madame Merrick's, Morcum Calstock bowing deeply as they passed. He must have made an impact on Celia Cavendish as she stopped and glanced back in his direction, prompting him to bow again. She passed through the door, looking pointedly at my parcel, and raised her eyebrows, smiling a mischievous smile as the blood rushed to my cheeks. Mother and Elowyn came rushing forward and would have curtseyed had not Arbella Cavendish stumbled as she reached the top step.

Gripping Mrs Jennings' arm, she steadied herself against the door frame, looking so white, I thought she would faint. Mother must have thought so too. She came rushing over with a chair as Celia Cavendish and Mrs Jennings waved their fans to create some air. As her colour returned, she smiled faintly.

'I'm sorry, it's the heat and the smell. I've never smelt anything so strong. It just made me feel ill, but I'm fine now.'

She was clearly struggling and, for a moment, I felt sorry for her. Did she know people were gossiping?

Her fainting attack had certainly not surprised Mother or Elowyn. 'I'm afraid it's the pilchards, Miss Cavendish,' said Mother kindly. 'They're pressing the fish – it's the oil that smells and this hot weather's making it worse. If it's too much for you, we can take your gowns to the hall and do your fittings there.'

Celia Cavendish flashed her impish smile. 'Oh, Mrs Pengelly, don't for a moment suggest that! What would we do if we didn't have you to come and visit? Life at the hall can be very dreary – Arbella and I need diverting, and there's nowhere more diverting than coming here.' She glanced in the direction of an elaborate glass punch-bowl which stood in pride of place on the table. It was a very large punch-bowl, with eight glass dishes hanging delicately by their handles. The punch bowl was empty and Madame Merrick nowhere to be seen. 'Are we too early?' she continued. 'I know we're not expected for another hour but Aunt Martha has a fearful headache and Mamma needs the carriage. We've escaped on our own for a bit of excitement!'

Crossing to the window, she looked down on the yard. Morcum Calstock had joined Tom and Mr Melhuish, and all three of them were sitting on the forge steps, drinking jugs of ale. Mrs Jennings frowned across at her.

'Don't look at me like that, Mrs Jennings, you know I don't mean anything by that. It's just we've been so cooped up lately and I've finished all my books.' Elowyn stood gazing at Celia Cavendish and I could see she had taken a great liking to this grand lady with her hint of rebellion. 'Miss Pengelly?'

Celia Cavendish turned her lively eyes to mine. 'Where's the circulating library? You do have books, as well as pilchards, in this little town of yours, I hope.'

'I'm afraid I don't know if there's a library – there may be one but I've never used it. I don't read novels.'

'You don't read novels? Miss Pengelly – that can't be true!'

'No. I've never read a single novel.'

Celia Cavendish's eyes widened. She looked genuinely astonished. She glanced at her cousin, who, looking much recovered, shrugged her shoulders and smiled back. I resented the glance that passed between them and would have made my excuse and left, but Celia Cavendish turned straight back to me, her face suddenly serious. 'Then you're wiser than I thought, Miss Pengelly. Why waste your time reading novels when you've so much to occupy you?' She coughed slightly and glanced out of the window. 'Your life is already full of excitement. You've used your time far more sensibly and you lead a much more productive life because of it. Indeed, I envy you.'

'Envy me, Miss Cavendish?'

'Absolutely. You do accounts and keep books. You're practical and sensible and you haven't filled your head with romantic nonsense. Novels are all lies, Miss Pengelly. They peddle nonsense to us poor women who are silly enough to believe them. They do us no favours. What man do you know would fall on his knees to declare his undying love? And even if he did, what woman would be foolish enough to believe him?' She spoke harshly, almost with bitterness.

Mother glanced nervously at Mrs Jennings, who smiled

fleetingly. Elowyn looked stunned by the intimate turn the conversation was taking. Arbella Cavendish, however, leapt to her feet, her sickness quite recovered. 'Cousin Celia – I'll not have you be so cynical – of course such men exist.' A beautiful pink blush was spreading across her cheeks. Her eyes were shining, her voice strong. 'I can't have you say that. Men do love – passionately and with undying devotion. You're too hard on them.' She watched our astonished faces and her blush deepened. There were tears in her eyes as her bottom lip began to tremble. 'They do exist,' she repeated more softly. 'I've found such a man.'

Celia Cavendish's smile was full of sadness. 'Then I envy you, too, dear cousin. I would wish the same for all of us.' She paused for a moment. 'But one of us has to be a *Countess* and Mamma is counting on me marrying Viscount Vallenforth. I cannot, as yet, see any evidence of his *undying devotion* but I can live in hope. One day he may prefer me to his horses though I won't hold my breath.'

Her tone held such resignation that, for a moment, nobody moved. A flash of sadness crossed Mother's face, then relief as she glanced out of the window. Madame Merrick had seen the carriage and was hurrying across the yard. 'Madame Merrick will be that sorry to keep you waiting – she only went out to buy some—'

'Some ingredients for the punch, Mrs Pengelly?' interrupted Celia Cavendish, her usual high spirits returning. 'I can't tell you how much we're looking forward to tasting some of Madame Merrick's punch. Poor Aunt Martha will be so disappointed she didn't come!'

I could have enjoyed Celia Cavendish's teasing. I could have enjoyed the irony that Madame Merrick had been out to buy inferior brandy when a bottle of her best cognac lay concealed in her bottom drawer – but all sense of fun had left me. All I could hear were empty words, echoing round my empty heart. *We are like strangers, nothing more. There is nothing between us.* I curtseyed to Celia Cavendish, wishing everyone a good day. I was not good company. I would go home and get under Jenna's feet. Better still, I would curl up with Mr Pitt and eat my sugared almonds.

As the ferry crossed the river, I sat in the bow, trailing my fingers through the water like I had done as a child. I would do that, or I would pretend to be a figurehead, standing with my hands behind my back, my chin held high, ploughing the waves on a journey to foreign lands. Whether it was the sugared almonds that made me think of my childhood, or the intimacy of the conversation we had just had, I found myself wishing for my sisters that lay buried in the churchyard.

The conversation had unsettled me. I had never shared such intimacies before, always shunning the frivolity of feminine chatter. I had never had occasion to dress prettily: never been to an assembly, never read novels. There had been little laughter in my childhood, next to no teasing and no suppressed giggling. Everything had been so political and intense. I could see now, what a very lonely child I had been and what a sad life Mother had led.

At the cottage, I could hardly squeeze past the enormous trunk that filled the hall. We were to move the next day and Jenna had clearly been busy. We did not have many possessions but what we did have, had been carefully packed. Father's papers were nowhere to be seen, the borrowed chairs returned to Mrs Mellor. The dresser was empty, the table standing uncluttered against the wall.

The parlour was similarly sorted with baskets of pots and pans neatly stacked, one on top of another. One large pan remained on the table and, lifting the lid, the delicious smell of boiled ham and potatoes filled the room, but Jenna was nowhere to be found. Even the chickens had gone. The yard was swept, the clothes line empty, the slops rinsed and cleaned. Upstairs, my clothes had been placed into a trunk and though the bed remained made, everything else had been packed away.

Disappointed not to find Jenna, I called out, squeezing back along the hall to check if she was coming up the hill. I felt a rising sense of sadness. This would be our last night in the cottage and, though I hated it with vengeance, I began to feel strangely reluctant to leave. I would miss the intimacy of these shabby rooms with their damp discolouration on the walls, the tiny casements blocking more light than they admitted. I would miss the memories they contained – the sound of a soft thud, the silhouette of a man in the moonlight, the crush of hot lips.

On the step, Jenna was clutching Mr Pitt in her arms.

'Didn't you hear me calling, Jenna? Are you turning deaf in your old age?' My teasing died on my lips. She had been crying. Tears streaked her face. 'What is it? Why're you crying?' I gathered up my skirts to sit next to her on the step. She shrugged her shoulders, fresh tears forming in her eyes. With a faint smile, she buried her face in Mr Pitt's soft fur. 'Is it because of Mr Pitt?' She nodded then shook her head, her mobcap slipping to one side. 'Is it because we're going back to Coombe House?' She nodded again, shrugging her shoulders once more.

'But, Jenna, I thought you'd be happy we're going back. You've worked your fingers to the bone here…all that fetching water and scrubbing and having to go the bakehouse every time you wanted something cooked. You'll be back to a proper range and running water. I thought you'd want that – to have a proper bed to sleep in, not having to sleep under the kitchen table any more – surely that's got to be better?'

She nodded and tried to smile. Freeing one hand, she used her apron to wipe her tears. 'I know, don't mind me, Miss Pengelly – I'm just being stupid.'

We sat in silence. It felt strangely lonely. Over the last year, the differences between us had been almost swept aside. She was our maid, yes, but she was also my only friend. She had been with us for seven years. I had taught her to read and write and Mother had taught her to sew almost as well as she could herself. She was the nearest thing I had to a sister, yet she was still our maid. It seemed so wrong. 'No, Jenna, *we're* not going to go back to how it *was*. We can't…not now – not after what we've been through – things will be different.'

'No, they won't – ye know they won't.'

'Yes, they *will*, Jenna.'

'No, they won't. They can't. Mrs Munroe's very particular. You know she'll never let a cat in her kitchen—'

'I don't care how *particular* Mrs Munroe is. From now on, things are going to be different.'

Jenna wiped away her tears, clutching Mr Pitt closer, her face breaking into a smile. 'Ye're beginning to sound just like Madame Merrick!'

'Am I? Well, I'm glad. She's a woman who gets what she wants – Mr Pitt's coming with us whether Mrs Munroe *likes* it or not. Find him a stout basket and butter his paws – he's family now and our whole family's going home.'

She smiled a watery smile. I put my arm round her shoulders and we sat lost in our own thoughts. The breeze was cool against our cheeks. Above us, gulls circled, their wings spread wide as they glided effortlessly on the rising draughts. Suddenly I remembered the sugared almonds. 'Look, Jenna, we've got a treat. Sugared almonds – that's got to make everything better.' I undid the ribbon, holding out the delicate white bonbons looking like birds' eggs in a silken nest.

Her eyes widened. 'Where'd they come from?'

'They're a present from Mr Calstock.'

'Well, Miss Rosehannon Pengelly, this *is* a turn up!' she cried, her tear-stained face breaking into the biggest smile. 'Ye sly old puss – ye've kept that very quiet. So it's Morcum Calstock who's in love with ye? Well, of course he is…who wouldn't be? And Mr Pengelly likes him too. It's wonderful!'

'Jenna, stop it! It's just his way of saying thank-you for a very small service I rendered him. It doesn't signify anything.'

'No – and my name ain't Jenna Marlow and summer don't follow spring.'

We lingered over our choice of bonbons but, as I bit into the delicate treat, the anticipation of pleasure died on my lips. My stomach began churning in disgust. The sugared almond was too sweet. Instinctively, I spat it out. How much blood had been shed to cover these almonds? How many African men and women forced from their homes, shackled and whipped, transported across oceans in horrific conditions? How many tortured, degraded or died so that these almonds could be dipped in sugar to be given to someone who did not need them?

Handing the pouch to Jenna, I wiped my mouth, trying to rid myself of the taste. 'I can't eat them Jenna – I should never have accepted them. They're tainted. All I can taste is the blood of slaves.'

Chapter Forty-eight

Thursday 22nd August 1793 5:00 a.m.

The early light of dawn crept through the casement. The dairy herd was ready for milking, the cows moaning impatiently below my window. I should have been grateful it was the last time I would wake to the sound of their bells, but my heart felt heavy.

Father had once again made it clear Mother was to end her employment with Madame Merrick. She was to lay down her needles and resume her duties as mistress of Coombe House. In an angry tirade, he had insisted the servants would need supervising and that she should be at home for anyone who called. He, and he alone, would provide for his wife and family.

No-one spoke at breakfast. Jenna cleared away the last of the plates, her face pale through lack of sleep. Mother remained withdrawn, her tone resigned. She spoke softly to Jenna, giving a few last-minute instructions: Sam would come with a cart, they might need a few journeys, but everything should be cleared by noon. The next time we sat down for a meal would be in Coombe House. In the meantime, Mother would spend her last day with Madame Merrick and I would go as usual to the yard with Father.

We did not speak as we crossed the river. Father's face was stony, his expression resolute. Mother gazed across the river mouth and out to sea, her restless hands pulling at the cloak she wrapped around her. It was a grey day with black clouds heavy above us, the southerly wind whipping the waves, the sea getting rougher. More ships than usual crowded the river. Barges, brimming with tin, were rafted together, waiting for reloading onto ships that would take them to London. Several fine cutters, at least four brigs, and a naval brigantine lay at anchor, their masts tall above us. The ferryman dodged their hulls, cursing them for lying across his route. Even the sight of an imposing three-masted barque did not tempt Father out of his sulky silence. I could see him study it carefully, but he would not share his thoughts.

Neither did we speak as we crossed the town. We walked quickly, lost in our own thoughts, each step increasing my sadness. I could feel Mother's emptiness. At the foot of the steps, I paused, telling Father I would not be long. I followed Mother through the door, with the gleaming new sign hanging so proudly above. Word had been sent to Madame Merrick so she knew it was to be Mother's last day. Elowyn's face crumpled at our entrance and Mother rushed to put her arms around her, but she said nothing. I knew she could not speak; her heart was too full of longing.

The four commissioned gowns hung gracefully on the dressmakers' dummies. Mother insisted they needed another week's work but, to my mind, they looked perfect. Arbella's dress was breath-taking. Shimmering even in the dull light, the silk had a glow of its own. Lace covered the whole of the bodice and exquisitely embroidered flowers, with pearls in their centre, decorated the neckline. The sleeves were delicately puffed, caught into layers of lace below the elbows. The skirt fell in soft folds. It was delicate, exquisite, and perfect for her. Mother, Elowyn and Mrs Mellows had gone through to the back and I found myself alone with Madame Merrick.

She stood behind me and cleared her throat. 'I shall miss your mother considerably. There is *much* still to be done and I shall have to do it *all* myself now. But I have to thank you for your *intervention*…without you, the gowns would never have been finished and I would have been in *difficulties*…' She stopped, blinking for a moment before getting out her handkerchief. 'I am not insensible to what I owe you. First the patronage…then your insistence your mother should remain…and *look*, I have a letter from *Sir James Polcarrow*. I am to go to Polcarrow to measure Lady Polcarrow for some new gowns. Her name will be added to my list of *patrons* and if I could *only* find another seamstress as good as your dear mother, my business is set to thrive.' Trying to maintain her composure, she struggled to find her words. 'Eva is a lucky lady, Miss Pengelly — she is very *fortunate* to have you as a daughter…and I, in my turn, have been very fortunate to have had your *intervention*. If I had been lucky enough to have had a daughter, I would *wish* her to be like you.'

I thought my heart would burst. Though her lips were

pursed, I could see them tremble and I knew what it had cost to say those words. I had learnt so much from this extraordinary woman and, though we often did not see eye to eye, I realised the respect I had for her had long since turned to affection. To her obvious surprise, I reached forward to kiss her on the cheek.

Raising her lorgnettes and both eyebrows, she stared at me with that cool, hard look that always made me think she could read my mind. She had attended to her face with extra care: she wore more rouge than usual and a thin pencilled line had been drawn through her eyebrows. She had extraordinarily high cheekbones and a good complexion, but even behind the rouge, she looked strained. I knew she was a woman who would always put on a brave face.

'Madame Merrick,' I said, looking straight into those hooded eyes, 'You may find I haven't quite finished *intervening* just yet.'

Her focus sharpened. 'Indeed, Miss Pengelly?' she said slowly, a flicker of understanding crossing her unsmiling eyes. 'Now, why does that not surprise me?'

I put my finger to my lips. Mother came through from the back room, tying her apron round her for the last time. Elowyn was inconsolable.

The yard was already busy but, entering the office, I could see immediately Father had not been at his desk. He was pacing the room and at my entrance turned abruptly round, squaring his shoulders, a frown clouding his face. I watched as he put his hands behind his back, his feet apart. I had been expecting this. I recognised his stance and was ready for what was to come. 'This is your last day in the yard, Rosehannon. Your place is now at home with your mother. A boatyard's not a suitable place for a woman – a child perhaps, but not a woman. You distract the men too much.'

'They shouldn't look. It's not my fault they can't keep their eyes to themselves.'

'It's wrong you've so much freedom. You can't continue goin' where and when you please. It's not safe, nor seemly.'

'I don't need to be chaperoned. I'm never alone. I come to work with you or Mother and if I go into town, I take Jimmy Tregony.' I should not have lied so easily but I had spent too long surviving without a chaperone and, besides, why did he care now? Had Morcum Calstock told him he had seen me alone with two men or mentioned my dreams of running the yard?

'I shan't always be in the yard, settin' up the Friendly Society will take me away and I'll not always be here to keep an eye on you.'

'Then stay with us, Father,' I pleaded. 'Build the boats you're known for. That's what'll secure our future – good boats built to good designs.'

Father's face flushed. 'That's quite enough – you've grown too bold, too quick to question. Your place's now at home. You've few, if any, domestic skills and it's time you learnt some. You'll not make a good wife if you have all this freedom.'

So that was it. 'And what if I don't want to make a good wife?'

'Rosehannon, this nonsense must stop. Morcum Calstock's very taken with you and if he joins the family, he'll run the office. He'll do the accounts, pay the men and order our stocks. This is a man's world and no place for a woman.' He walked to his desk, looking down at the piled-up papers. 'My mind's made up. There'll be no more discussion.'

I paused to take breath. 'What d'you mean join the family?' Our eyes locked and I had never seen him look more resolute.

'You know exactly what I mean. There'll be no more discussion.'

'If you insist, Father...' I replied, trying to sound calm. 'I'll spend the morning bringing everything up to date and you can ask Mr Calstock to start tomorrow.'

'I knew you'd be reasonable. I'm proud I've taught you to reason. This is your future – my grandson will inherit my yard.'

So the yard was my dowry and negotiations had already started. 'Do we know enough about Mr Calstock, Father?' I said, my resentment held in check. 'After all, we've only just met him. Does he know anything about boat-building – perhaps he's no wish to build boats?'

'His interest in the yard leaves me in no doubt. Leave the details to me...' A smile began playing on his lips and he looked like he always did when he secured a contract – not arrogant enough to look smug, but complacent enough to look self-satisfied. 'It's like a dream come true.'

'I'm glad for you,' I managed to say.

I took off my bonnet, hanging it on the hook I always used.

Straightening my dress, I walked to my bureau for the last time. There was very little to do as everything was up to date. I felt surprisingly calm. A month ago, I would have been angry: I would have been pleading with Father to let me stay, but I had grown tired of struggling in a man's world. It was not my place – I could see that now.

I glanced at Father, reading the newspaper with the confidence of a man who had just secured his future. 'You've the chance of making someone else's dream come true,' I said, in a matter-of-fact tone.

'How so, Rose?'

'As you no longer need me, I'm going to start a school of needlework. It won't be my school, of course – it'll be Mother's – but I intend to do all the accounts. I'll set it all up for her. Mother will be the proprietor and as Jenna's so skilful with the needle, she'll be another teacher – she won't be our maid any more…'

Father's newspaper slammed onto the desk, crushed beneath his fists. 'Absolutely not! I forbid you to talk such nonsense!'

'As well as doing the accounts, I'll teach the alphabet and any calculations they'll need to learn as I intend our girls to be able to read and write and…'

'Didn't you hear me? – I forbid any more talk.'

'We'll start with no more than five or six girls, chosen by Mother and Madame Merrick. The mornings will be spent in lessons, but the afternoons will be spent making what we'll sell. I intend to make a profit – Mother and Jenna will get a fair wage for a fair day's work and I'll get an income too. I'll order all the materials, balance the books and do the accounts…'

I knew Father would be angry, but I did not expect such icy coldness. 'Stop at once! Your foolishness has gone far enough. Not another word an' I'll try to forget what's just passed.'

I could not stop myself, excitement making my heart race. We could do it, we really could. 'As you want Mother and me at home, we'll start our school in Coombe House. We've got far too many rooms — we don't use the half of them. We'll use the top bedrooms — unless you allow us the room next to your study.'

'I'll not listen to another word.' Rising from his seat, he made for the door. 'I forbid you to start a school…and the fact you even thought of it being in Coombe House! You're more foolish than I thought.'

'I hoped you wouldn't refuse, Father, but I suppose I should've known. It was worth asking though…'

He had his hand on the doorknob. 'Good, I'm glad that's settled.'

'It's a pity, though…because now I'm going to have to ask Sir James for a suitable place. I know he'll be obliging. In fact, I think we both know how very obliging he'll be – especially when he knows how grateful I'd be to him. He'll find a place with a very low rent – he may even charge me no rent at all…' All colour drained from Father's cheeks, he looked haunted, too shocked to speak. Making his way slowly back to his desk, he stood leaning on it for support.

'Father,' I continued with absolute clarity, 'here's your choice. Either go to Mother and tell her you've just had an idea she should start a School of Needlework in Coombe House, or I shall send word to Sir James.' I hoped I looked convincing, sounded resolute. I had no intention of ever asking Sir James Polcarrow for anything again.

Father's shoulders sagged, his face seemed to age and whereas before I would have done anything to spare him pain, I stood my ground, tightening my lips.

'Have you discussed this with your mother?'

'No.'

'Then she'll never agree to it. If I forbid it, she'll never do it.'

'Why not make her dreams come true?'

'Because she doesn't want it.'

'Of course she wants it – and if you didn't trample on her good nature all the time, you'd know it's exactly what she wants. She's been lonely and neglected for too long and we could put things right.'

'It'll fail – I give you less than a year.'

'It'll thrive. Mother's granddaughter will inherit her school.'

'You've changed, Rosehannon, and not for the better.'

'I haven't changed, Father. I'm what you made me, but I've become my own woman.'

'Not your own woman – someone else's woman! The town's already talkin' and I'll not have my daughter called...'

'As you say, but it's your choice.'

My voice sounded calm but I was in turmoil. I tried to look busy, staying at my bureau, hoping, praying, he did not call my bluff. We sat in silence until he rose from his chair and strode out of the office, steadying himself by the door as he grasped his stick. If he turned towards the boatyard I was lost, but he turned towards Madame Merrick's and I felt almost giddy with relief. Climbing the now sturdy steps, he paused at the top, reading the sign carefully before opening the door and entering for the first time.

For too long, I had struggled in a man's world. I could see that now. From now on, I wanted to thrive in a woman's world. Like Madame Merrick, I wanted to be surrounded with fun and laughter, share the intimacies of the dressing room, be privy to the gossip and confidences that it brought. I was going to wear lace and ribbons. Maybe even silk. Jenna would no longer be a servant. A whole new world was opening up – we lived in changing times – and I, Rosehannon Pengelly, had every intention of helping them change.

Closing my account book, I retrieved my bonnet, casting my eyes round the room for one last time. This office had seen me change from a girl to a woman. I saw the mark left by my first peg before I could reach the taller pegs; the stool I used to stand on before I could reach the top shelves. I saw the models I had so lovingly held as I sat by Father's feet, the vast number of box files I had created, the account books I had so meticulously kept. I loved everything about the place but my eyes were dry.

I would never set foot in here again. Not unless Father begged me to do so, and not unless he paid me an honest day's wage.

Chapter Forty-nine

I shut the door behind me, pleased when Tom joined me to cross the yard. He was carrying some broken caulking hammers and was looking for Mr Melhuish. 'I can't think where he's gone,' he said, leaving the hammers on the anvil. 'Jimmy's gone too – they must be fetchin' something.'

'That's a shame. I was hoping Jimmy would come with me.'

'D'you need an errand doing?'

'No. I just felt like company, that's all.' Seeing Tom was fortuitous. 'Tom, just because we're moving back to Coombe House doesn't change anything – I'll still expect you and Elowyn to come on Sundays.'

Tom looked at the ground. 'I'm not so sure we should, Miss Pengelly.'

'Tom, it won't make any difference. We can sit in the kitchen if you like, Mrs Munroe won't mind – in fact, if you give her one of your smiles she'll pile you with more food than you can eat.' I hoped the thought of food would do the trick.

'It won't seem right, Miss Pengelly. We'd better…'

'Nonsense,' I said, cutting him short, 'I'll expect both of you. We're not stopping now you've come so far.' Giving him no chance to protest, I skipped beneath the arch with a new lightness in my step. I never thought I would ever want to leave the yard but my mind was racing with plans for Mother's new school.

We would train dressmakers to sew top-quality gowns for Madame Merrick, but as our sales would determine our success, we must not compete with her business. I had lain awake most of the night trying to think what could be sewn by inexperienced seamstresses, yet sold for profit and now I had an idea. What if our school produced clothes for the domestic sphere, like my *working gown* which Madame Merrick so detested? Housekeepers' gowns, maid's dresses, aprons and hats to reflect the wealth of the households they came from? Every garment bearing the interwoven initials of the family buying them – just like Elowyn had sewn on mine? New money was pouring into Cornwall and, after all, the aristocracy had their livery, so why would the newly rich not want their servants recognised?

Clouds, heavy with rain, darkened the sky. The wind showed no sign of lessening but I needed to be out in the air where I could think clearly. I pulled my cloak round me and headed to the town square. The town was deserted, everyone busy sorting the pilchards, all hands salting or gutting the fish. The cellars would be teeming, every last ounce of flesh stripped, every drop of oil pressed, the bones sent to the fields.

I sat on the edge of a horse trough. We would benefit from a patron, but could I ask Celia Cavendish or would her forthcoming marriage to Viscount Vallenforth prevent her? I had only seen Viscount Vallenforth that one time but I had not liked what I saw and felt saddened at the thought of such a lively lady married to such a man.

The streets seemed so empty and even planning our new school could not stop my growing sense of loneliness. The sight of Arbella's wedding gown still lodged in my mind and I had no idea it would make me feel so empty. At any other time, I would have been happy to study the ships laying three abreast against the quayside, but the thought of doing that now left me cold. I felt strangely numb, not wanting to go back to Coombe House to see the tree with the recently cut branch. Seeing the open window in my room would bring back too much pain.

A man came towards the trough, leading two plough horses by their halters. They were beautiful animals, slow and dependable, their soft eyes belying their enormous strength. I left them drinking and wandered up the road to where a shop was selling household goods. I had not looked before at aprons and caps and if such things were for sale, I would make a note of their quality and price.

So many new shops seemed to have opened and I was glad of an excuse to see what they were selling. A bow-fronted window, full of bonnets and matching parasols, caught my attention and I stopped to look. Behind me, a woman rushed quickly past and I caught her reflection in the window. She was clearly in a hurry, wrapped in a large cloak, the hood pulled well down and I swung round to get a better look. She had already disappeared round the bend but I could have sworn it was Arbella Cavendish. Who else had ringlets of golden blonde hair? I felt suddenly curious. After all, if it was her, she was bound to be lost and may need some help.

As luck would have it, the man with the two plough horses was making his way up the lane and, as the bend narrowed, the horses blocked the way. The hooded woman stood to one side, waiting for them to pass and I gained some ground but as she heard my footsteps, she drew her cloak round her, covering her head completely. There was no trace of blonde hair and immediately, I felt so foolish, thinking my mind was playing me tricks. Ever since I had seen her beautiful dress, my thoughts had been far too full of Arbella Cavendish.

I should have left it at that. I should have gone back to Coombe House to help Jenna unpack, but as I watched the woman disappear down an alleyway, something drew me forward. It was the alley that Jim had led me down and in the daylight, I saw it for what it was – a rat-infested hell-hole, home to some of the poorest people in Fosse. It was shameful: no-one should have to live like that. I may have quarrelled with Father, but I still believed him to be right. The Corporation was failing in its duty and whoever owned the buildings should be held to account.

The stench was overpowering. Rats, the size of cats, seemed unconcerned by my presence. Everywhere was black with scum. Puddles of putrid water filled the path. The build-ings were rotting, mould covering the few remaining doors. None of the windows had glass and I looked around searching for the woman but she had vanished, probably stepping into one of the doorways. I should never have thought to follow her and, lifting my skirts high over the filth, I started back the way I had come.

My heart sank. A tall man was coming down the alley towards me, his hands held wide on either side. He was walking slowly, deliberately, his feet squelching the mud, his huge frame blocking the entrance. Just one glance at his tall hat, the familiar set of his huge shoulders and my fear turned to panic. The knife glinted in his tattooed hands and I screamed. There was no-one there, no-one to hear me. I picked up my skirts and ran. I had no choice but to run deeper into the maze of rotting buildings, the foul stench suffocating me as I ran.

Darting between barrels, I jumped the discarded fish crates, dodging between the piles of rubbish strewn across my path. My shoes sank into the ground, the mud slowing my progress, but I did not dare to look round. Zack was behind me. Ahead, I could see the tops of masts visible above the rooftops and I remembered the alley led to the wharf behind the brewhouse. My bonnet had long since fallen off, my hair flying behind me in a tangled mess. A terrible stitch stabbed my side but if I could just reach the wharf, I would stand a chance.

The alley widened and I reached the water. There was no-one there, only a gig moored along the quayside, a sailor carving a figurine in his lap. I looked frantically around. The dark walls of the warehouse rose high beside me, pressing down on me, the river rough; huge swells tossing the gig against the wharf. I had no choice. I had to ask the sailor to help. Throwing myself towards him, I stood clasping the boat, gasping heavily, almost too breathless to speak. He seemed not to notice, but continued carving, slowly whittling away at the wood in his hands.

I saw the pipe before I smelt the tobacco. Pungent fumes filled my nostrils – the scent of vanilla smoke wafted around me, choking me. Not a sailor. Not an ordinary sailor, but the man who had been watching me, waiting for me. I was powerless to run. From the corner of my eye, I saw Zack raise his fist and pain gripped the side of my head – a searing pain so severe it felt like a thousand knives were plunging through my skull. I thought I would vomit. I tried shielding myself from the second blow but it was too late.

Bright lights flashed inside my head, exploding like gunpowder in my brain. I was spiralling downwards, whirling deeper and deeper down a spinning black tunnel. Falling and falling. Spinning out of control, swirling weightlessly through nothing but darkness, nothing but blackness. Then nothing at all.

Chapter Fifty

I could hear voices drifting around me, wordless and indistinct. Angry, abrupt voices, one moment barely audible, the next pounding in my ears. My head throbbed. I felt such pain. Blinding pain and such intense nausea, I thought I would vomit.

'I said use force...not kill her, for chrissake.'

'She'll live.'

'She better wake soon – damn her.'

I could feel swaying, rolling. I tried to move but my limbs were lifeless, my head clamped in a vice. I could not open my eyes but lay listening, fighting my nausea, trying to make sense of my surroundings. The air was thick with tobacco smoke but other smells, too, filtered through my swimming senses – dampness, wood polish, the smell of tar.

'We leave on the tide. We've got till four.'

'She'll wake I tell you.'

Through the pain and blackness, their words made no

sense. I could hear and I could smell but I could not move – like living, but being dead.

'The bitch's wakin' – look, her eyelids are movin'. She's comin' round. Fetch a bucket of water, for chrissake.'

A violent splash of cold water must have jolted me to my senses. As my vision cleared, I could make out the shapes of three men towering above me.

'Get her to the chair but keep her gagged – she's got a scream like a witch's cat.'

Half-pushed, half-carried, I was grabbed round the waist and heaved onto a chair. My head was forced back, my hands tied behind me. I could feel my legs already bound and a gag bit painfully into my mouth. My head was swimming but as they tossed me about like a rag doll, my vision began to clear. I was on a ship – that much was easy.

I could see highly polished wood, elaborate carvings and such grandeur could only mean I was in the cabin of a very large ship. My chair was pushed against the central table, which was bolted to the floor. A painted chest lay roped by my feet and a solid brass lantern swung freely from the deck-head above. A man was glaring at me, his thick-set figure looming over me through the half-light. Built like an ox, his huge hands pressed down on the polished table. To my muddled mind, he looked familiar.

'We meet again, Miss Pengelly,' said Sulio Denville.

The gag was pulled from my mouth. I tried to speak but my tongue was too dry, my lips too swollen. 'What d'you want?' I managed to whisper.

'We want the creek.'

'The creek's not ours.' My head was throbbing. 'We've nothing to do with the creek.'

A man stepped from the shadows, the light flickering on his bald head. Without his wig, Thomas Warren looked older, greyer, and I hardly recognised him. 'Lying whore! You bid for it right under our noses and now you're going to do exactly what I tell you to do. You're going to write to your father and tell him if he ever wants to see his precious daughter again, he's to sell us that creek.'

I had to concentrate on what he was saying. My senses were hazy, my hearing muffled. 'He can't sell you the creek… you've made a mistake – we don't own it…we wanted to lease it…and I even suggested it to Sir James…but we never bought the creek. Father doesn't own it.'

Sulio Denville laughed. I remembered his laugh. I also remembered the look on his face when he had tried to kill James Polcarrow. 'You expect us to believe that? I'm afraid you've to do a lot better than that. I want that creek and I always get what I want.'

'It's the truth…on Father's life, I swear it's the truth… we don't own the creek or the land…I swear it.' Though I sounded weak, my mind was clearing.

Sulio Denville leant across the table, his eyebrows slicing angrily across his forehead. His beard was grey and wiry, several of his teeth missing. He glared at Thomas Warren. 'You said they owned it.'

'The whore's lying. For chrissake, I was there. I saw her. It was her, alright. Beat it out of her – you'll see I'm right.'

'I'm not lying…and I'll do anything you ask. I'll write to

Father but he'll know something's wrong. He'll go to the constable and have the town searched...he'll know to alert everybody...' My mouth felt bruised, every muscle in my body aching. I knew these men were ruthless. 'Please, please let me go.' I pleaded. 'The creek was bought in Sir James's name – he owns the creek.' I was struggling to hold back my tears.

'Don't trust a word she says.' Beads of sweat were glistening on Thomas Warren's bald head. Wiping his brow with his shirt sleeve, he lurched as the ship rolled. 'She's a lying whore.'

'No, it's the truth, I promise. On Father's life, I promise.'

Sulio Denville slammed his huge hands on the table. 'Dammit!' He stood glaring at Thomas Warren across the table. 'She may be tellin' the truth. Why didn't you confirm it, you damn fool? You said they owned it.'

'I thought...'

'Either way, it makes no difference – your father's got the lease so we'll re-lease it from him. He won't see you again till we have an agreement.'

My mind was racing. Thomas Warren had never returned to Polcarrow, so they had no idea Father had refused the lease. 'No...' I said, 'Father's been in Mevagissey and hasn't signed the lease. A meeting's been planned for next week – I presume that's when he'll be offered the creek.'

'Presume be dammed, you conniving bitch,' Thomas Warren hissed in my ear. 'Your father's your puppet – everyone knows who runs that yard.' He paused, his eyes glinting. 'Your father doesn't even know about the log pool, does he?' He gripped my hair, forcing back my head, 'You haven't told him, have you?'

'No,' I replied, turning my face from his stinking breath.

'That's more like it – we'll get the lease for ourselves.' A gleam crossed Sulio Denville's eyes. 'Zack, get to Polcarrow and ask to lease the creek.' Zack had been watching from the shadows. I saw him nod, unsmiling. Sulio Denville's eyes narrowed, tobacco fumes swirling round his face. 'But that's not goin' to help you, *Miss Pengelly*,' he said, drawing the smoke into his mouth. 'You know too much so you're comin' to the Ivory Coast.'

I tried to scream but Thomas Warren's hands clamped my mouth, his hand forcing my chin upwards, hurting my neck. The cabin was rolling, pitching in the swell and I could hardly breathe: my legs were tied so securely, my arms bound behind my back, I could not wrench free.

'It's not that easy,' he said, my head pinned against him. 'James Polcarrow's too infatuated with this bitch. He knows she wants the lease and he won't give it to anyone else – not until he's discussed it with her. The only way we'll keep that dammed man at bay is if the bitch writes to say she no longer wants it.'

Sulio Denville's eyes remained narrowed. 'That'll work well for us – she can tell Polcarrow to lease the creek to Zack. We'll change his name, make out he's a timber merchant – that way we'll be sure to get it.' Grabbing some paper, he checked to see if both sides were clear of writing and my hands were freed from their bindings. As I stretched my arms, rubbing my wrists, I felt a pistol press against my back.

'Write only what I say,' said Thomas Warren, his lips brushing against my hair. 'We've a long voyage ahead and we wouldn't want you to get hurt. Not for what I've got in mind. No, we're going to have to keep you as fresh as a daisy, my little beauty, because in case you've forgotten, we've unfinished business...' Slamming down the pistol, he seized my hair, twisting it painfully in his hands as he piled it on top of my head. Forcing my head against the table, he began to lick the back of my neck, his foul rasping tongue making me want to retch.

'For chrissake, get on with the letter,' snapped Sulio Denville.

Thomas Warren released me and I seized the quill, trying to steady my shaking hand. He coughed, clearing his throat. 'Write this...*Dear Sir James...You will think it strange for me to change my mind, especially as I've been so adamant....* No, don't write adamant, write...*especially as I thought I wanted the creek so badly. However—*'

'Wait!' I cried, my hands still shaking, 'you're going too fast...'

'*However, I have found a timber merchant in Plymouth and have decided to buy our logs directly from him as I trust him to supply us with the quality we seek...*'

'The tip's smudging – the end's too blunt,' I cried, throwing down the pen.

'For chrissake sake, woman – it's your heavy hand,' Sulio Denville shouted, crossing the cabin to open a drawer, his gait swaying with the movement of the ship. The storm must have intensified. It must be well into the night. Through the aft windows, I could see lanterns burning on the stern. I dipped the new pen into the ink and waited for Thomas Warren to continue.

'...and though I said I wanted the lease, please feel free to offer it to someone else. However, I do have a friend who would benefit from a log pool. His name is Zach Trewellyn... Yours, in gratitude, Rosehannon Pengelly...'

I finished writing the letter. Nothing I had written would alert James Polcarrow. He would assume I had tried to reason with Father but had been unsuccessful in persuading him to change his mind. He would merely think I was bringing the whole business to an end and would never know how much danger I was in. James Polcarrow was my only hope. I needed him more than I had ever needed anyone, yet the formality of my letter meant he would never guess my danger. I took a deep breath, signing the letter with shaking hands.

Sulio Denville grabbed it from my hand, holding it to the light, his face furious. 'What's this nonsense?' he said, slamming it down on the table. 'Have you lost your senses?'

Both men were staring at the drawing of a rose I had hastily sketched under my name. I, too, looked at it, my voice breaking. 'I'm sorry – it's a childish habit I haven't yet broken. My name's Rose and I often do it without thinking... it was foolish of me... I can rewrite the letter if you like.' My heart was pounding. *Please, let them believe me. Please.*

Sulio Denville frowned. He glanced at the brass clock on the panel above the desk. 'Oh, for God's sake, woman – we haven't time,' he said, folding the paper and sealing it with wax. He handed it to Thomas Warren. 'It's already past one, so you'll have to hurry. Leave the letter so James Polcarrow gets it after we've sailed. And get a message to Roskelly. Make sure he knows about the creek…and, for chrissake, be back by four.' His eyes turned to me.

'Zack, before you leave, get this woman below and hide her well. I don't want any of the men seein' her – it's a long journey and we'll want her for ourselves.'

All my childhood, I had imagined evil in the shape of goblins, pixies and phantoms that lurked in shadows, hiding in crevices to catch me unawares. But the look that passed between those three men was worse than any evil I could ever have imagined.

Man's inhumanity to man.

Chapter Fifty-one

Bound in a sack and tossed over Zack Denville's shoulders, I was powerless to struggle. With every new turn I could feel we were going deeper into the hold. When the lack of height meant he could no longer stand, Zack dragged me along like a bag of provisions. He spoke to no-one and I heard no voices.

The sack was suffocating, the smell unbearable. The ship was lurching and I could feel Zack stumbling to keep his balance. My back banged painfully against something hard and furious squawking filled the air. My head was spinning, my nausea rising, the gag around my mouth so tight I knew I would choke if I vomited. I wanted to scream, fight back, but I was trussed so tightly I could barely move.

The dragging stopped and I felt myself being wedged into a tiny space. A space so small, my knees were jammed so I could not move. For a moment I lay suffocating in the darkness, rolling with the motion of the ship, the damp sack pressing against my face. I thought he had gone and I had been left alone but, suddenly, the sack was ripped open, the damp cloth removed from my face. As if drowning, I gulped the rancid air, feeling Zack drag a wet chain across my body, securing it firmly to a shackle beside me. For a moment, I was relieved: I was gagged, I was bound, but at least I could breathe.

I watched the lantern sway across the vast hold, Zack's huge outline bending double under the close confines of the deck above. The darkness enveloped me and I was left crammed into a space hardly big enough for a dog. I knew which ship it was – the huge three-masted barque lying off Porthruan. I recognised the large windows in the stern which Father had studied so carefully. I remember thinking it was destined for a long voyage, but had never imagined it to be a slave ship.

Shackles and chains lay in coils around me. I could feel the slaves' fear. Suffering had seeped deep into the timbers, and lay thick in the air around me. I could smell death, pain, agony, absorbed by the black hull, once so lovingly carved and meticulously crafted. I was one of them now. I was at the mercy of men who knew no mercy.

Like a child, I closed my eyes, shutting them tightly to block out the terror. As a little girl I would think myself in a safe place. I would imagine Father holding me, laughing at my foolishness, telling me there were no such things as demons. But it was not Father who was holding me now. It was James Polcarrow whose strong arms folded round me in the darkness, his lips brushing my forehead. James Polcarrow, keeping me safe, never letting me go.

Above the moaning of timbers and clucking of hens, I could hear pigs squealing and cows stamping in their stalls. I could see nothing, but strained my ears to hear, every new noise making me turn in its direction. Rats were everywhere. One ran over my legs and for once I was grateful for the sack. It was unbearably hot and wet. Dampness rose from my dress and I found myself blushing in helpless shame.

He would not come. There were only three more hours before the tide turned. He would get the letter too late and would never find me. No-one would ever know where I had gone. But perhaps Jenna would think to alert him? Jenna and Mother would be so worried – they must be doing everything in their power to find me. The thought of them made my tears flow.

I had no concept of time. Perhaps an hour passed, perhaps several. I had no way of telling. My fingers were numb, all feeling in my legs gone. The ropes were biting into my wrists, the chain pressing heavily against my body. Jenna would not alert James Polcarrow – she would think I was with him. I had spent too many moonlit nights in his company and she had been aware of every single one of them. Her loyalty was too strong. I knew she would shield me from my parents. She would be waiting in my room, furious with me, ready to scold me, ready to hold me.

My body was shaking, my face burning. I was thirsty. My lips were crushed, my tongue swollen. I was shaking with cold yet felt unbearably hot. I could feel my mind begin to wander and shut my eyes, going deeper into my safe world again – deeper into the arms of James Polcarrow. I was past pretending. I ached for him. He was as much part of me as I was myself. I could see him leading me to a low couch covered in soft blue velvet. We were on the cutter, the waves rocking, the cabin gently rolling. He was smiling…his eyes burning…

I must have passed out. I woke to hear voices and see a lantern swaying above the steps to the upper deck. I started writhing in the sack, grunting and moaning, but any sound I made was drowned by the chickens and pigs. I tried twisting, jangling the chain, but I could not move. The light dimmed and I was left in darkness, tears rolling down my cheeks.

Once again the lantern swung across the hatch. The voices had returned. I could hear heavy objects being scraped across the deck. This time the men were climbing down the steps. A flint was struck and the lantern, hanging from the deck, began to glow, its light flickering steadily across the vast hold.

'She's here somewhere – look again. Look down here… and behind the pigs. Here, give me the lamp. We're not leaving this ship until we find her…even if we have to start all over again.' It was the voice of James Polcarrow.

'Don't tell me they put slaves down here as well…'

'They cram them anywhere and everywhere – even on those platforms where they can't even sit. Look under all the sacking and pull out those crates. She's here. I know she's here.'

'They're pistols, Sir James – the ship's loaded with firearms.'

I could see the lamp coming nearer. My body was shaking, tears streaming down my face. James Polcarrow was coming.

Bent double, he was thrusting his lantern into every corner, looking behind each timber, searching every possible place. Soon, he would find me. Soon, I would feel his strong arms around me. I should never have doubted he would come. I watched him pause, wiping the sweat from his brow, his handkerchief catching the light. The lamp shone on his jacket and I could see he was formally dressed. He lifted the lantern and, through the darkness, our eyes met.

He said nothing, but crouched by my side, his eyes black in the half-light. I saw his jaw tighten, his face change from relief to anger. Immediately he rose, turning his back on me, handing Joseph his dagger. 'Use this to cut the ropes,' he said, 'wrap her in your jacket and keep her warm. Take her straight to her mother.'

Joseph cut the gag, cradling my head in his hands, soothing me as if I were a child. 'Ye'll be alright now, Miss Pengelly,' he whispered gently. 'I'll get ye back to Jenna – she'll know what to do.' Once again his kind hands helped me. He reached across, pulling back the chain, his face angry with compassion. Ripping through the sack he freed my hands. Turning me gently, he cut the straps that bound my legs. If he noticed my soiled dress, he made no sign. I felt too numb to move, too exhausted to help. I wanted to smile, to thank him but, more than anything, I wanted to cry. James Polcarrow was making his way down the hold, away from me.

'What time is it, Joseph?' My mouth was almost too sore to speak. 'Tell Sir James, Thomas Warren will be returning to the ship – he expects to sail with the tide. Tell Sir James, Thomas Warren was responsible...'

'Don't ye worry, Miss Pengelly,' soothed Joseph, 'Thomas Warren's goin' nowhere – he's tied up with Sulio Denville and now Sir James's found ye, he'll send for the authorities.' I started shaking, tears of relief flooding down my cheeks, clutching Joseph tighter now I knew it was all over.

James Polcarrow paused at the foot of the steps. 'Make sure no-one sees you row Miss Pengelly ashore,' he called back across the hold. 'Tell everyone you found her in the alley. Miss Pengelly's name must not be linked to mine. Tongues will wag and I must not be implicated.'

It was Joseph who scooped me up and carried me home, Joseph's strong arms that rowed me across the river. Joseph who carried me through the streets, holding me to him, never putting me down. It was Joseph who calmed my fears, seeing me safely home and as I leant against his broad shoulders, burying my face in his neck, my heart howled.

It should have been James Polcarrow's strong arms who rowed me ashore, James Polcarrow who carried me so tenderly in his arms. James Polcarrow holding me as if he would never let me go, but James Polcarrow was not to be implicated. He had made that quite clear. So close to his wedding, he could not risk any scandal.

Ebb Tide

Chapter Fifty-two

Coombe House
Saturday 24th August 1793 6:00 p.m.

The sitting room in Coombe House lay directly across the hall from the dining room. After the confines of the tiny cottage, the huge ceilings and elegant proportions seemed so much grander than I remembered and I had forgotten how pretty it was. The stone mantelpiece had carved scrolls at each end, two vases carefully positioned so their reflections showed in the large gold mirror behind them. They were Mother's pride and joy – one was green, covered with brightly painted birds and flowers, the other pale blue with white, raised figures of gods and goddesses. Between the vases a carriage clock stood encased in a dome of glass.

It was the first time I had been allowed downstairs. I had been nursed in my room, the days passing in a restless blur of snatched sleep and haunting nightmares. Jenna and Mother had asked no questions, bathing the rope burns on my feet and wrists in pursed silence. They had sponged my bruised head, put ointment on my lips, but had said nothing.

411

I had not been entirely honest when I said I was better – a dull ache lodged in my head, the fire was blazing, the room the temperature of an oven. I was confined to the chaise longue and uncomfortably hot, but Mother was convinced I still had a fever and was determined to keep me warm.

'Jenna, no…not another log…please – I'm already sweltering. If I'm perspiring, it's because I'm too hot, not because I'm feverish…'

Jenna put the log firmly on top of the others. The wood crackled, sparks flew. 'It's time for yer next drink,' she said.

'I'm not ill, but if you bring me any more of that nettle brew, I'll be sick.'

'It's not nettle, its yarrow,' she said, smiling as she shut the door behind her.

Before Father's bankruptcy, I had spent little time in this beautiful room and seeing it with new eyes made me feel sad I had treated it with such contempt. It was peaceful and elegant and I loved the pale blue and gold colours. Mother's chairs were light and feminine, their elegantly curved backs and dark mahogany wood sitting delicately against the stripes of the wallpaper. I had always found her room dull compared to the excitement found in Father's study, and I regretted that now.

Mother was happy. Now I was better, she was relaxing. She sat at the foot of my chaise longue, busily embroidering a handkerchief but I could tell her mind was not on her stitching.

'Go on, Mother, tell me more. What exactly did Father say?'

'He said for a long time he'd thought my talents were being wasted. He said if I could teach girls to sew they'd have a trade for life and it would keep them from poverty. He cares so much about the poor that he wants me to start a school of needlework.'

'I can't think of anything better. I'll help you...if you want me to.'

'Well, of course, I do, Rose – I couldn't do it without you. I'll be depending on you and Jenna.'

I shifted Mr Pitt to one side. I was wearing my lemon sprig gown and was worried that the butter might stain the material. It was the only dress I could wear, my other dress still soaking in the laundry, but somehow it felt right to be wearing my beautiful dress in Mother's sitting room. Besides, everything was going to change. From now on, I would never go anywhere unattended. I would never roam the countryside, chasing butterflies, or go scrambling over rocks. I would never ruin my clothes by lying on my back, watching skylarks hover above me and I would never again venture down stinking alleyways.

Instead, I would spend my time addressing my woeful lack of domestic skills. Mother and I would pass our evenings sitting cosily by the fire. There was still plenty of time to learn to sew and plenty of time to discuss what we should ask Mrs Munroe to cook. Besides, we had the school to plan. 'Mrs Munroe's going to wonder where all her butter's gone,' I said, scratching Mr Pitt behind the ear.

'Rose,' said Mother, her voice at once serious, 'I don't like to scold ye in front of Jenna, but now we're alone, I have to tell ye — ye were wrong and very foolish to go down that alley. What were ye thinking? If Joseph hadn't chanced upon ye, anything could've happened. Ye could've been killed.'

I had been expecting this. 'Mother, please don't scold. I'll never go anywhere alone again. Honestly, I've learnt my lesson. I promise.'

'I scold only because ye're so precious to me,' she replied softly, putting down her sewing and folding her hands in her lap. She was wearing a dark-blue velvet gown, a delicate butterfly brooch pinned to the lace at her throat. Her shoulders were back, her spine straight, a beautiful soft curve to her neck. Only her hands looked at odds in her elegant surroundings. 'Rose, I know there's something ye're not telling me. I won't ask and I'll never pry — ye can tell me when you're ready, or not at all. It's just a mother knows things without being told. I can't explain it very well, but I just wanted to tell ye — a mother just knows…in her heart… that's all.'

I lowered my eyes. Was she talking about Father's idea for the school or had she guessed James Polcarrow had been involved in my rescue? I could not tell. She had told me Sulio Denville was behind bars; held for assault, false witness and the theft of the cutter and Thomas Warren had been seized for embezzlement, false accounting and misappropriation of land, but had she guessed more?

Jenna came through the door balancing a tray with yet another evil-smelling, steaming potion. Mother stood up, smiling down at me, straightening her gown. 'Mrs Munroe wants to discuss menus. She's promised us whortleberry pie

– can you believe that? It's your father's favourite and she's determined to spoil us. Here, Jenna, let me hold the door...'

The two of them were clearly in league. Ever since I had been brought home, they had not left me alone. Either one was with me, or the other – or both. Jenna had even moved her bed into my room but I did not mind. I wanted her there.

I had stopped Mother from scolding but Jenna was always a different matter. 'Don't look at me like that, Jenna – honestly, I think you're worse than Mother. Anyway, I know Joseph must have told you what really happened, so there's no need to talk about it.'

'It ain't my business where ye go – or who ye choose to spend yer time with. It would just be nice to know whether to expect ye home or not!'

'I wasn't *spending* my time with anyone – I was minding my own business...' I said, taking the cup. It smelt worse than any of her other brews but I held my tongue, sipping the bitter contents without complaint.

'Well, it's a good job Sir James was on hand,' she said, crossing her arms and staring down at me, 'And a good job he found ye...though what he thinks of all yer cavorting...'

'I wasn't *cavorting*, Jenna, and he doesn't care, even if I was. He made it very plain he doesn't want anything more to do with me and I don't blame him. We abused his good intentions and Father was rude to him. He even called Father an English Jacobin.'

Jenna had dressed her hair differently. She was not wearing her usual maid's cap but a delicate lace mobcap, like Mother's. Her hair lay beautifully coiled on either side of

415

her head and tiny ringlets bobbed against her forehead. The new style suited her – it was elegant and dignified and made her look quite enchanting. Her eyes, however, remained stern and disapproving. 'It's got nothing to do with Mr Pengelly. Sir James don't care a cat's whisker what yer Father does.'

'Well, he doesn't want anything more to do with me. He was angry – I could see it in his face. He doesn't want his name linked to mine – that's why he told Joseph to tell everyone he found me in the alley. Even Mother doesn't know he was involved. No-one knows and that's how James Polcarrow wants it.'

'Course he don't want people to know – Sir James's too honourable.'

'Honourable! It's got *nothing* to do with honour! He's afraid Arbella Cavendish will hear – that's all. He doesn't want to be implicated in any scandal. I heard him say so.'

Jenna raised her eyes in exasperation. 'Ye're meant to be the clever one, Rose Pengelly. I may've nothing like yer brains but at least I think straight…It's not *hisself* he's thinking of… he don't want his name linked to ye because t'would ruin *ye*. Now ye're spoken for, ye must be above gossip…'

'What d'you mean spoken for? Of course, I'm not spoken for!'

'Well if ye ain't, ye soon will be. Are ye alright? Here, ye're spilling yer drink.' Taking hold of the cup, she knelt by my side, her voice softening. 'Can't ye see he's protecting ye? Sir James knows ye're to marry Morcum Calstock and he's that concerned for yer reputation. If word gets out he

416

searched a slave ship for over two hours before he found ye
– ye'd be ruined.'

'But I'm not going to marry Morcum Calstock! I never
was. I never will. How can he think that?'

'Not marry him?' Jenna seemed completely bewildered,
'but it's all over town. Yer father's told enough people to
make it common knowledge. I thought ye admired Morcum
Calstock – I thought he was the man we've been waiting
for.'

'You know very well he isn't, Jenna. He's a very fine man
and I like him very much – he's kind and courageous and
very handsome…and where Father sees him as the son he
never had, I see him like the brother I've always wanted.
But as to marrying him…I couldn't, never. There's no spark
between us…no sense of wanting. He looks at me but his
eyes don't burn.'

''Twould be enough for most women if he looked at them
at all! And ye can hardly expect the poor man to go making
love to ye right under yer father's eyes. Ye needs give him
time – that's all.'

I shook my head, biting my bottom lip. Jenna put her arms
round me. She smelt of lavender, of green fields and fresh air
and I clung to her earthy strength, pressing my lips together,
determined not to cry. I was on the cliff top, my hair swirling
around me, rain lashing my face. My hands were stinging
from the rope, my borrowed clothes hanging heavily about
me. I was glancing back to the face of the sailor and my heart
was lurching from the force of his gaze. That hungry gaze
that sent my pulse racing and my loins aching.

James Polcarrow was shielding me from gossip. He had saved my reputation for another man and somehow that made everything worse. The heat in the room became unbearable.

'It's far too hot, Jenna, open the windows. I'm not ill and I don't have a fever – open the windows, please.'

The large sash windows faced the lane, looking directly over the river. Framed by pine shutters, they were positioned to catch the morning sun. I preferred them in the evening when the rays of the dying sun would linger on the fields opposite. As Jenna opened the windows, the smell of the sea filled the room.

'Wider, Jenna, open them wider. Let the air in.' I could smell the salt on the drying seaweed, the cockle-covered chains of the jetty where Father moored his boat and I breathed deeply, trying to rid myself of the sense of suffocation which I thought would never leave me. I could hear the gulls screeching for discarded fish guts and tried to block out the groaning of the ship's timbers. He had come for me. Even when he thought I loved another man, he had come. He had asked nothing of me, taken no credit, demanded no gratitude. I had summoned him and he had come.

'How did he find me, Jenna?'

'Henderson was at his niece's wedding and well the worse for drink…it was gone two and he was makin' a hell of a din tryin' to get back through the gates. The gatekeeper's a friend – or related…something anyway, and he thought Henderson wouldn't make it back along the drive. He thought he'd lose his key…or more like was too drunk to use it and would lie out all night. Well, he left his lad to mind the gate and went with Henderson – to see him into the house. Thought he may as well save himself a trip in the mornin', so he gathered up the post in the letterbox and took it with him. Sir James was in his study. He'd just had dinner with Sir George and his son Matthew – now there's a lovely looking man...'

'Jenna!'

'Well he is...anyway, Joseph says Sir James was just goin' to bed when he sees Henderson cross the hall – to leave the letters in the tray – an' Sir James stops him, takes the letters and when he sees one of them was from ye, he opened it there and then – like he knew ye was in trouble.'

'Go on.'

'Well, somehow he guessed ye'd be on one of the ships. He'd been goin' through all the land deals. They've formed a company, ye know, Mr Tregellas, Mr Warren the whole lot of them and he'd found evidence they owned a ship. He'd noticed the time of the tides scribbled on Mr Warren's blotter and it got him thinking...anyway...he got Joseph up and roused the harbour master and made him go through all the listings, looking for a ship owned by St Austell Holdings.'

'Jenna, how clever of him.'

'They've been leasing his land – all round the creek. It's the clay. Honest to God, he was that sure – it was like he was driven. I've never seen the like before. I think he was desperate.'

'You saw him, Jenna?'

'We were that worried ye'd not come home, Mrs Pengelly sent me to fetch Joseph.'

'She knows about you and Joseph?'

'Course – anyway, I was at the gate. The gatekeeper's lad wouldn't let me in but I was there when they came rushin' out. He asked if ye'd come home and I said that's what'd brought me to him...honest, he was that mad...he looked possessed.'

The air was cooling my face, sounds from my childhood filtering through the open window. Pack mules were passing on their way back to the fields, empty carts heading back to the farms, ready to be filled for the next day's market. Yawls would soon drift home on the incoming tide, gigs would start racing along the river. Children would stop searching for cockles, the taverns would soon start to overspill. It was all so familiar, so very dear, but knowing James Polcarrow loved me so much had just made my heart ache so terribly.

Suddenly, Jenna leant out of the window, her new-found dignity vanishing as her feet lifted from the ground. 'Well, I'll be jiggered,' she said, ankles in mid-air. 'That looks like ...yes...that's Madame Merrick alright...rushin' down the road. Something's wrong – she never runs.'

I dashed to the window to see Madame Merrick rushing towards the house. Not only was she running but she had a handkerchief held to her face.

'Quick, Jenna, get Mother,' I said. 'Something must have happened.'

Chapter Fifty-three

Running footsteps sounded across the hall: Madame Merrick entered the room in a whirl of green silk, the feathers on her turban fluttering in agitation. All composure lost, she stood flushed and breathless, clutching her chest in great distress.

'What is it, Marie? What's happened? Here, sit down. Jenna, pull up that chair...'

'The worst...Eva, the *worst*...Shut the door, Jenna, I cannot have the servants hearing. Oh, Eva...I am *ruined*... utterly *ruined*.' She held her handkerchief to her face, dabbing her tears. 'Nobody must hear – though how I can stop it becoming *common* gossip, I do not know. Soon it will be on everyone's lips – everyone will be talking about it. I will be ruined...my *reputation* will be *besmirched* and all my hard work will be for nothing...' With a huge sigh she sat, stiff-backed and upright on Jenna's proffered chair.

Mother knelt by her side. 'No-one can hear – tell us what's happened.'

'The worst, Eva...' No longer able to speak, Madame Merrick buried her head in her hands.

Mother looked desperate. 'Jenna, go upstairs to Mr Pengelly's study and bring down a glass of brandy. There's a bottle in the bureau, third drawer down — be careful not to disturb anything and he'll never know...'

Hardly able to conceal her surprise, Jenna ran to the door. She was just closing it when Mother called back. 'On second thoughts, bring the whole bottle and as many glasses as you can hold — I think we're all going to need a drop. Don't look so shocked — it's medicinal. Madame Merrick isn't well.'

Part of me was surprised to see Madame Merrick looking so vulnerable. I thought her iron will would be protection enough, but I could see in Mother's tender administrations, she knew her friend's formidable shell was not as hard as she would have us believe.

'It's not a fire, is it, Madame Merrick? The warehouse isn't in danger? I asked, fearful that Thomas Warren had carried out his threat.

'Good gracious, no...it is *far* worse than that...'

Mother's face turned ashen. On Jenna's return, she seized the brandy and, wasting no time, poured four large glasses. With trembling hands, she handed one to Madame Merrick.

'Why will you be ruined, Marie?'

Madame Merrick drank the brandy in one large gulp. She put her chin in the air and arched her eyebrows, hardly able to utter the unspeakable. 'That *odious* woman, Lady Cavendish, has decided to withdraw her patronage...she has gone *elsewhere*.'

'Elsewhere!' cried Mother. 'She can't – not now the gowns are finished.'

'I have just received this *note...*' Madame Merrick replied, fumbling in her purse to retrieve the offending letter, 'informing me she no longer *requires* her gowns...Nor does she *require* the gown for Miss Arbella Cavendish.' Madame Merrick looked anxiously at the door. 'She thinks nothing of *ruining* my reputation. My gowns are far *superior* to anything in Truro...or Bath...and certainly equal to anything found in London.' She held her lace handkerchief to her quivering lips.

'She can't withdraw her order – not like that. Not now the gowns are finished.' Eyes blazing, Mother reached for her glass, downing it with one swift gulp. 'She'll have to pay – there's at least two gowns' worth of material in each dress... not to mention all the extra stitching. Unpicking them will take for ever – no-one else's going to fit them!'

'It's not the *money*, Eva, or the work involved. I can recover the loss of payment but I can never recover the *loss of patronage*. That is what will *ruin* me...not the money.'

'People like her don't care two hoots about ruining your reputation,' I said, taking hold of my glass and sipping it slowly. 'Lady Cavendish doesn't care what grief she inflicts – or how unjustifiable it is. I'm just sorry I got you her patronage.' The brandy was strong and burnt my throat, adding more warmth to my already flushed cheeks. 'But has Miss Cavendish cancelled her order?' The prospect of never seeing Celia Cavendish again seemed suddenly rather sad, and by the look on Mother's face, I could see she was thinking the same. The success of our school was being threatened – even before it had started.

'Not yet – but I expect she'll follow. They are cousins, after all, and *very* close.' Madame Merrick dabbed her eyes again. 'Oh, Eva, I'll have to take down my *beautiful* new sign and *everyone* will *talk*. Soon everyone will know I no longer supply the aristocracy.' Her shoulders began to shake as a sob caught her throat.

Mother's cheeks had taken on a rosy glow. She poured Madame Merrick another glass, glancing at Jenna's untouched glass before pouring herself a second. For a moment, she brightened. 'Sir James Polcarrow won't let you down. You can get the sign repainted with Lady Polcarrow's name on it. She's got nothing to do with the Cavendish family, so she won't withdraw her patronage. Ye aren't ruined, Marie, ye still have good prospects.'

'You're forgetting Miss Cavendish will soon *be* the new *Lady Polcarrow* so Sir James will have no say in the matter – especially if Lady *Harridan* has her way! Mother could no longer resist her second glass. With a sad but encouraging smile, she shrugged her shoulders, her cheeks glowing pinker.

The room seemed hotter than ever. Madame Merrick looked around, noticing Mother's furnishings for the first time. Reaching inside her bag, she found her fan which she opened with a deft flick, before waving it vigorously, cooling her cheeks. 'You have a very *pretty* room here, Eva…but… goodness me…do you always keep it so hot?'

'Not usually,' replied Mother, a little flustered, 'but Rose's been unwell – I'm afraid she has a fever.'

Madame Merrick reached in her bag for her lorgnettes and peered across the room at me, her concern at once giving way to relief. 'Nonsense, Rosehannon looks the picture of health,' she said, her fan still flapping furiously. 'She looks very well – of course, it's the *colour* of the dress that shows off her great beauty...I chose it deliberately to compliment her colouring – but all that is in the past, if my business is to fail. There will be no more gowns...'

She stopped to blow her nose, as the sound of horses' hooves drifted through the open window. Jenna was sitting on the window seat and as a firm command rang out for the horses to halt, the three of us looked at Jenna to satisfy our curiosity. It was too late for callers; the clock on the mantle-piece having just chimed eight, and it could not have been Father, as he did not have a horse. Jenna peeped through the window, a huge smile spreading across her face.

'Good grief, child, stop *ogling*' cried Madame Merrick sharply. 'Come away from the window – it is extremely *vulgar* to stare like that. It will give people the impression you are a *half-wit*...'

Jenna was not listening or, if she was, she gave no sign of hearing. Men were dismounting. I could hear the horses shaking their heads, the jangle of their bridles, the stamping of their hooves. Footsteps scraped on the step outside and a knock sounded on the front door.

'Jenna, who *exactly* are you...*ogling*?' said Mother, smiling. It must have been the brandy talking.

'It's Joseph,' replied Jenna sweetly. 'He's holdin' the horses.' She stood a little longer, smiling out of the window before adding, as if in after-thought. '...while Sir James visits us.'

'*Sir James Polcarrow?*' Madame Merrick cried, sitting bolt upright, fanning herself in greater earnest. 'Sir James Polcarrow calling *here*...? He must have business to discuss with Mr Pengelly. But why would he come *here*? Why does he not send for Mr Pengelly?' She stood up, straightening her gown, her long fingers flying over imaginary creases. Glancing in my direction, she paled in horror. 'Miss Pengelly, *quickly*, you are covered in *cat hairs*...Make yourself present-able, child, and Jenna...stop gawping, sit here – remember if Sir James comes into the room, curtsey *very* low and *do not look him in the eye*. Oh, if only it was not so hot in here...'

A great flurry of agitation resulted in us taking up poses Madame Merrick deemed proper. I was to sit bolt upright on my chaise-longue, Jenna was to sit elegantly on the window seat, while Madame Merrick and Mother would perch on the edge of their chairs, facing away from the fire in an attempt to lessen their heightened colour. Mother remained surprisingly calm, all of us sitting in dignified silence as Sam opened the door. Adopting the gravity such a prestigious visitor required, he announced, in his best voice, that Sir James would like a quiet word alone with Mother.

Madame Merrick's eyes widened and if my heart had not been hammering so hard, I would have enjoyed her incredu-lity. Mother steadied herself on the arm of her chair, glancing in the mirror to readjust her mobcap, which was leaning slightly to one side. With a little smile, she followed Sam out to the hall, leaving the door slightly ajar. Blood rushed to my head, pulsing at my temples. I began straining my ears, trying to catch snatches of their conversation.

'Good evening, Sir James, it's always a pleasure to welcome you into our home.' Her next words were lost – I think she was thanking him for his part in restoring our good fortune. His reply was also indistinct, but I thought his tone sounded urgent. He seemed to be explaining something. Suddenly his words became audible.

'…it is a letter addressed to me and must be kept confidential – but I believe Miss Pengelly should read it. It concerns her, and if you're sure she hasn't received a letter of her own, then I believe she has a right to read it…'

'Then please, Sir James, come in and give her the letter yourself. Let her read it…'

'No, Mrs Pengelly, I've no wish to trespass on your hospitality. I ask only for you to give her the letter and, at your own convenience, return it to me. I'm content to entrust it to you. Goodnight, and please forgive me for troubling you.'

I tried breathing deeply. I expected Mother to say goodnight and was waiting for the front door to close, but she spoke again. 'Sir James, do give the letter to her yourself – after all, it can only take a few moments to read, and you wouldn't be trespassing on my hospitality. In fact, I'd consider it a great honour if you'd join me in my sitting room. Please…I absolutely insist…come through…' She sounded so assured and I could only imagine it was the brandy giving her courage.

Her words said, the door opened and Mother ushered James Polcarrow into the room. Madame Merrick swept an elegant curtsey, falling deeply to the floor with the grace of a duchess. Jenna followed suit, biting her bottom lip, concentrating hard on keeping her back straight. I, too, dipped a curtsey, keeping my eyes averted. James Polcarrow glanced fleetingly round, looking at odds among the feminine furnishings, his tall frame and broad shoulders somehow too strong and powerful for the delicate room.

'I don't think you have met my dear friend, Madame Merrick,' said Mother.

'No,' replied Sir James, bowing formally, 'I have not yet had that honour – although I know you by your reputation, Madame Merrick. Lady Polcarrow speaks very highly of you.'

'And of course you know Jenna…'

'Good evening, Miss Marlow. I hope I find you well. I did not mean to interrupt your evening,' he said, bowing formally again.

Jenna beamed with pleasure, her eyes sparkling, the dimples in her cheeks creasing. She looked coyly at Madame Merrick as if to remind her not to ogle, but James Polcarrow looked preoccupied. He was not dressed for riding. He was dressed formally in a silk jacket and breeches, his cravat neatly secured by a silver pin, but his hair was ruffled, his movements restless. In Mother's beautiful room, he looked like a caged bear – captive and confined. I could feel the tension in his body, my own body responding to his nervousness.

With the briefest of glimpses, he thrust a letter into my hand, his own hand shaking. Our fingers touched. My hands were clammy, my mouth parched. I knew by the frown on his face how serious this letter must be and how only the most pressing business would bring him to my door.

'I'm very sorry for what this contains, Miss Pengelly, but I feel you have every right to its content – though I wish I could have spared you such unhappiness...' His face was drawn, unsmiling. He would not look at me. His eyes darted around the room, to the window, to the fire, to Jenna, to Mother, anywhere except at me. His spoke as if the words were being dragged from him. 'And I'd have preferred not to witness your distress, but your mother was quite insistent...' He turned abruptly away, looking out of the window, straight-backed, shoulders braced, head high. Clasping his hands behind his back, he stared across the river, the familiar stony mask closing over his face.

Madame Merrick and Mother sat stiffly in their chairs. Jenna seized her chance, slipping quietly out of the room. I took the letter to the other window. I needed the breeze to cool my forehead and clear my head. There were two pages of tight script, confidently written in a flowing hand. A knife twisted inside me.

I knew at once it was from Arbella Cavendish.

Chapter Fifty-four

Dated 22nd August 1973, the letter was addressed from Pendenning Hall. Everything about the quality of the paper and the elegance of her writing spoke of her grace and gentility. I could see her beautiful head bent in concentration, her hair glinting in the sun, her silk sleeves rustling as she leant to dip her pen. Swallowing my jealousy, I began to read.

Dear Sir James,

If I could, in any way, spare you the pain I am about to inflict, then please believe me when I say I would have done anything, anything at all in my power, to change the course of events which lead me to take the action I am about to take. You of all people deserve better. You have shown me nothing but politeness and honour. You have behaved with the utmost chivalry and yet I am about to treat you so shamefully. I cannot ask your forgiveness because I doubt even you could grant that, but I do ask you for understanding; for a little bit of that compassion for human suffering which I know is in your soul.

From the moment we met, I knew you harboured a cherished wish that I could be yours. To my shame, I trifled with your affection and never loved you as you deserved. Believe me when I say there could be no finer man than you, but even at the tender age of seventeen, I already knew the depths of true love. I was not free to love you then, and I am not free to love you now.

The man I love, and with whom I will elope, is the man who will always hold my heart. His name is Morcum Calstock. He was my father's steward before you came to Government House. He is strong and courageous, noble and clever, highly educated, accomplished, and destined for great honours, yet to my parents he is worse than nobody. He has no family to speak of, no fortune, no connections, but his worse crime is that he has no title. My mother made it quite clear I was to marry, if not a duke, at least an earl.

When my father found us together in the gardens of Government House, he dismissed Morcum from the island, and took pains to spread vicious lies and slander about him to all the plantation owners in the area. Morcum's prospects lay in ruins and he had to flee, promising me that when he returned, we would start a new life together back in England. He had returned to the island shortly before you declared your love for me, yet Father's hold over every ship that came and left the island left us desperate for a means to escape.

I dismissed you then, if you recall, telling you that you stood no chance without a title. Imagine my surprise when *you revealed your true identity. Suddenly doors seemed to open. I was free to hope and free to dream. Fleeing the island became a possibility, even if I had to lie and use you so shamefully. I could not risk sailing without Father's knowledge, so when you offered me a way to escape, I grasped it.*

I knew I could probably persuade Mother to accept a baronetcy even though she aimed for greater glory, so I seized the opportunity of your proposal, gratefully, selfishly rejoicing in my good fortune. My plan was to follow you to England, somehow convince you that we had made a mistake, (maybe even tell you the truth) and elope with Morcum before Father had me shipped back to Dominica. I believed that though you would have been appalled by my action, you would be more hurt than heartbroken. But no, I must not lie. The truth is, I had only my own interests in mind. We were desperate and you were the sacrifice.

The weeks following your departure saw the worse storms the island had ever witnessed. We heard nothing but the loss of ships and as we waited to follow you to England, I began to doubt the success of my plan. I grew fearful and anxious, worrying that your ship had gone down, that you had never returned to England and I would soon have news of your death. But, added to that, Mother began to question whether she had been too hasty in her decision to allow the marriage.

My anxiety turned to panic. Father had accepted your disguise as being part of a boyish prank; he himself had run away to sea and saw your spirit for adventure as a worthy attribute, but Mother was beginning to waver. Even now I thank God we heard nothing of the fact that you were a convict on the run. It was only because your estate neighboured my uncle's that kept my mother from cancelling the engagement. You will wonder why I bother to write what must now seem irrelevant, but I need you to know the depth of my desperation, seeing my one chance of happiness unravelling before me. There were rumours Morcum was back on the island and Mother was watching me like a hawk. I was confined to the house, followed everywhere, my maid now my gaoler.

Believe me, what I did next I blush to remember and I blush with shame as I write. Only desperation could have made me sacrifice my good name, and only my own self-interest would make me sacrifice yours. I used you with no compunction. You, who would never have acted in such a way and could not defend yourself. You, who had done me no harm and had only sought my good opinion.

I told my parents we must make haste and leave for England because I was carrying your child. This will shock you, I know. My hand shakes knowing the anger this will evoke. Your honour is in doubt even as my name is in ruins.

You will ask yourself how I could even countenance the idea, let alone execute my plan, but once my mind was made up, I found it was easy. I revelled in my mother's fury. I rejoiced in Father's inability to control me. There was nothing they could do. I was ruined, unfit for any earl or passing duke. The only way they could salvage the situation was to hurry me onto a ship and come in search of you. And that is what they did, advertising and proclaiming the marriage to everyone before you had a chance to change your mind.

That you never guessed my treachery is what makes me feel so guilty. I could tell at once your affections for me had changed. There was no love in your eyes, no joy in your greeting. Yet you kept your word and would not break our engagement, and my heart ached, knowing you deserved so much better.

Time is running short. I will arrange for you to get this letter well after we have fled. Morcum sailed soon after we left Dominica and followed me to Fosse. We met soon after he arrived – outside a dressmaker's shop in town. He has since sent me word and we sail tonight – though when and where we are to go shall remain our secret.

Please find it in your heart to forgive me in time, or, if you cannot forgive me, please understand that my actions are born out of desperation. I leave you with joy in my heart and happiness in my step and I can only wish that soon, you too, have the same good fortune in loving someone as deeply as I love Morcum Calstock.

Yours in haste,
Arbella Cavendish

My eyes raced across the tightly written script, gasping with amazement every time she sought to justify her actions. How dare she use James Polcarrow so abominably? Lie so blatantly? Fool everyone so openly and completely? I looked up. James Polcarrow was watching me, his blue eyes staring from across the room.

'I'm sorry you had to find out this way,' he said softly. 'It seems Morcum Calstock is an unprincipled man.' His face was rigid with control.

I stared back at his fine features; his strong jaw, straight nose, dark eyebrows and the shock of unruly hair that had yet to be tamed. My heart was leaping, whirling, doing somersaults in my chest. 'I couldn't care less about Morcum Calstock. Father will be disappointed though – in fact I'd like to see his face when he finds out Morcum Calstock's only interest in the yard was because it was next to a dress-maker!'

'You're not upset by the letter?'

'Of course I am. I'm absolutely furious – though not with Morcum Calstock. He means nothing to me and never has.' Mother and Madame Merrick had not spoken. Like dress-makers' dummies, they sat unmoving, unspeaking, staring straight into the flickering fire. Mother had long ago given up all pretence of sewing. Their backs were turned, their eyes averted, but never had two pairs of ears been more eager to hear, four eyes more desperate to look. I could only guess the thoughts rushing through their minds, their instincts telling them this unprecedented visit had something to do with the suddenly discarded wedding gown.

The clock ticked across the silent room as James Polcarrow fought to control his emotions.

'You knew about her deception…?' There was accusation in his voice, even betrayal.

'Yes.'

'When?'

'The night of the creek.'

'Yet you said nothing?'

'Of course I said nothing. I assumed you knew!'

He looked saddened, hurt, his eyes full of disappointment. 'And you believed me capable of abandoning her?'

My heart dived. Yes, I had believed him capable; I had listened to tattle and not my heart. In my hand, the letter trembled. 'I could not love a man capable of abandoning a woman and her unborn child,' I whispered.

His eyes blazed, burning like they did in my dreams. 'And I could not love a woman capable of less.'

Our hearts were calling to each other across the silent room. Aching for each other, speaking without talking, loving without touching, held rigid by protocol and formality. I wanted him to take me in his arms, feel his lips against mine. I wanted to feel the strength of his body pressing against me. Two hearts beating with the same beat. Two lovers joined as one. Two souls united by destiny.

Madame Merrick reached for her fan. Mother's eyes were full of tears. She picked up her sewing but I could see she held her needle in her left hand. I found I was smiling. Smiling and smiling, like Mr Pitt with a stolen sardine.

James's eyes held mine. His frown disappeared. His smile was tentative, shy, slightly secretive but, as it grew, it filled his face with such joy, smoothing away all pain. In that moment, I saw the man he should always have been, the man he really was, and I loved him so tenderly, so passionately, so terrifyingly completely, that my heart lurched in pain.

Outside, dusk had fallen. A slight drizzle had dampened the cobbles and cooled the air. It would soon be time to shut the windows, light the candles, draw across the shutters. Mother would ask Sam to see Madame Merrick safely home and Sir James Polcarrow would bow politely, bid me good-night and mount his horse. This life-changing, wonderful day would soon be over.

James was still smiling as he turned to Mother, 'Would it be too much to ask if I may visit you again?' His voice was courteous, full of love.

Mother smiled, her beautiful face as flushed as mine. 'Course it wouldn't, Sir James. Ye just come when ye like – ye know ye'll always be welcome in my home. Come tomorrow – we'll be here, won't we, Rose?'

The End

Acknowledgements

I would like to extend a huge thank you to my family and friends; to my agent, Teresa Chris and editor, Sara O'Keeffe and her team at Atlantic Books. Also, to everyone in the Cornwall Record Office, Truro. Thank you, each and every one of you for your enthusiasm and support.